PICKETWIRE VAQUERO

FIVE TRAILS WEST, BOOK III

PICKETWIRE VAQUERO

ONE FAMILY'S WESTERN ODYSSEY

JAMES D. CROWNOVER

FIVE STAR

A part of Gale, Cengage Learning

GALE
CENGAGE Learning·

Farmington Hills, Mich • San Francisco • New York • Waterville, Maine
Meriden, Conn • Mason, Ohio • Chicago

GALE
CENGAGE Learning®

LIBRARY OF CONGRESS CATALOGING-IN-PUBLICATION DATA

Names: Crownover, James D., author.
Title: Picketwire vaquero / James D. Crownover.
Description: First edition. | Waterville, Maine : Five Star, A part of Gale Cengage Learning, [2016] | Series: Five trails West ; book 3
Identifiers: LCCN 2016004078 (print) | LCCN 2016009181 (ebook) | ISBN 9781432832919 (hardcover) | ISBN 1432832913 (hardcover) | ISBN 9781432832872 (ebook) | ISBN 1432832875 (ebook) | ISBN 9781432833541 (ebook) | ISBN 1432833545 (ebook)
Subjects: LCSH: Families—Fiction. | Frontier and pioneer life—Fiction. | GSAFD: Western fiction. | Historical fiction.
Classification: LCC PS3603.R765 P53 2016 (print) | LCC PS3603.R765 (ebook) | DDC 813/.6—dc23
LC record available at http://lccn.loc.gov/2016004078

First Edition. First Printing: September 2016
Find us on Facebook– https://www.facebook.com/FiveStarCengage
Visit our website– http://www.gale.cengage.com/fivestar/
Contact Five Star™ Publishing at FiveStar@cengage.com

To Kristine, whose enthusiasm
keeps me going

Hiram Harris
Anglo-Saxon
Born: 1767
Place: South Carolina

Sarah Fourkiller
Cherokee
Born: circa 1774
Place: Tennessee

Ruth Harris
Born: 1790
Place: Tennessee
Married: Tom Finn 1806
Married: Samuel Meeker 1815
Place: Village on the Middle Fork

Samuel Harris
Born: 1794

Jerry Harris
Born: 1796
Place: Tennessee
Married: Kansas 1822

Joseph Harris
Born: 1805
Place: Tennessee

| John (Pony) 1833
| Jacob 1835
| Luzina 1838
| Parlee 1842
| Zenas Leonard 1844

Jesse Meeker, nee Finn
Born: 1807
Place: Pirate's Island
Married: Amira Dreadfulwater 1831
Place: Chewey, Cherokee Nation

Born: 1844
Place: Arkansas
Married: Sophia
Maria Gomez 1876

Sarah Fourkiller Meeker
Born: 1816

PROLOGUE

Enter now the last three trails on the Harris/Meeker trek west; the third trail was the California Road, which is the southern route to California mapped out by Captain Randolph Marcy in 1849. Originally called the California Road, it was later called the Southern Route.

The fourth trail the family followed was the Cherokee Trail. It was established by the Cherokees on their way to California in 1849. It ran west from the Northwest Arkansas–Indian Territory border and was the preferred trail for many Arkansas drovers and Indian Nation travelers, having plenty of water and grass and avoiding overgrazed trails and passes of the Oregon Trail to the north. A man named C.C. Seay took a herd of cattle, quite possibly white-faced, over this trail from Cincinnati, Arkansas, to California in 1853.

Whether you call it Purgatory, Picketwire, Las Animas, or El Rio de Las Animas Perdidas en Purgatorio, the little river played a large part in the early settlement of the country. Uncle Dick Wootton and the Bents both had ranches there very early. It was here that Zenas first began to handle cattle.

Let's get one thing straight at the gitgo: "cowboy" is a misnomer, a corruption. The Mexicans were the first to herd cattle in the new world and they were called vaqueros—"vaca" meaning cattle or beef, more broadly, livestock. The true meaning of the word "vaquero" (pronounced *bakero*) is cowherd. Whether he was fifteen and fuzzy-cheeked or forty, bearded, and stove-up, he was *not* a boy. He didn't herd cows, he herded cattle—livestock—mostly of the neutered horned class. Therefore, he should most properly be called a stockman, but in our culture, the stockman has taken the nomen of cowboy. Call one of these men cowpoke or cowpuncher and you would most likely wake up to find yourself gazing at the sky and counting the stars as they float by. Cowpokes or punchers were the ones who rode the cattle trains and used a pole to poke up the steers that had laid down in the cattle cars, since any steer that remained in that position would eventually be trampled to death by his fellow passengers. Compensation for stooping to the status of cowpuncher was a round-trip ticket in the caboose and a chance to see a big city like Kansas City or Chicago.

Though the name *vaquero* originally referred to the Mexican, it became generalized, and there were Mexican vaqueros, white vaqueros, and negro vaqueros, the black vaquero being much more common than we suppose today. I must add here that the vaquero on the range was *in the whole* judged on his abilities and not his race. Be he black, Mexican-American, Yankee, or Rebel, he *earned* a place in the vaquero class by his ability to ride, pop brush, rope, and in his general willingness to hold up more than his end of the log—laziness was not tolerated.

For several years, Zenas Meeker worked up and down the last trail west, the Santa Fe Trail. He was born in 1844 and he relates most of this book from firsthand knowledge. We hope you enjoy the ride.

The reader is reminded that two languages are used in the telling of this story, Cherokee and English. When a character is using proper English, he is probably speaking Cherokee. English used by the speakers in this story is spoken with the colloquialisms of the time and place.

CHAPTER 1
JESSE MEEKER LEAVES HOME

1826

"Pa told us a lot about his life, but he never told us about why he left th' Village on Middle Fork. No one talked about it much, but from what I have gathered from Grandma Ruth and Uncle Riley, it must have been a pretty rough time for all of them.

"I gathered that Pa became involved with some girl in th' village and by the last of 1825 was ready to marry her. Th' girl's family objected on th' grounds that Pa was too young an' unproven an' it led to some strong feelings in Pa an' Uncle Riley. It took some straight talk from Sam an' Uncle Lonza to keep peace, upshot of it all was that Pa and Uncle Riley left th' village."

Pa, Riley, and Uncle Jerry were raising horses and th' boys took their share of horses an' left. They traded at the Village at the Forks for a time, then moved on up to Bear Creek Springs. They did very well, the improved breeding of their horses giving them the advantage over other horse traders. In late 1826, Pa and Uncle Riley moved over on Osage Creek b'tween Snow Knob an' Crystal Mountain outside Cherokee lands where the grazing was good an' they could keep closer control of their stock.

They did a little farmin' in th' bottoms an' traded horses around the area. The hedge apple fences they planted around both places were so thick a horse couldn't push through and made a very effective barrier. We made our arrows out of th' shoots an' bows out of hickory wrapped in sinew.

★ ★ ★ ★ ★

Carroll County, Arkansas Territory, was organized in 1823. Th' county seat was established at th' village of Carrollton in a log courthouse built in 1825. In 1829, Cherokees signed a treaty giving up their Arkansas territory in exchange for lands in the Indian Territory and the bulk of th' tribe moved. Fishinghawk an' Laughing Brook were too old and infirm to move, so the clan, along with many of their Cherokee neighbors, remained on Middle Fork.

Pa built a large dogwalk-style cabin on Osage Creek an' married my ma, who was Amira Dreadfulwater from th' old Bear Creek Village. They were married in th' fall of 1831 at Chewey, Cherokee Nation. Uncle Riley returned to Middle Fork. My oldest brother, John (we always called him Pony), was born in 1833. In 1835, Jacob was born and sister Luzina was born in 1838. She died in 1842. Sister Parlee was born in November of 1842 and I was youngest, born in 1844.

Some time late in the fall of 1836, Pa heard about a trader who had set up a store at old Fort Osage on th' Missouri, so in th' spring of '37 he rounded up a string of horses an' with several men from Park Hill, Cherokee Nation drove them up to Fort Osage.

Th' trader's name was Zenas Leonard, an ex-trapper turned trader who catered to mountain men and traders bound for Santa Fe. He took a likin' t' Pa's horses—Cherokee Ponies he called them—an' told Pa he could sell all he could get his hands on. He also said that Santa Fe traders was getting away from oxen an' more an' more wantin' mules. With that in mind, Pa traded for a dozen played-out mares in from th' trail at th' rate of two or three of the ganted mares for one of his horses. Somewhere, Mr. Leonard come up with a big jack an' practically gave him t' Pa with assurance that Pa would bring his mules to him for trade.

Well, Pa was subject of some funnin' b'cause of his herd of played-out horses an' that jackass, but he knowed what he was doin'. He hired a couple of Park Hill men t' help him herd them back t' Osage Creek. They went slow, feedin' on spring grasses an' by th' time they had reached home, th' mares were fat an' happy.

Now, Pa had to keep his two herds separated. He penned up Jack as we called him, an' put his new mares with him as they came in season. By th' time another summer rolled around, he had a bunch of mule colts rompin' around th' bottoms.

This was th' year Uncle Riley came back out with his wife, Lavica Standing Bear, an' helped with th' stock. They were in partnership for several years then. Everyone was involved in breakin' horses and mules. Pony and Jacob an' later Parlee an' me had th' job o' tamin' foals an' gettin' them halter broke. As they grew older, Pa an' Uncle Riley took on th' breakin' of them to saddle and harness. By that time, th' animals was so tame there was little danger of buckin' or runaways, though some of us got throwed once in a while.

It was everyone's job, includin' Ma an' Aunt Lavi, t' keep th' horses used to saddle an' ridin'. I was partial t' mules, always have been. For intelligence, bottom an' gait, they'll always beat a horse. Some people say they are stubborn, but I say they are just very patient. If they don't want t' do something, it's usually for some good reason an' a patient man can sooner or later find it out.

Horses have their place, especially around herds or when you need t' travel fast. They can handle cows much better than mules, but for just plain work or endurance, a mule is better. He can live on things a horse won't even eat an' go longer without water. Get him tangled in this durned bobwire an he'll stand still until someone rescues him. A horse will fight it until he is all cut up an' more than one has died from it.

Th' mule's pappy is an animal of a different stripe. Donkeys aren't patient, they's just plain *stubborn!* Try as you might, you can never understand him completely. He has great strength and will carry near as much as a horse, but at his own speed. He and the Mexicans get along well, for their speeds pretty well match and when a jackass balks, th' Mex finds it a good time t' sit down an' rest 'til ol' jack is ready t' resume. A mule gits his ability t' live on weeds an' such from th' donkey, for he can live on even less than a mule.

Still donkeys are handy animals t' have around, always gentle an' patient with children an' a lot of men have had a special regard for them. I once knew a prospector named Pittinger who had three donkeys he kept after he retired. One day I asked old Pitt if he would sell one of them. He thought a minute and said, reluctantly, "I might sell a couple of them, but that one over there I would never sell. We were down in a mine working one day an' that jackass broke loose an' ran out of th' mine. 'Course, I had t' chase him down an' just as I got out of th' hole, th' whole shaft collapsed. When th' dust settled so's I could see, that donkey was standin' there looking at me noddin' his head an' rollin his eyes!

"He saved my life an' I owes it to him t' see that he has a good life. We left that claim an' never went back—didn't pay too good anyway an' th' skimpy ol' vein was too far underground t' be worth goin' after."

CHAPTER 2
OF LAW AND JUSTICE

1845–46

Even b'fore th' treaty of 1828, whites were movin into th' Ozarks. They were a mixed bunch, some good honest neighbors an' some rotten to th' core. Mostly, they lived off huntin' and what little bit of garden th' women kept. They would have moved in on Pa an' Uncle Riley, but th' bois d'arc hedges marked their land an' they stood pat, no one encroachin' on them. Time to time, some new pilgrim cast his eye on their places, but they soon learned that they were not goin' t' move us an' they went on somewheres else.

Well up Osage Creek from our place was a large bottom just right for farmin' an' a little settlement grew up there. Pa thought it was around 1836 that two brothers, James and Alexander Fancher, settled in that valley. Later, in th' early '40's, they were joined by more of th' Fancher clan, namely their nephews John an' th' younger Alexander. They became quite prosperous cattlemen, runnin' cows on th' open ranges across Carroll and Boone counties.

Pa an' Riley had considered settling where Osage Settlement grew up, but had moved on down th' creek where water was more reliable an' there weren't so many people. There wasn't any more settlers down th' creek from our place for fear of th' Osages, but Pa knowin' th' language an' some of the people got along with them pretty well.

Pa an' Uncle Riley took a bunch of horses up to Fort Osage

15

in th' fall o' '39. Pa told Mr. Zenas about th' mules an' he said he would take them when they were four years old an' harness broke. B'fore they got home, Aunt Lavi gave birth to a boy. They named him Wesley Fourkiller, but we just called him Wes.

In 1842, th' year Parlee was born an' Luzina took th' fever, Pa took his first mules to Fort Osage. There were eighteen an' Mr. Leonard was well pleased with them, especially when he learned Pa an' Uncle Riley had broke them to work as teams. He paid Pa premium prices for them an' held them until spring when caravans started forming up. They sold out fast an' still there was a demand for more.

Pa assured Mr. Leonard that he would have a bunch ready every fall from then on. He an' Uncle Riley noted that if they would bring mules in springtime, they could trade directly with th' Santa Fe traders at better prices. For th' time bein', they determined t' continue tradin' with Mr. Leonard because he had been so fair with them.

Actually, there were nineteen foals in that bunch, but Pa kept th' prettiest one for Parlee. She kept her all her life, some twenty-five years. That was a long time for a work animal t' live in those days, but Parlee's mule never worked hard, only plowin' garden plots an' servin' as a ridin' mule for my sister an' her kids.

I was born in 1844, September 3rd, baby of th' family. They named me Zenas Leonard Meeker after th' trader b'cause he had been so good to our family. When I was a boy, I made several trips to Sibley, th' name o' th' town that grew up around old Fort Osage, an' Mr. Leonard always paid me special attention.

Arkansas became a state in 1836 an' of a sudden everyone was concerned about "The Law." There were lawyers an' county officials pushin' "The Law" on people like they couldn't live

16

without it. Pa said he had spent most of his life without it an' if they wanted to live by it, ok, but he didn't need it. Th' county kept pushin' him t' deed up his land an' he even tried to a time or two, but couldn't b'cause he was Cherokee out of th' reservation an' th' lawyers he hired had their eyes on his farm. Uncle Riley got disgusted with th' whole thing an' when word came that the folks on Little Red could use some help, he packed up an' left his place for Pony.

Still, th' pressure t' move was on. Th' two places were th' best land in th' bottoms an' it galled some of th' settlers that "Injuns" could own it an' do better than whites with it. One day a lawyer Pa had hired rode up an' showed Pa a deed he had in his name to th' two farms.

"You couldn't get a deed for me in spite o' th' fact I am three quarters white, yet it was easy for you to get a deed for yourself. How much did you pay for my land?"

"I didn't have to pay anything for it," Mr. Law replied, "it is open for settlement for anyone who files on it."

"Well, I was here before there was any law about settlement or a place to file. That means that the land is mine and no paper you wave in my face is gonna change that."

"You mean you won't yield to the authority of the law?"

"Not when it is used by shysters like you to pervert justice an' steal from honest folk, I won't."

Pa pulled that lawyer down off his horse an' gave him a thorough thrashin'. "Your deed is as worthless as th' paper it's written on!" An' Pa burned it right there in front o' th' lawyer. Then he hoisted him across his saddle an' tied his hands an' feet together under th' horse's belly. "Now you get off *my* land an' stay away! It'd be good if you hurried before my temper gits th' best of me an' I shoot your sorry ass!" He slapped th' horse's rump an' sent him on his way back to Carrollton.

Someone found him still tied across his saddle an' instead of releasing him, led his horse into town an' around th' square b'fore tyin' up at th' tavern where th' boys had a grand time hurrahin' him. Seems no one liked lawyers much. Finally, Sheriff Sims Rowe come along an' untied him.

A few weeks later, he rode up with Sheriff Rowe, our neighbor up th' creek. Pa got word they were comin an' met them down at th' gate, his rifle under his arm. "Welcome, Sheriff, light down an' come on in," he called, not even looking at th' lawyer. Mr. Sheriff was awful uneasy, you could see he would had rather be somewheres else.

"Don't have time, jist now, Jesse," he replied. "This lawyer here has a deed t' this propity an' I am here t' serve you notice that you have ten days t' vacate th' primesis."

Pony said Pa studied th' paper a minute, then looked at th' sheriff. He hadn't once glanced at our lawyer. "When did you come into th' valley, Sheriff?"

"It was in th' fall o' '30 me an' th' family pulled in t' this very yard," he answered.

"So I was already here then?"

"Yep, an' you heped me find my place up th' creek there. We built a cabin an' finished 'er b'fore Christmas."

"Seems Riley an' I helped you some on that."

"Heped? Without'n you two, that house wouldn't have been built by spring!"

"When did this lawyer come into th' valley?" His rifle barrel swung up t' point at th' lawyer's chest. Pa still didn't look at him.

Th' sheriff looked at th' lawyer an speculated, "I think it was in th' summer o' 38, wasn't it?"

Mr. Lawyer swallowed an' nodded, his eye on th' mouth o' that gun barrel.

"I been here since 1826," Pa continued, "well b'fore any law an' order was 'stablished. I had t' be my own law an' keep order myself. Then th' state come in 1836 an' took over lawin'. Things didn't git any better, may have got worse in some cases. Two times I tried t' go by what th' law wanted an' deed up this place, even hired this lawyer t' see to it for me," the gun barrel lifted some, "but got denied for some reason. Then some days back he comes out here with a deed to my property in *his* name. *No piece of paper changes who possesses this land so long as I live here!*"

He looked straight into th' sheriff's eyes. "He couldn't take th' place in his own strength or in th' strength of a piece o' paper, so he perverts law by hidin' b'hind it, hopin' someone else would do his dirty work an' take th' heat fer stealin' what ain't rightly his." The gun barrel lifted a little more an' th' lawyer shifted uneasily. "Sheriff, we been friends an' neighbors a long while, but if you are backing this thief, th' friendship stops here!"

Sheriff Rowe nodded, liftin' his hat an' wipin' his face with his bandanna, mostly to hide his grin from th' lawyer an' wink at Pa. He turned to th' lawyer. "Seems I'm caught b'tween justice an' th' law here, an' I am gonna light down on th' side of justice. Jesse was here b'fore any o' us an' he welcomed ever upstanding man to th' valley. So far as I'm concerned, this land is his, deed er no deed an' that's that!"

If it could have, th' lawyer's face got redder, "Seems like we'll have to wait until we have a new sheriff before the law prevails," he said.

"Shore 'nough." Th' sheriff grinned. "An' I plan on bein' sheriff a long time!" With that said, he turned and ambled off toward home. "Seems I hears th' dinner bell ringin'," he cast over his shoulder, "Good evening, gentlemen."

Pa's gun never wavered an' he never looked at th' lawyer. He must hev remembered th' last time he "rode" away, for he hurried after th' sheriff, passin' him on his way back t' town. Not long after that, facin' th' fact that he would have t' work with his hands or starve for lack of lawin', he left th' country.

His deed to th' farm remained recorded in th' courthouse until th' building burned. There were no more attempts t' use law t' take th' farm away. In fact, it was still common fer folks to own their farm without a deed. Some time after turn of th' century there was a scramble t' deed up these lands when th' first children inherited th' ole homestead.

In actuality, th' country was civilized in name only; law and order by state or county was practically nonexistent and men took care of their own problems without resorting to the law. Anyone b'sides women an' widows who applied for protection from th' sheriff was viewed as weak and the target of scorn. His life was made miserable by th' rough elements of th' community. Civilization had caught up with th' lawless in their march to th' western sea and there was many a clash between th' two until the lawless were conquered or moved on. It was so in Carroll County and th' rowdies put up quite a struggle b'fore givin' up.

Efforts t' steal horses an' cattle continued unabated. Many a time Pa an' Pony patrolled their land all night t' keep thieves out of th' horse herds. Once Pa noticed a thinning of th' hedge in a place an' pushin' through, he found a clearing in th' middle with only a thin layer of trees inside and out t' hide th' opening. Thieves would only have t' chop out a few trees either side t' have a clear path t' run horses through.

While Pony patrolled, Pa slept by th' clearing waitin' on visitors. In a few nights, he was wakened by th' sound of muffled chopping an' knew his "guests" had arrived. There were four of them, two working on th' outside an two on th' inside. Quietly, Pa slipped out an' found th' thieves' horses. After he had moved them a ways out of reach, he returned to th' hedge.

Th' two working on th' outside were resting on their axe

20

handles when Pa's shotgun loaded with rock salt hit their posteriors. In a trice, they were running toward where they had left horses. Th' two working on th' inside had t' flee past Pa t' git to th' horses an' when they were lined up just right, he let them have th' other barrel. Bullets an' confusion flew for a few moments, then all was quiet, except for th' baying of dogs following their retreat.

Pa retrieved th' would-be thieves' horses an' put them inside th' hedge. It wasn't hard t' close th' path that had only been partially cleared. They hung th' four saddles, such as they were, on th' fence by th' front gate an' put th' word out that they had "found" four horses tied in the brush and would gladly return them if their rightful owners could accurately describe them.

The community had great fun trying to identify the culprits by evidence of their wounds. There were strong suspicions about a couple of rowdies who only drank at th' bar an' never offered t' sit. One of them was caught out alone by parties unknown an' when he was roped and stripped, it was found that his backside was spotted with pockmarks from shoulders to knees. Soon after, he was called away by an urgent need t' visit a sick mother.

The horses were never claimed and after a year Pa turned them over to the county, which eventually sold them. Three of the saddles disappeared one night, tracks of the departing horses being lost in road traffic. The last time I was by there, that fourth saddle or what was left of it was still astraddle the fence, slowly melting into the ground, a monument and warning to anyone who contemplated thievery.

CHAPTER 3
THE CHEROKEE TRAIL & THE
CALIFORNIA ROAD

1849

In 1848, news of gold strikes in California spread like wildfire over th' whole country, even President Polk spoke of it. Th' Fanchers heard about th' country and mild climate where they could graze cattle year round and decided t' investigate th' possibility of movin' their operation t' California. In th' fall of '49 they started gatherin' cattle an' when they set th' herd on th' trail in early '50, Pony was with them.

They followed th' trail of a company of Cherokees that went to California in '49. This became known as the Cherokee Trail, *not* to be confused with th' Trail of Tears, which was a whole 'nother story.

Basically, th' trail began anywhere along th' Arkansas border from Fort Smith north. C.C. Seay made cattle drives from Cincinnati, Arkansas, going west until he intersected th' trail somewhere along th' Arkansas River. This portion of th' trail was already established as th' Santa Fe Trail and th' next part known as th' Cherokee Trail is where it left th' Santa Fe near Pueblo, ran north along th' front range of th' Rockies to a place south of South Pass where they found another pass that wasn't overgrazed and used up. There the Cherokees turned west over the mountains and somewhere near Bridger's fort it intersected with th' Oregon/California Trail.

The Fanchers drove their herd down th' Humboldt River to th' Sink of the Humboldt, then made a dry drive to th' Carson

River and on into California. In April, th' Fancher women an' all th' children left Cape Girardeau for California by boat. They crossed th' Isthmus of Panama and caught a boat to San Diego where they were to meet th' men. They found their ranch near Visalia and spent the next two years establishing their range and building a home and outbuildings. Pony stayed with them 'til Alexander and his family came back in '52. He came with them by boat to Cape Girardeau.

I hardly knew him, he had filled out, grown a beard an' wore a sombrero and gun outside his pants all th' time. Ma made him take th' gun off in th' house. He hung it on a peg high up where I couldn't reach it. He was glad t' git back and had all kinds of tales t' tell, but after a while I could tell he got a little bored.

Pa traded a lot around th' country, goin' down th' Fallen Ash Military Road as far as Fort Smith. Th' Army was always needin' horses an' he did right smart tradin' with them. In th' spring of 1849, he took Jake and a bunch of horses down to th' fort, knowin' th' demand would be high for th' summer's activities. He didn't get close to th' fort with a single horse for sale. Th' country was crawlin' with people, wagons, and livestock, all headed for California gold fields. Demand for horses was so high that Pa could have asked almost any price for them an' gotten it.

It had been his intention to drive the horses to th' fort for th' Army t' buy, but when he got to the edge of th' settlement, folks was stoppin' him every few feet askin' to buy his horses. He finally pulled back to th' edge of town an' put th' horses in a corral there an' let buyers come t' him. He didn't have t' keep one horse overnight, and had so much trouble keeping his own mounts he slept in th' corral with them to prevent stealing.

Captain Randolph Marcy heard Pa was in town and came

out very early th' next morning, catchin' Pa as he was packin' up t' come back home. Th' captain was ordered to survey a new trail across th' southern plains an' escort wagon trains to Santa Fe and he prevailed on Pa t' go with him as scout an' interpreter for th' various Indian tribes they would encounter. I doubt that it took much persuadin' t' git Pa t' agree an' he sent Jacob home with neighbors who were returning from visiting in Van Buren while he stayed with Captain Marcy.

I was only five when Jake came in. He was still mad that Pa hadn't taken him, an' Ma had a time keepin' him from turning around an' catchin' up with th' train on th' trail. After he had cooled off a bit, he figgered he could buy up a bunch of horses an' sell them easily at Fort Smith, and that's just what he done, even takin' some of th' mules with him. He made good an' came back with quite a bag of silver and th' news that Pa had left Fort Smith with Captain Marcy April 5th.

They would mark a trail for the wagons to follow, mostly up th' south side of th' Canadian River. Forty wagons had left on the 11th and another group had left the 16th of April. From then on, it looked like a steady stream of wagons crossing th' prairies on Marcy's trail. All in all, it's been estimated that 20,000 people took this trail to California in '49.

Jake said th' town was fairly bustin' with people an' more arriving every day. Trains were made up of companies of people, each one having a captain and a charter that all the members of th' company had to sign. There was the Fort Smith Company, the Clarksville Company, the Little Rock and California Mining Association, and the Tennessee Company, among others. He laughed an' told us about some of th' charters th' companies had made up. One required that no member was to have offensive body odors and had to change his underwear once a week!

Gold fever was sure running high and a few folks around got

a bad case of it. It must not have been all they said it was, for after a year or two, they began filterin' back into th' country as poor or worse than when they left. Mostly, those that made good were th' ones who provided goods and services such as livestock and tools to th' miners. They came back with gold jinglin' in their pockets while most miners was scrounging for their next meal. Pa didn't get back until early in 1850.

This is some of what he told us about th' trip:

We started out several days ahead of the trains an' marked a trail. It went from Fort Smith to the Choctaw Agency, northwest across the Canadian River to North Fork Town and Edward's Post, recrossed th' river at Choteau's Crossing an' stayed on th' south' side of the Canadian all the way to its headwaters in New Mexico and then on to th' Santa Fe Trail.

Captain Marcy had hired a Comanche named Manuel El Comanche as a guide. Manuel had just guided Josiah Gregg from Santa Fe to Van Buren and was preparing to return to San Miguel, New Mexico, where he lived with his Mexican wife. He was interesting to talk to e'en though he could barely speak English. I learned a lot of Spanish on that trip and between English, Spanish, and sign language, we communicated pretty well. He told me about living wild on the plains and about guiding Albert Pike to the mountains in '33. By that, I deduced he had done a lot of traveling across the plains. He proved to be very reliable and valuable to th' captain.

Between Edward's Post and Choteau's Settlement, we waited for th' trains t' catch up an' mainly traveled with them. At Edward's we picked up Captain Black Beaver, a Delaware who knew English, Spanish, French, and eight Indian languages. The Army didn't need me for interpreting too much after that and I set myself to scoutin' an' getting meat for th' soldiers.

A lot of trailblazin' was in th' form of finding prominent

landmarks along th' path an' riding back to tell th' trains what t' steer to next. In this way we stayed ahead of them, but were near enough t' be of aid should they need it. It involved a lot of riding and we probably traveled enough up an' down that trail to have gone to Santa Fe from Fort Smith three or four times.

I enjoyed th' work an' it was interesting seein' all that new country an' tryin t' determine th' best routes for wagons t' follow. Th' river bottoms were too sandy and boggy for travel and we stayed up on th' divides above th' breaks as much as we could. Where it showed, th' soil was red and so were th' sandstone rocks. One interesting place Black Beaver showed us was Red Rock Canyon. Traveling across country, you could miss it entirely, as it cuts into th' prairie and out of sight until you are almost on top of it. There is a spring-fed stream running through it an' it is well watered with plenty of grass. Our trains stopped there for a couple of days to rest and repair wagons and equipment. While they rested, we scouted th' road on ahead.

Th' next prominent landmark we found is only about six miles from that canyon, but as it turned out, it was the next stop for th' train as they had a very hard pull coming out of th' canyon an' it took most of th' day for them all to get on top. This particular landmark is a tall hill shaped like a potato hill standing out by itself on th' plain above th' breaks to Sugar Creek. It could be seen almost as soon as we climbed out of Red Rock and Black Beaver said there was a spring southeast of it.

Two of the young officers, Lieutenants Simpson and Harrison, made it up to race to it with th' first one who got there earning th' right t' name th' hill. Off they went in a cloud of dust and it was a matter of good-humored controversy which of them got there first. Lt. Simpson climbed the hill and planted a flag on th' peak. They named th' hill Rock Mary after young

Miss Mary Conway, who was a party in th' train. She was the niece of ex-Governor Conway of Arkansas.

I'm pretty sure th' name would have been th' same regardless of who won as this young lady was th' sweetheart of th' trains. Her father had given her a fine horse, which she rode the whole way, much to the surprise and admiration of everyone. Along th' way, she became betrothed to young Lt. Montgomery Pike Harrison, a story I will continue later.

Here, the editor must interject his own experience and knowledge of Rock Mary: A few years ago after reading references to the Rock in various accounts of early western travels, I determined to find the hill for myself. On a trip to Oklahoma City, two companions and I rode out to find Rock Mary. We knew we were very close to it, but could not determine its exact location. Seeing a car approaching on the sparsely traveled road we stopped and I flagged the car down. It was driven by an elderly man with a pleasant demeanor and I asked him, "Can you tell me about Rock Mary and where it is?"

"Can I?" he replied, "I can tell you more than you want to know about it!"

With that, my two companions joined me in the middle of the road and this gentleman relayed his story. "My grandfather homesteaded the land Rock Mary is on and after he had owned it a while and built up his ranch, someone from the state came out and said that they wanted to make it a state landmark and would he mind if people came out and climbed the hill? Grandpa was afraid of what trouble that might cause with his cows and fences and gates and said he would not allow public access to the hill.

"With that, the state man went down into th' breaks and found a strange rock formation there and named it Rock Mary. It certainly can't be the correct rock for it is well hidden and can't be seen more than a quarter mile away!

"There used to be a good spring on the southeast side of it, but it

has dried up. We used to climb it all the time and play there. You can still look out in both directions and see the old California Trails coming in to the spring. My father inherited the place and passed it on to me. I'm retired and have leased the land out, but I'm sure it would be ok if you wanted to climb the hill."

We declined the invitation and then he showed us how to get to the correct Rock Mary. I have always regretted not climbing that hill and seeing those old traces converging on Rock Mary and its spring.

We marked our trail south of hills later named Dead Woman and Wagon Wheel Mounds. From there, we followed th' divides staying on th' headwaters of creeks an' skirting those red canyons. The land was gradually rising and it began t' get harder t' find good water. A lake on Middle Buffalo Creek still had water and th' train stopped there for a rest while we scouted the country for th' next two days.

It was decided that we should turn southwest from Middle Buffalo to Sweetwater Creek and follow it across th' Staked Plains as it was our only chance for water. This we did all the way to th' very head of th' creek. From there we crossed an area that was dotted with lakes, most of them not much more than muddy buffalo wallows, but some larger with water in them. At th' west end of the lakes, we cut northwest across the upper end of White Deer Creek to Spring Creek, which was still running. It was a hard pull of twenty-five dry miles and that runnin' water sure looked good.

It was here that we met a band of Northern Comanche, th' most warlike branch of th' Comanche tribe. Their range was th' Staked Plain an we were in th' very middle of it. Th' train was thrown into a dither, but Captain Marcy eventually calmed everyone down, assuring them that we outnumbered th' band an' that they were not likely t' cause any trouble, only have a "big talk."

That afternoon, Chief Wolf's Shoulder rode into camp in war paint and headdress. When the headmen were seated on th' ground around th' captain's tent we had our smoke and a big talk. Marcy assured them through Black Beaver that we were not a war party, but we were leading the trains to California and intended no harm. It is the Comanche custom that they give gifts at the big talks and Wolf's Shoulder had brought two Comanche wives to present to the captain. He told the chief that he was honored, but that it was the white man's custom to have only one wife and he was already married.

To that the chief replied, "You are the strangest man I ever saw. When Comanche goes on a long trip, the first thing he wants is a wife!"

After the big talk, the chief challenged Marcy to a race with any of the Army stock against their ponies. Black Beaver warned the captain not to race, knowing that the Indians had ponies that could easily beat anything the Army had. He related that the Kickapoo had a thoroughbred racehorse and challenged the Comanches to a race, betting everthing they had on the race. Black Beaver, who was visiting the Comanches, also bet heavily on the thoroughbred. The Comanche chief refused to bet with him because he was a guest, but Black Bear insisted. The Comanche pony easily won the race and the chief refused Black Beaver's goods, telling him never to bet against a Comanche pony again! We parted company with the Comanches on friendly terms and the whole train breathed easier.

Speakin of th' train an' Indians, they had met Wildcat the Seminole chief an' some of his half-drunk Indians when they crossed Seminole territory. He was obnoxious an' insulting, but didn't abuse them any. I didn't see him when we crossed their lands. He was quite a woodsman and it took Jackson a long time to root him out of Florida.

I never saw land so flat and barren o' trees as those Staked

Plains. They were so lackin' in features that it was hard t' navigate in them. They got their name from th' Spanish or Mexicans who had to plant stakes or pile rocks t' mark their trail so's they could find their way back home. Comanches had no trouble navigating on th' plains. Their sense of direction was uncanny an' they could find their way without fail. We would have done good t' hire one of them t' guide us across, but for th' fact that we followed streams an' didn't need them.

From Spring Creek we cut northwest to th' Canadian River and followed it the rest o' th' way almost to th' Santa Fe Trail. That Canadian is a nice stream with steep banks and clear water. There is plenty of vegetation, with plum thickets and grape vines aplenty. Grass there was short an' brown, but stock loved it and actually fattened on it. That country sure would make good cattle growin' if it weren't for buffalo. That whole country was covered with them. I never saw th' like of wild life, from buffalo and horses right down to prairie wolf an' badger. We never lacked for meat of all kinds. There were turkeys an' grouse in th' thickets and we almost always had eggs. Some o' th' best pan fish an' catfish I ever tasted came out of that river. At The Crossing of the Canadian we camped an' the first Anglo babies born on th' Llano Estacado were born—twins!—we rested a couple of days until they were ready to move.

One evening, th' sky was streaked with those dark streaks we sometimes see here and Black Beaver said, "River will rise tomorrow." Th' next morning, Captain Marcy steered th' trains away from th' banks some. One train complained about us takin th' long way and cut across th' neck of one river bend, goin' down into a large bowl-shaped valley next to th' river.

They were almost even with th' lead train when a wall of water three feet high was seen coming down th' river. Behind it, water rose—and fast! It roared past in a rush and spread out over th' bowl, flooding wagons up to th' boxes before they could turn out of th' way. Oxen were panicking an' drovers were near washin' away in th' current. There was a mad scramble for high ground an' we all rushed out to help. That train ceased to be, with every wagon turnin' for higher ground. Most of those who were walking had run ahead of th' water, but those wagons were too slow an' got caught.

Water swirled through th' bowl, wagons were pushed sideways by th' current so that they were bunchin' up downstream. I threw a loop over th' leaders of one of the wagons, an' by pullin' led them out of th' water. No sooner than they were out, I was throwin' my rope to a man who was being washed by an' pulled him out. It seemed like forever, but we had everyone out in half an' hour, mostly wet and muddy.

Th' captain was as mad as ever I saw him. "Maybe next time you will follow along like you're supposed to instead of takin' your own trail!" he shouted at th' train captain loud enough for th' whole company t' hear. "There was good reason we went where we did, but I guess you found that out, didn't you?"

Th' poor man just hung his head and kicked dirt.

"Now get your train to th' back and stay there until you learn to stay in line!"

I had expected that we would stop there an' let them dry out, but we pushed on, th' soggy train soakin' up dust. When we stopped for noonin', they were a sorry looking bunch, covered with mud where dust hit their wet clothes an' canvases. They worked th' whole time cleanin' themselves and their belongings. I guess Captain Marcy cooled off a little, for this noonin' was a little longer than usual and we only traveled about six miles before sunset. After that, we didn't have any trouble with stray wagons or trains.

Th' Canadian stayed high all day but by next morning it was back in its banks and falling to its normal level, still muddy. I kept an eye out for those streaks in th' sky after sunset and almost every time we saw them, that river would rise. Th' best explanation we could come up with was that they were shadows of thunderheads up on th' headwaters somewhere, an' in that country runoff was high, causing th' flood.

The trains had trouble with oxen th' whole time we were in buffalo territory, for they would run off and join a buffalo herd every chance they got. The herders were forever chasing them down and the trains lost several head to buffalo herds.

The river got more crooked as we went up it an' we had t' work to find our best route without travelin' all th' crooks an' bends. Some days we left it an' didn't see it agin until dark. We could see Tucumcari Mountain stickin' up way south for a couple of days an' measured our advance by it.

Leaving th' Canadian, we traveled up Rio Conchas. The rainy season caught up with us an' travel got heavy in mud. Those trains split up an' drove abreast of each other t' avoid makin' deep ruts. Our first night on th' Conchas we camped just east of Variadero Mesa and there wasn't another landmark until we saw Mesa Montosa rising in th' northwest. We left th' Conchas and made a dry run to Gallinas River where we had trouble crossing because of high water. From there, we went south of a mountain called Mesas Cuatas to Aguilar Creek, up that creek a ways an' around th' base of some hills to Apache Springs. From there it was less than a day's travel to th' Santa Fe Trail. When th' train got to th' trail, we left it an' rode on ahead to Santa Fe.

I'm not sure when it happened, but somewhere along th' way, Lieutenant Harrison asked Doctor Conway for his daughter Mary's hand. The good doctor and his wife readily agreed but stipulated that any marriage would have to be after they arrived in California. This was sensible, for to marry right away was out of the question. The young couple was popular with all the people of the train an' it was a sad time when they parted, the train bypassin' Santa Fe an' our troop goin' on into town to resupply.

Captain Marcy's orders directed him to find an alternate route back to Fort Smith, so he determined to travel down th' Rio Grande to El Paso del Norte and return from there. Moving south, we heard that the Arkansas trains had stopped at Albuquerque and were just a few days ahead of us. Lt. Harrison secured permission to ride ahead and catch th' train for one last goodbye to Mary Conway. He caught up with them somewhere before they got to Socorro and stayed with the train until it left th' river at Socorro for California. He waited there for us to catch up.

When we left El Paso, we had two Mexican guides t' show us across th' Chihuahuan Desert and what a desert it was, th' first *real* one I ever saw. Up 'til then, I thought th' Staked Plains were dry, but I didn't *know* dry. If it wasn't knee-deep sand, it was rocks and cactus. Some places it was too dry for cactus.

First water was thirty miles away at a place called Hueco Tanks. From there, it was seventy miles to th' next reliable water at Pine Springs on th' eastern slopes of th' Guadalupe Mountains. We set our sights on El Capitan Mountain and starting just after midnight, trudged on. Th' road was plain, for it led to th' salt flats below El Capitan and Mexicans and Indians had gone there for their salt supply for centuries. It made a good trading item all over th' southwest and way down into Mexico. Th' salt flats were wet and there were pools here and there, but th' water was too salty t' use—it just made us thirstier than ever.

It was a steep climb, maybe a thousand feet up th' western foot of El Capitan to a bench that ran around th' south end to Pine Springs. Looking south from this height, you could see nothing but flat desert between th' Sierra Diablos and Delaware Mountains. East and southeast, th' land was rolling and broken, falling off like a series of benches down to th' Pecos River flats.

Not many of us stopped t' take in th' scenery, bein' dry as those salt flats and knowin' water was near. Coming around into th' shadows, our animals caught th' scent of water and picked up their pace. It sure was a blessing t' see that trickle of water! We drank our fill and th' animals were greatly refreshed after that seventy mile dry run.

Our guides were jumpy as barefoot kids on hot rocks. This was Apache country—Mescalero they said—and they was sure they were watchin' us. After a good rest, we moved up th' draw a ways and made camp where there was some forage for our stock. We didn't make much fire an' Captain Marcy set a double guard for th' night. In th' morning we watered up again. It was sixty miles to th' Pecos and we were not sure of water in b'tween.

Th' Mexes' nervousness was contagious an' most of us rode with their rifles across our laps. With others all armed up, I felt safe an' rode comfortable with my rifle in th' boot, but I kept a sharp eye out.

About six miles from th' springs was a draw the Mexicans called Rio Delaware, though it proved out to be mostly dry all th' way to th' Pecos. There was an occasional pool and by digging anywhere in th' channel you could hit water, so we didn't suffer any.

After two days we left that river an' headed southeastward to hit th' Pecos at Red Bluff. Th' water was slickey with alkali, but in small amounts it didn't make you sick. It wasn't strong enough t' ruin th' coffee.

That river's banks were steep and we rode far downriver before we found a place we could cross at Horsehead Draw. East of th' river was flatiron level and without guides we would have been lost. They struck out a little north of due east across th' best grassland you could have found.

It was th' last of August when we were at our driest in Arkansas, but here, thunderheads started building about noon and th' whole countryside was dotted with rain by mid-afternoon. When one of these storms caught you, it was sure you would get a soakin'. Some of them got real violent, mostly th' tall ones, and th' lightning was terrible. Out on those tree-less plains, we were th' tallest things around an' if it looked to git bad, we stopped and throwed th' horses an' laid down b'side them.

Once one of our horses was out grazing when a little storm came over an' he was struck by lightning. When we got to him, he was still smoking. His hooves were burned off an' there wasn't a hair from his ears down his neck an' forelegs to th' ground. His meat was cooked to a turn and we had a big meal of horsemeat roast for supper.

One towering storm came up on us from b'hind an' th' first thing we knew of it was when it started hailing out of a clear sky when th' cloud was still a good ten miles away. We watched and when we saw it was coming our way, found a place t' hide in a draw. Now, finding a draw t' hide in out there has mixed advantages, for you have t' weigh th' risk of a flash flood comin' down on you agin th' risk of gittin fried with lightning. We would watch th' storm and th' gully bottom, usually getting forced out of th' draw as th' water rose. Some draws had real flash floods. We watched a six foot wall coming down one of them one day and never felt a drop of rain. After a week of travel across this plain, th' ground b'gan t' gradually break into rolling hills of red soil and there were trees around numerous lakes and ponds we encountered.

Soon, we came upon a well-worn trail and followed it for several miles. On th' edge of Calf Creek below a tall mesa, we came to Big Spring bubbling up out of a bottomless hole in th' ground. From a height on th' side of th' mesa, you could see trails coming from all directions converging at th' spring.

This was Comanche-Kiowa country, and it seemed th' more

nervous we were about that, th' more relaxed those two Mexicans were. We camped well hidden and protected an' next morning when we got up, our guides were gone with their mules and packs. Black Beaver nodded and grinned. "Comancheros," was all he said, meanin' that the Mexicans were traders with th' Comanches and had no fear of them. Their trail led off southwest.

"They will go to Horsehead Crossing and probably hook up with some Comanches they can trade with," Beaver said.

We were now in well-watered country and not restricted to following streams. Captain Marcy set our path a little north of east an' we were soon on our way. This time, my rifle rode across my lap with all th' others. It was pleasant rolling country we rode through. Buffalo were plentiful an' grass was deep, turning green in th' rain. Along creeks, trees were thick and big, live oak, walnut, cottonwood, and almost all other kinds we have around here.

CHAPTER 4
THE MURDER OF LIEUTENANT HARRISON

Our sixth day out from Big Spring we camped on Bluff Creek. After supper, Lt. Harrison mounted up and rode up th' creek exploring. He often rode out alone, though we had warned him time an' agin about th' danger.

"Don't worry about me," he said, "if I see Indians, I won't run, but I'll face them calmly. I don't believe they would harm a man who shows no fear or threat to them."

When it grew dark an' th' lieutenant hadn't showed up, Captain Marcy ordered th' howitzer fired to signal our location. We spent a restless night waiting for him to come in, but he never came. That morning th' men were uncommonly quiet. Captain Marcy had th' howitzer fired again with no results. After breakfast he detailed five men to ride with him an' put me and Black Beaver on th' lieutenant's trail.

It was easy t' follow and went up th' creek quite a ways. His pace was a steady walk until we came upon a place where he had stopped his horse and turned to face away from th' creek, then proceeded on his new route. Maybe a hundred yards on, he stopped and was met by three sets of tracks. We soon determined that it was a horse and two mules. The four turned back to th' creek and rode a ways together, then stopped an' we found where they had sat and smoked a while.

Somehow the two Indians overpowered Lt. Harrison and got his weapon. There was quite a scuffle, but we found where they had put him back on his horse and ridden off up th' edge of a ravine into some timber, one on each side of the prisoner. A little ways on, we found th' lieutenant's saddle spotted with blood and gore and knew that violence had been done. Scuff marks led to th' edge of th' ravine and there in th' bottom was Lieutenant Harrison's body, stripped except for one boot, shot in th' back of th' head.

All was quiet for a moment, our anger rising. I wheeled my horse and trotted up th' trail, black thoughts of revenge in my mind. Black Beaver was right behind me and the rest followed. The Indians left in a run still going up th' edge of th' ravine, making no effort to hide their trail and we followed at a trot. Several miles along we came to their camp where they had spent th' night. We must have surprised them, for th' fire was still smoldering and there was meat hangin' on a spit. They had to be close, but try as we may, we could not catch up with them and th' captain finally called off th' chase about noon. We were too far from camp and probably too near a larger Indian camp from th' leisurely way those murderers had acted.

Back at th' ravine Captain Marcy said, "Let's get him out of there." Four men went down to recover Lieutenant Harrison's body while we stood guard. They had t' carry him down th' ravine quite a ways to where they could get to th' top.

We laid him out and Captain Marcy covered him with his blanket. One of th' troopers walked away and threw up. Two of th' men cut poles for a litter and we took Lt. Harrison's body back to camp on a travois.

Where the Indians had come up to th' lieutenant, Beaver motioned to me an' we backtracked their trail. We found where they had galloped down th' hill, then slowed and walked up to where the parties met. Probably they stopped running when they saw that Lt. Harrison wasn't running away. Further back we found where they had topped th' hill and caught sight of th' lone man. They had sat there for a while, probably determining that he was alone, then broke into a gallop. Beyond that, the trail was plain enough that we knew that we could easily backtrack on it. With that, we returned and caught up with th' troop.

It was a black day for us, th' worst time on th' whole trip. Everyone was greatly subdued and sat around in groups talking low. Captain Marcy doubled th' guard and ordered that we remain armed at all times, an order given just for a formality since it was already put in effect by our seasoned troops.

Th' doctor examined th' body, finding bruises on th' wrists where he had been tied and other indications that the lieutenant had put up a struggle. He probed th' wound and removed the bullet, which proved that he had been shot with his own gun.

His name was Lieutenant Montgomery Pike Harrison, grandson of President William Henry Harrison, older brother of future President Benjamin Harrison.

Because he was from a prominent family Captain Marcy went to pains t' write down all circumstances of the incident. He questioned us as to our impressions of th' happenings and especially Black Beaver and I about our ideas of what happened. Th' sign was plain and we could read it like a book. There was no doubt in our minds how it went down.

Our only unknown was who the Indians were. Beaver's opinion differed from mine an' we agreed that either of us could be right, but when th' captain asked us for an opinion, we didn't say anything. To make a mistake in this case could bring grief down on a whole innocent tribe and neither of us wanted that. We were curious where they had gotten mules, for it was sure they had come from white men too.

We turned northeast from Bluff Creek, makin' good time across th' grasslands. Ocassionally we would come across some abandoned cabin or ashes of one. Sometimes there would be a grave or two nearby, giving testimony to violence that had occurred there. Th' whole countryside had been abandoned by white folk because of Indian depredations. It wasn't until we reached Jacksboro settlement that we saw any people. What few that was there were in a fort built by one of th' settlers. They lived with a constant threat of attack and worked their fields in groups, part working an' part standin' guard. All of them were armed.

We stayed there a couple of days restin' an' reprovisioning as we could. There wasn't much available from these people for they needed all they had to get by themselves. Captain Marcy spent much time talking to them. At night he would make notes of what had been said that day. From Jacksboro, we took th' trace to Colbert's Ferry on th' Red River, then back to Fort Smith.

It must have been September, 1850 when Pa got home. It was a great relief t' see him safe and sound. Demand for horses remained high an' Pa worked hard t' keep up his herd and have horses for sale.

The younger Alexander Fancher began gatherin' all th' cattle and horses he could get his hands on and in April, 1854, he left with four hundred head of cattle and a wagon train of thirteen families. He left his wife and children on th' Osage, intendin' to come back and take them on his third and last trip to California. Of course, Pony went with him, only this time he took along a small herd of horses t' sell.

Those horses didn't get past Fort Bridger where old Jim Bridger bought up th' whole herd at Pony's price. Pony always grumbled that he must have priced them too low if Jim bought 'em without dickerin'.

From Fort Bridger they went down th' Humboldt again,

across th' Sierras to Grass Valley an' down th' western foothills to their ranch. They sold off th' steers in th' gold fields, making a fantastic profit and leaving th' heifers to replenish th' ranch.

Pony didn't stay at Visalia long, but took up with a bunch of men who were going back to th' states by th' southern route. These men were well off, but when they got to Yuma, they traded their fine horses for mostly played-out mounts th' pilgrims coming in to California had. Pony was attached to his horse and intended t' keep him until th' men told him he would not have him three days in Indian country, but the Indians wouldn't steal nags from ragged men goin' east. So he ended up with four tired horses and a pack mule. The men laughed at him again, for th' 'Paches' favorite meat was mule and shore 'nough, he was stolen before th' week was out on th' Gila Trail.

They followed th' Gila past Casa Grande into New Mexico, past th' copper mines near Silver City an' across th' mountains to th' Rio Grande. Pony got to Elephant Butte with one poor nag. He bought a good horse there that he kept for the rest of th' trip home. They rode on up th' river to Santa Fe where th' company broke up.

Bein' by now th' dead of winter and with Utes on th' warpath, no trains were going east. Pony spent th' winter an' th' rest of his money in Santa Fe. He got word about a herd of cattle Mr. St. Vrain was gatherin t' send to th' Arkansas t' replace those th' Utes stole from Uncle Dick Wootton and William Bent and hired on to help with th' drive.

They left th' middle of March, 1855, an' Pony said he never came closer t' freezin' t' death. A blizzard hit them at th' Pecos crossing an' they spent three days huddled up in a 'dobe at San Jose waitin' out th' storm. They had their herd stuffed in a 'dobe corral an' they milled around bawlin' th' whole time.

The fourth day, they crossed th' Pecos where th' cows

41

watered. They pushed them off th' trail to where th' snow had blown off the grass an' they ate their fill, then th' whole herd bedded down in th' middle of th' day! Pony said that was one time they let cows tell them what to do.

Late in th' evening, they got up an' drifted a little, grazing but by sundown they were bedded down again. They barely made five miles that day, but th' herd was up at sunrise an' moved out, makin' Las Vegas by night. From there, they went up by Fort Union an' on to th' adobe ruins of Bent's Old Fort where Mr. Wootton picked up his cows t' drive to his ranch at th' mouth of Rio Huerfano.

He told about th' Utes murderin' people at The Pueblo an' nine Cherokee drovers who declined his offer t' stay at his forted house an' got slaughtered not far from there. The Utes came around his place, but a couple of well-placed shots discouraged them from making any kind of attack, so they stole some cows and left. "For bein' on th' warpath agin, th' Comanches, they shore took it out on a bunch of other folks along th' way!" he said.

After deliverin' th' rest to Mr. Bent's ranch, Pony drifted on down to Bent's new fort in Big Timbers. Th' new fort was backed up to a bluff an' was made out of stone instead of adobe. Everything was first rate an' he was impressed.

There was a village of Cheyenne camped there, getting ready for their spring buffalo hunt. Pony was invited t' go with them, but instead hired on to a train goin' back to Westport that had lost a driver when he had broken his leg. So Pony turned his horse in to th' train's herd an' walked all th' way t' Westport b'hind four spans of oxen pullin' two wagons loaded with furs.

Th' lame man rode in th' wagon an' taught Pony how t' drive. Pony wore out his boots an' learned right quick that boots beat moccasins for oxen drovin'. He bought th' lame man's boots an' wore them out by th' time they got t' Westport.

He got paid, bought a new pair of boots, an' scooted straight for home, bypassing Osage country. I guess he was home by th' middle of June.

CHAPTER 5
THE HOG BUTCHERING

1855

One of th' most memorable events in my boyhood happened when I was eleven. A bunch of wild people had moved into th' hills around. They were shiftless and mean, an' enjoyed bullying people, even women were not spared. Sometimes fifteen or twenty of them would git together and do a little night ridin', terrorizing an' stealin' whatever took their fancy. They would burn barns, haystacks, an' houses that were left unguarded and even some that were guarded if one or two of 'em had powder an' bullets.

One night when Pa was out patrolling th' farms an' Pony was still out west, they rode down our gate an' headed for th' house. Ma heard th' ruckus an' put a couple of shots at 'em that made them rethink chargin' th' house. They started t' leave when one of th' pigs squealed.

"I shore hev a hankerin' fer some bacon," one of them shouted.

"Why don't we have a pig roastin'?" another called.

With that, th' whole bunch swung back to th' pigpen. There was lots of shoutin' an' pig squealin' an' soon a shot rang out an' one hog squealed his last.

Shouts of "Swing him up here, boys!" "Bleed him out" "Whur we gonna throw th' offal?" "Leave it fer th' Injuns, they like th' stuff!" and much more was shouted loud enough for us to hear at th' house.

A couple of shots hit th' door an' someone shot out one of th' windows. Pa had come to th' house to see that we were safe an' had all of us kids lie down on th' floor. He an' Ma stayed by th' window an' kept watch.

"I can get one of them from here," Ma said. She was so mad Pa had t' hold her back from chargin' out th' door.

"I could git one or two of them too, Mira, but th' rest would be on us in a minute an' we couldn't hold 'em off, or they would come back another night an' git revenge. We got th' kids t' watch after, let's see how many of them we can put a name to. I want *all* of 'em!"

I crawled to th' fireplace an' pulled out a charred stick an' carried it to Pa. I wrote on th' floor as he named th' ones he could identify in th' light of their fire or by names they called out in their hilarity.

"There's Hiss Clayburn."

Someone called out, "Raney, bring yore knife here."

"Only one Raney in th' country an' that's the Hensley boy."

"There's Demps Barnes," Ma said. She was calmer an' set herself about getting as many names as she could.

A shot spattered against th' logs an' someone hollered, "You still sleepin' in thur, Jess? Bring that girl o' yourn out an' let's dance!"

"That's Barnes Arnold!" Parlee whispered through clinched teeth, "I'll kill him first time I see him!"

On an' on we watched an' identified; Joe Whimpee, Fletch Parsley, Hirm Crook, Dillis Griggs, Noah Musick, Tom Griggs, Moss Weaver, Wylie Goodwin.

"I see that Whimpee boy," Ma said, "That's thirteen of them."

"I already have Joe down," I said.

"There's twelve of them, Ma," Parlee said.

"Good, we got them all," Pa said.

There was a sudden squealing at th' pigpen an' Ma's temper

rose again. "There's only twelve of them, Jesse, we can take them!"

Pa shook his head. "We could git three or four o' them b'fore they got to us an' then we'd all be dead, else they'd be feuding us. Better we take them on one or two at a time 'til we git them all."

Ma started t' say something else an' Pa cut her off sharp, "I'm no coward, Mira, and we will do this my way and be sure of ridding this place of that trash once and for all without shedding one drop of innocent blood!" He reached over an' gently took th' gun from her an' put his arm around her shoulders. Ma laid her head on his chest an' cried, more from anger an' th' loss of her pigs than from anything else.

Th' sky was grayin up an' th' raiders b'gan readyin' t' leave.

"Jess must be gone, else he'd be out here hepin' us butcher," one of them called.

"I bet he's out patrollin' his hedge agin horse thieves!" another said.

"Bein's these're his pigs we ought t' leave him most o' th' meat."

"Yore right, there, but we need t' git somethin' for our work."

"Let's take th' sow an' leave him th' rest."

"They killed my brood sow!" Ma gritted an' Pa held on to her tight. I think she was mad enough t' take on th' whole crowd then.

Th' gang mounted up an' galloped out of th' broken gate, draggin' th' sow's carcass b'hind them an' shootin' at th' house. Later, I dug out nineteen bullets from th' walls, inside and out.

Pa stepped out th' door, gun in hand, an' Parlee followed with Ma's gun. Ma slipped around them an' headed for th' pigpen. I trotted along b'hind her an' we got to th' pen t'gether. Every pig was dead an' scattered around were twelve or thirteen baby pigs they had cut out of th' brood sow. Ma just stood there starin' an' working her hands into fists. Tears of anger were runnin' down her cheeks an' I cried too for th' poor little pigs that never got a chance t' even squeal.

Pa came up an' surveyed th' carnage. He stood there a minute with his arm around Ma, then said, "Well, Miry girl, we might's well make applesauce outta th' windfall. You an' Parlee git a fire goin' under th' pot an' boil water while Jacob an' Zenas an' I gather up what's left of th' meat here."

We all set to an' were soon cleanin' an' butcherin' what meat we could save. Good, hard work served t' work off a lot of anger that day. We put up th' meat in little hams an' bacon slabs, not near as much as would have been if th' pigs had grown. Pa went looking for th' sow's carcass an' found her 'bout a mile from th' house, but she was too tore up t' be any good. He jist let her lie there in th' road where they had left her so's others would see an' know whut hed happened.

Word got around an' lots of neighbors gave their regrets, sayin' somethin' ought t' be done about those night riders. Th' sheriff rode down an' asked if we knew any o' them, but Pa wouldn't tell him a one. He figgered it was his responsibility t' see that right was done by them.

There were lots of sly grins an' comments when Pa was on th' town square, but he paid no mind, even when he saw one or other o' th' ones that did th' deed. Pony come back seethin' mad an' had more than one fight with th' hill boys whin' somethin' untoward was said or muttered. 'Nough o' them got whupped that they stopped sayin' anythin' when he was around. Still, someone took a shot at him one night when he came home late. It was looking like this would develop into a feud for a while there.

A new pilgrim came into th' country lookin' for a place an' Pa sold him both places at a good price. He was a tough veteran o' th' frontier an' looked likely to take care o' hisself an' his family. We packed up an' moved back to th' Village on th' Middle Fork.

The Village at th' Forks was gone an' a white settlement had grown up nearby. Even th' whites failed t' take into account th' amount of water that could come down th' valley an' th' village was subject t' floodin' now an' agin.

Everyone was glad t' see us and we had a grand reunion. Pa rented a place up Weaver Creek that had some good meadow bottoms an' we set about raisin' our stock an' plantin' a garden in th' spring of '56. Early August when most o' th' gardenin' was done, Pa said one night at th' table, "Now that the crops are mostly laid by, I think I will take Jake and Zee and do a little hunting, if Pony will take care of the place while we're gone."

It was ok with him, since that left him home an' free t' court a little gal up on Dodd Mountain. You couldn't have said anything more exciting to two boys than, "Let's go huntin'," an' th' next few days flew by with work or seemed t' drag whin we weren't busy. Pa was makin' some funny preparations for a hunt in our eyes, but we didn't care as long as we were goin' along. It seemed he had a lot more rope than necessary an' he gathered three extra rifles an' came in one night with three pistols he had gotten from somewhere. There was an awful lot of powder an' he sat up late makin' lead for th' guns—a whole lot of lead.

Th' day b'fore we left, Pa made us pack all th' packs an' taught us how t' do it properly. More than one o' them had t' be repacked to his satisfaction. We hardly slept that night an' were up b'fore anyone had stirred. Horses were saddled an' tied in front o' th' house b'fore breakfast. We all hauled packs out after we ate an' Pa showed us how t' load th' mules. We were anxious t' go but Pa took his time making sure everything was in good shape. Ma made us both kiss her goodbye like we was little kids an' Parlee give us both a big hug. It was like we were off on a long trip.

CHAPTER 6
INTO THE ABYSS

1856

We was excited about gittin' under way an' it didn't take us long t' deduce that Pa was up t' somethin' big. Me an' Jake speculated on what might be goin' on, but couldn't figger it out. Just b'fore we got to Pee Dee Creek, Pa turned off th' trail an' headed north up th' mountain. It was slow goin' 'til we got out on top. We avoided what few settlers were in th' country, never once nearin' house or farm. Pa kept to th' ridges an' mountainsides like we was hidin' an' we near busted with curiosity, but neither one o' us would ask a question.

There was a few settlements growin' up in th' country an' we avoided them too, which was not in Pa's character t' do, bein' a horse trader an' all. After several days, we recognized th' country around Bear Creek Springs, but agin, Pa avoided bein' seen or stopping t' visit friends he knew that still lived around there.

Turnin' west, we rode up over th' hills an' down into Long Creek valley. That night instead o' campin', we kept on across th' valley an' up over th' pass where Alpena is now and into th' drainage o' Dry Creek. Now, we *knew* somethin' was up, for we had left th' best huntin' grounds and were back in our old territory where game had been hunted out.

"Maybe Pa's goin t' visit folks at Carrollton an' take us on west to th' buffler grounds," Jake whispered.

"That don't 'splain why we're hidin' out like we are," I answered.

"Betchya we are," he persisted.

But he was wrong, for where th' trail crossed Dry Creek, we turned southwest up Dry to th' gap b'tween Round Mountain an' Blacklick Mountain. Over against Pine Mountain, there's a canyon an' bluff where one o' th' branches of Dry comes off th' mountain an' there's where we made camp, up under a bluff. It was brushy and rocky an' we had t' unload th' mules so's they could push through brush, around an' over rocks to th' bluff. There might have been a half acre of open land there where animals could be comfortable.

All morning, we gathered firewood an' made camp, so it looked like we were gonna be there a while. Pa picked a place under th' cedars where we could build a small fire an' smoke would disburse through th' trees so's not to be detected. He instructed us not to make a big fire an' to stay hidden from sight at all times. We was bustin' an' Jake tried t' git me t' ask Pa what kind of game we was huntin', but I wasn't about to.

By midafternoon camp was made up an' we cooked some meat and ate. Pa pulled a piece o' deerskin out of his bag an' studied it, then turned to us an' said, "I suppose you will bust or die off if I don't explain what we are doing here and just what we are going to be hunting. I have a list here of our game," an' he handed Jake th' skin. Jake took it an' started readin', his eyes bugged out an' he drew in a big breath, then near forgot t' breathe.

His face got pale, then red, then he started grinnin' an' whisperin', "Yeah, yeah . . ."

I couldn't wait any longer an' snatched th' skin out'n his hand. When I turned th' writin' up, this is what I read:

Hiss Clayburn	Rany Hensley
Demps Barns	Barns Arnold
Joe Whimpy	Fletch Parsly
Hirm Crook	Dillis Griggs

| Noah Musick | Tom Griggs |
| Moss Weaver | Wyly Goodwin |

I felt th' blood leave my face, my scalp crawled, an' my eyes dimmed. I've had that feelin' other times in my life at various moments, but I still remember that time like it was yesterday. Me an' Jake had talked about th' hog butcherin' an' how Pa had handled it an' we was near decidin' Pa was ascaired o' th' bunch. We had made our own list an' plotted for near a year how we were gonna git even. Somehow Pa or one o' th' women had found it an' deduced what we were thinkin'.

Pa looked at us an' said in Cherokee, "When I saw the night riders that night, I knew that there was no way of resisting them without exposing the family to mortal danger. Those fellows are sneaks and backstabbers, cowards at heart, and find strength only in bunches. If we had fought that night, there would have been more than hogs and pigs killed and they would have not stopped until we were ruined and some of us dead. The whole countryside would have been drawn into a feud on one side or t'other and the Osage would have run red for a long time.

"My first responsibility was to see that my family was safe and I have done that. My second responsibility as I see it is to spare bloodshed to my friends and neighbors in the valley, and my third responsibility is to stop night riding and bullying, which is what we are here for.

"Taken one or two at a time, we can rid this country of the whole bunch for the good of the community and to let them know that their behavior will not be tolerated." He thought a moment, and I could hear him breathing it was so quiet.

"Appeasement never brings peace when bullies rule. When all they know is the force of violence, they have to be met with equal and greater force until the lawless know that their actions come at a cost too high to risk. Rarely do they learn to live peacefully, but turn their attentions elsewhere to weaker quarries. Only when they are completely destroyed or driven out will there be peace and order—until the next bullies appear.

"A man or a clan or a tribe or a community has to be strong enough in the eyes of their enemies to make them know that to attack would be too expensive and painful to attempt. We were isolated from the rest of the community when we lived on Osage and were vulnerable to a mob. It was not possible to resist them without loss, but now we can choose our battles and battlefields and by isolating them into smaller numbers, we can defeat the whole if we are careful and a little lucky."

It was quiet for a long time. I think me an' Jake both were ashamed of ourselves.

Finally, Jake said, "Ok, Pa, we'll help all we can."

I wondered what a twelve year old could do to help, but that didn't stop me from agreein' with Jake!

"I'm going to scout around for a day or two to see what the lay of the land is, then we can make some plans," Pa said. "For the time being, I want you two to stay here and lay low. It'll be boring for you, but I don't see any alternatives until I know more about things."

"That's ok, Pa," Jake said, "It'll give the stock time to rest and me and Zee can gather hay for them."

"Don't be seen and *don't* make trails for someone to follow!"

"We won't."

"If I'm not back by sunset in two days, you two pack up and head back home by way of Bear Creek and the Village at the Forks Trail, you understand?"

"Yes, Pa."

"I'll know where you are and will catch up with you if I can. You promise to do as I say?"

"Yes, Pa."

"Don't leave until the morning of the third day."

"We won't."

With that, Pa rolled up in his blanket and was asleep. Me an' Jake was too excited t' sleep an' we sat an' talked a long time, plannin' out what we was goin t' do while Pa was gone. By th' time th' sun set, we were so sleepy, bein's we hadn't slept in thirty-six hours, that we rolled up an' were soon sound. Pa must have left some time in th' night, for when we woke next morning he was gone.

We worked hard all day, sneakin' out an' gatherin' hay from some o' th' meadows around that hadn't already been mowed. Carrollton was on t'other side o' Pine Mountain an' th' countryside was settled up some, but we were out o' th' way under th' bluff, it bein' rough country not good for any kind o' farmin'. Next day we spent makin' th' camp more secure. We even built a wall around th' shelter under th' bluff where we could fort up if necessary an' stowed all our gear there. There wasn't room to sleep in there so we made our beds agin th' outside wall.

Sunset an' Pa hadn't showed up. We was *some* worried an' Jake said we would not even pack until morning an' give Pa more time t' come in if he had been delayed. I took th' first watch, hidin' myself under th' haystack where I could watch while Jake slept. It must have been not more than two hours later that Pa give th' signal that he was comin' in. Jake sat up, but I didn't move. Purty soon I heard a leaf turn an' a shadow moved an' sat by Jake.

"Where's Zee?' Pa asked.

"Here, Pa," I whispered, "I'm on first watch." I sure was relieved he had come back.

"No need t' watch, but you stay there an' I will roll up under the cedars across from you. I'm too tired to talk now, but we'll talk in the morning."

I didn't mind settlin' down under th' hay where it was warm. Cold air settled in that hollow at night even in August and it was right chilly when th' sun went down. Us sleepin' in separate places was standard procedure when we camped. It gave any prowlers of th' two-legged or four-legged kind problems determinin' just how many of us there were an' where we were.

In spite o' my intentions, Pa was up an' stirrin' b'fore I got up. Jake kicked me when he came t' git hay for th' stock. I was up an' about when he come back. We ate, then Pa set back an' told us what he had done.

"When I left here, I went over the hill and through the gap by Bradfield's down to Carrollton. I was sneaking up to the back of the saloon when I stepped on a body. It was none other than Fletcher Parsley, passed out cold drunk. I left him laying there and went to the window. Most of the night riders were there whooping it up and drinking. By and bye someone stepped out back to relieve himself. I saw by the light it was Demps Barnes.

"It took a little persuading, but he agreed to pick up old Fletch and come back up the mountain with me. Just so he wouldn't get lost, I tied a rope around his waist and around the saddle horn. He kept complaining that Fletch was wet and stinking and even once threw him down, but I convinced him it was better if he carried his buddy with us.

"There's a sinkhole on the first bench to the left of the trail through the gap and I took the boys there. Just before we got to the hole, Demps gave out and begged to leave Fletch on the ground. I augered with him some, then give in to his wishes. He led on and must not have known about the sinkhole, for all of a sudden he let out a yelp and the rope went taut. He had fallen right into that hole and was dangling in the air! Wasn't anything I could do but ease him down to the bottom. I got down and eased up to the edge of the hole. It slopes off at a steep rate, then there is a sheer fall to the bottom where Demps was.

" 'Demps, air ye ok?' I called in English.

" 'Where am I?' and I knew he was ok.

" 'Looks like you done fell into a sinkhole, didn't you know it was here?'

" 'No,' he said with some other words throwed in you shouldn't hear, 'git me out!'

" 'I'll have t' go for help, untie th rope an' let me have it back.'

"He untied with a lot of talk that must have warmed up that hole considerable and I pulled it up and went for help. Wouldn't you know th' only help I could find was ol' Fletcher layin' back there by th' trail still sleepin' it off?" In Cherokee he continued, "I tied the rope tight under his arms and had a time waking him up. He finally came around some and I told him about Demps' dilemma. Well, that got his attention and he was all about rescuing his friend. We set out an' darned if that boy didn't fall into the same hole! The sudden stop at the end of the rope dislodged one of his boots and it must have hit Demps, for he hollered out.

"There wasn't anything to do but lower Fletch to the bottom. Then butterfingered me, I let that rope slip and it fell into the hole too! There was consternation above and below. Demps tied a rock to the end of the rope and tried to fling it out, but it's a good thirty feet to the top and it kept falling back.

" 'Demps, you might as well be throwin' Fletch as that rock, it'll do just as much good,' I called.

"He agreed with some more o' those warmin' words.

" 'I'm gonna have t' go get some more rope t' git ya out, may be late afore I get back. If they's no rope at Carrollton, I'll have t' go up t' Hittson's at Osage.'

" 'Hurry up,' he says, 'they may be snakes in here!'

" 'You got Fletch's bowie knife if you need it, but don't you go cuttin' on that rope, we'll need it t' git you out.' He was still talking an' yellin' when I left.

"On th' way out, I stopped off at Bradfield's an' told him what had happened. He said he would be glad t' watch over th' boys 'til I got back. He had a rope long enough, but his wife needed it t' draw water an' couldn't spare it."

Me an' Jake was cryin' we laughed so hard. When we had caught our breath, Pa said, "I went down to see Sims Rowe and talk over what we needed t' stop th' night riding. Things were worse than ever.

" 'With folks guardin' their homes an' not able t' gather enough t' fight, th' gang holds sway over th' whole country,' he said. 'I can't keep deputies and I can't do anything by myself, not havin a jail t' keep them in. I swear I don't know what to do!'

" 'Well, I've got a jail for you,' I said, 'and they can't get out of it on their own.' Then I told him about th' sinkhole and its two inmates.

" 'Well I'll be damned,' he said, 'couldn't be a better jail in th' country!' He was all enthused an' we talked about how we could get th' rest into it.

"We decided to take our time and catch them one at a time to avoid getting into a battle with th' bunch of them. Sims said that they did th' most of their night ridin' when th' moon was bright. Rest of th' time, they hung around town an' drank or scattered into th' hills to their cabins."

"Th' Griggs boys are gone, shot up tryin' t' make off with some Osage horses up on White River. Word has it that th' Osages had a scalp dance shortly after that. Th' rest of th' gang rode back pretty subdued for a while, then they were worse than ever."

"What are we gonna do, now?" I asked.

"Most of our work will be at night for a while until we get them thinned out, then when they can't bunch up, we figger th' community will turn out t' help. Sims figgers Wylie Goodwin will be pretty easy t' take. He swamps at th' tavern days an' can be lured away by a jug. We plan t' add him tonight. Last night I happened on Arnold and Hensley and persuaded them to help me rescue Parsley an' Barnes, but my hands are so beat up I couldn't handle th' ropes." He held up both hands and they were red, skinned up and swollen. He must have had a time "convincin' " Parsley an' Barnes t' help. I could see some red splotches on his face an' there was a little split in his lip, but he didn't say anything about it.

"I came here to get you to help. The boys are tied to trees an' Jasper Bradfield is watchin' over them 'til we get back."

Well, I can tell you it didn't take any time for me an' Jake t' be saddled up an' ready! Pa traded his horse for our biggest mule an' we were soon on our way. Instead of goin' by way of th' gap, we rode up th' hill to th' west an' came around th' bench to th' sinkhole. It was funnel shaped with steep sides a feller couldn't stand up on. We could see th' other side where th' men had slid down an' I gave a shudder thinkin' about stumblin' into that without a rope anchor. At th' bottom of th' funnel was a black hole some twenty feet across. Layin' on our stomachs at th' rim, we couldn't see far into it.

"Air ye still there, Demps?" Pa called.

"What d'yuh *think*, you blankety-blank-blank, when I get out of here . . ."

"I got help here an' Barnes an' Raney are on their way, we'll have you out in no time," Pa interrupted. "How's Fletcher doin'?"

"Pukin' on ever'thin' an' beggin for water!"

Pa grinned. "Seems I remember a drip over to th' back there, you find it?"

"Shore, but it don't quench *his* thirst! Send us down a jug."

"Sure 'nough, Demps, think I hear them comin' up now, hope their rope's long enough." With that, Pa motioned us to follow an' we rode around th' hole. I gave it a wide berth. Brad-field was sittin' on a log smokin' his pipe, a rifle across his knees; th' two thugs were tied to trees nearby. They looked pretty beat. Barnes Arnold had both eyes swelled near shut an' Hensley had blood stainin' his shirt. His nose was cocked at a funny angle.

"Been havin' a good conversation with th' boys here, seems they run into a buzz saw er somethin'." Bradfield grinned.

"Whin I git loose, I'm gonna . . ." Raney growled.

"Now Raney," Pa said softly, "what makes you think th' outcome will be different . . . unless you can use some kind of equalizer . . ." Pa mused.

"I don't need no equalizer," he snarled.

"Well, we can all right ready see that!" Bradfield laughed, then he got dead serious.

"Didn't need no 'equalizer' whin' yuh held Simmons an' fired his barn, did yuh? I guess them three rifles poked in his face was jist there for th' fun o' it! Made a good light for th' bunch t' dance around, didn't it?" He barely held his temper in check an' his rifle raised some. Hensley closed his eyes tight.

"Boys, I just ran into Fletch an' Demps over on th' bench. They're in a might o' trouble an' I told them we would come back an' rescue them," Pa said. "Zee, you an' Jake, untie Raney an' we'll take him with us. Don't think we'll need Barnes, he cain't see too well. He can stay with Bradfield. If we need you, we'll come back for you, Barnes."

We went an' untied Raney. He was wrapped up pretty tight an' we went round an' round unwinding him. When th' last strand was loose, he fell to his knees. His hands were tied b'hind his back.

"Slip th' end o' that rope under his arms and tie it close in th' back," Pa instructed.

I tied it while Jake handed Pa th' other end. Raney stumbled ahead of us on th' way to th' hole an' I almost felt sorry for him. Almost. He stopped short when he saw the sinkhole and his face turned white. His knees buckled some an' I thought he was gonna fall.

Pa got down an' checked th' cinch on th' mule. He tightened th' knot on th' horn an' th' one b'hind Hensley's back. He nodded. "Nice knot, Zee, but I'm gonna add another one fer safety. Now, Raney, Fletch an' Demps both stumbled into that hole at night an' th' rope fell in with them. I spent all day diggin' up this rope an' it's th' last one in th' country long enough t' reach. I'm gonna lower you down t' th' boys so you can take that end to them. When you get down, untie th' rope, tie that other one to it an' I'll pull it up for Arnold t' use. They's not much room in th' bottom down there an' if I have to let ol' Arnold down without a rope, three or four o' yuh will get hurt." He looked Raney in th' eyes, almost nose t' nose. "Understand?"

Raney nodded, pale as a ghost.

"I'm gonna let you down slow an' easy so's you don't get hurt. You sit down on th' edge o' th' hole and we'll let th' mule walk forward slow and easy. You'll swing some over th' lip, but th' rope will reach bottom easy enough." Pa was almost gentle with him. "When you git to th' bottom, better stuff your nose with rags so's it'll heal open. Now sit down there an' dangle yer feet over th' edge. I'll git on my ol' mule, Joe, there an' tighten th' rope up."

Raney hesitated a moment an' Pa said softly but sternly, "Go on, Hensley, make it easy on yourself."

Th' bully sat down an' pulled himself to th' lip with his heels, only he went too far over and some of th' lip gave way. He slid down th' slope screamin' an' yellin'. Luckily I had stayed back by Joe's head an' when I seen what was happenin' held th' mule. At th' same time, Pa had grabbed th' rope an' he and Jake slowed it down so th' shock on th' saddle was slight.

Ever'thing was quiet fer a moment except for th' boys in th' hole who were bein' showered with gravel an' rocks an' didn't know what was goin' t' follow.

Pa got up an' brushed his pants off as he was looking over th' lip. Raney had stopped halfway down th' slope, feet spread wide to keep himself upright.

"Yuh went too far, Raney, but I guess you was never one t' do things halfway, was yuh?" Pa called.

For th' first time, Raney found his voice an' let out a string of curses that fairly turned th' air blue. I moved Joe ahead a couple of steps an' th' cursing stopped.

"That's good, Zee, bring him on slow," Pa said. He lay at th' lip watchin' Raney an' signalin me t' move up slow. "Hold there, Zee. Rainey, we're gonna ease you over th' lip an' you'll dangle fer a little, not more'n twenty-five—thirty feet t' th' bottom now, might be easier if ya lay down afore you go over th' edge."

He watched a moment, then signaled for me an' Joe t' come forward. I felt Joe's muscles tighten b'fore I moved him. That mule was watchin' Pa an' knew what he was t' do as soon as I did! We started walkin' forward again and I could feel when Raney swung over. I pulled Joe a little faster until th' rope slackened an' Pa signaled us t' stop.

"Now, boys, untie that rope an' we'll pull it back up."

"I'm not letting go 'til you pull me up!" Demps called.

"Now Demps, you know that's not gonna happen for a while. If you don't let go, I'll jist let 'er go up here an' you'll have th' only ropes in th' country long enough t' let you out o' thet hole. It would take me weeks t' go to Little Rock or Sibley t' git more rope, *if I was disposed to*. Untie it an' let go, I got more use for it up here b'fore you can git outta there."

All was quiet an' in a minute I started pullin th' rope up an' loopin' it over Joe's saddle horn.

We got Barnes an' brought him to th' sinkhole. Bradfield

came with us. At th' hole, Pa called out, "Fletch, Demps, ol' Barnes is mighty worried about you boys an' begged me t' take him to ya. I told him it warn't necessary you was all right, but he insists, so here he comes. He cain't see too well, so you need t' help him all yuh can."

With that, we lowered Barnes Arnold into th' hole. Joe an' I stayed farther back so th' first part wasn't a free slide an' Pa signaled us like b'fore. I didn't do nothin' but let Joe act accordin' t' Pa's signals. When th' rope went slack, he took one more step, then stopped. We pulled th' rope up without any discussion this time.

Jasper Bradfield chuckled. "Best durn jail in th' country! We shoulda thought o' it long ago!"

Pa called down to th' men in th' hole, "Boys, we're gonna go git ya some more company, now. Only four o' us knows where you are, so you'll know yore buddies won th' war if'n we don't come back in a day or so. Don't waste your breath yellin', no one but birds flyin' over kin hear you. If you climb up that rock pile above th' big boulder, they's a hole that goes somewheres. You can feel a little breeze comin' through it sometimes, so there's another outlet sommers, but it may be a long way in th' dark. Be careful for pits in th' floor if yuh have to try goin' thataway."

"What we gonna eat or drink down here?" Raney called.

"Demps, show him th' seep, it's purty good water, Raney, but don't be a pig about it. I'll bring you back some chow if I'm lucky enough t' get back."

With that, Pa an' Bradfield turned t' leave, both of them grinning like possums up a gum tree. "I don't think you need t' worry about guardin' that bunch," Pa said. "We'll hide our tracks and they will be secure there."

"I'll watch, just th' same t' be sure they ain't any rescuers come along," Bradfield said.

"Sheriff may bring up Wylie Goodwin 'bout sundown. I'd be obliged if you hold him 'til we get here."

"Be my pleasure," th' old man said. "I'll have him at th' tyin'-up trees if they show. Ma might let me borry th' well rope for a few minutes." He chuckled.

"Keep this rope an' spare th' missus th' trouble," Pa said.

CHAPTER 7
JAKE LENDS A HAND

1856

With that, we took off over th' gap t' camp. Pa was hungry an' gittin' mighty sore from his fightin'. We made him some food while he soaked his hands in cool creek water. When he had finished, he turned in an' slept.

I pulled out th' list an' we went down by th' branch an' studied it.

"We got Demps Barnes, Fletcher Parsley, Raney Hensley, an' Barnes Arnold in th' hole, th' Griggs boys is gone an' Wylie Goodwin may as well be, he's so soft," I said.

"So that leaves Clayburn, Whimpee, Crook, Musick, and Weaver t' go, don't it?"

"Clayburn may be hardest t' catch," I said.

"Nah, I bet it'll be those Cherokees Musick an' Weaver."

"What about Crook, he's half-breed," I said.

"Yeah, half-Osage mean an' half-white-trash lazy," Jake mused. "I don't think he'll be all that hard t' handle."

"What about Joe Whimpee; he's only a couple of years older'n you, ain't he? He shouldn't give too much trouble."

"He's three years older an' he whipped me a time or two. Loves t' pick on smaller kids. I'd shore like t' give *him* another try." Jake's jaw tightened.

"He usta brag he run away frum some blacksmith he was 'dentured to up Sibley way, wonder if they want him back up there."

"Prob'ly not, he don't seem too keen on workin'."

"So-o who d'ya think th' next one after Wylie'll be?"

"That's prob'ly up t' Pa an' Sheriff Rowe," I said. "It may even be th' luck o' th' draw who's next. We better git some rest ourselves, Pa's gonna need some help next time he goes out, he's so sore."

And with that we both turned in. It was just after noon an' I wasn't sleepy, but we napped some. 'Bout midafternoon I had all th' restin' I could stand an' got up. Jake saw me up an' he got up too. Pa was still sleepin' so we went down by th' branch an' sat a while.

"Pa shore could use some rest while his hands healed up a bit," Jake said.

"It'd be hard t' keep him still 'til this is all over," I replied. "Wonder what he's gonna feed th' prisoners."

"Prob'ly nothin'."

"Be good if we could find a pig for 'em, they like it so much."

"Sa-a-ay, that's a good idea, Zee, lets go see if we can find one for 'em an' maybe Pa would take it easy tonight."

"We could get Joe out easy enough an' both of us could ride him."

"Ok, you get Joe an' I'll get th' saddle. We can saddle him on th' way."

"On th' way *where*?"

"I dunno, maybe back north th' way we come in an' find a farm where they have hogs. It isn't likely anyone would know us."

He went for th' saddle an' I found Joe dozin' in th' shade, swishin' flies. He seemed ready t' go an' it wasn't too long afore we was headin' down toward Low Gap south o' Round Mountain. To th' northwest a ways, we ran across a place. They didn't have any hogs, but said there was a man with some by Tanyard Spring, so we rode over there.

"We're gonna ride plum 'round that Round Mountain," Jake grumbled.

"How we gonna pay fer a hog?"

"Maybe we can tell them it's for some prisoners th' sheriff has an' they kin collect from him, I don't know."

It was about three miles to Tanyard an' gettin' late when we got there. Th' farmer had some hogs an' when we told him what it was for, he agreed to let us have one.

"Yuh kin take yore pick. Tell Sims not to let Arnold an' Demps Barnes loose 'til I git there. They owes me fer Ma's milk cow they run off—an' I aims t' collect in cash or flesh!"

He led us down to th' pen an' we were lookin' over th' lot when he said, "I found th' runt dead this mornin' whin I come down t' feed. Don't know whut was wrong, but th' rest seems ok." He indicated th' half-grown pigs rooting around their mammy.

"What'd ya do with 'im?" I could see Jake's wheels turnin'.

"Throwed him over by th' trees, hadn't got time t' bury 'im yit . . . Sa-a-ay, you ain't gittin' any idees, air ye?" His grin said he knew th' answer.

I hopped down an' ran over to th' carcass. "He ain't swelled too much yet," I called.

"Why, you scalawags, I'll *give* you that pig if you feed it to them two!" Th' farmer was fairly dancin' with glee.

Well th' upstart was that we tied that pig on back o' th' saddle an' I walked. Th' old pioneer was still laughin' an' wavin' his hat when we left. It was gittin' late an' we were afraid Pa would wake up and leave b'fore we got there, so halfway up th' branch, Jake hurried on to camp. Pa still wasn't up when I got there, so we got around an' cooked supper. Th' smell of food woke him up an' we ate.

"Pa, we found some food for th' prisoners." I couldn't wait to tell him any longer.

Pa looked up, "You boys been huntin'?"

"Not 'zactly, Pa," Jake said.

"We found a farmer that had some pigs an' got one from him," I explained.

"Well, I s'pose it'd be proper t' feed them pork as much as they like it. Where is it?"

"Layin' over there by Joe."

Pa got up an' walked over to where th' pig was layin'. He nudged it with his foot, "Looks a little ripe, don't he, boys?"

"He only died last night sometime, but th' price was right," I replied.

"Th' farmer at Tanyard Spring said it was good enough for those boys, since they run off his milk cow," Jake explained.

"Tanyard? That must have been Alf Weaver. Was he 'bout fifty, walked with a little limp?"

"Yep, that was him, but he didn't act like he knowed *us*," I said. "Wants us t' hold Arnold an' Barnes for him."

"Let's saddle up and take the boys supper b'fore it gets dark," Pa said, so we hurried up, finished supper, an' got goin'.

We could hear hollerin' before we got to th' tyin'-up trees an' there was ol' Wylie Goodwin trussed up cussin' a blue streak at Bradfield who was sittin' on his log calm an' collected.

"Good thing you boys showed up when yuh did, I was gittin ready t' throttle that noise down."

Wylie looked at us an' began cussin' again, then he saw who Pa was, turned pale, an' shut up. Pa walked over to him an' spoke right in his face, "Hello, Wylie, it's been a while, hasn't it? Seems you were at a butcherin' last time I saw you."

"Thet wasn't my idée an' I had nothin t' do with it," he whined.

"Well, that must have been someone else I saw holdin' up that suckling an' slingin' it out in th' yard."

Wylie whimpered an' hung his head. Pa grabbed his hair an'

pulled his head back. "If that wasn't you, who was it, Wylie?"

"I don't know!"

"Must have been some other 'Wylie' th' boys was talking to, who could that be?"

"I don't know," th' coward whimpered.

"It was you, Goodwin, I heard you brag it!" Bradfield said.

"Th' boys here got supper for your friends and I thought it would be nice if you took it to them." Pa started untying the man. "That ok with you?"

"Shore, Jesse, I'll take it to them." Wylie brightened.

"Ok, let's git goin'." Pa slapped him on th' back.

"Ain't you goin' t' untie my hands?"

"Not just yet, th' boys might want to do that for you."

Wylie groaned at the thought that his buddies would see him trussed up. They only let him run with them so he could be the butt of their crude jokes. He was kind of simple.

We started toward th' sinkhole, Wylie following along b'hind Pa and Bradfield and jabbering away. He didn't see th' hole 'til we were right on top of it.

"Whoa!" he said, backing away, and I think if Joe an' Jake and I hadn't been in th' way, he would have bolted right then.

Pa grabbed him an' whirled him around, stringin' th' rope under his arms an' tyin' it b'tween his shoulder blades. "They been askin' for you, Wylie, an' it'd be nice if you visited them an' took them their supper."

I tied th' rope to th' saddle horn. Bradfield tugged it an' nodded approval. Joe backed up to his usual spot for beginning an' Pa struggled t' get Wylie to th' edge of th' slope. He kicked Wylie's feet out from under him an' he sat with a thump. Before he could move, Pa shoved him over th' lip an' he slid down a few feet. At th' same time Pa signaled an' Joe started his slow walk. Wylie was screamin' in holy terror, but it was suddenly silent when he went over th' edge. We lowered him until th' rope slacked.

"Untie him boys, he's brought supper to you," Pa called.

A rough laugh came from th' hole. "He's done fainted dead away!"

"Rope's loose, send us thet food," Demps demanded.

I backed Joe up about ten or twelve feet while Pa an' Jake tied the pig's hind feet to th' rope. Thinkin' I had backed up all th' way, they shoved th' pig over th' edge while Bradfield was watchin' all this an' laughin' to hisself.

Mr. pig shot down th' slope in a shower of rocks an' gravel an' out over th' hole. I braced Joe for th' impact an' he knowed what t' do. There were shouts an' yells from th' hole an' th' pig swung back an' forth like a pendulum for a while, then we lowered it to th' floor. Pa and Jake had jumped back when th' pig started sliding, then, when it stopped, they looked at me in surprise. "Be careful, boy, you don't send one of us down there with a trick like that," Pa said, then he grinned.

"How's your supper, boys?" he called.

"How long's this thing been dead?"

"We can't eat him raw!"

"He ain't cooked?" Jake asked incredulously.

"Do you want some firewood?" Pa called.

"Yeah, yeah," sang a chorus, then, "No! Don't be throwin' no sticks down here, we can't dodge 'em!"

"We'll lower a bundle of sticks down, but we can't get any fire to you," Pa called.

Jake an' I got busy an' all four of us had a big bundle of sticks gathered in no time.

"Here they come!" Pa called. He an' Jake lowered them by hand an' th' rope was soon gathered in an' stowed.

"Enjoy your meal, boys. We'll be back in a while," Pa called. A chorus of curses replied.

On th' way back, Bradfield said, "Sims said there was a lot of curiosity about th' disappearances an' Hiss was callin' for th' boys t' meet him at th' tavern tomorrow night. That usually means night ridin'.'"

"Moon's still kinda dark for that, ain't it?"

"Yeah, an' it rises late, too. Sheriff thought you might want t' talk to him, said he'd be in town if'n you wanted t' send one o' th' boys for him."

Pa looked at us, "That means you would get there after dark, think th' two of you can find your way back here in th' dark?"

"Yes, Pa." We were disgusted he thought we might not be able to, but dared not show it.

"Tell you what, tell th' sheriff I'll meet him where this trail meets th' Huntsville Road any time b'fore daylight. Ride Joe, but go slow, he isn't that good in th' dark."

We didn't need promptin' an' were on our way. I got on first an' got th' saddle for a change.

"I get th' saddle comin' back," Jake demanded.

Joe could be surefooted in th' dark, but not at more than a walk, so we walked an' it was slap dark when we saw th' lights of town. Smithy was working late, but Sheriff Rowe wasn't there when we rode by. Th' only other place still open would be th' tavern, but just as we were goin' t' look in, I saw a light at th' courthouse.

"Bet that's where th' sheriff is," I said, so we rode over t' take a look. Sure 'nough, there he sat, feet up smokin' his pipe. Without getting off Joe, we tapped on the window (it was real glass!) an' he motioned for us to come to th' back door. He got there just as we rode up.

"Pa said he would meet you where the Bradfield Trail meets Huntsville Road," Jake said.

Sheriff Rowe nodded, tapping out his pipe. "I'll go right now," he said, "you want t' ride with me?"

"No, sir, we've got another errand t' run an' this mule don't

70

go more than a walk after sundown," Jake said, punching me in th' off ribs.

"Ok, boys, I'll tell your Pa you'll be coming along b'hind." He turned back to turn out th' light an' we rode on.

"What are we gonna do now?" I whispered as we rode away.

"Let's look around an' see what's goin' on," he says, so we rode up an' down th' square, but th' only signs of life were lights in th' blacksmith shop an' tavern an' it was pretty quiet there. Jake slid down an' sneaked up to th' side window.

In a moment he was back. "Joe Whimpee's in there talking t' Hiss Clayburn. I heard Hiss tell him t' git an' to meet him here tomorrow night. Whimpee's growed a little, but so have I an' I think I could take him!" He stuck his foot in th' stirrup an' swung on behind again. We pulled up close to th' corner o' th' building and waited. In a few minutes, Joe come out. He looked around for a moment, then started off down th' road out of town.

"Follow him," Jake hissed in my ear. A touch of reins was all Joe needed. We weren't far behind an' when Joe kicked a rock, Whimpee stopped an' turned. Jake got up on his feet, squattin' behind me holdin' onto my shoulders.

"Who's that?" Whimpee asked.

"Zenas Meeker," I said low as we walked up.

"Oh yeah? an' who's that ahind yuh?"

"Just me, Jake," and he leaped right into Whimpee's chest, takin' him to th' ground. Th' blow knocked th' breath out of Whimpee an' Jake rolled off an' stood over him. "When ya catch yore breath, I'm gonna whip yore sorry bee-hind."

"Like hell, you will!" Joe grunted.

I rode th' mule, Joe, off a ways an' tied him to a tree. By th' time I turned around, they were goin' after it an' I couldn't tell who was who in th' dark. They fought for what seemed an hour. Sometimes I could tell one from th' other, but most o' th' time

I couldn't. From th' noises, I took it that Whimpee was getting whupped, but he wasn't givin' up. Th' mule was restless with all th' noise an' stir an' th' fight was gittin' closer to him, so I untied him an' rode him off a ways. Suddenly, one of th' boys turned an' ran back toward town.

"Catch him, Zee, afore he gits t' town an' spreads th' word about us!"

This was scary an' I urged ol' Joe into a trot. He caught up with Whimpee almost before I could shake out a loop. I lassoed him as I passed him an' th' rope tightened below his knees. He fell with a thud an' lay there pantin'. Just as he got to his knees, Jake hit him from b'hind an' he sprawled out agin. I got down an' we hogtied him pretty quick. There wasn't much fight left in him, and I doubt that Jake had enough left in him t' tie him up if I hadn't been there.

"Now what?" I asked.

Jake spit an' I smelled blood. "Put him 'cross th' shaddle an' we take 'm wif us." Jake was talkin' like he had a mouth full of mush.

"You ok?"

"Yeth, I whipped 'm, didn' I?"

"Made him run!"

We laid Whimpee acrost th' saddle an' he gurgled a couple of times. "Get him down, get him down, he's choking!" I hissed. I pulled him down an' he stood up pantin' for breath.

"Can't ride him thataway," I said. We untied his feet and hoisted him astride th' saddle. Jake got on b'hind him an' I led th' mule.

"Thought you was gonna ride in front goin' back," I said.

"Phut up!" came th' muffled reply.

That was a long three miles back to th' trail. After I seen Jake in th' light o' day, I knowed he felt ever step that mule made. I must have started givin' th' signal half a mile b'fore we got near an' Pa finally heard me about th' tenth time I gave it. I saw th' sheriff's horse first, then the three men came out.

"Who's that ye got with you, boys?" Bradfield asked.

"Joe Whimpee," I said. Th' other two wasn't talking any.

"Good for you," Sheriff Rowe said. "I would have got him this afternoon if I could have caught him away from Hiss for five minutes."

"Nobody knows we got him. He left Hiss sittin' by hisself in th' tavern."

CHAPTER 8
BLANCHE BRADFIELD TAKES CHARGE

Sims says, "Let's see, that leaves . . ."

"Four," I said.

"Three Injuns an' Hiss Clayburn," Pa added.

"Might be two or three more ridin' with them since you left," th' sheriff said.

"Those are th' only ones we have a quarrel with," Pa said. I noted he included me an' Jake.

"Wouldn't be bad t' get th' whole bunch," Bradfield commented.

"Brad, do yuh think we could git some help from others now that they are thinned down some?"

"I think we could, Sims, yuh want t' try?"

"Why not? If we got around early in th' morning, we could talk to fifteen or twenty men that would maybe give us a hand, 'specially if they knowed we had six o' th' worst ones already."

"It would be good if we could get some help, maybe we could gather th' whole bunch up at once," Pa said.

"Good!" Sheriff Rowe was all business now that it was decided. "Brad, you get th' ones down Huntsville Road an' I'll spend th' night in town an' go out toward Bear Springs an' get those boys involved. If we could borry those two boys, Jesse, they could go down Osage Creek from Huntsville Road and git some o' them in. Might be best if you laid low an' not take a chance you would be recognized by any o' th' gang," he said. "We'll meet right here tomorrow afternoon 'bout midafternoon an' I'll swear 'em in."

"You boys good with that?" Pa asked, an' I said "Yes, sir" for both of us.

"What're we gonna do with Whimpee?" Sims asked.

"I reckon he'd be safe with his buddies in jail," Pa said.

"Pa, I ain't seen him in th' light, but he an' Jake had a fight afore we tied him up, he may need a little attention, they's a awful lot o' blood on both o' them."

Bradfield snorted, "Depends on whose blood it is."

There were two muffled growls from th' mule's direction.

"We'll have a look at those two in th' light 'fore we decide what t' do with 'em," Pa said. "That jail might not be good for th' boy if he's too beat up."

"I'll leave that to you two," Sims said, "I've lost a might of sleep lately an' tomorrow's gonna be a long busy one." With that, he mounted up and was gone. I started up th' trail. Pa an' Mr. Bradfield followed.

When we got to Bradfield's cabin, we helped th' two battlers down from Joe the Mule. We almost had t' carry Joe Whimpee to th' house. Mrs. Bradfield brought a light out on th' dogwalk an' we studied th' two gladiators. It would have been hard looking at th' damage done t' tell which one had won, but Jake an' I knew who had run. Jake had his front teeth loosened an' there was a little chunk bit out'n his ear. One eye was swollen shut an' it was on th' way t' bein' a good shiner.

Joe may have been a little worse off, but not much. His nose an' mouth were smashed an' he had a swollen eye, too. His half-torn-off clothes revealed a big red an' blue welt on his left ribs. He seemed t' have trouble breathin' an' when Pa touched his side, he cried out in pain.

"Looks like a broken rib or two," Pa said. "We can't put him in jail with that." They were bein' careful not t' say what th' jail was an' Mrs. Bradfield caught on t' th' drift of things.

"No, you're not about to put this boy in jail in that condition, we'll keep him right here where I can take care of those
ribs and see he gits good feeding."

Ol' man Bradfield nodded. "I think yore right, Ma, d'ya think
yuh kin keep him frum runnin' off while I'm out an' about?"

"T'won't be hard with those ribs and by th' time those knees
finish swellin', he won't *want* t' move!"

She tugged his pants legs up t' show two raw and bleeding
knees already swelling. It must have happened when I roped
him an' Jake tackled him. I almost felt sorry for him. Almost.

Whimpee was looking worse and worse by th' minute. Tears
streaked down his face, washing away blood an' dirt an' he gritted his teeth in pain. You could tell all fight was gone out'n him.
Suddenly, his knees buckled an' he sat down right there on th'
floor.

"Now, let's see about th' other boy." Mrs. Bradfield swung
th' lantern over toward Jake and clucked in sympathy when she
saw he had leaned against th' wall an slid t' th' floor. His head
was on his chest an' I swear if he wasn't asleep!

"You boys, you boys!" she fussed. "Cain't there be anything
better t' do than beatin' up on each other like this?"

Jake lifted his head an' grinned a lopsided grin. He looked
funny with that grin on his face, one eye swelled plumb shut.
"Hes-s s-swhupped me s-stwiss, but I s-swhupped 's-sim
s-slast!" he lisped through swollen lips.

"Well, it sure cost you aplenty!" she replied. Standing up, she
put her hands on her hips an' said, "Ok, let's git these two into
th' kitchen an' cleaned up some." To her husband, she said,
"tear us some strips of cloth about this wide," indicating the
size with her fingers, "for a wrap around those ribs while I mix
up a mustard plaster." Lookin' at me, she said, "Young man,
you an' your pa git these two into th' kitchen. There's a pot o'

water on th' fire, get it and let's see if we can clean them up some."

We started t' lift Joe up, but he cried out an' held his side tight.

"Wait a minute, Zee," Pa said an' stepped into th' house an' came out with a chair. "Joe, we're gonna set you in this chair an' carry you on it. Can you git into it?"

I'll have t' say he was game an' with our help, he got on th' chair. Pa on one side an' me on th' other, we carried him into th' kitchen. It was warm an' clean an' sure smelled of good food an' coffee. Mr. Bradfield came in holdin' Jake by th' elbow an' led him to another chair across th' table from us. Pa poured a pan of warm water an' th' missus throwed him a rag. He b'gan t' wash Joe up. Pa took th' remains o' that shirt off an' washed his topside, then rolled his pant legs up an' removed his moccasins. When he washed his knees, little gravels rolled out from where they had stuck in them. They looked bad.

When he had finished, I took th' pan outside an' throwed it out. Th' water was dark with dirt an' blood. I got clean water an' started t' wash Jake, but he jerked th' rag out'n my hand an' washed hisself. He shore was a mess.

As soon as th' mustard plaster was ready, Mrs. Bradfield spread it on a folded cloth an' gently applied it to Whimpee's ribs. They must have been skinned, for he winced a little at first. Pa an' Mr. Bradfield wrapped th' ribs tight an it seemed t' ease him some.

"You're gonna have t' lie flat o' yore back, young man," Mrs. Bradfield said, "I have you a robe on the floor there by th' fire. It won't be very soft, but you don't need soft as much as you need a firm support for those ribs. Help him over there, now an' let's git him t' bed."

As easy as they could, Bradfield an' Pa led th' boy to th' buffalo robe an' lowered him down on it. Nurse Bradfield put another robe over him and tucked it around his feet and legs. She slipped a small cushion under his head.

"There, now you stay there and don't move."

You could tell he wouldn't be movin' around much fer a couple o' days. He was soon asleep.

Meantime, Mrs. Bradfield examined Jake carefully, "No broken bones? That's good, but those teeth look awful loose. You need t' pack your lips t' hold them in place and help th' insides heal a little. In th' morning, we'll git a slab o' meat fer that eye. Let's see yore hands." She clucked at th' bruised and swollen hands. "A little soakin' in cold water oughta help that, then we're gonna prop you up to sleep so you don't choke on your own blood!"

Another robe was spread on th' floor opposite side o' th' fire over a chair back that had been laid down t' make an incline. Jake eased himself down an' Missus Blanche covered him up to his chin.

"If your hands get too warm, lay them on top of th' covers, but you should keep as warm as possible," she told him.

Jake nodded sleepily.

"I don't think those two will give any trouble for a day or two." Bradfield grinned. "Just th' same, I'll sleep in here t'night an' keep watch on 'em."

Pa didn't say anything about Jake stayin' there, I guess he figgered he'd git better care than in camp.

"We shure appreciate this, Mrs. Bradfield, sorry t' impose on you like this."

"If it means riddin' this area o' those night riders, it'll be worth th' little trouble those two'll be!" she replied.

"We need t' get back to camp b'fore we go out tomorrow . . ."

"You just go right ahead," th' lady interrupted. "I'm sure I can handle these two for a day or two th' way they're beat up!

78

It'll be a pleasure t' have company. If'n they cain't talk, they can sure *listen!*" She smiled.

With that, we said our "goodnights" an' headed for th' gap. Pa rode Joe the Mule with me b'hind 'cause he said Joe could get us there surer than if we walked an' stumbled around. At camp I gave him some grain we had an' left him munchin' on hay. We wouldn't need him on th' morrow, horses bein' best for what I was goin' t' be doin'. It must have been after midnight afore we laid down an' it seemed my head had just hit th' bedroll when I heard Pa up movin' around getting breakfast.

"I'll go watch th' boys an' th' sinkhole while you and Brad-field are gone," he said.

"I think I'll go down to our old place an' work myself up th' creek to th' road," I said. "That way I won't ride th' creek twice."

"Good thinking," Pa said, "Take th' bay, he's had a good rest and I'll meet you this afternoon."

CHAPTER 9
THE FINAL ROUNDUP

There was a dim trail along th' Osage past our old place, but th' land was rough, not good for farmin'. Mostly mountain folks lived up on th' ridges an' not many o' them at that. Anyhow, they wouldn't be sympathetic to our cause and it would not be any use talking to them.

It was Tom Sowell from Tennessee that bought our farms an' he had kept them up very well. That old saddle Pa hung by th' gate was still there, only it was weathered. Mr. Sowell said he left it there t' warn away all varieties of thieves. It had worked for us 'til th' hog butcherin'. He said he would be there t' help us out an' I moved on up th' creek. There must have been a dozen or more houses scattered along th' bottoms and every one of th' men said they'd be glad t' help us round up th' gang. By th' time I got to Huntsville Road, I could count fifteen men who had committed t' join us.

Only one man said he wouldn't be there. "I ain't gonna be any part of no vigilante lynchin'," he said.

"It won't be a lynchin', we're just gonna catch 'em an' put 'em in jail 'til th' law can take care of them," I said, but he wouldn't believe me.

"Lynchin's wrong an' I ain't gonna go 'long with it."

There was no use arguing with him, so I left. I only hoped he wouldn't go about stirrin' up trouble by warnin' night riders what we were up to. I caught up with Mr. Bradfield on th' road. He had two men with him that I knew by sight, but not name.

"How'd ya do, Zenas," he called as I rode up.

"I got fifteen yes's an' one no," I said.

"Let me guess," one o' th men said, "it was ol' Witt!"

"That's right, said he wouldn't be no part of vigilante lynchin'. I told him we wasn't gonna lynch anybody, but he didn't b'lieve me."

Th' three laughed at that. "That's him all right, only time he comes t' town is t' vote agin whoever we all like, most contrary man in th' county."

"We'll have enough," Bradfield said, "be more pleasurable without 'im!"

Pa was sittin' by th' road whin we rode up. We tied th' horses in th' shade an' waited for th' sheriff an' th' rest t' show up. Out of all th' men that had told me they would help out, only Tom Sowell an' one other showed up by th' time Sheriff Rowe got there. He swore us all in, me included, bein' only twelve at th' time. "I got four men o' th' Fancher clan swore in, an' they're watchin' things in town. We'll mosey over thataway an' lay low 'til th' gang gits in. I hope t' catch 'em without any shootin', but just in case, we'll let them git out of town afore we hit 'em."

Near town, Sheriff Rowe split us up in pairs an' set us t' watchin' trails fer th' gang. "I'll go on in to town an' look around, won't be natural for me t' disappear so sudden-like. They'll wait t' ride after I head for home, so we'll watch which way they go an' foller."

Me an' Pa were watchin' Pine Mountain Trail. We tied back in th' trees an' eased up under some brush where we had a good sight o' th' trail. I knowed it wasn't a good time, but something was botherin' me an' I had to know, so I asked, "Pa, how come so many men said they'd help us, then didn't show up?"

Pa didn't even have t' think about it, he knew why. "It wasn't because they meant t' lie or they're scairt, Zee, it was b'cause they said what was in their *hearts*. Later on when they thought it over in their *heads*, they realized th' danger they might be puttin' their family in if this thing failed and they decided they couldn't afford th' risk. After all, no one has thought ahead much about what they are gonna do with that bunch once they are rounded up. They can't keep them in that hole long an' th' law will have t' handle them sooner or later. Nowadays, law is fickle an' weak a-a-a-nd it's just as likely to turn those fellows loose as keep them. Then where would these deputies—an' th' sheriff for that matter—be?"

"I guess they might be worser off, wouldn't they?"

"Very likely. I had t' make th' same decision when they killed our hogs. Them shootin' at th' house told me they didn't care if they hurt someone or not and they knew womenfolks an' you boys were in th' house.

"It took me a year t' get th' family out of harm's way so I could deal with these men without endangerin' you all. Law an' order in a new country is very weak and a man has t' purty much be his own law an' keep his own order. That don't mean he has t' go around killin' ever'body who gets in his way, but it *does* mean that he has t' be prepared for any event. Maybe that preparation an' readiness will discourage bullies an' lawless men from messin' with him and his. Problem with these galoots is they bunched up so's it was hard t' resist them on an individual basis."

"So, are we gonna leave when they're all caught?"

"They're not all caught yet, let's get that done b'fore we take th' next step. I've gotten my 'pound of flesh' from three of them an' I intend t' extract some more before we're done. No one will ever threaten harm or try t' harm my family without answerin' t' me!"

I've thought a lot about what Pa said that night an' it's

b'come my philosophy too. Family is important an' if a man is gonna have one, he has t' be strong enough t' protect it no matter whether in a civilized land or on th' frontier. I've found that there are as many wolves in town as there are in th' woods, an' it pays t' keep an eye out fer what's your'n wherever they are.

Pa had whipped th' strongest of th' bunch he had caught up with. First, it was Demps Barnes, th' meanest, then he must have whipped Hensley and Arnold together, though he didn't say. All three o' them were pretty beat up when I saw them. He didn't do anything with Fletcher Parsley, prob'ly 'cause he was so drunk, an' he didn't do anything t' that wimpy Wylie Goodwin. Jacob had taken care of Joe Whimpee b'cause he had bullied him b'fore—it was just like Pa was doin' with his enemies—only I'm sure Jake didn't think it through like Pa did. Maybe you don't have t' think about those things, you just do what you have to t' git along.

A hoof klinked agin a rock an' Pa nudged me. In a moment, a rider came in sight from th' mountain an' we watched him approach. It was Hirm Crook! When he was near opposite us, Pa stood up. "Hello there, Hirm, how are you?"

Th' man stopped an' turned t' face us. "Hullo yersef, who is that hidin' in the bresh?" Pa stepped out on th' trail. "It's Jesse Meeker. I've come t' collect fer th' hogs o' mine ya butchered last year."

Hirm laughed. "I done paid all I aims t' pay fer them pigs o' yourn!"

"We-e-l-l, I don't think so, step down an' let's talk about it."

Crook stepped down opposite side o' his horse an' as he did, he drew his bowie out of his belt. I had stepped out t' take th' horse an' he heard me cock my rifle. "Put th' knife in th' saddlebag, Mr. Crook, an' I'll git this horse out'n th' way," I said. My voice squeaked a little, but he saw that th' gun barrel was steady on his chest. He put th' knife in th' bag an' stepped

83

back so's I could move th' horse.

I backed up pullin' th' horse with me an' keeping my gun aimed. We were out o' th' way when I tripped on a limb an' fell backwards. Th' gun went off in th' air right near th' horse's head an' he bolted, runnin' down th' trail towards town.

Crook didn't wait an instant, but charged Pa, head down like a bull. Pa sidestepped at th' last second an' kneed him in th' ribs hard as he went by. Crook fell to his hands an' knees, but was up in a flash an' when he turned, he ran into Pa's fist in th' chin. Th' blow turned him around and he kept on turnin', his fist swingin' like a ball on a string an' catchin Pa just b'hind th' ear. He stumbled back an' Crook was on him like a cat on a mouse. They went down with Hirm on top, but b'fore he was set, Pa throwed him off. I was reloadin' as fast as I could an' determined to shoot th' man if he went past fightin'.

They both rolled over an' come up swingin'. Pa caught Crook in th' temple with a left, an' pushed Hirm's right off with his arm. Hirm charged in agin an' this time, Pa stood. His knee came up an' caught th' man full in th' face an' as they both went down, Pa slapped him one-two on th' face with both hands open. It sounded like a flat board slapped on water. It stunned Crook, not th' force o' th' blows, but th' fact that someone would slap his face with their open hand infuriated him.

You could see him getting madder an' madder as he backed off a moment, then he rushed Pa again. Pa feinted one way, then moved t'other. He grabbed Crook's hair as he went by an' when he whirled around, slapped him again on th' face, open handed. Hirm Crook bellered like a mad bull an' rushed Pa again. This time, Pa ducked an' Crook flew over his back. Pa raised up an' threw him backwards, fallin' on top of him. Th' impact knocked th' breath out of him an' Pa was astraddle of him in a flash, slapping his face left an' right as hard an' fast as he could.

Crook couldn't do anything, but try to fend off th' blows. About th' time he caught his breath, Pa bounced on his gut an' knocked it out'n him agin. He never let up slappin' th' man's face an' I almost laughed out loud. Th' third time Pa knocked th' breath out of th' man, he quit an' just covered his face from th' slaps. Pa jumped up an' pulled Hirm to his feet, th' fight gone out of him. Pa shook him like a dog on a snake.

"You gonna come into my yard with a crowd o' bullies an' shoot at my house an' kill my hogs any more?" He was th' maddest I ever had seen him an' 'most scared me.

Hirm shook his head.

"Is it fun t' shoot at wimmin an' children from th' dark?" Pa was still shakin' him so he couldn't answer. "D'yuh think ya'll ever be man enough t' stand up t' another man an' fight fair, *do ya?*" Still th' man couldn't answer. Pa flung him down like a sack o' feed, though he must have been forty pounds heavier. "Bring me that rope, Zenas," an' I ran for the horses.

I tied Crook's hands b'hind his back while Pa stood in front of him. "I been easy on you, Crook, but th' next time this happens, it won't go so easy with you. You're gonna leave this country an' go to th' reservation an' you're gonna stay there, understand?" The man nodded his head.

"He's tied up, Pa, what do you want t' do now?" I was tryin t' get Pa's mind off'n the man.

"We'll take him to town an' then to jail! Maybe his buddies ain't eat all that pork yet." Pa took a big breath an' grinned an' I knowed he had got his temper back. I was shore relieved. I thought for a minute there he would do something *really* bad.

I tied th' rope from Crook to my saddle horn while Pa mounted up an' we headed for town. We met Hirm's horse headin' back towards us, probably thinking he would head back home, an' Pa caught up his reins.

We met th' sheriff an' Tom Sowell comin' from town. "We

heard a shot an' thought you might need help," Sims said, "but looks like you got things in hand. Was anyone with him? Anyone git shot?"

"No, he was alone an' th' shot was in th' air t' git his attention," Pa answered.

I was glad he didn't tell them more about that shot!

"They heard th' shot in th' tavern an' come runnin out t' see what was goin' on an' we got all five o' them right there in th' open an' unarmed!" Sheriff Rowe explained. "They are corralled at th' courthouse, an' madder than red wasps in August!"

We rode on an' I heard Pa rippin' cloth. When I looked, he had torn his shirttail off an' wrapped his hands with it. I knew more was comin' up.

Th' sheriff rode ahead an' by th' time we got there, had herded th' prisoners out, tied up an' ready t' march. They were defiant an' mouthin' all kinds o' threats on ever'one. In th' light, Hirm Crook's face looked terrible. It was blood red an' startin t' turn purple in places. Some o' those purple spots was busted blood vessels an' they probably would stay like that th' rest o' his life.

Pa got down an' looked the prisoners over, walkin' from one to th' other, looking them straight in th' face. Hiss Clayburn spit at him, but th' two Cherokees, Musick and Weaver, didn't say anything.

"Sheriff Rowe," Pa called, "these three men owe me for some pigs they took. Since I'm not going t' be here when they come to trial, I would like t' collect from them now, if you don't mind."

"Don't mind at all, Jesse, go right ahead."

"You ready t' pay, Hiss?"

"I got my hands tied right now, Harris, or I'd pay yuh what's comin to ya."

"Someone untie him."

Mr. Jim Fancher untied Hiss' hands an' he stood rubbin' th' circulation back into them. "Think I'm ready, now, Harris," and he stooped an' brought a bowie out of his boot. Pa drew his knife an' th' rest of us made a circle. Me an' Mr. Sowell stood b'hind th' other prisoners.

I couldn't see much of th' fight. They circled for some time slashin' at each other, but wary too. It scared me when Hiss made a slash at Pa an' caught him down th' ribs. His shirt was cut an' in a minute was wet. Hiss made another lunge an' Pa dodged t' one side, whippin' his knife down across Clayburn's knife hand. Th' knife fell an' Pa kicked it out of th' way while Hiss backed up, cussin' an' looking for a place t' run.

Pa throwed his knife down with th' other an' th' blacksmith picked them both up.

Hiss grinned an' ugly grin an' said, "Think yuh kin beat me with fists, Harris, looks like you're all stove up already. Now, I'm gonna teach *you* somethin'!"

They circled a time or two, Hiss swingin' an' Pa dodging an' waitin his chance. Hiss was patient, but careless an' once when he swung, Pa ducked in an' come up under his chin with his head, straightenin' him up for a couple of blows to th' gut. Hiss backed off, spittin' blood an' a tooth chip or two, tryin t' catch his breath. Pa didn't let him, movin' in an' givin' him a haymaker to th' jaw. It knocked him down on his knees, but Pa reached out an' pushed him up on his feet, b'fore givin' him th' other fist in th' face.

Blood was streamin' down his face, but Hiss still caught Pa in th' head with a swing, then tripped him to th' ground. He rolled to his hands and knees an' Hiss kicked him in th' gut. He grabbed Pa by th' hair an' was swingin' for his face when Pa come up with both fists together right under th' chin before Clayburn's blow hit his ribs. Hiss went over backwards an' Pa got a chance t' catch his breath. They circled agin, but Hiss was slower now an' not mouthin', just trying to breathe and rest some. There was a lot of blood from his slashed hand an' I noticed that Pa's pants had turned dark b'low his cut ribs.

Suddenly, Pa charged in an' Hiss dodged, trippin' him to th' ground. He dove for Pa's back, but Pa rolled away, then was on top of Hiss, swingin' for his head. Hiss hooked his leg under Pa's chin an' flipped him over, but he couldn't clear his head enough t' take advantage. He just stood there on his knees shakin' his head. Pa came to his knees, an' smashed a left to his face, followed with a right to th' jaw that knocked him out cold.

It was real quiet for a minute an' Pa stood up a little shakily. "Guess I got my pay for th' pigs, Sheriff."

"I'd say ya did, Jesse . . ." but that was all he got to say, for right at that moment a company of soldiers rode into th' square.

CHAPTER 10
JUSTICE SERVED

Th' head officer rode up to our circle. It was th' first army man I had seen an' I thought th' gold bars on his shoulders meant he was a gen'ral, but Pa said later he was only a lieutenant, which I took t' mean he was something less than a gen'ral.

"Hello, men," he said, "Do you know where I can find the sheriff, Rowe, I think his name is?"

"I'm Sheriff Rowe and these are my deputies. We have just taken these men prisoners for night riding." I noticed the sheriff spoke formally, as we called it.

"Very good, Sheriff, the Army will not interfere with civilian activities. However, I have warrants here for the arrest of certain men said to be in this area. I would like to go over them with you."

"Fine, fine," said the sheriff. "Let me secure these prisoners in the courthouse and we will go over your list in my office. I will be glad to assist you any way I can."

He instructed th' deputies t' take th' prisoners back into the courtroom an' guard them there while he talked with th' gen'ral. Th' blacksmith came up an' took Pa to his house. Someone said his wife was th' nearest thing to a doctor they had an' by that, I knew they would take care of Pa. I jist stayed t' watch th' soldiers.

Th' gen'ral eyed th' tavern, then called out "Sergeant!" Another soldier with stripes on his arms rode up and saluted, "Yes, sir!"

In a low voice, th' gen'ral said, "Give the men one pint of beer in the tavern and no more. Not a drop of whiskey, then make camp over in the wagon yard. Pay the keeper for the drinks, then close the tavern for the night and post a guard at the door. I will hold you responsible for any drunkenness. You may assure the keeper that the tavern can be opened as usual tomorrow. We will be giving him more business tonight than he will get in a month and I am sure he will be satisfied with that. If you need me, I will be in the courthouse with the sheriff."

"Yes, sir!" the sergeant said and saluted.

He rode back to th' army while th' gen'ral dismounted an' went into the courthouse. I heard th' sergeant givin' orders to th' men an' there was a cheer an' rush for th' tavern. Through th' front window I could see that th' barkeeper an' helper had poured up a bunch of glasses of beer. They had used all the glasses an' there were not enough for th' whole army, so th' sergeant made th' ones without glasses wait until the others had finished.

As soon as one glass was emptied, another took it an' had it filled while the first soldier sat an' laughed an' talked with th' others. As soon as all the army had their drink, th' sergeant went up to pay an' get his beer. Barkeep shook his head sadly, there was no more beer left, but he did pour the sergeant a drink from a bottle, which he downed quickly.

We could hear wagons coming and soon they pulled into th' light, three army wagons driven by men dressed in ever'day clothes. "All right, men," the sergeant roared over th' noise, "to horse and camp!" With that, the men filed out, some laughing an' talking an' some grumpily, prob'ly 'cause they didn't get more beer.

They rode east to th' wagon yard an' I heard them makin' camp. Th' barkeeper closed up an' I went over to th' courthouse.

Pa was soakin' his hands in th' horse trough an' th' other

90

men were guardin' prisoners. Sheriff Rowe an' th' gen'ral talked a long time; when they finally came out, th' sheriff was grinning like a possum eatin' green grapes. Th' gen'ral mounted an' rode off to th' wagon yard.

"Jesse, it looks like th' lieutenant has solved all our problems. He has warrants for 'most th' whole gang an' is goin' t' take them off our hands an' out'n th' country!"

It turned out that Fletcher Parsley and Barnes Arnold were deserters from th' army an' they were goin' back t' Fort Smith with Raney Hensley who was wanted by th' sheriff at Van Buren. Th' Cherokees Musick and Weaver were wanted by th' Cherokee Police an' th' lieutenant had agreed t' deliver them there on his way to Fort Scott. Hirm Crook was goin' to th' Osage Council.

"Demps Barnes an' Hiss Clayburn are both wanted at Potts Landing on th' Arkansas River an' th' Army will deliver them there an' collect a reward for them for th' company t' split. That just leaves us with Joe Whimpee and Wylie Goodwin to take care of!"

"That sounds real good, Sims, I was wonderin' what you were gonna do with all those prisoners t' keep."

"Only thing is that the company is going to stay around a day or two to rest up the stock and look for some other wanted fellows an' the lieutenant wants me to hold the prisoners for him."

"Looks like it's gonna git purty crowded in th' jail." Pa grinned, then winced an' touched his jaw tenderly. "Is there gonna be room enough?"

"I suppose so, though it'll get close to just standin' room. Now, yore gonna have t' feed an' water them for sure."

"That won't be too hard, th' county has money in my budget for that, though it may be all used up by th' time these fellers leave."

"They looked well fed, maybe you can get by easier since they won't be doin' much work afore they leave."

Th' sheriff grinned. "It's gittin late, best move th' boys out an' git 'em secure. I'll have t' be haulin' them water an' feed soon's they're in jail."

There was quite a bit o' curiosity by th' deputies *and* th' prisoners about th' "jail" Sheriff Rowe was usin'. They were getting belligerent now that they were all together. We heard comments like, "Ain't no jail held me fer long yet" and "Wait til we git out, th' whole country's gonna pay!"

We just grinned an' kept them marchin' for th' gap. It was just grayin' up dawn when we reached Bradfield's place. Jake an' Joe Whimpee both were out doin' chores, though Joe was movin' slow an' didn't do any stoopin'. Seemed like Joe an' Jake had made some kind of peace. We rested an' watered th' prisoners. A couple of them were drinkin' awful careful, must have had sore mouths or somethin'. They weren't mouthin' too much now. Maybe they were tired from th' walk, not bein' used to such work an' all.

When we started around th' bench to th' sinkhole, Jake motioned t' Joe t' come along and watch. It was an' awful quiet walk, ever'one sensing they were nearing th' end of th' trip. It might be that some o' th' prisoners were thinking they might be endin' up swinging from a limb. Me an' Jake an' Joe hurried ahead so's we could see their faces when they saw th' hole. Joe blanched some when he saw it hisself.

It was funny reading th' expressions of th' men as they realized what th' "jail" was. Th' deputies first stared, then grinned when they realized what had been goin' on. Th' prisoners jist bunched together an' stared. They didn't make a sound.

"Fletch, Demps, we brought yuh some visitors, move back an' we'll let 'em down," th' sheriff called.

The call started a lot of hollerin' an' beggin' from th' hole an' it took a few minutes t' get them t' calm down so we could understand what they were talking about.

"You gotta git us out'n here, Sheriff, they's a bear or something wooly tryin t' git at us through that hole!"

"What's he look like?"

There followed an argument among th' prisoners as to just what was tryin t' git to them, th' final word bein' that th' bulk o' them thought it was a bear.

"I'll bet he smelled your meat a cookin!"

"It don't matter *what* he smells, he's still tryin t' git in here an' we don't want him!"

"Seems like they's two things ya oughter be doin'; throw all th' bones an' leftovers in th' hole, then cover it up with rocks."

"We done that, but he keeps diggin' th' rocks out!" The voice was almost crying.

"Well, we're sendin' you some help. Maybe if th' bear gits through, you can kill him an' have some meat an' a robe for th' chill."

"They ain't room down here for more!" someone whined. Th' deputies chuckled.

"Guess you'll have t' climb up an' perch on th' rocks, 'cause more's a-comin!"

They got busy lowerin' prisoners into the hole, some o' them fightin' an' resistin' an' some o' them jist calm an' meek. They was lots of hollerin' an' cussin' from b'low, but the work continued 'til all was lowered.

"How's that pig holdin' out, boys?" Sheriff Rowe called.

" 'T's all gone."

"We're hungry."

"And thirsty, they ain't enough water."

"We need more firewood, it's cold down here."

"Don't ever'one talk at oncet, I'm makin' a list," th' sheriff replied, while pretendin' t' write the things down on an imaginary piece of paper. Everyone grinned, even Joe Whimpee.

All was quiet for a minute, then Sheriff Rowe called, "I got that all down, boys, anything else you kin think of?"

There were a lot more requests, but they were not items prisoners should have. "I ain't writin' them things down, boys 'cause you ain't elegible fer them," the sheriff called. "By th' way, send up that other rope, we may need it in case this one breaks. It's a long way to go t' git another one an' you might be there longer than we planned without a spare."

It was quiet for a moment, then there was a lot of yellin' an' cussin'. "These idiots burned th' rope up when they ran out o' firewood!"

It must have been one of the new prisoners talkin'.

Ever'one laughed at that an' th' sheriff grinned an' shook his head. "It's a wonder you fellers grew up t' be men! I guess we'll jist hev t' hope this rope holds out. Th' Army's gonna take th' whole lot o' you except Wylie in a day or two soon's they git their business done. I'm gonna get you water an' food and maybe these deputies'll git you some wood fer a fire. Don't burn it all at once, now!"

To th' rest of us, he said, "If you men will gather some wood, we'll lower it down t' them. I want t' haul Wylie out of there, he's mostly harmless an' I think th' barkeeper can use him an' keep him out of mischief. Th' county will pay you a dollar a day for your work an' I think you have put in th' most of two days, so I'll have your money for you next time I see you."

We soon had a big bundle of wood tied an' ready t' lower into th' hole. Th' sheriff had t' call several times t' be heard over th' uproar. "We're lowerin' firewood, boys, when you get it, put Wylie in th' rope an' we'll haul him up. You do that by tyin' th' rope under his arms an' b'hind his back so he can use his hands to help. Any funny business an' it'll come out of your food and water, understand?" Sheriff Rowe sure had a handle on th' antics o' th' gang.

Someone down there knew how to make a harness, for when Wylie crawled up over th' lip of th' hole, he had th' rope looped around his chest an' was sitting in a loop made for his rump t' fit in. With th' pull o' th' rope holdin' him up, he actually walked up th' slope only slippin' once or twice.

"Good work, boys, you sure improved on what we had an' that earns you a little extry provision. I'll have t' think of what that will be."

"We jist didn't want Wylie makin' water or fallin' back in on us," someone called.

"Those boys are soundin' like old-timers down there," Pa said. "If it weren't for th' bear, I'll bet they would be looking for a way out."

"Ol' Ephraim jist might be our friend." Jim Fancher laughed.

We could tell Pa was havin' a sinkin' spell so we said our "good-byes" an' moved on over th' gap t' camp. Pa washed in th' branch while me and Jake cooked a meal. He ate an' rolled up in his bed an' slept. I was sleepy too, but Jake had t' know ever'thing that had happened an' we sat down by th' branch an' talked. After I told him what had happened to us, he told me about stayin' at th' Bradfields an' how good Mrs. Bradfield had treated them. She seemed to take a special interest in Joe Whim-pee.

"I wouldn't be surprised if she ast th' sheriff t' let her keep him," he said.

That was th' last thing I remember Jake sayin' an' when I woke up, I was layin' in th' same place, only Jake had throwed a robe over me. It was sundown an' th' smell of meat cookin' woke me and Pa up. We ate, then rolled up proper in our bedrolls an' slept for real, leavin' Jake t' care for camp an' stock.

Th' next couple o' days, Pa was real sore an' didn't move around much. It was ok with us. We took advantage o' th' time t' do some critter huntin'. Now that we didn't have t' hide our whereabouts, we moved pretty freely about th' country. It was surprising th' number of deer we saw this close in to th' settlement an' we got a couple of nice does.

Pa took over camp duties, dryin' meat an' working up th' hides. We was concerned about his hands, but he said the exercise done them good, which I doubted. Soakin' them in cold water helped a lot an' he rendered some fat from th' deer an' rubbed that on his hands.

Me an' Jake visited th' old place an' talked to the Sowells. Jake told them about th' hog butcherin' an' I showed them some of th' bullet holes they hadn't found.

"So that's why you men came back!" Mr. Sowell said. "I knowed a man like your pa wouldn't jist tuck tail an' run like that. Folks around here didn't think about him gittin' his family out'n th' way afore takin' care o' business, but that was th' smart thing t' do. You shore done us a service gittin' rid o' that bunch. That pa o' you'rn shore is *some* fighter!"

Mrs. Sowell insisted on us takin' dinner with them an' we didn't take long t' agree. It was just like old times eatin' in th' house we had grown up in—an' th' food was great. Th' sun was sinkin' when we rode out th' gate an' we got to camp after dark. Pa had dinner fixed, but we weren't too hungry. Pa teased us about fillin' up on Mrs. Sowell's Sometime Biscuits an' we didn't deny it.

Sittin' around camp was shore borin' for all of us an' Pa allowed he could heal just as well on th' back of a gentle-gaited mule as layin' around in th' rocks, so th' fourth day we packed up an' hauled out. We went over th' gap an' said our "goodbyes" to th' Bradfields. Joe Whimpee was there. He said th' Bradfields told him he could stay as long as he wanted and he was happy with that.

We rode into Carrollton just as th' Army was forming up t'

move on. They had converted one of the wagons into a prisoner wagon an' it bulged with prisoners chained to th' floor. All th' ones from th' jail and a few more were there. Them soldiers sure cleaned out th' vermin from th' country. We got a lot o' sullen looks an' there was some mutterin' goin' on in th' wagon, but none we could hear. Pa never looked their way. I hope that rankled them some.

Townfolks an' some from th' country around had come in t' see th' Army off an' they sure gave us a warm welcome. We got a lot o' invitations t' visit an' have a meal, but we were anxious to see home so after visitin' around some, we hit th' trail.

Bear Creek Springs was mostly abandoned except for a few cabins around. Pa looked a long time at th' old village grounds. He allowed Ma had cried when she saw it abandoned. It was sad, but we knew th' tribe was happy bein' closer to buffalo grounds. Seems like th' politicians didn't know how t' treat Indians that built cabins an' tilled soil like our people did.

Ma an' Grandma took Pa in hand when we got home an' they doctored him up. Grandma fussed about th' way they had sewed up Pa's side, but it healed pretty good anyway. It wasn't long b'fore Pa could work with his hands agin, but I don't think they were ever th' same after that. Pony was sure put out that he didn't git in on th'action an' even Parlee was in a snit about it. Pa just grinned at them.

"And that's how Carrollton got shut of th' night riders an' we got paid for the hog butcherin'." Zenas rocked and rubbed his hands up and down his thighs, grinning. "I never doubted Pa's courage after that! We heard later that Demps Barnes and Hiss Clayburn couldn't stay out of mischief and were found swingin' from a white-oak limb down in the Arkansas Valley. Noah Musick an' Moss Weaver stood trial in th' Nation an' both served time in jail. We never heard or run across any of the others."

CHAPTER 11
AMIRA'S PREMONITION

1857

Not long after we got back from Carrollton, a young man came to Pa an' asked for Parlee's hand. Pa was some surprised, not knowin' that Parlee was bein' courted, so he put th' feller off until he could talk to Parlee an' Ma. That night after supper and we were sittin' around th' fire, Pa said, "Parlee, that young feller, Bob Crow, came by today an' asked me for your hand . . ."

"What?" Parlee fairly screamed an' came out of her chair. "What did you tell him, Pa, what did you say?"

We were all taken aback an' Pa didn't know what t' say for a minute. Parlee's face first turned as pale as a sheet, then she got red as a beet an' you could tell she was crazy mad.

"I told him I would make my decision after talking to you an' th' family, Parlee. What's this all about?"

Parlee relaxed a little an' rocked a minute b'fore answerin' th' question. "He's been botherin' me ever since you went on th' hunt an' has gotten t' be a real pest. He knew that someone else was gonna come see you an' wanted t' git in ahead of him."

She blushed an' hid her face. Me an' Jake just grinned for we had seen her holdin' hands with Joe Beavers down by th' creek. Seemed like Joe spent a lot of time up here lookin' for stray cows.

Me an' Jake was sittin' on th' floor in front of th' fire. "Looks like Joe found his heifer," Jake whispered to me an' Parlee kicked him so hard under th' ribs he lost his breath. Ma gave us a hard look.

"So this Crow feller wants to marry you afore someone else does?"

"Yes, Pa an' that rapscallion won't be in th' way when I meet him in th' mornin' with my gun!"

"Now, now, Parlee that won't be necessary. He came to me proper like an' I will handle th' situation without bloodshed." There was a smile tuggin' at th' corners of Pa's mouth. "Ma, you take Parlee's gun an' keep it safe, we don't want any wedding takin' place in th' jail."

I giggled an' Ma said, "Zee, go bring in a load of wood."

"But there's plenty here," I protested.

"Do as your Ma says, Zee, and Jake, you go with him!" Pa sounded stern but he winked at us with his off eye. They was always sendin' us off when they wanted t' talk business secret.

"Awww, Pa," Jake was already up an edgin' toward th' door, "we already know it's that Joe Beavers courtin' Parlee."

"*Jake Meeker,* I'll skin you alive!" Parlee yelled, th' last part came through th' closed door. Me an' Jake had both known Parlee's wrath. "You better lay low an' watch your back for a few days," I said.

"You don't have t' worry about that," Jake snickered.

We stayed outside 'til we froze out, then loaded up with wood an' went for th' house. Th' wood box b'hind th' chimney was already full so we piled wood b'side it an' threw a couple more logs on th' fire, then sat down on th' floor t'other side o' Pa from Parlee. It was quiet for a few minutes with only Ma's rocker creakin' an' th' click o' her knittin' needles.

After a while, Pa says, "Looks like we'll be gittin' some weather soon, we need t' round up horses an' put them in th' corral for a day or two. You boys go out after breakfast an' bring them up while I fork down some hay for 'em."

After breakfast, we saddled up an' rode to th' back of th' pasture an' drove our horses to th' creek. While they was drinkin', Joe Beavers rode up. "Howdy, boys, how's things?" he called.

"Jist fine, Joe," I replied. He sorta sat there not sayin anything for a minute. "Parlee at th' house?"

"I guess," Jake said.

"She's been in some kind o' fettle since Bob Crow asked Pa for her hand," I said.

Joe's head swung around an' his mouth flew open b'fore he caught himself, then his jaws tightened. "Ast yore Pa t' marry her?"

"Yeah, Pa was gonna give him his answer t'day," Jake said, wavin' one o' th' mares back to th' herd an' tryin t' act unconcerned, but his last words were lost in th' wind, for Joe had turned his horse an' was in a high lope for th' house.

"Well, that lit a shuck under him," I said. "We better stay scarce for a while."

"That's what I was thinking." He hazed a couple of mares out of th' herd back toward th' back o' th' meadow an' I turned th' rest toward th' corral. At th' house, Joe's horse was tied out front an' we shooed horses into th' corral.

"Looks like we're a couple short," Pa called from th' loft.

"Yeah, that bay mare an' her sister bolted out o' th' creek an' headed for th' back pasture," I called. "We'll go gather 'em up."

'Bout that time, Parlee an' Joe come out o' th' house an' headed for Pa at th' barn. We sat still a moment, then Pa called, "You boys get those horses in, it's startin t' snow a-ready!"

"Aawww . . ."

"*Git, now*, or they'll be up in th' cedars an' you'll never catch 'em!"

When Pa used that tone, you done it, so off we rode. When we looked back, Pa was sittin' in th' loft door swingin' his feet an' Parlee an' Joe was standin in th' corral talking to him.

"Don't know why we have t' miss all th' fun," Jake growled.

"Cain't say we didn't have *some*," I replied.

"Yeah, did yuh see his head spin an' eyes bug whin we told him 'bout Bob?"

"I'm thinkin' we better take a long time t' git those horses in," I replied.

Th' mares was standin in th' middle o' th' pasture watchin' th' snow come down an' curious 'bout what we were up to. We rode on by an' they snorted at us, obviously expectin' us t' haze them back to th' house. They knew we always came for them when th' weather got bad and our actions puzzled them. We rode up under th' cedars an' sat there a while, watchin' snow fall. It was gittin' heavier an' heavier, you could hear it swishin' softly as it fell. It was real quiet an' what sounds it made came clear in th' cold air. Not a breeze stirred.

"Shore is purty, ain't it?"

"Yeah, so long's yuh know yuh have a warm fire at th' end o' th' day," Jake replied.

Th' two mares stomped a little, shook off snow, an' headed for th' house on their own. Jake started after them an' I held him back.

"Let them go an' we'll ride in after a bit," I said, so we sat there a few minutes longer, then started for th' barn in a slow walk. Our horses kept wantin' t' pick up th' pace an' we finally let them. When we got to th' barn, th' two mares was hangin' their heads over th' gate waitin' for someone t' let them in. No one was in sight an' it was all quiet. We put th' horses up an' rubbed them down with hay a few minutes. Joe's horse was still standin' slaunch-hipped in front o' th' house so I took him to th' corral an' tied him in th' barn where his saddle wouldn't git any wetter. Jake was splittin' wood when I got back an' we both hauled in another armload an' piled it b'hind th' chimney.

Ever'one was sittin' around th' fire, Ma rockin an' knittin', Pa smoking his pipe, an' Parlee an' Joe makin' goo-goo eyes at each other.

Me an' Jake stood by th' fire dryin' out an' not a word was said. After a while when I got good an' agervated, I said, "Well, what kind o' secret are you keeping from us now? Ain't we *ever* gonna be big enough t' be included in th' family?"

"Zenas Meeker!" Ma said sternly, but Pa said, "Th' boy has a point, Mira, after all they *are* a part o' th' family an' carry their share o' th' load. Joe, tell th' boys what has happened."

Joe grinned, "I ast t' marry yore sister an' Mr. Meeker agreed . . ."

"—And I said yes!" Parlee put in.

"That's a good thing," I said as if I didn't know it all along.

Me an' Jake went over an' shook Joe's hand. Parlee stood up an' hugged us both in a big bear hug. She was beaming like I never saw b'fore.

After that, ever'one relaxed an' there was a lot of small talk as we sat an' watched th' snow fall. Joe stayed for dinner an' didn't leave until th' middle o' th' afternoon. I went t' get his horse an' as I rounded th' corner o' th' house, he was kissin' Parlee goodbye. I didn't say nothin' an' stood with her, watchin' man an' horse disappear into th' snow. Parlee hugged me agin as we turned to th' door. I was glad she was so happy, but I didn't need all that huggin'.

Th' next days an' weeks was awful busy gittin' ready for th' weddin'. They decided t' git married in th' spring an' have a blended Christian and Cherokee ceremony. Our preacher was a practical man, country-born an' familiar with th' Cherokee way. He didn't have any problem with th' way our folks wanted t' do th' ceremony an' worked it out with th' Cherokee priest.

Parlee wore th' wedding dress that Aunt Lydia an' Grandma Ruth got married in. It fit to a 'T' and by th' time Grandma an'

Aunt Lydia got through, it was th' prettiest dress in th' valley. Parlee was all aflutter an' fairly glowed all th' time.

Pa, Pony, Joe, Jake, an' me built an arbor down by th' creek an' that's where th' weddin' was th' 15th of May, 1857. It looked like th' whole county was there an' after th' ceremony, there was th' biggest potluck feast on the ground you ever saw. I never saw such a feed.

Joe had a place up on Holly Mountain and they lived there, had a house full of kids. I never knew what Pa said t' that other boy. He didn't want Parlee bad enough t' come through th' snow to find out Pa's decision. Guess he knew what th' answer would be.

Cattle buyers came into th' country in th' winter of 1856–57 buying up good cows for the younger Alexander Fancher and Captain Jack Baker, a part Cherokee who lived by a big spring on Crooked Creek a few miles south of the old Bear Springs settlement. The two were planning to leave for California in th' spring of '57. This was to be th' last trip for th' Fanchers as they planned t' settle on th' ranch John was building.

Of course, Pony was all ears an' eyes for goin' along an' it appeared that he would go. He sent a note with th' buyers back to Mr. Fancher that he would be willing to hire on as a drover for th' train if he could bring a small herd of horses along. His experience with th' first two Fancher trains made it a sure thing that he would be welcome t' go on this trip.

Th' only fly in that ointment was his Dodd Mountain sweetheart, Dicy Endaly, who had patiently waited through one long drive to California. He hurried off t' tell her th' news an' didn't come in until late that night. In th' mornin', his long face an' ill temper told us that th' news had not been well received.

We mostly avoided him for a few days, but a second trip to th' mountain only made things worse. He was fast getting impossible t' live with an' Pa was gettin' out of patience with him.

"Pony, if you can't be civil with th' family, git out an' settle things with that Endaly girl an' git your head on straight!"

Ma gave Pa one of those looks and after a while Pony left th' house. We heard him saddle up an' ride out. He didn't come back for several days, but that didn't make living around Ma an' Pa any easier. It was just too quiet to be anything but dangerous an' me an' Jake found it a good time t' be scarce.

We had learned that in times like this when something big loomed or there was a fork in th' trail, Ma always had special insight into th' matter an' could give reliable advice, so one day when Pa was out, Pony rode in an' had a long talk with her. Ma told him that she saw a dark cloud hanging over th' Fancher-Baker train an' that she didn't think it would ever reach California. That troubled Pony a lot, for he loved th' trail life an' wanted t' go real bad. He left for th' hills again an' spent th' day ponderin' his options. In the end, he rode up Dodd Mountain an' asked Dicy's pa for her hand in marriage. This was gladly received an' Pony returned home in high fettle, apologized to th' family, and all was well agin. When th' train departed Baker's Prairie in April, Pony wasn't with it.

Pony found a farm he wanted t' buy an' he and Pa rounded up a herd of horses t' take to Fort Smith for th' cash needed t' buy th' place and set up housekeeping for him an' Dicy. Since I was considered too young t' be left in charge of th' farm chores, Jake had t' stay home an' I went along with Pa an' Pony t' help with th' drivin'.

Th' road we took joined th' river road near where Morrilton is an' we drove on past Potts Tavern to th' fort. Th' town of Van Buren was all abuzz about a killin' that recently happened up in th' hills near Rudy Settlement. A prominent Mormon missionary named Pratt had been murdered by a man whose wife had been stolen by th' missionary in California.

Th' story was that this Pratt had eleven wives in Salt Lake, but had lured th' other man's wife away. This man McLean had taken his two sons to his wife's wealthy parents in New Orleans to live and Pratt and th' woman plotted t' steal th' children back. She was to get the boys and meet Pratt at Fort Gibson. Pratt was arrested in th' Cherokee Nation an' sent to Van Buren for trial for theft. Th' judge found him not guilty an' released him, but begged Pratt t' stay in his protective custody as there was much unrest about th' matter and th' judge feared for th' man's safety. Pratt refused and left only to be caught up with and murdered by Mclean.

People were mostly in sympathy with McLean, there being a lot of anger about th' Mormons and their polygamy. I cannot understand why a man would want more than one wife and this case reminds me of David in th' Scriptures when he had many wives, but stole th' only wife of his neighbor, only to be cursed by his own pronouncement after th' parable of th' sheep.

News of Pratt's murder in Arkansas got to Salt Lake City before the Fancher train and when the train got to a place called Mountain Meadows in Utah, the Mormons massacred them in revenge.

Dow High was supposed to go with th' Fancher train, but was held up by th' illness of John Standlee, who along with his brother Isaac was driving a herd of heifers t' stock a ranch in California. They were a few days behind th' Fancher train and discovered th' massacre. Some of th' bodies were piled in an open pit, but many lay where they had fallen, stripped of their clothing. It must have been a horror beyond imagining, for John Standlee went mad after they reached California. He made his way back to Arkansas alone and lived in th' woods a mad man until he died.

CHAPTER 12
BENT'S NEW FORT

1858

The year 1857 was good for th' family with Pony an' Parlee both getting married and all, but it was a bad year for business. Some kind o' depression or money panic hit th' east an th' land was flooded with ragged pilgrims with no money. We fared well, not dependin' on silver or gold for our trade, but even the barter trade was slow an' we didn't have much demand for our horses except for those that wanted t' do some night appropriation. Pa musta used ten pounds o' rock salt th' winter of '57–58. He was gittin' awful restless.

Some of Joe Beavers' folks from th' Nation had come to th' weddin an' talked about a bunch of them goin t' Arapaho County, Kansas, huntin' gold on Cherry Creek. That's up where Denver is now.

Pa talked a lot about goin' on th' trip too 'til Ma told him that if he was so bent on goin', t' go ahead, but we was all goin' with him. That set him back some, but me an' Jake was all for it. It was all we could talk about. Without sayin' a word, Pa bought a couple of wagons an' broke th' mules we had t' pull them.

Early February 1858, we loaded all our gear on th' two wagons an' headed out t' Park Hill, Cherokee Nation. It like t' killed Pony t' see us go without him, but Dicy was expectin' in th' summer an' couldn't take th' trip. Me an' Jake took turns drivin' one wagon or herdin' th' horses an' Ma an' Pa led in th' other.

It was colder'n blue blazes, but travel was pretty easy with th' ground froze hard as rock. Th' route we took was th' most direct, for th' party was scheduled t' leave in March. We went through Carrollton to Alabam, Fayetteville, and Cane Hill. We crossed into th' Nation west of Dutch Mills. Pa rode on ahead to see when th' train would leave an' Ma had t' drive a wagon.

We camped that night where th' road leaves Caney Creek south of Bidding Springs and were past Tailholt nigh to th' Illinois River when Pa met us. Th' look on his face told us that all was well and he said th' train wasn't planning t' leave for another week. He said he had a big surprise for Ma but he wouldn't say what it was.

Th' Illinois wasn't high, but th' crossin' was deep an' we doubled our teams t' pull across. That way part of th' mules was on solid ground while others were swimmin'. Me an' Jake pushed th' herd across upstream t' block some o' th' current from th' first wagon so's Ma wouldn't get wet, but in th' shallows, th' horses splashed her good. She drove while Pa led th' mules. By th' time she got out, th' water on Ma's clothes had froze solid. Pa hurried up an' unhitched th' teams an' he and I went back for th' other wagon while Jake built a fire. Th' second wagon was lighter an' we didn't have any trouble getting it across.

When I stood up in th' wagon, my pants were so frozen they crackled. Jake had th' fire goin' big an' Ma had dry clothes laid out for us. My legs were blue an' those pants would have stood by themselves from th' knees up. We was shiverin' so much we couldn't talk. Pa got us busy rubbin' down th' mules an' that warmed us up. We got back on th' road as fast as we could so th' stock wouldn't get so cold an' by midafternoon pulled into th' wagon yard at Park Hill. That yard was chock full an' th' yard master opened a pasture gate for our herd an' motioned us to a back corner o' th' lot b'side a small Studebaker wagon an' fire.

No one was in sight at th' wagon an' Pa lifted Ma down. He had a big grin on his face an' we knew something was up. Suddenly a woman stuck her head out of th' canvas on th' Studebaker an' squealed "Miry." Ma's eyes got wide an' she didn't move for a second, then ran to th' wagon while th' other woman jumped down an' they hugged an' both were talkin' at once. It was our Aunt Janey, Ma's sister! She and her husband, Joal Kelly, were going in th' train.

Uncle Joal stepped out o' th' wagon grinning great big. "We sure pulled a good one on 'em, Jesse," he boomed. He was an Irishman full of fun an' jokes an' we called him Uncle Jolly. He made t' shake my hand an' suddenly grabbed me in a big bear hug instead. "By golly, Jake, you seem mighty spare!"

"I'm not Jake," I grunted.

"Might you be th' second Zenas Leonard?"

I could only nod an' he laughed an' set me down so's I could catch my breath. Lookin' at me serious-like, he said kinda low, "Don't know if yuh knowed it or not, but Mr. Leonard died last year."

I felt bad about that an' Uncle Jolly tousled my hair. "It's ok, Zenas, he had a good life an' died easy an' peaceful." Then he was off hurrahing Jake.

That night after supper, Uncle Jolly told some about th' train. A man named William Green was married to a Cherokee an' had a farm in Kansas. He heard about th' Cherokees finding gold back in '50 an' about some Delawares having a goose quill full o' gold taken from Cherry Creek. It was more than he could stand so he talked to his brothers and wrote to th' Cherokees an' got up a train o' gold hunters. All we were waiting on was Mr. Green t' show up an' lead th' train out. Uncle Jolly an'

Aunt Janey were goin' along t' dig some gold an' see th' country. They planned to return t' their farm in th' Nation after that, mostly, I think, t' be near their children an' grandkids.

It was purty interesting t' see th' camp an' talk to new people. Park Hill was a modern town an' th' Cherokees were a mixture of modern farmers an' merchants an' those who refused t' give up old ways. I could tell there was a lot of animosity among th' people with parties opposing each other. There was a lot of fightin' an bloodshed amongst them. There were two seminaries there, one for boys an' one for girls. Except for their darker skin, you would have taken them for white kids by their manners and dress.

Late Friday evening Mr. Green rode in, with wagons an' riders. He called a meeting for Saturday morning. They spent most o' th' morning organizing th' train. Uncle Jolly was elected a lieutenant an' put in charge o' th' herds. There was a small number of cattle an' a large horse and mule herd t' tend to an' me an' Jake knew right off what our chore was gonna be, which was all right with us as Pa never trusted his horses to some stranger herdin' them. Ridin' herd would give us a chance t' be more mobile than ridin th' seat o' some wagon. We'd see a lot more country that way.

Pa an' Uncle Jolly decided t' hitch th' Studebaker t' one o' our wagons eliminatin' th' need for a third driver. Ma an' Aunt Janey were pleased, for they could ride together on one o' th' wagons. There was one other woman goin' along on th' train, a Mrs. Kirk an' her children. The three struck up a friendship an' visited back an' forth a lot. Mr. Kirk saw to it that the two groups camped together an' we shared fire an' found.

Departure was set for Monday morning an' th' camp was abuzz all day with preparation. Sunday, we went to church meetin' an heard a stem-winder of a sermon from th' Baptist preacher. We finished our preparations early that afternoon an' sat around th' fire wonderin' if there was anything we might have missed. Other than a few minor things like extra wagon grease (we used bear grease), stuff like that, we were ready.

We went t' bed with th' sun an' Jake an' I hardly slept at all we was so excited. We had our fire goin big b'fore anyone else in th' whole camp was up. By th' time th' women were out, coffee was boilin', Jake was warmin' lard in th' skillet, an' I was slicing bacon. "My, my you boys are anxious to go," Ma said. "I was afraid you would bring my breakfast to me in bed."

"We're just tryin' t' help," I said.

"Go help the men round up th' teams and we'll have breakfast ready when you get back."

We caught up our horses an' rode out in th' pasture bareback an' brought th' whole herd up close to th' gate. There was a lot of commotion and confusion gettin' th' teams separated from each other an' it took us some time. There were seventy people in th' train, b'tween forty and fifty wagons, th' number varying as we went along. Our wagons an' Mr. Kirk's were th' only ones very heavily loaded, none o' th' rest o' th' people planning a permanent move. Pa wasn't interested in gold, he just wanted a good market for his horses.

Th' sun was up before we had all th' horses sorted out an' in harness. It seemed awful late t' me for th' train t' get movin', but no one seemed to hurry, bein' this was only a sort of shakedown trip th' first day. We would only go about ten miles before camping. That way any problems could be ironed out early. A lot of men on horseback didn't start with us, they would catch up later.

Uncle Jolly had extra men helping drive th' herd since th' animals would not be trail broke an' hard t' handle. He rode with us an' th' women drove th' hind wagon. We had our work cut out for us with half of th' horses wantin' to go home an' th' other half not wantin' to go anywhere. Th' only docile ones were th' ones we switched from halfway because they were too tired t' resist. If we had gone too much farther, we would have tired out our third mounts that day. I swore it would have been easier t' tie all th' working stock together an' driven them.

This may have been the first time any wagons had taken th' Cherokee Trail. I know it was one of the first ones and no one in our train knew of one b'fore. That bein' so, we sought th' easiest way t' drive. Going due west was out of th' question b'cause of rough hills an' havin t' go through th' Cross Timbers twice, so Mr. Green led us in a big arc north and northwest across prairie land.

Crossin' th' Neosho River was a chore. We got wet and cold. One o' th' wagons tipped over an' they lost considerable equipment and one mule drowned. By th' time we got to th' upper Verdigris we were pretty seasoned to th' trail an' crossed easily, it bein' no bigger than some of th' creeks we had crossed.

Me an' Jake shore enjoyed herdin'. When th' horses got trail broke, they were pretty easy t' keep bunched an' half th' time one or t'other of us was free t' explore a little. We didn't stray off too far, but in this tall grass prairie th' grass hid lots of interesting features such as deep gulleys an' limestone bluffs you couldn't see a hundred yards away. Further north in Kansas th' grass grew so tall an' thick a man on horseback couldn't see a man ten feet away, but this growth we went through was shorter, mostly belly high on a horse, though some places it was higher.

Up along th' Kansas border we came to a burn where a fire had swept through th' previous summer or fall. Grass was comin' back green an' thick an' grazin' was real good. That fire must have been thirty miles wide. It would have been a real trial t' cross right after it had burned, but in that spring it was a grass eater's paradise.

Most o' th' time we herded to one side of th' train except

111

when buffalo were thick, then we lined up b'hind th' cattle an' th' wagons while men at th' head of th' train shoved buffalo aside. There wasn't any trouble keeping supplied with meat in buffalo country. Some men enjoyed shootin' buffalo from horseback, but that required a good buffalo horse, which were few in our train. Most experienced hunters hunted on foot an' would shoot from a stand, getting two or three animals as needed by th' train. We feasted on hump, ribs, and tongues and never got tired of it.

We hit th' Santa Fe Trail some days before th' Great Bend o' th' Arkansas an' followed it th' rest of th' way t' Bent's New Fort in Big Timbers. When we got there June 12th there were only three men caring for th' place, William Bent having left for th' States, but they made us welcome. There were plenty of supplies on hand including whiskey at a dollar a pint. Some o' th' men got pretty drunk.

Th' gold seekers were anxious to move on to th' gold fields, but when they found out that is was near 200 miles away instead of 'fifty or so' as told back east, Mrs. Kirk said she and the children would go no further. Her husband was in a quandary about what t' do, having gotten so close to th' gold fields. They talked it over an' since we were not going t' leave for some time, it was agreed that she would stay at th' fort with Ma an' Aunt Janey while Mr. Kirk an' Uncle Jolly took th' Studebaker on to Cherry Creek. In a day or two the train moved on, not a few of them with throbbing heads from whiskey.

Th' Santa Fe Trail was already busy with loaded trains movin' west and mostly empty trains hurrying east for more goods. It was good business for horse traders an' Pa had traded off all th' horses he wanted to in a few days, regrettin' he didn't have more, mules especially.

We took th' tired stock and our others we wanted t' keep out on th' prairie t' rest an' fatten—and out of sight of people desperate for new stock. Pa stayed at th' fort buying up played-out stock that became available an' runnin' them out to us.

It seemed strange that out there in th' prairie wilderness there was more silver an' gold trade than in th' states, but it was so. Pa traded horses for silver after his stock was depleted an' he accumulated a right smart supply of Mexican pesos. He an' Ma were always concerned with keeping the money safe. Problem wasn't with th' Cheyennes, who didn't see any use in th' coin except for decoration. I have seen many a silver coin pounded out t' make conchos for saddles and belts and trinkets for th' women's hair. What thieving of cash came from th' whites an' Spaniards passin' through. Th' fort had a safe where Pa was welcome t' keep his excess an' he wore his tradin' money in a belt under his shirt.

Me an' Jake did a lot of visitin' with Cheyenne boys an' got t' be good friends with them. When we weren't herdin', we were in th' river or fishin' or racin' horses. They had some fast mustangs, but we had a couple o' Cherokee Ponies that could hold their own with them an' there was lots of spirited competitions. Th' braves would come out t' watch th' races an' bet on them. I've seen some o' them lose everything but their moccasins and breechclout an' walk off looking for something of value t' bet with. I heard that some even bet their wives away, but never saw it happen. They sure loved gambling.

Th' Cherry Creek gold hunters returned in early August, mad and disgusted at finding no gold. They got drunk—those that had money—an' left for th' Nation in a day or two. Mr. Kirk and family packed up an' joined a train headed west for Santa Fe. They settled around Las Vegas and I saw him years later at Fort Union. He had done quite well for himself.

Uncle Jolly stayed with us an' helped Pa in th' horse trade. Aunt Janey gave him fits about losin' out on th' gold while Pa got rich with silver. Uncle Jolly would just grin an' jingle some pesos in his pocket. "I'm gonna catch up with him, Janey and buy you the fanciest sulky in the Nation with a white stocking bay t' pull it!"

There was a lot of bustle and excitement when Mr. Bent arrived from St. Louis. He rode in a day or two ahead of his train an' th' place got real busy preparing for new goods and unloadin' th' train when it pulled in. Th' fort was fairly bulging with gear an' people an' stock.

Mr. William's wives lived in tipis instead o' th' fort an' one evening when he was sittin' in front of th' tipi, Pa went over t' meet him. He was a quiet man, easy to talk with an' had a keen mind for business. There was already a chill in th' air an' he told Pa that winter was near an' there were no more trains comin' west after him. What few trains goin' east would be lightly loaded an' not likely t' need remounts. Horse tradin' was about t' shut down for th' winter.

Pa was in his fiftieth year an' felt th' need t' settle an' avoid a harsh winter on th' prairie so he determined t' get back east b'fore snow flew. Me an' Jake weren't at all interested in goin' back east with all th' activity out here an' we argued agin leavin', but Ma an' Aunt Janey sided with Pa an' they were determined t' quit th' west, at least for th' time bein'.

Pa an' Mr. Bent struck up a deal where he would buy out Pa's herd for silver an' hire me an' Jake t' keep herd on them through th' winter. That was satisfactory with us but Ma was upset about leavin' us on our own. She came near t' changing her mind about leavin', but we all assured her we would be ok and would go back east t' see them in a year or two. Little did I know it would be ten years b'fore I laid eyes on her agin.

Things got busy for a few days while Pa wrapped up his business an' packed th' wagons. They had determined t' leave th' Studebaker an' pack ever'thing in th' two big wagons. A day or two b'fore they planned t' leave, Pa hitched up th' Studebaker an' drove up to th' fort. To our surprise, he returned with the wagon loaded with camping gear.

"I thought you were gonna sell th' Studebaker an' take th' two big wagons back," I said to him.

"We are. I thought you boys might need an outfit of your own if you're gonna stay out here," he replied.

"Wowee," Jake's eyes widened, "look at that stuff!"

We were like two kids at Christmas goin' through that wagon. Th' folks gathered around an' watched with much amusement. In addition to all th' cooking an' campin' gear, there was a small keg of powder and some lead bars.

Uncle Jolly lifted a blanket corner an' exclaimed, "I swear, Jesse, yore gonna spoil these boys rotten, why if I had this much when I started out, I'da felt like a plantation tycoon!"

Jake lifted th' blanket an' whispered, "Looka here, Zee!" He started diggin' things off an' come up with a new Hawken rifle.

"Wow," I said, reaching for the gun.

Jake pulled away, "This-un's mine, yours is in th' wagon."

I couldn't b'lieve Pa had bought *two* rifles, but shore 'nuf there was another one in there. They had walnut burl stocks an' were both brand new. Each came with its own bullet mold an' there were two powder horns made and ornamented by Cheyenne squaws.

"We didn't need you t' spend all this on us, Pa," Jake said.

"You boys earned every bit of it on this trip and I got th' benefit if anyone did."

There were two wooden cases tucked under th' seat an' I thought I recognized what they were. Sure enough, inside was a Colt's revolver with spare cylinder. The one I held had been used and "K.C." was scratched on th' butt.

"Mr. Bent said that Kit Carson had traded it in for a newer model with a bored-through cylinder, but he said he would guarantee that one," Pa said.

"Trade yuh my new one for that one," Jake said, but there was no deal in that for me. I used it for several years until th' price came down on bored-through guns an' cartridges got plentiful.

We sure were surprised an' pleased with th' gear Pa had bought us an' we made good use of it in th' coming years. Ma came over from their tent an' handed each of us a buffalo robe. "I traded with the Cheyenne women for these. They will come in very handy in the cold."

"There are Mackinaw coats and boots paid for at th' store. You need t' get up there tomorrow and get ones that fit," Pa said.

I don't believe I have ever been so speechless and surprised. Pa must have spent upwards of a hundred dollars each on us. All in all it was to be th' most money—for its time, you see—that anyone has ever spent on me—before or since!

In addition to all that, we had a team for th' wagon an' two mounts each for us t' ride. We made sure t' keep th' two racing ponies and they came in handy later on both as racers and life savers.

A couple of days later, Pa an' Uncle Jolly hitched their wagons on a train to Freeport an' we parted company. We rode out a half-day with them, then left after they nooned. Ma stood on th' wagon seat an' waved her kerchief until they dropped down over a ridge and we could see them no more. There was a lump in my throat and a tear in my eye for a while, but excitement for our new life soon overtook.

We got a letter from Ma in th' spring of '59 sayin' they had gotten back safely an' that Pa had bought a large farm on Archer's Fork between th' horseshoe bends an' Hartsugg Creek. There were good bottoms for crops an' lots o' pasture for Pa's horses.

As usual I sat scratching on my pad for a few minutes catching up with Zenas' narrative. Zenas stoked his pipe, lit it with a kitchen match, and sat puffing to the rhythm of his gently creaking rocker. I heard the screen door squeak and Mrs. Meeker stepped out with an old cherrywood box in her hands. Zenas took it and opened it. There lay an old Colt's 1850's revolver, much worn, but clean and well oiled. I didn't want to touch it, but Zenas handed it to me. It was heavy and solid feeling, probably .40 to .44 caliber and scratched plainly on the butt were the initials K.C. *"I lost th' spare cylinder crossin' a river one night, but th' gun was in my hand an' th' barrel was hot." Zenas chuckled.*

There weren't any notches in th' scales, but I wager both owners could have put some there if they had wanted to . . .

CHAPTER 13
PURGATORY

1859

Just before the end of the 16ᵗʰ century, an expedition was sent out of Mexico to subdue rebellious Indians in Nuevo Mexico. After the mission of the army was completed, the captains, against orders, took up Coronado's quest for the cities of gold. The leaders of the expedition quarreled and one was killed, prompting the priests to leave the army to its own devices. The soldiers followed a pleasant little stream flowing down from the Spanish Peaks to its conjunction with the Arkansas River. There in a verdant meadow, they camped.

In the early morning light, Indians set fire to the tall grasses. Only one man and a young girl survived, the remaining soldiers left their armor and their bones bleaching in the sun.

Santa Fe was established in 1608. Years passed, and a band of explorers discovered the rusting remnants of the army scattered across the meadow. They named the little stream El Rio de Las Animas Perdidas en Purgatorio. A hundred years later, French traders stumbling over the stream's name, said to be longer than the stream itself, shortened it to Purgatoire. Thick-tongued Americans shortened the name to Las Animas while others corrupted Purgatoire into Purgatory or Picketwire. Today's maps label the stream Purgatoire, but the locals still call it Picketwire. The little stream still flows down from Stonewall to the Arkansas as it has for millennia without regard of the many names man has given it. It is the Picketwire country that Zenas now becomes familiar with as he and Jacob enter the employ of William Bent.

We threw Pa's horses in with Mr. Bent's herd an' Jake was made head herder over me an' a half-dozen Mexican boys. Most of our time was spent huntin' graze, for th' summer's traffic had eaten up everything around th' fort and we had to range out further and further t' find grass. This made us nervous for it exposed th' herd t' roamin' bands of Indians. If we lost th' herd, we'd be out in th' middle of th' plains without a job. Jake had a talk with Mr. Bent an' it was decided that it was time to take th' herd up to th' Purgatory ranch for th' winter. There was plenty of grass an' th' stockade would give protection from prowlin' varmints of all kinds. The men there had been instructed to cut hay for th' herd for th' winter.

It didn't take us long t' be ready t' move, most o' our gear packed in th' Studebaker already, and early next morning we put our herd on th' trail. This was in th' first week of October, 1857, and it was already pretty cold at night. Th' sun soon melted th' rime of ice off th' river an' warmed things nicely, but in shade it was pretty nippy.

Our Mexican boys went along t' help us, then they would return to th' fort. They were a ragged bunch, half of them barefooted with only a blanket for cover. They would herd most o' th' time afoot an' their feet must have been hard as whet leather. When we moved th' herd, they would catch a horse an' ride bareback—some o' th' best riders I ever saw. Jake sent one of th' boys ahead to tell them at th' fort we would arrive about sunset and we moved at a leisurely pace, letting th' herd graze as we went along. We splashed across th' ford an' into the meadows of th' bottoms just as long shadows of th' Sangre de Christos reached th' rough stockade.

We hazed our herd into a corral next to th' stockade an' Jake sent hungry boys ahead t' get supper. A good bait of buffalo short ribs and strong coffee set us up nicely for a long night's rest. Th' Mexes rolled up in their blankets, feet to th' fire an' were soon soundly asleep. After a good breakfast, they were on their way back to th' fort sure of walkin' twenty-five miles afore dark.

It was along about this time we began getting word of th' massacre at Mountain Meadows. At first, Jake and I were relieved because we knew that th' Fanchers would take th' Humboldt trail as they had on all their other trips an' that was far north of th' Meadows. Then news came in that it *was* th' Fancher train and that all had been murdered.

Rumors flew that Mormons had attacked th' train an' many an argument resulted on whether white men could treat other white men so. Gradually, the truth came out with Captain Carleton's report an' later revelations of th' sorry event. Th' great question we have always had is why the Fanchers would choose an unfamiliar route like that and th' best I can determine, they were misled into taking it by Mormon plotters.

We knew many people in th' train and it saddened us t' think of what happened to them. Ma's premonition had proven true, though she took no comfort in it. Nevertheless we were glad Pony had not gone along.

Purgatory Ranch was th' first place Charles and William Bent settled after they had traded with Indians a while. It was here that a chief suggested that they build a permanent trading house in Big Timbers, but the men wanted to keep their fur trade as well as Indian trade and chose a spot between Big Timbers an' th' mountains north of a bend in th' Arkansas River. There they built the old adobe fort and operated it for nearly thirty years until William burned it down.

Earlier in '57 he had built a rough stockade in th' Purgatory bottoms an' started ranchin'. Th' men working there welcomed an' made room for us an' we settled in. There were cattle in addition to horses an' we all rode herd on th' mixture. Most days

120

were clear an' mild, but when a norther roared down th' front range, we penned up our horses an' left cattle to their own devices. They would drift some, but rarely left th' confines of th' valley, choosing to hole up under cedars instead. When weather cleared, we would ride up th' valley several miles an' start hazing cows back to th' bottom meadows. It got to be such a routine that when we started out after them, we would meet cows comin' back. Still, there were a few stubborn ones that had to be choused out an' driven back, mostly th' same ones ever'time.

Spring comes slow on th' high plains an' by th' time those last spring blizzards were through with us it was late April or early May. That first spring we penned up our horses an' began gelding out th' weakest studs so we could upgrade our stock. With Mr. Bent's permission, we weeded out older and weaker mares an' sold them off. There was considerable pressure from trail traffic t' trade off brood stock, but we held firm on keeping them.

We got a big Jack from Uncle Dick Wootton up on th' Huerfano an' started our mule herd. He had gotten it off'n some traders hangin' around th' remains of The Pueblo twenty miles upriver from his ranch. He drove a hard bargain, but we got it back when he came down an' traded for some of our mules. Mr. Bent was pleased with th' way we managed his herd an' enjoyed watchin' young stock cavorting in th' bottoms.

In 1860, Mr. Bent came up an' greatly enlarged th' stockade. We moved out of th' way an' spent all summer well up th' river. The new building was something to behold. It was fully a hundred feet on a side with fifteen-foot-high pickets a foot or more in diameter and rooms built around north, west, and south walls. Th' east side held stables and a blacksmith shop. The gate was in th' south wall an' that whole north side was Bent's quarters. It looked like he was planning to spend a lot more time there.

There weren't many Indians hangin' around th' ranch. Th' Cheyenne were greatly decimated by a cholera epidemic in '48 an' mostly stayed away from us. We had to keep our eyes out for Apaches from th' southwest, Utes from those mountains west, an' that Comanche-Kiowa-Arapaho bunch from th' plains. We had scouts out all th' time watchin' an' we all rode armed. We lost a few stock to individuals raiding—never got any of them back—but th' herd as a whole stayed safe.

CHAPTER 14
A WILD COW ROUNDUP

1861

It gets pretty boring closed in waitin' out winter an' when we had heard th' same stories umpteen times we were all ready for some action. This was th' second year we were at Purgatory Ranch. Horse herdin' had settled down to just keepin' Injuns out of th' herd an' managing our breeding stock.

Jake wasn't in such a need for me an' I was thinkin' about branchin' out on my own some. I had ambitions of doin' more in life than herdin' a bunch of stock for another man. Little did I know that would be my lot for some years t' come. I had a lot t' learn b'fore I was ready t' step out on my own.

Well, it was in this bored state o' mind that we were sittin' around th' fire one blizzardy day when John Hatcher started telling us about Bent–St. Vrain Company's first ranch on th' Upper Purgatory.

"Back in '47 when th' army was takin' over th' territory an' war with Mexico was ragin', I was runnin' a ranch on th' Upper Purgatory for th' company. Injuns, seein' their chance, stole all our mules an' horses an' told me t' skedaddle. I didn't take them too seriously until one mornin' I woke up t' th' music of war cries and gunfire. Those rascals killed ever cow in sight 'cept fer three an' tol' me t' leave pronto, this was their land. It was along about this time my scalp got that crawly feelin'—an I don't mean lousy either—and I decided I had urgent business elsewhere. Th' oxen they left couldn't pull fast enough fer us, so

123

we cut our wagon in half an' made a cart out o' th' front end, hitched up, an' pulled out at th' highest speed my whip could induce in those ol' steers.

"That seemed t' please th' savages an' they gave us an offi-ci-al escort out'n th' country. We left b'hind a good amount of plunder that soon disappeared, our shanties goin' up in smoke.

"What those Injuns didn't take was cattle scattered around along the river an up th' draws. They stayed an' multiplied, becoming a nuisance to th' welfare o' wild life. Last time I was through there, th' brush fairly bulged with cattle. I saw only a few that still had brands, th' rest were unmarked."

It was quiet for a minute while that bit of information was digested, then Jake said, "I suppose Mr. Bent would lay claim to th' whole bunch . . ."

"Sí but hee not able to catch theem up by heemself, maybee he let us catch theem for a price," a Mexican American we called Hillside said. He had that name because one leg was shorter than the other an' we said he could only walk straight on th' side of a hill an' then only in one direction. But he could ride a horse better than any of the rest of us. He and his cousin Juan were practically inseperable.

"D'yuh think he would give us a part o' th' ones we could catch?" I asked.

"Might do," John said, "they's been runnin' wild all this time an' I s'pose if'n one pushed it, those cows don't rightly b'long t' enybody, leastways that's what those Texicans claim."

"Bet that's not what Mr. Bent claims," Jake said.

Well, we jostled that around for some time an' finally d'cided to proposition Mr. Bent for a roundup where we would keep a portion of th' cows for ourselves as pay.

"Better ask fer a high percent, for it's sure that ol' trader won't take your first offer. He'll have yuh jewed down t' th' bone afore he gits through," John observed. By that, we decided t' ask for sixty percent straight run herd an' we would provide our own camp.

Ol' Bent musta knowed somethin' was up for he came down an' took supper with us that night.

When we made th' proposition to him, he smiled an' nodded his head. "Thought you boys had your heads t'gether for somethin'. I suppose I could lay claim t' *all* th' increase up there if I wanted to, an' hire you boys t' gather them up. If you want paid in stock, that would be all right with me but not for sixty percent of th' gather. Seems more likely I should get seventy percent an' you should get thirty."

There was quiet fer a moment while we mulled that around. "Them cows ain't marked anyway, what would you pay us t' brand 'em fer ye?" someone asked.

"Don't see as how I need 'em marked if you boys mark yours."

"Thet way, he could lay claim t' all unmarked stock left in th' country," Jake whispered.

"Mr. Bent, th' army needs cattle an' those should be plenty fat for sale. If we branded yours along with ours, we both would have a ready an' eager market," I said.

He rubbed his chin for a moment. "Guess you're right there, son. Maybe they *should* be carryin' my brand."

John Hatcher spoke up, "That's a awful hard job with a bunch o' cows that wild, Bill, what say we gather them seventy-thirty like you say an' you see to th' brandin'?"

"Now, John, why should I worry about that when you boys would be right there an' all geared up t' do th' job yourselves?"

"Guess yore right there," John mused for a moment. "We could brand our cows an' your'n at th' same time . . . say for forty percent o' th' herd straight run."

Now straight run meant that we would brand an' separate th' herd as they come to th' fire without selectin' bull or steer nor cow or calf. Not bein' good vaqueros, that was about th' peak

125

o' our ability.

"Cain't see that forty percent, John."

"Could you see forty percent if we cut th' bull calves at th' same time?" Jake asked.

Now things were gittin' involved and Ol' Bill Bent sat back an' studied a minute. "Tell you what, boys, if you brand *and* cut my portion o' th' herd . . . I'll go sixty-five–thirty-five if they are penned an' ready for sale."

I nodded. "That sounds good . . ."

"I don't know . . ." John Hatcher interrupted, ". . . Thet's a purty low price t' pay fer all th' work it's gonna take. I want to waller that aroun' an' see what's on th' underside b'fore I commits myself t' it."

Mr. Bent chuckled, you could see he was enjoyin' th' back and forth play more than worryin' about those cows an' who got what.

"Well, you just do that, John, an' let me know what you decide in th' mornin'. I got t' get to th' house, it's been a long day." With that he got up, nodded to th' rest o' us, an' left, trottin' across th' yard in wind an' snow.

John watched him go, then turned to me, "Don't ever show that yore eager t' take a deal like thet, 'specially with Mr. William Bent, he'll git th' idée he's bein' too easy on yuh an' drive a harder bargain next time. I'll go in there 'bout noon tomorry, hat in hand an' shakin' my head sayin', 'I guess we'll take yore offer, Bill, but you shore drive a hard bargain' He'll know I'll be lyin' through my teeth, but thet's part o' th' game we're playin' here. He'll prob'ly try t' add somethin' else to th' deal, but I'll hold fast an' maybe 'bout sundown he'll come over an' say all right."

An' you know, that's just th' way it played out. John told Mr. Bent we would accept his deal, then th' boss wanted us t' trail th' herd to Purgatory Ranch. John pretended t' get mad an'

126

throwed his hat down an' said, "Dammit, Bill, yuh ain't never satisfied, air ye? Yuh know good an' well those cows ain't gonna trail an' a whole army o' men couldn't hold 'em. Best we can do is sell them right there an' let th' army worry 'bout herdin' 'em sommers!"

John grinned when he told us. "Well, Bill laughed an' said 'you're sure right there, John, you boys go ahead an' I'll send word to Fort Union we have cattle t' sell, range delivery. Th' quartermaster'll probably come out to see 'em and buy.' "

Th' next days were busy plannin' an' getting things ready. All of us couldn't go an' it was decided that Jake would take care o' th' stock, cows an' horses, with four Mexican boys t' help him an' keep things goin' at th' stockade. That left us with ten men t' go after cows. I remember John Prowers an' Tom Boggs was there an' young George Bent was back from school in St. Louis. He was quiet and even sullen at times an' in th' end didn't go with us. Mr. Bent outfitted him with fancy clothes an' a five-hundred-dollar horse from Denver. He had a place on th' Purgatory if he wanted it, but he ran away an' joined his mother's family on th' plains.

We decided t' take three horses each, knowin' there would be some hard ridin' t' do an' there'd always be one or two horses stove up on top o' that. Hatcher left early t' go palaver with th' Indians an' let them know what we were up to. He sent word back that it was all well with them and they wouldn't bother us if we rid th' country o' those pesky cows. Th' "not botherin' " part was met with not a little skepticism, but th' word was encouragin' anyway. We loaded th' ol' Studebaker with our bedding an' what provisions we could wrangle by hook or crook.

We pulled out th' second week in March on th' tail end of what we hoped was th' last blizzard o' th' year. It was blitzy cold but th' wind was at our backs an' those buffalo robes shed wind purty good. After a day or two, th' wind turned south an' it warmed up considerably.

John Hatcher an' the boys with him had set up camp under th' north bank of a draw opposite th' mouths o' Trinchera and Trementina creeks. It was ideal for firewood, water, and shelter.

Riding out on th' flats where th' ranch had been, we saw lots of cow sign, but no cows.

"If you look down in th' canyon an' in th' trees, you'll scare up a bunch of 'em," John said, "they's got t' be fifteen hundred t' two thousand head within a five mile circle o' here, no telling how many hev wandered off, been killed, or rustled away."

"Feed mostly at night, do they?" Hillside asked.

"Late in th' evenin' 'til early in th' mornin'."

"How d'yuh propose t' catch them?" Tom asked.

"Not havin' any tame cows t' neck 'em to, I s'pose next best way would be like we catch mustangs by trappin' them," John replied. "There's a good bluff down in th' canyon that would be one wing an' we would have t' build th' other one an' a pen at th' end that would hold 'em."

"What we need is a good box canyon with grass an' water," I said.

"Good luck on finding that," John said. He pulled out his pipe an' began building a smoke. "I guess next best thing is th' falls in Bent Canyon. We could run 'em up agin that an' maybe build fence where th' slope ain't steep enough t' hold 'em."

"I ain't gonna spend my time building fences. If we don't git those cows fast an' turn 'em fast, there won't be no money in it fer us." Ben Lott was one o' th' men with us. He was a scrawny little fellow, hard as iron an' one o' th' best scrappers I ever knew. I've seen him beat men twice his size in half th' time it would take anyone else. He never said much, but when he did we listened. "What we need is a natural pen that will hold five hundred to a thousand critturs for several days, maybe weeks, till we're done with 'em."

"You're right there, Ben," I said. "John, you sure they ain't any box canyons fit for our purpose?"

"Nope, not a one. We looked fer one when we came into th' country, would hev been th' ideal thing fer a ranch, but there just ain't one. We ended up settin' up on th' flat where we could see anythin' comin at us, 'twas th' best we could do."

"Thee can-yon of thee Purgator-r-r-y has two sides an' plenty agua and gr-r-r-ass, señors, eet just don't have no eends for thee box," Hillside observed.

"Too bad we don't have some powder, we could blast a wall t' plug th' canyon."

"Then yuh 'ould have a lake, dummy," John Prowers said.

"We ain't gonna have room t' keep a thousand cows until they're sold," Tom Boggs said.

I nodded. "Looks like we're gonna have t' catch small bunches an' drive them somewheres afore we catch up some more."

Hatcher had been quiet for a few minutes, then he said, "Hillside had th' glimmer o' a idée there, we could use th' canyon fer our pen an' th' cows would have all th' water an' grass they wanted. All we would have t' do would be t' keep th' ends plugged so's they couldn't scatter or git out."

"We need a long stretch with a bottleneck where we can have two holdin' pens, one t' hold th' gather . . ." I said.

". . . An one t' hold th' branded!" Ben put in.

"How rough is that canyon on down to th' bottoms, John?" Tom Boggs asked.

"Not too bad." John pulled thoughtfully on his pipe. "You boys might have something there. When we got th' herd branded, we could funnel them right on down th' canyon without loosin 'em an' by th' time they got to th' bottoms, they might just be so tired an' hungry they 'ould stay there where we could git aholt o' them when we needed to."

"D'yuh think we could sell them there?" I could tell Prowers had plans for his portion th' rest of us hadn't considered.

"Oh yeah, th' army there has t' eat just es much es th' one at Union."

"Well, let's find us a pen," I said and turned back to th' river.

We had pitched camp near th' upper end of th' canyon an' from there on down, it got deeper, th' sides got steeper. Ridin th' rim, we followed it for several miles. Th' southeast side o' th' canyon wasn't so steep as t' hold cows an' there were a lot of drainages comin' into th' river from that side where cattle could escape. Th' northwest bank was ideal for our purposes if th' south side had been th' same. Finally we reined in on th' rim of a deep draw we couldn't cross.

"No use goin' any further," John Hatcher said, "it's several miles more until both sides are steep enough for our purposes."

Hillside was standing on the point looking down into th' ar-royo. "Eef wee can't use thee reever, why can't wee use these draw? Thee sides are verrry steep for a cow an' eet look-es like eet ees long enough to hold our herds."

"Well I'll be switched if yuh ain't right!" Tom exclaimed, "All we got t' find out is if it's long enough an' we can fence off th' upper end."

We rode up th' rim o' that draw an' it looked pretty good. Th' brush wasn't too thick an' it looked like there was plenty grass on th' lower slopes t' hold a pretty good herd for a while. It was near three miles to where th' arroyo shallowed out enough t' where it would do us no good, but steeper walls a little below there were only about a quarter mile apart an' a fence could be made easy.

"This looks pretty good," Ben allowed, "I can live with that little bit o' fence building."

"We need t' find us a place 'bout halfway down t' build us a fence an' holdin' chute fer brandin'."

Not quite halfway back to th' river, there was a narrow place with steep rock bluffs just right for our purposes. It just meant we couldn't build up too much of a herd b'fore we branded. It was near dark when we rode back to camp an' there wasn't much cookin' done b'fore we turned in. Last thing I heard was John Hatcher sayin', "We'll lay out our plans in th' morning, boys . . ."

I woke just as th' sun peeked over th' horizon an' shined its rays into my eyes. One or two others were stoking th' fire, but most o' us were still in our blankets.

Ben was sawin' thick slices out of a ham. "Grab a slab an' cook yer breakfast, Zee," he said cheerfully, "It's on Mr. Will'am Bent!"

I soon had two ham steaks sizzling over th' fire an' people started stirrin'. Me an' Ben sat down an' started eatin' while th' others scrambled t' start their own breakfast.

John Prowers musta finished early, for he sat smoking his pipe an' joshin' th' others fer bein' so lazy an' slow. He was another of those little men who wore like iron, one o' th' ugliest fellers I ever knowed, but with th' biggest heart of all. He had trapped th' mountains afore Kit Carson an' traded with Indians almost as long as anybody. I never knew him t' meet any tribe he couldn't talk with. He knew sign language just like he was born with it. In '53 or so, he had driven a flock of sheep to California an' made a killin' on it. I don't know what he did with all that money, though some said he had a big ranch sommers. He just enjoyed frontier life too much t' settle down, like a whole bunch of those old-timers I knew.

After breakfast, we gathered around him an' he laid out th' arroyo on th' ground, markin' three places we would hafta build fences at and dividin' us up into work crews.

"Me and Zee and Hillside will start buildin' th' middle fence and chute while you other two bunches build end fences. Be sure t' make 'em tight, those cows'r strong as buffalo an' jump like deer, so weave brush high an' tight. You boys on th' upper end can build wings out a ways t' funnel them into th' gate. Be sure you make 'em wide enough at th' mouth so's it don't spook th' critters away."

Turnin to th' other crew, he said, "you don't hev t' make a gate, just make th' fence up solid an' we'll tear it down when we're ready.

"Th' chute is gonna have t' be strong an' it'll take a long time t' make, so when ya git through hie yoreselfs down and lend us a hand. We may es well move camp now, so round it all up an' we'll set up camp by a spring I know of closer to th' arroyo."

We sure hated t' leave that cozy camp an' didn't relish campin' out in th' open on top, but it was necessary. Camp was broken in record time and we were on our way. John led us northwest a few miles 'til we came to a little draw where th' spring was. This drained into our arroyo an' th' upper fence was only about a mile away. There wasn't a lot of wood there so we would have t' drag it up, but that wasn't any problem.

We set up camp by droppin' th' wagon an' leavin one man there t' watch horses an' boil ham bone an' beans, an' hurried on to our tasks. John walked up an' down th' rock bluff on th' right side o' th' arroyo 'til he found a spot where th' solid rock was smooth an' footing good. We laid out our chute here, about thirty feet long, four feet out from th' rock, then taperin' back away from th' bluff t' form a funnel.

Hillside an' I started cutting poles for th' chute an' John trimmed th' brush off an' dragged it up for th' fence. We worked all afternoon cutting poles an' stackin' them by th' wall where th' chute would be. Ever once in a while we could hear th' sound of choppin' echoin' down th' draw.

Sunset was early down in th' bottom an' we were just quittin' for th' night when th' crew from downstream rode up. The boys at th' upper end had made good progress and had a pile of poles laid out for our chute.

"That should be enough t' finish th' chute," I said.

We found ham and beans thick an' bubblin' hot an' th' coffee made strong. Th' cook was complimented on his work. We chose camp keeper for th' next day by th' one that had th' most blisters.

"Yuh kin only count th' ones on yer hands, not yer rear end," Boggs called.

"You ain't got any blisters on yer ass, they's all turned t' calluses," came th' retort, to which there came another smart reply an' th' whole camp turned into an' uproar for a minute or two. Mostly, though, we were all tired an' sore an' stars weren't hardly out b'fore we were all asleep. Last thing I remember was seein' John's pipe glow as he sat on his robe finishing his smoke.

There were a lot of stiff and sore muscles next morning, but we were mostly youngsters toughened up to work. Hillside an' I spent th' day digging holes an' settin' poles while John wove a brush fence. After noon, he came an' tied in runners at th' top an' middle of our posts for strength. We poured water in th' post holes and tamped dirt hard against th' posts. There was room left between th' uprights for brandin' irons and an' extra brace against th' top upright every few feet.

John kept shakin' th' fence an' we had t' reinforce and tamp several loose ones two or three times b'fore they were good and tight. A couple o' boys from th' river rode up about mid-afternoon sayin' they had gotten far enough along t' be spared t' help us an' we made good progress with th' brush fence. Two more days of hard work an' th' fences were done. So were we for a while. We ran our stock into th' upper pen an' took time t' rest up and prepare for th' roundup.

John and a couple of others were up b'fore daylight ridin' out an' scoutin' th' countryside. They were back by late afternoon ridin' tired horses. When they were fed, we gathered 'round t' hear about what they had found.

Ben Lott whittled him a toothpick an' wiped off a big area of sand with his boot. With his stick, he drew a big arc that looked like a smiling mouth. "This here's th' Purgatory. It makes a big bend like this an' th' north side of it is th' old ranch." Up on th' right side a ways he drew another line that ran a little north of west an' almost touched th' other side of th' smile. "An this is our draw. It almost goes to th' river up here on th' upper end where th' divide is pretty narrer."

"This is gonna be our first area t' gather," John put in, "th' bottoms ain't th' only place cows are. We scairt up a passel o' cows layin' around those waller tanks scattered all over th' place."

"So we thought th' best way t' approach this is t' ride up th' arroyo scarin' out th' ones we find there an' runnin' them out on th' flats, then turn right around an' head 'em south towards th' river," Ben added.

"If'n we can keep them movin' south and east, pickin' up what we run acrost on th' flats, we can gather most o' th' ones there an' push them toward those holdin' pens." John said, packin' his pipe. "Th' Purgatory is on th' rise an' not many o' them cows is likely t' swim it, so it'll act as a fence t' keep them goin' our way."

Ben squatted back on his heels an' looked at John expectantly.

John took a few puffs on his pipe an' pointed his stem at th' upper end of th' arroyo. "That's a good fifteen mile from here and it looks like we'll hev t' spend at least one night—maybe two—on th' flats, so we'll need all horses an' enough grub t' last us. If we work up th' draw fast, we can get to the top a little after noon an' change horses there for our drive back acrost th' flats an' down th' river. We should have a good bunch by sundown an' it may be if we do a little night ridin', we could keep most o' them in front of us."

"Thee moon ees nearing full an' r-r-r-ises just after Meester Sol sets, so we can see thees cows good," Juan said.

"Yer right there, Juan, it'll help a lot."

We divvied up chores an' next mornin' two boys gathered th' cavyyard and food. The rest of us left t' drive cows. Anglin' northwest a ways, we hit th' draw a couple of miles above camp an' spread out in a long line startin' a little ways north of th' draw an' tailin' back on th' flats south. Whatever got pushed out was hazed toward th' middle and we kept them bunched an' movin' all morning. It wasn't to those cows' likin' an' we had t' work hard t' keep them in front of us. By noon, our horses was tired out an' we stopped t' remount.

"It don't make sense that we are drivin' this mob *away* from th' pens," I said as we rested a moment. "There must be a couple hundred there, why don't we drive them back an' put 'em in th' fence?"

"I been thinking th' same thing," Tom said.

The rest began t' see th' logic of it.

"We should have gone around an' made our drive *toward* th' pens instead of away," I heard Prowers say.

"Yer right," John Hatcher said. "I cut off too big a quid for us t' chaw, guess my eyes were too big."

"I bet if we made smaller sweeps so that we could be back in camp each night, we would do better an' not be so hard on th horses," I added.

"Good idée Meester Zee, let's do eet!" Hillside said an' mounted up.

"Take th' cavyyard back t' camp, boys, an' graze them up on th' flats away from th' pens an' we'll drive this bunch back along th' draw nice an' easy. One of yuh open th' gates an' we'll have them penned afore they know it," Hatcher said.

By th' time he had finished, we were all mounted an' movin' out to th' bunched cows. Th' drive back down th' draw was more leisurely than th' mornin's work, those cows bein' near as tired as our horses were, and with fresh horses, we were able t' keep them bunched good. I had time t' take notice o' things and look around some.

'Way to th' north there rose a steep ridge that could do as a barrier for rounding up cattle agin. Later when we examined it closer, th' ridge turned out t' be a hogback. We used it to good advantage when we gathered up there. To th' south stretched th' flats. It was dotted with buffalo wallows filled with water and was ideal short-grass grazin' land. 'Way to th' south, th' line o' the river showed green. I wasn't used to gauging distances out here yet and it looked like maybe five miles away. In reality, it was more like ten or twelve miles. Clear air and high skys make everything seem nearer than they are.

Th' cattle were mostly longhorn with a few blacks o' th' Mexican strain thrown in. There was every color of cow in th' world there, from black to brindle to yeller. Most were multicolored like a paint horse. I counted five different colors on several cows.

Their horns were long and sharp an' when they were bunched, you could hear them clack as they bumped each other. Some of those things spanned six to eight feet. They were mostly well fed and sleek, but stood tall and narrow hipped. This was b'fore cowmen had coined th' term *mossyhorn* or *mossyback,* or Shanghai Pierce called his steers *sea lions,* but they were a lusty bunch of mixed cattle—from old cows and some steers still car- ryin a Bent–St. Vrain brand to snortin', slick-sided bulls and cows with calves at their sides. Several looked like they would drop a calf any day.

As I learned more about wild cows, I found that few of them would drop a calf in winter time, their chances of survival bein' slim. This trait ain't in tamer cows kept in fenced pastures, pampered with hay an' shelter. These young cowmen of today would be awed at th' wild cows we had t' handle in those days.

We drove these cattle loose and slow until we were close to th' pens, then we bunched them close an' pushed so hard they were in th' pen b'fore they knew it.

It was a tired but happy crowd that rode into camp an' filled cups with boiling hot coffee. We finished off th' last of our ham and beans an' sat and talked over th' day's events. Everyone agreed that we had struck on a good method of roundin' up cows an' with a few modifications here an' there, we could be pretty efficient.

We decided that there needed to be two men caring for th' horses all th' time an' two boys were appointed to that job. I kept quiet about my horse herdin' experience for I wanted t' be in on cow gathering. These two worked things out so that one was with the cavyyard day and night.

In th' mornings, John Hatcher would map out th' area we were going t' clear an' after we caught our morning mounts, the horses would be taken to a designated spot or area where they were allowed to graze until we needed t' change mounts. Then they would be taken back to the area of the camp to rest an' graze more until they were needed again. A good number of us got t' catchin' up a fresh horse at night an' picketin' him near camp in case he was needed before daylight. I was sure glad I did that a time or two. After th' war in big drives and roundups it became a general practice for us all t' keep a good night horse near every night.

After three gathers, we had four hundred and eighteen head by later count an' we decided it was time t' brand this bunch an' let th' horses have a little rest.

"I been thinking, John," said one o' th' boys who was *never* strong in that discipline, "how we gonna divide up these cows?

Out of ten cows we get three an' one half an' Mister Bill gets six an' one half. How we gonna get *half*-cows?"

"Yeah, an' who would get th' front half an' who would git th' back portion?" I added.

"I don' want none o' mine t' bee thee fr-ront half, them big horns is pl-en-ty ba'ad!" said Juan, who had gotten a taste of th' business end of a mad cow an' lost a large portion of his pant leg along with a good amount of horsehide on his mount.

"Don't worry, Juan, them horns'd keep 'em tipped up on their noses all the time," Tom Boggs called.

"Th' question seems t'me to be where you would brand that front half . . ." I started t' say.

". . . Yeah, an where yuh gonna notch th' ear o' th' back half?" Prowers interrupted.

We all laughed at that and John studied a bit. "Wel-l-l, son, if'n you doubles th' numbers, you will see that out of twenty critturs we'd get seven o' them an' ol' Bill'd git thirteen. That way we wouldn't have a bunch o' half-cows draggin' around an' tryin' t' keep up with th' herd."

The man grinned an' nodded. He was used t' takin' ribbin' just like th' rest of us an' didn't mind, since he gave as much as he got.

CHAPTER 15
BRANDING

We had t' learn some things about branding th' same way we did about roundin' up cattle, but by th' third day we had it down and things went smoothly after that. Our chute held four critters at once, so we would brand th' first cow, whatever it was, cow, calf, or bull, with our own brand, which consisted only as an X under th' Bent brand if there was one. Th' next three were branded and marked Bent–St. Vrain until we got to th' fifth bunch, where we branded th' first three ours an' only one Bent's.

Our slow friend was puzzled and had t' git down in th' sand an' make twenty marks b'fore he was satisfied that it would work that way.

"By gum, Hatcher, yore shore right with your math, it's a good thing we let you come along with us, yuh jist mought pay yer way!" he called as he scrubbed out his ciphers with his boot.

We were all kept busy; two men on horseback drove cattle into th' chute, four men slid bars b'tween cows t' hold 'em in place, then notched ears or cut bulls as needed while three men did th' brandin' an' fed th' fire. One man kept tally, me an' John sharing that chore. I would much rather have done something else, but John insisted that I run th' book since I wrote neater.

We didn't cut any bulls over three years old, fearing it might damage them too much but we still got so many fries we were tired of them by th' third day. Needin' all ten of us t' do th' brandin' left no one t' herd horses, so we eased them in to th' upper pen an' that seemed t' work out, cattle keepin' their distance from horses an' th' ones on horseback watchin' 'em. We branded one hundred and ten first day, one hundred thirty-one second, one hundred fifty-seven th' third day, and there were twenty old cows an' steers already branded (how I know that exactly is that I still have my tally book). Th' last day we finished up after dark jist so's we wouldn't have t' come back.

That was one tired bunch of cowmen when we dragged into camp that night an' we still had t' cook our supper.

"Seems like we air a man or two short fer this operation," someone muttered.

"Sho' 'nuf," Ben agreed, "we don't have anyone t' watch th' cavyyard while we're brandin' an' they spend that time eatin' up grass that should be saved for cattle."

"We need us a cook, too." Tom wasn't very happy about bein' his own cook.

"And more food!"

"Those horses are shore gittin' a workout, wouldn't hurt if we had another mount apiece."

"I think yore right," John Prowers said. "Zee, take a sheet out'n that tally book an' write all this down an' we'll go see what Mr. Bill Bent thinks about it all. Tomorrow we will rest up an' after that, we're gonna start a cattle drive down th' Purgatory!"

Well, you can rest assured we were glad to hear that an' soon all were fed and asleep save for me, Ben, and John. They kept me busy for an' hour writtin' things down t' talk t' Mr. Bent about.

Sunrise didn't find much stirrin' in camp b'cause we didn't sleep too much. Th' smell of blood brought wolves an' coyotes out an' they set up such a howl no one could sleep. Several of us rode out to th' point over th' lower pen t' see if everything was safe. With moonlight we could see several places where cows were holdin' off a pack an' one bunch already had a calf down an' fightin' over th' carcass. On th' count, we fired into th' mess an' five of those scoundrels fell with one runnin' off yelpin' an' screamin'.

There was some speculation as t' who was th' poor shot that only winged his target while we reloaded, but no one owned up to it. After that we took potshots at whatever we could see an' soon th' only noises were our guns. Wolves would slink away when we fired, but soon were back an' more of them would eat lead.

Every once in a while some grumpy sleepyhead would show up until we were all lined up along th' ridge except for th' nighthawk with th' horses. He came in all tuckered an' grumpy b'cause th' noise had kept horses stirred an' he had a time keeping them together an' not striking out for parts unknown.

Those varmints began creepin' off as th' sun rose an' we did th' same. A cup or two o' coffee an' I rolled up in my robe an' slept 'til noon—would have slept longer but th' sun was too hot. Tom Boggs came in with a deer draped over his horse an' we set to makin' it disappear. He had ridden out north when we quit th' ridge an' didn't see sign of game until he got north o' th' hogback. That's how scarce it was around the cattle range.

Sunshine dried up that blood smell some, and wolves were not so bad th' second night. We broke up into three watches with orders t' keep shootin' t' a minimum so's th' rest of us could sleep. I was on first watch an' we only shot a half-dozen times. When I rolled up in my robe an' went t' sleep, I didn't hear any shots until time t' git up.

Wagon an' cavyyard pulled out headed north and we opened th' gate just as th' sun started over th' horizon. We hadn't gone a hundred yards until we saw that it wouldn't do t' herd them through th' bottoms because of high water. It took a lot o' yellin' an' ridin' t' git 'em turned around but we got them back in their pen an' those boys that were still in there ran to open a gate in th' middle fence. Th' cows were stirred up now an' milled around bawlin' an' mad at us. We had a time getting them started through that gap, but once they started, they went—and right on through th' next gap at a good trot.

Men outside the pens kept them bunched. We moved them at a good trot for near an hour 'til they were good and winded, then we slowed them down to a walk an' let them spread t' cool off. A herd hot an' bunched like that puts off a lot of heat you can feel several feet away and if you aren't careful, they'll start droppin'. Fortunately, our weather was still cool an' we didn't lose any that time. Later we were not so fortunate.

I guess time in th' pens had made th' cattle mostly ferget their home range, for they stayed together except for a few stubborn ones, mostly cows about t' come fresh. They were huntin' a good place t' hide their calf. We always had a new calf or two every morning when we started. Usually, we put it in th' wagon for a day or two 'til they got their legs, mama following an' bawlin'.

A little after midafternoon we would let th' herd stop an' graze 'til near dark, then we drove them together for beddin' down. John Hatcher had considerable experience herdin' across th' Santa Fe Trail an' he taught us how t' ride herd around th' bed grounds. Now, I don't know how those cows changed their habits from night grazin' except that they were a little tired from travelin' an' full from their afternoon meal.

At least once a night th' herd would get up an' stand a minute, then lay back down. It was real scary first time they did this, we thought they were about t' do somethin' bad, but John was there an' kept *us* calm. This was th' first time I heard someone singin' to cows, but John must have sung most every hymn he knew. It had a calming effect an' covered any unusual noises we might make. By th' third night, all night riders were singin'.

Before we got to th' ranch, we had quite a drag o' mammas an' calves and by th' time they had been at th' ranch a week, there were a *bunch* o' new calves. It was good we didn't have t' drive them any further.

Those long-legged cows could travel an' we made those eighty miles on th' morning o' th' fifth day. Mr. Bent knew we were comin' in an' rode out at breakfast th' fifth morning. He seemed very pleased with our job an' asked a dozen questions about th' operation. We made a late start for talking t' him an' knowin' we only had a little ways t' go.

After we had talked a while, John Prowers said, "Bill, we learned a lot with this bunch, an' they's a lot more cows up there we can gather. I would guess there are at least a thousand more head up there . . ."

"We rounded up four hundred and eighteen cows in three days, Mr. Bent," Tom put in.

"And we got here with four hundred and twenty-seven, ten of them dropped on th' way and one killed by wolves," I said from consultin' my tally book.

"Three days' gather, you say?"

"Yessir," came a chorus.

"It took three days t' brand 'em, but we got better at it an' we'll be more efficient next time." Whoever spoke threw in that "next time" t' drop a hint that we wanted t' go back.

"Wee started out divideng thee cows ten at a time, Meester Beel," Juan put in, "but thee three and a haf an seex an' a haf deedn't wor-r-r-k so well, for thee haf calfs both died, so Meester John, he say wee divide thee cows twenty at a time an' thee haf cows go away—an' you know they deed yust that!" Open hands palm up, he shrugged his shoulders and seemed amazed at the mathematical magic.

Everyone laughed and Mr. Bent asked, "Well, Juan, what did you do with those calf halves?"

"Wee ate heem!" Juan said with a big grin.

"You ate *my* half too?" Mr. Bent feigned shock.

"Sí, Meester Beel, you wer-r-r-e not ther-r-e to take heem an thee meat, she would hev spoiled—an' you all-time tell us no eeat our own vaca." Juan shrugged and grinned.

When th' laughter died, Mr. Bent said, "Well I guess you did right by that. I'm glad you figgered out t' eliminate that half business early afore you lost too many cows."

That broke up our conference an' we went t' work lining out on th' trail while John Hatcher an' Mr. Bent sat to one side watching. Mr. Bent stayed with us until we scattered th' herd out in th' bottoms, then headed for th' stockade.

Ben Lott unsaddled an' lifted his nose high sniffing like a hound. "I kin smell it now, boys, that there's a hog roastin' on th' spit an' it's jist fer us!"

"Shore glad it ain't salt pork er beef er fries," John Prowers put in.

"Maybe they'll hev sides like rice er corn 'nstead o' beans."

"An' bread!"

"But señors, wee must hev thee *frijoles!*"

"Not none o' me today, Juan, I'm eatin' a little higher on th' hog than that!" Tom Boggs rubbed his belly.

Sure enough, when we went into th' stockade, th' fire pit had *two* hogs spitted up an' a Mexican boy was turning each of them while Cooky fussed about. We could tell there was a feast a-formin' an' hurried off t' clean up an' put on clean clothes. What a feast that was! About midafternoon th' hogs were roasted an' we ate slabs of steaks, ribs with sauce, and there was rice and corn with those mandatory frijoles. There were four kinds of bread that disappeared on th' order of biscuits, flour tortillas, cornbread, an' corn tortillas.

I ended up with a big slab of cornbread smothered in beans and bean juice. That pot o' beans had a whole ham in it an' there was nothing t' beat it. You can bet that feast put us out of commission an' we were not worth anything the rest o' th' day. By sunset we were all ready t' sleep it off, especially those who had washed it all down with an ale or two—or three.

After a breakfast of rice pudding and flour tortillas, John Hatcher gathered us and said, "Boys, Bill is mullin' over sendin' us back fer th' rest o' those cows, same deal as b'fore 'cept'n he's gonna send more help an' provisions. It'll mean a little less o' th' cut but we will catch more cows in lesser time, so things might even out."

"We gonna git more horses?"

"—An' a cook?" Tom was sure worryin' about his eats.

"Horses an' cook included. It works out that we can move them in batches o' four to five hundred at a time, about what he can turn with th' army and other buyers. We will probably have t' trail several bunches t' Fort Union. It's a longer run, but we'll be paid direct in silver an' Las Vegas ain't that fer off. We could spend a day er two there afore headin' back."

"Loma Parda ees much closer than Las Vegas, Señor," came from back o' th' crowd.

"Too many get lead poisonin' in Loma fer my taste," Hatcher replied, "I'll take Las Vegas any day. Their pizen ain't near so potent an' they look you in the eye when they shoot you."

I wasn't near so interested in *where* I got shot as I was in *not* getting shot. I determined then an' there not to trouble Loma Parda with my presence and not t' delve too deep in th' social amenities o' Las Vegas, but more about that when we get there.

We rested that day, but near sunset, Mr. Bent gathered us together an' laid out his plans. "You boys did good with this gather and with th' looks of things in th' east, we will need every cow we can get our hands on. I have decided to send you back to clean out as much of that country as you can. Gather and brand bunches of four hundred to six hundred at a time and head them down this way. If we need to send them to Fort Union, I'll send a crew to drive them and you can keep on gatherin'. The seventy-thirty deal . . ."

"Sixty-five–thirty-five," came a chorus.

Mr. Bent grinned and nodded, ". . . stands not only with you and the three others I am sending with you this time. You will have to include the cook and the five that are left here with the horse herd."

Well that suited us just fine, it was much better than sitting around th' ranch an' herdin' brood mares all day. Jake was fit to be tied that he wasn't included in th' gathering an' had a talk with Mr. Bent. He argued that with th' Injuns callin' a truce while we were catchin' cows, th' horses would be safe an' grazin' good for them, but Mr. Bent felt that it would look too much like ranchin' if a big herd of horses was up there an' b'sides, he needed them near the fort for tradin' during travelin' season so Jake was stymied from th' second gatherin' expedition. Still, he profited from it well with a lot less work an' trouble th' rest of us went through.

Next morning we went out to th' horse herd an' cut out our horses plus enough t' make a fourth mount for every rider except nighthawk an' cook. We were done about noon an' instead o' waitin' another day for wagons t' be ready, we struck a leisurely pace up th' river with our horses. Third day out, th' wagons caught up with us an' we all stayed together after that.

Back at th' pens, we got ready t' make another gather. A goodly number of cattle had wandered into th' area we had first cleared an' a sweep brought in near a hundred the first day. After that, we started over new territory, where stock was thicker. It took us four days t' gather six hundred head, then brandin' started. We began t' notice that a number of cattle

146

were getting away well b'fore we werc close enough t' stop them.

"Those wild ones air gonna be harder t' catch than ropin' jackass rabbits," Ben Lott observed.

"If they all get bunched up in one gather, we'll never hold 'em," I said.

"Yeah, let's talk it over t'night an' d'cide what we need t' do about them," Tom said, wiping sweat out of his hat band.

Discussions about what t' do with those really wild cows was long an' sometimes loud. It started off with John Hatcher suggestin' that we neck them to more tame cows.

"That might make th' *tame* cow wilder," I said.

"Maybe so, but it would also make th' *wild* cow tamer," Tom said.

"Theen wee would have two *haf-wilder* cows eenstead of one wild one an' one not so wild?" Juan asked.

Hatcher chuckled. "Sounds like that's what they air intendin', don't it?"

"We could hamstring 'em, but then they'd be no good fer travelin'," Tom mused.

"Jest who d'yuh think is gonna be dumb enough t' git close enough to one o' those critters t' cut him? I'll tell yuh who'd git cut an' it wouldn't be th' one with th' knife!"

"Not interested in gittin' skewered on one o' them horns, air ye, John?" Hatcher chuckled.

"Ther-re is one way to keep them out of thee br-r-rush when we catch theem," Hillside said. "Een thee br-r-rush countrree, wee catch thee cow an' prop her eyelids open. Theen she ve-r-ry careful where she steek her head."

It was quiet a moment while we considered that. "I think that might work, but we're shore handling them cows a lot, fer what they're worth, why don't we just shoot 'em or leave 'em be?" John Prowers asked.

"Seems t' me we see about one really wild cow for ever'

fifteen-twenty head o' reg'lar cows, that could add up t' quite a number by th' time we're through here," I said.

"Yuh don't see them out on th' flats much, they stays close to th' bottoms where they kin duck into th' bresh quick," Ben observed.

"Be a lot less trouble, just t' shoot 'em," Prowers persisted.

"I guess we could bring th' carcass in for th' cook . . ." Hatcher began, but th' cook, a grizzled old trail driver we called Stumpy who was too stove up t' drive any more, cut him off. "You ain't gonna bring no tough stringy beef in here fer me t' make food out'n, I'll shoot yer onery hide!"

He was a good cook who took pride in his work, something not found in every range cook I've come up agin. When we ran low on meat he would ride out to th' herd an' pick out th' one he wanted. We always made sure it wasn't a branded critter; it was always a yearlin' heifer an' we would drive her close to th' wagon before we shot her. He rigged th' tongue up so's he could hang th' carcass up by th' hamstrings on a singletree. Soon's she was hung, he shooed us off an' did his own butcherin'. Made th' best son-of-a-gun stew.

"I seen a way t' tame down a wild cow that might work here," Tom Boggs said. "Vaqueros in Californy would hobble 'em, front foot, t' back. After a few days, they would tame down so's they could be cut loose."

"Seems like any way we do it, we're gonna hafta use three or four riders t' handle one cow," John Prowers said. He was an impatient kind o' feller, always in a hurry t' git things done.

"Shore don't seem like a better way, do it?" Ben mused.

"What if we spent our time catchin' four or five o' them wild cows every day after our gather?" I asked. "We don't need all of us t' drive a herd in, maybe three could be spared t' catch wild cows."

"Hillside an' Juan is th' best ropers, if'n they could git th' cow down, eny one o' us could hobble 'em," Ben said.

"Eet weel take fr-resh horses."

"Yeah, so we would be ridin' three mounts a day 'nstead o' two," Tom Boggs said.

"Not if we began work right after noon when we have our second mount an' most o' that time we're drivin' back t' th' pens," I said.

"We could probably spare three riders after noon, even if we aren't through with our gather," Hatcher said. "Let's jist plan on that an' we'll see how it works out."

So it was set an' th' very next day Hillside, Juan, and Tom took after th' wild ones right after noon. They started out a ways from th' bunch after some that we had seen scamperin' for brush that morning.

First thing they tried was sendin' Tom into th' brush t' chouse out a critter so Juan an' Hillside could get their lariats on it, but th' one they went after was too wily t' leave th' bushes. This was something new for man and horse and it took two men t' get him out. Once he was in th' open, it was only a moment until he was spread out, a rope around horns and hind leg enough t' hold him while Tom hobbled him front and back hooves on th' same side. When that cow got up, snortin' fire an' seein' red, he charged after Tom, who was scrambling for his horse. He would have had him, too, on about his third leap, if'n th' hobbles hadn't stood him on his nose his first lunge. Puzzled, he jumped up only to go down again when his feet wouldn't do what his brain told them to do. Thoroughly puzzled by this turn of events, he got up slowly, forgetting about th' man, who had by now gained his seat and was safely out of reach.

That cow took a step or two an' found that (in this case) his right front leg would not take as long a step without a strong pull on his right hind leg, thus he was reduced to takin' little steps, which greatly hampered his mobility. He stood still, not knowing exactly what t' do. Cautiously, the men approached him an' hazed him further out on the flat away from the thick brush. This was not good, but every time he tried t' turn back or charge man and horse, he was brought up short by those infernal hobbles. Soon he was tired o' th' game an' turned his head toward a nearby wallow for a drink. Satisfied, th' boys headed back into th' brush for another wild one.

There have been many an argument about which was hardest or wildest, cow, steer, or bull, and my conclusion has been that any one of 'em can be just as bad as t'other in th' extreme. There are various stages of "wildness" depending on age, size, health, and other factors, but when you get a critter in his prime, about four to seven years old and *wild,* it don't matter what his gender or state of virility is, he's a handful. Bulls might be first t' wear down if you stay after him for several days, for he soon gets sore reproductive organs an' can't continue like a steer who doesn't have that baggage banging around.

If a cow has a calf hidden sommers, she may be th' fiercest unless you can find th' calf. Then with it in hand, she will calm down considerable—most o' th' time. But let one o' those gals lose a calf an' she has enough temper t' keep fifty acres cleared o' anything that moves bigger than a mouse. I've seen a mama cow standin' over th' carcass of her calf, fendin' off coyote an' wolf with a coyote impaled on her horn that she couldn't shake off. We had t' rope her an' tie her down t' get that coyote off. She had gored him so hard that her horn had got stuck b'tween ribs on both sides o' his body. When we left her, she was back guardin' her calf an' scavengers was keepin' their distance.

CHAPTER 16
WILD COWHANDS

I haven't mentioned anything about Indians lurkin' about, but they were there watching us work, sometimes sittin' out of range just lookin', but other times we would detect that some cow or two come bustin' out o' th' brush b'cause there was someone back there pushin' 'em. Once in a while we would glimpse a piece of horse or man in th' shadows as they retreated. I guess cows were a problem to them, for there was very little game about where they should have been plentiful.

On th' whole, the Indian much preferred buffalo meat to beef and only accepted beef after th' buffalo was gone. I would have t' agree with him; th' buffalo was better all around for meat *and* hide. Too, he didn't make such a mess where he lived. By that I mean that at least where grass was plentiful he didn't eat it to th' ground like a cow. An eight-, ten-year-old buff still had his teeth where th' beef would have his teeth worn to th' gums from eatin' sand and grit with his graze. A buffalo didn't fowl streams like a cow does and it was sure his thinner pelt didn't last like a buffalo robe. Yuh never saw a body wearin' cowhide like we wore buffalo hide.

It was interesting to us that our horses were safe so long as we were roundin' up cattle. After that was over they became fair game again.

Back at th' wild cow hunt, th' boys started back into th' brush for a second wild one an' it turned out t' be partner to th' first one, a branded steer just as stubborn. Gittin' him out in

151

th' open was hard, but down an' hobbled easy. After he had got used t' his new handicap, he hobbled off t' commiserate with his buddy.

A strange thing then happened. As the boys were riding along the edge of the brush, they were startled by th' noisy emergence of a cow of th' variety they were huntin'. A short chase brought her down and two Indians watched at a distance as th' hobble was applied. As soon as the boys were remounted, those Indians turned back into th' brush and soon out came another wild one to be caught and hobbled.

Instead of mounting up as before, Tom had Juan hold th' cow down while he walked toward the two Indians, signing friendship. The Indians held their place an' he got close enough t' speak. It turned out that they were two Utes, about fifteen to seventeen years old. They had been sent to watch us as we worked. The tribe had been concerned about cattle that were escaping, knowing how fast they would repopulate. When they saw the three mopping up strays, and th' trouble they had, the two Indians decided t' help by chasing critters from th' brush.

They said that they knew of two more hiding nearby and they would run one of them out by a certain tall tree a little ahead of our direction of travel. With that they disappeared and Tom remounted and told th' other two what had been said. No sooner had they got to th' designated spot than a slick cow with calf burst out of the bushes. In a moment she was down and hobbled, the Indians sitting nearer watching.

Now our Mexican boys were some nervous, their people having learned th' violent nature of this particular tribe an' their animosity toward those of Spanish descent. Tom was cautious too, but friendly and spoke to them as he worked. They showed interest in what we were doing and said they had been forbidden from interfering with our work in any way, so long as we minded th' agreement b'tween us an' their tribe.

When Tom remounted and turned around, the boys had disappeared. In a few minutes popping bushes told them another
target was on its way out to them. This time the two rode up
close to watch what was being done, staying opposite two ropers who eyed them suspiciously. When he finished, Tom turned
around an' sat on th' bull's shoulder, grinning at the Indians
who chuckled at his antic. Though he knew some Ute, Tom
"spoke" to them by sign because he was more fluent in that
language. "Do you like my seat?"

"Good seat for you, not for me," signed one of the boys.

"Are there many more cattle in the brush between here and
the pens?"

"Yes, many."

"How many, ten or twelve?"

Both boys shook their heads emphatically, "No, twenty—
thirty!"

The look of surprise on Tom's face told them enough without
any signing.

"They must not all be wild."

"Most are."

Tom relayed this to his two ropers who expressed as much
surprise as he did. "That's way too many t' catch quickly," Tom
said.

"Wee no hav rope for that meeny," Juan said, "but thee
r-rawhide, she be plenty."

"If we worked all day instead of just halves, we *might* git them
all." Tom was looking at the Utes an' thinking.

"Hillside, what do you think of putting these boys t' work for
us?"

The two Mexicans rolled their eyes, showin' their doubts.

"What if'n we made 'em promise not t' eat any o' our livers?" Not that any of us ever heard o' Utes eatin' livers of their
victims.

Hillside spoke up in Spanish, "My father's mother was a Ute bought from thee Navajos many years ago. When I was a boy, she taught me thee language. I haven't used it for many years, but I think I could weeth a little practice." Turning to th' Indians, he spoke haltingly in their language. They listened carefully, making a comment or questioning from time to time. At last, Hillside said, "Señor Tom, I theenk wee could wor-r-rk a deal weeth thees boys, but they will have to help us without thee tribe finding out."

They had let th' ropes go slack and th' bull gave a mighty heave an' almost got up b'fore they could pull him back. Tom jumped up, loosed the lariats, and ran for his horse while everyone retreated a safe distance. Toro rose, snorted an' pawed, spun, an' fell over th' hobbles. Getting up, he tried t' trot an' found that he couldn't, then limped off a few yards and stood there glaring at the world.

The five rode for shade, each group still wary of th' other. "It's gittin' late, Hillside, why don't you an' Juan mosey those hobbled critters toward th' pens while I auger with these two an' see if we can work out a deal?"

"No, sir, Meester Tom, I won't leeve you alone weeth thees two!" Juan interrupted, "Wee do not know theem and they might take thee hair you wear under that hat!"

Tom laughed an' lifted his sombrero, revealin' his receding hair line. "Not much of a prize here, Juan!"

The two Indians smiled uncertainly.

"I can geet thee cattle started by myself," Hillside said, "and Juan can stay her-re weeth you." He turned and loped off after th' first two steers grazing back by th' waller tank.

Tom rolled a long shuck cigarette an' lit it with a sulfur match while the Utes watched closely. After a couple of puffs, he offered it to them an' they both solemnly took puffs. I won't go into details o' their negotiations, but end result was that the two boys would help round up wild cows for two pair of chaps and two shirts in advance (clothes needed for protection in th' brush, th' boys dressed only in moccasins and breechclouts) and a horse apiece when the job in th' upper end o' th' arroyo was finished.

Now, Tom had made these negotiations without any knowledge o' th' rest of us and it was his intention t' keep th' deal hisself if'n we didn't pitch in an' help. 'Course, he didn't have any idea how he would keep his word beyond shirts an' chaps, but he had time t' work that out later. Th' deal was sealed with more solemn puffs an' they parted company, agreein t' meet at th' same place at noon th' next day.

When th' deal was explained to Juan, he was appalled, "How are you going to get all those things, Señor Tom?" He was so excited he reverted to Spanish.

"They's allus a pair or two o' chaps layin' around camp an' ever'one has spare shirts. I'll give 'em one o' mine an' buy or borry one from someone."

This was one of those occasions where th' Mexican mind was overwhelmed with th' antics o' his Anglo companion and called only for a rolling of eyes an' a shrug, which Juan duly offered.

No one thought anything about it next morning when Tom an' Juan rode out with chaps on an' the extra bulk of Tom's blanket tied behind his saddle wasn't even discernible. In th' excitement caused when they drove in thirteen hobbled cattle, not countin' calves-by-side, nobody took note that the three wore no chaps. It was a matter of much comment by th' end of their fourth day of wild cow gatherin' that the three vaqueros had brought in thirty-five head with ten calves tagging along where it was thought that only a dozen head could have been found.

After supper they were subject to right smart of questioning for it was a gen'ral conclusion that three men acting alone could not possibly have caught all those cows in four afternoons. Hillside an' Juan became scarce an' Tom steered conversation away from th' matter by askin', "If we got that many in th' arroyo, how many more air they in other draws scattered about? Seems t' me we've been skimming cream off'n th' top an' not gittin' much milk at all. If this keeps up, won't be long until th' Injuns dope it out an' our horses'll start disappearin' agin."

"Aww, they won't bother with a few head left here or there," Ben Lott said.

"Ben, we jist gathered forty-five bulls, cows, an' calves out'n that one draw while we was gatherin' near five hundred head on th' flats. That's near ten percent o' th' entire catch an' how long d'yuh think it'd take them forty-five head t' multiply?" I asked.

"Zee's right there, we better make a clean sweep if'n we want t' keep our horses—and our hair," John Prowers said.

"I seen two o' them sittin' on th' ridge watchin' us t'day," the other John said.

"We see two almost ever' afternoon when we're poppin' bresh," Tom said in all sincerity. That he kept a straight face was a matter of admiration when all th' truth came out later.

"Well it looks like we're gonna haf'ta . . . be more diligent in our sweeps an' pay more attention . . . to th' wild ones as we go," John Hatcher said between puffs on his pipe.

"I shore hate poppin' bresh," someone said, to which most of us agreed.

"Tain't so bad," Tom said, "but it's shore hard on horses an' clothes."

One of th' Texians spoke up, "Those Mexes down on th' border have horses that love brush. Men do too, but they's hardly a one of 'em's got both eyes er all o' their fingers. They got so many splinters in 'em their blood runs like sap."

There followed a general discussion of th' science o' cow gatherin' that tapered off as one or t'other drifted off t' sleep.

Th' next day started our second brandin' an it went much smoother with our experience and two more helping. I'll say here that brandin' in chutes is much better than brandin' on open range—a lot less work on everyone an' less hazard o' *any* critter gittin' hurt. It wasn't until th' fourth morning when we were roundin' up for th' drive, that we discovered that two horses were missin' from th' cavyyard. Boy, did those two herders catch it. It was then an' there that John Hatcher ruled that horses had t' be counted ever'time they were gathered. Ever' man was t' account for his bunch afore they were let out on th' range at night an' when they came in mornin's. Luckily, bein' on th' drive, those two horses were not needed as badly as when we were gatherin'.

CHAPTER 17
THE BLIZZARD OF '61

The trip down th' valley was purty uneventful until th' last day an' that day, th' fifth day of April, 1861, will ever be branded on my mind. We woke up to a warm south breeze that carried a fine mist with it, makin' us think that spring had finally won out over winter. Seemed like th' cattle were extra restless an' we had a time gettin' them on th' trail. They wanted t' mill an' it didn't seem too unusual t' us that they wanted t' head south. By th' time they were lined out goin' north they had man an' horse in a lather. Th' only way we could keep them goin' was on a trot.

I had just chased a steer back into th' herd when Tom rode by an' hollered, "Gittin' colder, Zee!"

I hadn't noticed until then, but it *was* colder. Th' wind had died an' th' drizzle had stopped. Lookin' north, I could see a black line down aginst th' horizon, away off. It seemed the more we tried, th' more stubborn those cows become. No one was leadin' th' herd, it took all of us just t' drive those cows, an' *drive* was th' word.

Someone yelled an I looked up t' see th' cavyyard bearin' down on us as determined as th' cows t' head south. We headed them off, but it took two of us and both horse wranglers t' keep 'em together. They sure were spooked, th' whites o' their eyes showin' like I had never seen in a herd b'fore. John Hatcher galloped by from th' back, th' rim o' his sombrero laid back agin his crown. I heard him yellin' up ahead, but didn't pay attention, th' horses were givin' such trouble.

Suddenly th' cow line turned sharply t' th' left in front of us, cutting off th' cavyyard an' we had to stop or mix horses with th' herd. There was nothing we could do but mill until th' cows had passed. They were hazing th' cows into Rock Arroyo. When th' drag was into th' mouth o' th' draw, they fired their guns t' scare 'em on.

Something wet and cold stuck on my eyelash. It was snowin' big ol' flakes. John fired his gun in th' air an' signaled us t' gather. We couldn't do that and keep th' horses, so we just headed 'em north. When we got up beside th' group, they started ropin' out another mount for themselves.

Ben rode up an' yelled over th' wind, "Storm's comin', Zee, git a fresh mount, we're gonna make a run fer it, cows'r on their own!"

I looked up north an' that black line was higher on th' horizon. When I unlimbered my rope, it flaked ice off. I had a time makin' a loop. I remember my fingers bein' so numb I couldn't feel th' rope in my hand. It scared me that it could get that cold so quick. I didn't even try t' find my mounts, just grabbed one near. Juan was tryin t' change horses nearby an' he couldn't get his saddle on th' new mount. I rode over an' held th' horse while he saddled up, then he helped me change. Our old mounts were frantic an' ran off as soon as th' bit was out o' their mouths, frozen sweat on their sides shinin' in that gray-green light. That black cloud lit up with lightning inside it. Just one time.

Juan was shivering so much he couldn't hardly talk. "C-c-come on, Z-Z-Zee!" he called as he rode off.

We drove those horses hard right into th' teeth o' th' storm, it gittin' colder by th' minute. Big fluffy snowflakes were all gone, replaced by a fine hard snow that stung when it hit. None o' us were dressed warm, just wearin' slickers t' shed th' mist we had started out in. I pulled my bandanna up over my face an' tied my hat down with a leather thong from my saddle, th' brim on each side coming down over my ears an' shieldin' them some. I was looking out of a tunnel made by that hat an' had to keep turning my head t' see what was goin' on around me.

That was th' blackest cloud I had ever seen an' it just kept climbin' higher an' higher in th' sky 'til it towered over us, seemin' like it would come crashin' down an' bury us. Sometimes we could see lightning flashing, but it never thundered. It was eerie. Th' wind was blowin' so hard that snow didn't lay, it just blew horizontal. Of a sudden we came up on th' rim o' Tarbox Canyon an' there lay our wagon on its side, th' mules tied t' one o' th' wheels. John Prowers an' th' cook were in th' lee o' th' wagon tossin' out our bedrolls as we rode up. I jumped down an' tied my horse to a wheel. Openin' my roll, I put on everything I owned, pullin' three pairs o' socks over my hands after I had put my slicker back on. My buffalo robe I stretched over horse an' saddle. I had a feed bag an' after I had brushed all th' ice off his face I could, I put it over th' horse's nose an' tied it on.

Just as I was mountin' up, John Hatcher rode up leading five horses tied head to tail. "Here, Zenas, take these horses an' head for th' stockade with them. You break trail for a while an' we'll all follow. When your horses tire, someone else will lead."

I wrapped my blankets around me with th' opening behind, turned my horse into th' wind, an' passed th' mouth o' Tarbox down by th' river. Already, th' little stream out of Tarbox was froze solid an' I never knew when we passed over it. It wasn't hard t' keep th' right direction, all we had t' do was head into that blessed wind. I could see why critters wanted t' drift th' other way, I did too, but t' do so meant t' die.

Snow blowin' along th' ground was buildin' up an' beginnin' t' drift. Looking down, it looked like we were wadin' through boilin' smoke, that snow was so fine an' loose. It rolled along an' piled up in gullies so that they all but disappeared. So long as we stayed near th' Purgatory, they weren't so hard t' cross. We had t' cross th' river some place an' I worried about it.

"Hopefully, Lord, you'll have th' water froze enough that we won't have t' wade," I prayed. I talked t' Him quite a bit on that trip.

My horse b'gan t' tire an' someone, I couldn't tell who, passed me by an' began t' lead. We were glad t' fall in line where travel was somewhat easier. Sometimes I couldn't see my horse's ears th' snow was so thick, but ever' once in a while I could glimpse th' rump o' th' horse two feet ahead of his nose an' knew we were ok. Periodically, I wiped ice off my horse's eyes. It didn't work too well t' warm his ears with my hands, for my socks were soon crusted with ice an' I couldn't help him.

This is where my faith in a horse's instincts matured. By some unknown sense, they knew where they were an' where we wanted t' go. They already knew th' stockade as their home, and that is where they wanted t' be too, so long as we had th' reins an' directed them. Otherwise, they would have drifted with th' wind or holed up under the brush somewhere. Either way they would have died.

I have never been so cold in my life. I tried walkin' some, but I b'came terrified o' losin' my horse, which would have been th' end, so I stayed in th' saddle. I couldn't feel my legs b'low my knees. Ever' once in a while, I kicked out o' th' stirrups an' swung my legs.

It was some twelve miles t' th' stockade from Tarbox Arroyo but for us it seemed like a hundred. I grew more numb an' sleepy. Suddenly my face hit my horse's neck an' th' saddle horn poked my stomach. I had fallen asleep an' it scared me.

"I can't do that agin, ol' horse, so I'm gonna have t' sing t' keep awake, sorry." With that, I began t' sing as loud as I could through that ice-crusted bandanna. Gradually, my singin'd get softer an' softer until I started awake, realizin' th' sound had stopped and I would b'gin again. I had just started singin' for it seemed th' hundredth time when my horse stopped. Arousing myself, I saw that th' horses ahead of me had stopped an' my horse had stepped aside t' avoid running into them. I pushed forward until I came even with th' rider. He was so wrapped up I still didn't know who he was.

"What's th' matter?" I called.

"We're at th' upper ford," came a muffled voice I still couldn't identify.

"How do you know it's th' *upper* ford?" I yelled in his ear.

"That you, Zee? It's th' upper ford, 'cause my foot is draggin' that big boulder on this side of it, an' 'cause I says so!"

My foggy mind still couldn't place th' voice comin' out o' that mound of icy clothes, but I took his word an' got down, leadin' my horse forward. We dropped down a steep slope that somehow felt familiar an' I b'gan t' feel my way forward, reaching out with my foot for water or ice. I couldn't feel anything with my feet so I got down on my hands and knees an' inched forward, with reins wrapped firmly around my arm. I felt th' ground suddenly level off an' even through my mittens I could tell I had reached ice. Now th' question was, how thick was it? Returnin' to my unknown friend, I found that someone else had ridden up b'side him an' they were waitin' on me t' come back.

"Edge of th' river is frozen, but I don't know what it's like out in th' middle," I shouted. "I'll start across and you wait here. We had better go one at a time. If I get across on top o' th' ice, I'll fire my gun once . . ."

"Better save yer powder, Zee, let's string our ropes across an' use them as a guide. We'll tie them to trees an' when one gets clear, you can jerk th' rope four times an' th' next one can cross."

It sounded like John Prowers, but I wasn't sure. "Ok," I shouted.

We tied our three ropes together an' I took one end and started walkin' across th' river. My horse felt ice under his feet and stopped for a minute. I encouraged him with my voice, not daring t' do more an' he slowly took a few steps. Th' horses tied to us followed an' I prayed that ice was thick enough to hold us all, though I didn't know how water could freeze that solid that fast. Slowly, we went on and th' ice held. I listened for it t' crack, but I doubt that I could have heard it above th' roar o' that wind. It pushed against us like a big hand, makin' man and beast walk with feet spread t' keep from blowin' over.

Suddenly I stumped my toe on something stickin' above th' ice. I was near shoreline and b'gan t' feel my way along with my feet. Another step or two an' I kicked aginst th' bank. Steppin' closer, I lifted my foot t' step up on th' bank an' only kicked it. When I reached out my hand, I felt th' bank rim shoulder high. Wind had blown us upstream an' I had t' walk along that bank a good thirty paces t' get back to th' ford.

We were all glad t' feel land agin an' I had a time keepin' horses from plowin' on to th' stockade before I found a tree t' tie th' rope to. I had barely gotten it tied when a shadow loomed out o' th' white gloom. Someone had started in after me b'fore I had gotten across! He passed by without sayin' a word and I followed after, givin' th' rope four hard tugs an' feelin answerin' tugs.

We were now quarterin' across th' wind anglin' for th' stockade somewhere to th' northeast, a mile away. I was concerned that by following those horses ahead we would miss th' walls, but my horse seemed confident an' picked up his pace. In a minute or two, or maybe it was an hour, I couldn't tell, I saw shadows on my right an' realized we were passing th' leader. Soon my horses were trottin' as best they could in two feet of snow.

Their halt was sudden an' looking up, I saw we had brought up agin th' stockade wall. Wind whirlin' around th' lee had scoured snow to th' ground for three or four feet from th' wall an' there was a big drift beyond that. We had hit near th' southeast corner an' we started toward th' main gate in th' middle o' that south wall, b'hind that other string of horses who had busted through th' drift ahead of us.

Of course, that gate was closed tight an' barred an' no amount of yellin' was gonna raise anyone inside, as if I could make any such noise. I fumbled in my bag for my pistol an' prayed it was not too wet t' fire. It clicked. There was nothing t' do but remove my mittens an' fumble for a dry cap with fingers so numb I couldn't feel. Finally, I got another cap out only t' drop it. More fumbling got another one out somehow. I knew I couldn't last long enough t' get another cap out. Pulling th' hammer back, I pointed to th' sky an' pulled th' trigger. It fired with such a boom man an' beast jumped.

It seemed like hours before we heard shouts an' stirring at th' gate. We heard th' thump of hammers an' logs bangin' ice off th' bar so it could be lifted. Th' gate gave with a shower of ice and snow and slowly creaked open a few feet. It was hardly open enough for my horse t' git his head through before he was pushin' his way in with his shoulders, th' rest o' my string following an' th' rider an' his string hard right b'hind, leavin' me standin' outside until they had passed. A noise behind me told me another string was comin' an' I ducked in agint th' rump o' th' last horse b'fore I could get pushed out o' th' way by another string o' horses.

I fell to my knees an' someone grabbed my arm an' pulled me out o' th' near stampede for th' stables. I got a glimpse of horses as they disappeared, th' mystery rider still on his horse. Then everything went black.

I could've been out a week an' not known it. Next thing I remember was hearin' th' boom of a gun far, far away. It seemed I was in a long black tunnel strugglin' toward a pinpoint of light. I had my eyes open—I thought—but it was black all around. My whole body ached and pain in my limbs was almost unbearable. It got black again, then someone 'way off was yellin', "Wake up, Zenas, wake up, wake up!" I turned away from that noise an' a streak of pain shot through my head. "Don't rub yer ear, it's liable t' fall off," th' voice called. It seemed nearer. I opened my eyes, but all I could see was shadows flickerin' on adobe walls an' fine crystals o' ice twinklin' in th' air.

"Looky here, Zenas, air ye back?" someone behind me asked. I turned my head an' through a haze o' pain an' ice crystals, I saw a figure in th' light of a fire. "How're yuh feelin', boy, here have a drink."

Somethin' very hot passed my lips an' I near chocked b'fore I swallowed. It felt warm all th' way down. I took three or four more swallows an' fell back into that black tunnel . . . Someone was groanin' an' wakin' me up. I tried t' open my eyes, but couldn't. Whoever that was groanin' was shure gittin' on my nerves an' I got mad. Suddenly I realized it was me makin' noise an' I woke with a start.

"There ye air agin, boy, want another drink?" Something hot passed my lips an' it tasted good. I savored th' warmth flowin' down to my stomach where it settled. "Nothin' like a good hot broth t' warm a body," the voice said.

The wind howled an' I started up. "Where am I?"

"Yore safe as ennybody kin be in this storm." I could see it was one of th' hunters talkin' to me out of a buffalo robe wrapped tight around him. I was layin' next to a fireplace, but it was cold, our breath makin' fog in th' air. Ice crystals an' fine snow filled th' air an' settled on th' floor. There must have been three feet of it piled agin th' corners an' the floor was covered some places inches deep. Someone kept sweeping it away to th' far wall where it kept seepin' in around door an' window. I realized I was in th' livin' quarters built agin outside walls of th' stockade. There were a half-dozen other bodies rolled into robes, some still, some sitting up, noses, cheeks, and ears in various shades of color from red to black.

"Where are th' rest?" I asked.

"They're in other rooms," th' old man said, "them that made it."

"You mean there's some still out there?" I started up, but my legs wouldn't do what I wanted them to.

"We think ever'one but a couple made it in, but we're still firin' signals in case they air near. First one in th' gate was dead on his horse."

I stared stupidly, "Dead?"

"Yup, froze to his saddle. We had t' cut th' saddle off th' horse an' we set man, saddle, an' all agin th' wall. Them horses brought 'im home sure."

"They led th' rest o' us from th' upper ford," I said, "who was it?"

"Hillside."

He could have hit me an' it wouldn't have felt any worse. "Hillside? Dead?"

"He was froze solid with th' reins in his hand."

I could have cried. Later on when I was stronger, I did cry when we buried him b'side th' wall, an' I wasn't th' only one an' I wasn't ashamed, either. Maybe it was proper that th' best rider in our bunch would die in th' saddle. It was proper that he would be brought home by horses he loved. And it was proper that they led us. Sometimes I think I can see him 'way off across th' flats ridin' tall an' straight in th' saddle, one stirrup shorter than th' other.

One other rider didn't make it. After th' storm passed an' all through th' next summer an' fall we looked for him an' never found him. In '74 or '75 when th' Goodnight outfit trailed a herd from Pueblo into th' Palo Duro, they found a bunch of bones and bits of rope where scavengers had scattered them just north of where Toonerville is now.

There was an' old saddle half buried in th' sand where one o' th' horses had fallen an' when they dug it out there was a boot still in the bottom stirrup with a leg bone stickin' out. That was all they found. If it was our friend, he had drifted across th' Purgatory an' near twenty miles from where he was last seen. Most likely he was dead or near dead most of th' way an' his horses drifted until they fell.

That storm lasted less than forty-eight hours. It left twenty inches of snow and drifts three to fifteen feet high. On th' flats, they were like waves on th' ocean. Draws runnin' east and west were full of snow so that th' ground looked level and you didn't know where they were. It wiped out almost all animal life. Ridin' along, you would see a jackrabbit sittin' by a clump o' grass or under a bush an' when he didn't move, you knew he was frozen. Wolves, coyotes, antelope, deer, and buffalo carcasses were scattered ever'where. We lost all th' herd we had gathered except for a very few. Some that we found still living had to be shot b'cause their feet had frozen an' they couldn't walk. They had drifted with th' storm an' we found them scattered clear to th' Purgatory, some still standing, frozen solid, others were piled up in th' bottoms of draws an' covered with snow.

Mr. Bent had a thermometer an' th' boys there swore it went from 64 degrees in th' morning down to 30 below in three hours. Those of us out in th' weather didn't argue with that.

When I woke up in th' fort, it was 36 below, for I saw that with my own eyes. Even with fires goin', it must have been near zero or below in th' buildin's. There were a lot of frozen ears, noses, toes, and fingers, a couple o' th' boys losin' toes. I lost th' end of two fingers on each hand back to th' quick, but by fall they had mostly grown back. We all looked like a bunch of lizards sheddin' their skin for a while, but mostly we came through pretty good. The only long-term effects for some of us is that we can't resist really cold weather anymore. If I have t' be out in freezing weather now, I suffer for it. I know I'm in trouble when my skin starts turnin' blue. That's one o' th' reasons I have sought milder climates in th' basin.

Our horses survived fairly well, though several shed their ears and a couple were lame for a while. About half th' herd was lost because we couldn't tie all of them to lead and those that made th' stockade had t' crowd into already full stalls or mill around in th' open. Th' men kept them busy, rotatin' them through stalls where they could warm some, still four died inside th' stockade.

That storm wiped out all of th' cattle and horses on th' range east of th' mountains an' Bent–St. Vrain would have been wiped out completely if they hadn't had th' bulk of their stock west of th' mountains where th' storm wasn't near so strong. As you might guess that put an end to our cattle enterprise. That storm eliminated cattle on th' old upper Purgatory range. This made th' Indians happy, though there were not any other critters there either for a few years.

Speakin' of Indians, they seemed to weather th' storm fairly well, only a few older folks died. Their suffering came later when there was no game to be had and they had to move far out on th' plains before they found any.

On th' third day a Chinook blew down off th' mountains an' th' snow melted. The ground underneath had not frozen much an' what little moisture was in th' snow mostly soaked in. With that extra moisture, th' prairies fairly busted with green an' flowers. It was a good summer for grazin'—if there had been anything left t' eat on it.

We have what we call th' spring blizzard 'most every year but those bad storms only happen every thirty or forty years. Th' next one I recall was th' winter of '85–86. That one started in November an' went plum through 'til spring. Folks said you could walk on carcasses from Cheyenne to Dodge and never touch ground. Down on th' Rio Grande above Brownsville they found cows with brands from Wyoming and Montana. That's a long way t' drift, ain't it?

I recalled the horrible blizzard of 1931. Many a farmer lost all he had and most of them left the high plains for better climates. You probably remember the five children and their bus driver that perished in the storm out on the plains east of Denver. (Ed.)

CHAPTER 18
WAR

1861–1865

Maybe that storm was an omen of things t' come, for it was that same April that th' Civil War started. It sure stirred things up here in th' West. There was a great shaking in th' military, most soldiers being transferred back east, a goodly number headed for south of th' Mason-Dixon. Jake an' me were in a quandary about what t' do. We were southerners at heart, but dead set agin th' institution of slavery because o' those experiences our family had. We couldn't support a Southern cause and if we fought with th' North, we would be fightin' agin some of our kin and friends.

Mr. Bent settled that question for us by insistin' we stay with him an' move freight for th' Union. Since that seemed our best way t' avoid slingin' lead at our friends, we agreed along with Ben Lott and John Prowers. Tom Boggs went t' work for Lucien Maxwell and did good. Some time later he drove a herd of Maxwell cattle to th' Purgatory an' set up ranchin'. John Prowers married the Cheyenne warrior One-Eye's daughter an' ranched along th' Arkansas east o' th' Purgatory startin' out with a hundred head of cattle.

We spent that whole war runnin' supplies for th' Union military—not that it was th' safest thing t' do, with Indians growin' more belligerent because of an absence of soldiers an' both sides takin' shots at us across Bloody Kansas. Missouri weren't no cakewalk. It had been saved for th' Union by a hair's breadth an' was actually a battleground for such bushwhackers as Quantrill and Anderson. History books tell you that th' war ended in April, 1865, but anyone in th' South and West will tell you that it went on long after that. Some'll auger it's still goin' on in places . . .

We hauled a lot of freight across th' prairies in those years, but towards th' end it got awful hard. We had t' fight Injuns goin' an' comin'. It all come to a head in th' summer of '64. We were headed for Westport when we were met by a company of troops headed for Fort Larned led by a Lieutenant Eayre. He boasted about whipping a village of Cheyennes on Ash Creek in Kansas. When Mr. Bent asked him why, he said he had been ordered t' kill Cheyennes wherever found.

Mr. Bent was furious. "How could eighty soldiers defeat a camp I know has at least five hundred warriors? That man was lying!"

He sure 'nough was right, for that very next day we met a messenger from th' tribe who told us what really happened. Those soldiers had murdered Lean Bear when he went out alone and unarmed to talk peace, then the Indians had attacked and were driving those soldiers back when Black Kettle rode out and stopped them.

Mr. Bent gave us instructions t' proceed on to Missouri an' he rode back t' see what he could do. We hurried on, loaded, and turned around in record time. This was where Ben Lott left us an' we never saw nor heard of him since. That trip back was th' most hazardous we made th' whole war an' was th' last one made for a long time. We couldn't hardly get any sleep for watchin' for trouble. Indians followed us all th' way, spending nights harassin' us an' our stock an' stayin' just out o' range during th' day. Our mules got awful ganted b'fore we got back t' Fort Lyon since they couldn't get enough grazing. It became

171

a race between Indians and starvation, which would get us first. It shows just how bad things had gotten when Cheyennes attacked and harassed William Bent's wagons.

Indian depredations became general now an' all commerce across th' prairies came to a standstill. We all retreated to th' Purgatory stockade and when th' Kiowa chief Satanta would have attacked on August 7, we were strong enough that he didn't want any of us.

Denver was isolated and began to suffer from lack of food. Ranches were burned an' between two and three hundred whites were killed, man, woman, and child. Th' whole country was depopulated, the whites huddled in blockhouses in th' settlements. No one was safe. We took an' army o' armed men t' cut hay for what stock that was left, it bein' too dangerous t' take them out to graze. Mr. Bent was determined t' keep his Purgatory ranches, and with his family, John Prowers, and Tom Boggs helping, we managed.

The Rio Grande valley was much quieter than th' plains and th' trail from th' Arkansas River to Santa Fe was busy for a while with people and herds of stock retreating to that area. We held on at th' stockade and watched from a distance the events that embroiled th' plains. It seemed that William Bent aged twenty years in that year.

Kit Carson under General Carleton had herded th' Mescalero Apaches onto a reservation an' settled th' Navajos at Bosque Redondo, and the Pueblos were quiet. General Carleton sent Colonel Carson to th' Cimarron to punish Comanches an' that's when they fought th' First Battle of Adobe Walls. I guess it was a close thing. Kit done some damage an' held th' Injuns off even though he was outnumbered ten to one. Some say he lost th' battle, but he avoided certain calamity by retreating. I say a draw is better than certain defeat.

It came to light that a portion of the Cheyenne tribe professed peace, receiving the treaty commodities and trading for supplies, especially guns and ammunition. This they passed on to the hostiles, thereby keeping them supplied. This sort of treachery went on for some time and the whites considered one party as guilty of depredations as the other.

Maybe it explains why Black Kettle allowed Dog Soldiers t' stay with him—an' maybe he didn't have any choice, those Dog Soldiers doin' pretty much what they wanted. The Southern Cheyennes had been on th' war path all summer and had not gathered provisions for winter, so in obedience to the Colorado governor's orders they came to Fort Lyon for safety and provisions. Major Wynkoop sent them t' camp on Sand Creek. Northern Cheyennes stayed hostile along th' Platte.

Mr. Bent's son George was with us and when he heard his sister Julia and her brother Charles were with Black Kettle, he went to visit them. Three days later a company of soldiers surrounded our stockade an' said no one could leave. We watched an army march by across th' Arkansas. No one had any doubt it was that rascal Chivington in th' lead spoiling for a fight. A couple o' old-timers said that Jim Beckworth was ridin' b'side him. It didn't look good . . .

We learned later that when th' army got t' Fort Lyon, old Jim had t' be lifted from his horse. He couldn't go on and Chivington forced Robert Bent t' lead them to th' camp with th' promise he would kill him if he didn't.

Four days after th' battle at Adobe Walls, they struck Black Kettle's village at dawn in spite of an American flag flyin' over a white one. One-Eye, White Antelope, Left Hand, and Yellow Wolf were killed, along with one hundred ten women and children and only fifty-three warriors. Jack Smith, son of John Smith and Blackfoot's grandson, was captured and executed after being forced to confess to outrages on th' prairie, and Charles Bent barely escaped th' same fate when Charlie Autobeas' boys saved him. There were four Bent children at Sand Creek, Charles, George, Julie with her husband Ed Guerrier, and Robert. George was shot in th' hip but made his escape. He later returned to th' stockade to heal.

It was a massacre plain and simple an' that old saying "two wrongs don't make a right" kept runnin' through my head. If Kit had been at Fort Lyon, it would not have happened.

Even the supposed discovery of a blanket in th' village fringed with blond scalps didn't justify what the whites did. There were savages on both sides and with blood from both races in my veins, I maybe saw that clearer than most. Th' result was that the Sioux joined Cheyenne, Kiowa, and Arapahos and their war along th' Platte.

As the truth of th' massacre leaked out, Chivington fell from his lofty perch and eventually had to leave. Congress investigated, but nothing much more than words thrown back and forth came of it. Mr. Bent and now General Carson were made commissioners to th' Indians, but they were frustrated in their efforts.

Mr. Bent had children on both sides, George and Charles with th' tribe, Charlie so vicious that there was a price on his head and Mr. Bent disowned him. Robert and Mary were at the stockade, as were Julie and Ed Guerrier from time to time. They say that Mary would put a candle in th' window as a signal to Charlie that the way was clear for him to visit. On his last visit to th' ranch, he was looking for Mr. William t' kill him. Mary went out to th' irrigation ditch t' talk to him, but he went away without coming in. He died in 1868 after being wounded in a fight with Pawnees and then catching malaria.

The Cheyenne were gone, th' remnant of our southern tribe joinin' their northern kin making war. This had the effect of removing protection our area had enjoyed from Indian depredations and opened us for "visits" from Utes, Apaches, Comanches, and Kiowas—and "visit" they did. It was hard times.

CHAPTER 19
STUTTERIN' STAN & COON DOGS

I could tell that Zenas was in a good mood before I got out of the car and I was glad. Maybe we wouldn't talk about hard times today . . .

"Come on up an' have a seat, young man, I was just sittin' here wonderin' what tale t' tell you today when I got t' studyin' stutterin'. You remember th' old story about th' sea captain an' his stutterin' mate?"

He ignored my affirmative nod and proceeded. "Well, th' captain was sittin' in his quarters when his first mate came runnin' in so excited he couldn't say anything but stutter. Captain listened a minute, then remembered that stutterers could sing without stuttering, so he said, 'Sing it, man!'

"Th' mate stopped, took a deep breath. an' rememberin th' tune t' 'Auld Lang Syne' began t' sing, 'Should auld acquaintance be forgot and never brought to mind, th' bloomin' cook fell overboard an' tis twenty miles behind!' "

Zenas chuckled. "That reminds me of a feller who drifted through an' worked at th' ranch for a while. Only his closest friends called him Stutterin' Stan. He was th' worst stutterer I ever saw. He wasn't genteel about it, either, if you helped him or finished his sentences for him, he would most likely slug you one if you was in reach. We would occasionally go up t' Pueblo or th' fort for a day or two, an' th' first thing Stan would do was find th' toughest man in town and whip him, then he would

176

say, 'M-m-m-my n-n-na-me is . . . S-S-Sta-a-n a-a-n I s-s-t-ut-t-er a-an' if-f'n . . . *e-e-eny* one-one la-laughs, I-I . . . wi-wi-will wh-wh-*whup* 'im!'

"An' he would, too. When most stutterers git a couple of drinks in them they quit stutterin', but not Stan, if anything he got worse. When he did, he mostly kept quiet an' that was fine with us. Conversations were much shorter that way."

Some of our horses strayed off an' Jake sent us t' find 'em. We tracked 'em up th' river, then lost them when a herd of cows covered their tracks. Along about midafternoon, we came upon a man watchin' over a bunch of cows an' as we rode up, Stan asked him, "S-s-s . . . ay, m-m-m-mis-ter, h-ha . . . ve y-y-you s-s-seen e-e-eny B-b-b-ent h-h-hor-rses a-a-a . . . p-p-passin b-b-by?"

"T-t-they c-c-came b-by h-h-here a-a-bout n-n-noon," he replied, then he added quickly, for Stan was dismounting, "Isn't-it-funny-we-b-both-s-s-stutter!"

Stan whirled around an' faced th' man who was backing up. *"You damn well better!"* he said without a whisper of a stutter.

It was quiet a moment, then someone snickered an' I couldn't hold it in any longer. We laughed 'til we cried. Those two stutterers stood there grinnin' at us.

We had a bunch of hounds hangin' around th' ranch an' me an' Jake got t' talking about night hunts we used to go on.

"I wonder if these hounds could hunt coons?" Jake said.

"Bet we could teach 'em to," I replied.

"Aww them hounds is too lazy t' scratch fleas, much less chase a coon," Robert Bent said.

Well, that started it an' a few days later, Jake rode in with a cub coon in a sack. We put him in a cage an' th' dogs got mighty curious, one that poked his nose too close got it bloodied, which made him mad an' he spent his time incitin' th' rest o' th' pack to a right smart hatred o' that coon. 'Course, a coon bein' a coon, he loved a fuss an' kept all dogs at bay, occasionally gittin' a piece of one or t'other.

After a day or two of that, I said, "It's time we put those dogs to th' test, let's take 'em down by th' river tonight an' see what they do."

Well I can tell you they did mighty good work treein' a coon after an hour or two, then our hunt ended with a battle with a skunk.

"Looks like we got a little more trainin' t' do," Jake said while Robert howled.

We continued working with them until they finally got th' message that coons was th' thing—th' only thing. We had some good hunts after that, most cleaned out th' coon population in our neighborhood, which was much encouraged by farmers an' truck gardeners. We had a hunt almost every week, with ever'one joinin' in.

Tom Boggs, John Prowers, Bent boys as was home, me an' Jake was th' main ones. Tom an' John takin' their own hounds for trainin'. Word got out what we were doin' an' folks would send for us t' come to their place to work on their coon population. Of course we were glad to accommodate them, for it usually meant a fine breakfast cooked by a grateful wife an' a chance t' visit with others up an' down th' valley. If we had far t' go, we would tie dogs in a wagon so they wouldn't be tired when we hunted, an' therein lies a story.

Tom Boggs had a young dog he was trainin'. We all got together one afternoon late, tied our dogs in th' wagon, an' headed up Purgatory for a hunt. This was long b'fore cars for sure, so I guess you would say Tom's dog got wagon sick. He wretched an' wretched, then just lay around groanin' th' whole way. When we got ready t' hunt, he was in no mood for it and just followed us along, his head in th' lantern while th' other dogs hunted.

After a while they bayed an' Tom's pup perked up, decidin' he wasn't so bad after all, he streaked out after th' pack, only it was dark an' with his face in th' lantern, he was night blind. About th' time he hit full speed, he dead centered a tree an' knocked himself silly. After he come to his senses he was back in line behind that lantern.

A few minutes later, dogs treed an' that pup *knew* he was needed so off he went again—right off a fifteen foot bluff into th' river. Well, it was river when he broke through ice. That done it for th' poor feller, he stuck his head in that lantern an' didn't move from it th' rest of th' night. We bagged three coons an' when we headed home, *that* dog walked.

It was along about that time that those two Ute cowboys came back into play. This is how it happened: With summer activity on th' Santa Fe Trail, we were always scrambling t' have enough stock t' meet demand. We went so far as to train our own oxen from time to time—tore up a bunch o' wagons doin' it, but I can't say it wasn't exciting. Anyhow, we were always lookin' for more stock an' sometimes we didn't ask a lot of questions when someone had some for sale. Out there in those troublous times, stock strayed, got run off or lost in other ways, an' it was mostly impossible t' find proper owners.

One day th' lookout called down, "Cattle crossin' th' river northwest, two men drivin' 'em." Jake an' I were bringin' in a bunch o' horses so when they were penned, we rode out t' find if they were for sale. They had crossed th' Arkansas an' thrown their herd out west o' th' Purgatory. It seemed kind of strange t' us that those riders hung back in th' trees. We only got a glimpse o' them once in a while. Somehow they seemed familiar to me, but then again they were kinda strange looking.

We rode through th' herd looking them over. There were a lot of strange brands with some not branded, indicating that they may have once been owned by an eastern pilgrim.

"Looks like someone's been gatherin' strays," I called.

Jake just nodded. "Lets go talk to the drovers."

We trotted over to where th' men were, but it seemed they were very cautious about meeting us. When we got close enough t' see them, I realized that they were Indians dressed in nothing but breechclout, chaps, and sombrero. They were on cow ponies, not Indian ponies, an' suddenly I recognized th' horses an' knew who their riders were.

"Buenos dias, señors," I called in Spanish. "It is good to see my friends again." I took off my hat so they could recognize me and one called back, "Buenos dias, Señor Zee."

With that, they rode out to us and shook my hand in white man's fashion. "I see you still have th' horses you earned when we gathered cows."

"Yes, they have been good and they helped us gather the cattle."

"Where did you find them?" I asked. Even though we played loose with th' ownership thing, we didn't want any that were out and out stolen, for th' owner might claim them back and we would be out what we had paid for them.

"We gathered them along the foothills south of the Cherry Creek village (meanin' Denver). They are not stolen, Señor Zee," one of them said.

I nodded. One thing you could depend on, especially in those days, was that Indians did not lie. That was a particular vice of white men an' Mexican Americans.

"Are they for sale?" Jake asked.

"Yes, that is why we brought them here." We had named this speaker Dos and th' older Ute we called Uno in order to differentiate b'tween them. They were amused and seemed to like the names.

"We like the cattle work and want to become vaqueros," Uno said eagerly.

"Always a need for that around here," I said.

"We will buy the oxen, but we don't need the calves and cows," Jake said, "we know someone who would buy them from you."

"That would be good," Dos said.

We helped them drive their' herd over Rio Purgatory an' with Jake and Uno counting, Dos an' I drove th' herd between them and into a holding pen. There followed a conference b'tween Jake and Uno, squaring up th' count. Jake had th' same number of pebbles as notches on Uno's stick, but they had a difference in oxen count, which was soon accounted for, the two agreein' that one ox was lame and could not be of service anymore.

Jake had to confer with our bookkeeper b'fore he bought th' cattle, so we all went to th' stockade where the offices were. While Jake did his business, I took them down to th' kitchen for some grub. You would have thought those people had never seen an Indian b'fore th' way they stared, but then I guess they had never seen naked Indians wearin' chaps an' a hat b'fore.

Uno an' Dos ignored their stares, took their bowls of chili, and squatted agin th' wall to eat. Jake soon returned and when they had finished eating we sat down on a blanket an' began negotiating a deal. The Utes knew their going prices and would not take less. The big kink in th' deal was that the Indian is accustomed to negotiating prices on each individual item so Jake had to buy the oxen one at a time, even though each brought th' same price. The amazing thing is that Uno knew which steer each notch on his stick represented and we had to see that steer before we could make a purchase. As Jake counted out silver, Dos and I ran that particular ox out of th' pen. When we finished, Jake tried t' teach Uno a little multiplication math, but it didn't take and he finally gave up with a laugh.

The Utes split th' silver evenly, bagging it in leather pouches which were then tied to their chap belts. When they walked the silver clinked musically.

"Señor Tom lives nearby and it may be that he will buy your cows," I said.

Their eyes lighted an' they were pleased to know that Tom was nearby. We rode over to his ranch after assuring them that Jake would guard their herd while we were gone.

"We bought their oxen and they have some cows they would like to sell. I thought you would like to look at them," I said to Tom.

"Shore would," Tom agreed, "I would like to add some more this spring." He showed real pleasure at seein' th' boys again an' they had a long talk with sign.

"They know th' goin' prices," I warned.

Tom grinned. "I'll treat 'em fair, Zee."

"No danger in that not happenin'." I laughed. Tom signed our conversation and the two Indians grinned.

We sat there an' conversed in four languages, English, Spanish, Ute, and Sign. It was the norm for th' times. With other people we might throw French and German an' maybe one or two of a dozen Indian languages into th' mix. It always amuses us when someone from th' east comes out an' starts talking about th' need for one language for the U.S.A. It never has been that way east *or* west an' we will lose something in our culture if one day it comes to one language for us all. Oh I know all about Babel theorists sayin' languages are barriers to communication, but I say that languages when they wash up agin each other enrich both cultures an' people who use them. Th' beauty of American language is that we have adopted so many words from others and included them into our everyday conversations. Wonder how we would sound if we were to say we all had to use the original language of the country? It certainly would not be King James' English or even Spanish.

Late in th' evening we parted with Tom, him promising t' come over next morning t' see th' cows. After supper Dos and Uno turned their horses in with their cows an' disappeared into th' brush along th' river to sleep. We were not used to Utes being friendly with us an' some of our Mexican Americans were awful nervous about having them around. I'm sure there were some light sleepers that night, but I wasn't one of them.

Next morning, Tom rode in with Juan who was working for Tom. The pleasant meeting between Utes an' Juan served t' relieve some anxiety among th' Spanish speaking community. Tom looked over the cattle an' soon a blanket was spread an' negotiations began. I saddled up an' as each cow was purchased, Juan an' I ran it out of the pen. When we were through, the only thing left was that lame ox.

Bent's cook appeared and after looking th' animal over, *ordered* Jake t' buy him, which he did in spite o' his vow he "wasn't gonna take orders from no cook." I imagine he had th' same idea I had and our suspicions were confirmed when we saw th' fire pit being loaded with wood an' th' spit brought out. The ox disappeared and shortly half of him appeared spitted up over th' fire. Cookie had a young boy faithfully turnin' th' crank and we all knew th' agony and ecstasy of smellin' roasting beef. Supper that night was a feast.

It took Tom some time t' persuade his Cheyenne wife that there could be some good Utes, but finally she let him hire Uno and Dos as cowhands. It was amusing and satisfying at th' same time t' see those boys change from Indian to cowhand wearing pants an' boots. No one would argue with their abilities handling stock, that's for sure. They would go back to th' tribe occasionally, always reverting to the old way of dress. Uno came back once with a wife and after Tom's wife got over th' shock, they became good friends an' worked together keeping hands fed and household chores done.

It was my observation then that women of th' Indian race were more flexible, accepting, and adaptable to the new things of our European culture than their men. Even with bad white husbands they were generally better off than with Indian men and if they got a halfway decent white husband, their life became a heaven on earth, for a decent man didn't beat his wife, provided for her year-round so there were no starving times, gave her a sound house t' live in, didn't up an' move ever'time th' moon changed, *and* he did much of th' work that would have fallen on her shoulders in th' tipi. In return, she made a good wife, adopted white ways, kept a clean house, cooked, and made her man feel like a king. It was men like William Bent and Uncle Dick Wootton who married Indian maidens an' stayed with them through thick an' thin that helped settle th' west, not those who "married" for convenience, then went back east turning their backs on wife and children, leaving them to fend for themselves.

Uncle Dick, by th' way, only stayed on th' Huerfano a few years, then moved on to more adventuresome pursuits when his first wife died. He freighted some, then ran a store and hotel at Cherry Creek, now called Denver. After he got flooded out of his second farm on the Fountaine River, he moved up to Raton Pass in 1866 and built and operated a toll road through th' pass until he sold out to th' Santa Fe Railroad.

CHAPTER 20
BACK TO NEW MEXICO

1866–1869

With th' end of th' war, things began t' settle down, though some would argue that point with good reason. I guess you would be more accurate t' say that things *changed* more than settled down. Indian depredations subsided in our region, th' main battlegrounds shifting to th' northern plains and Texas, while we were left in relative calm for a few years 'til 'Paches got good an' warmed up an' we began fightin' among ourselves.

Mr. Bent went to Washington to try to get the stone fort back from th' government and collect five years' back rent still unpaid. He didn't get either. He came back in th' spring of '67 with a new bride, Adalina, daughter of old river man Alexander Harvey.

Kit Carson bought some land and settled in Boggsville. He wasn't well an' we had watched him decline in th' last few years. He blamed it on a fall with a horse he had several years b'fore. Still, government and Indians looked to him for help only a man of his ability could accomplish and he was almost as busy as ever. Th' last thing he did was help th' Utes secure a reservation in southwest Colorado. He took Ouray and a delegation to Washington and was very influential in getting a deal made.

While he was there, he consulted several doctors about his condition, but got no relief. He was back in th' spring of '68 just in time for th' birth of his last child, a girl he named Josefita after his wife. He was so frail he could barely hold his baby.

It was painful to see. Josefa never recovered from the birth and died in Kit's arms April 27.

It was the last straw for him and he just seemed t' pine away. On sunny days, he sat outside and visited with his neighbor Tom Boggs, who he named guardian of the Carson children. His decline continued until Doctor Tilton, th' Army doctor, took him to Fort Lyon where he could better care for him. He lay on buffalo robes on th' floor, th' only way he could get some relief. He rallied some May 23 an' asked for a real meal of buffalo steak and coffee and after that he smoked his pipe. Later, he began coughing violently, spittin' up blood. His last words were called to Doctor Tilton, *"Doctor, compadre, adios."* We laid him beside Josefa. They were married twenty-five years and died within a month of each other.

There have been thousands of words written and spoken about Kit Carson, most o' th' written pure fiction. T' hear th' Buntlines talk, you would think he was ten feet tall an' rode buffalos for mounts. In truth, he was a small man in stature, probably never weighed over 150 pounds in his life, preferred ridin' mules to horses for long hauls. But he was *active* and went at all things he intended t' do with energy and determination. He was a leader men listened to an' willingly follered. He spoke seldom, listened often—not just to big talkers, but to little men, too.

He had learned t' be cautious at all times. At a campfire, he was never in th' light, but stayed back in th' shadows never looking into th' fire t' keep his night vision, ever alert to th' night. On th' trail, he was always ahead of us in seein' things t' come an' readin' sign none of th' rest of us could see. Many a wily Indian has been put in th' shade by ol' Kit when it came to follerin' a trail. He knew every nook an' cranny of th' whole west an' could tell you where he was at any moment an' how far it was t' wherever.

Yeller pulp would have you believe he killed Injuns by th' tribe, but I heard him say he probably had not killed more than a half-dozen Indians in his life. I only heard tell of one white man he killed an' that was in a fair fight agin a big French bully at one of those trapper rendezvous. In so doin', he won th' heart o' his first bride.

All tribes held him in as high esteem as his white friends an' when they needed help, they always turned to Kit Carson. I suppose he will always be hated by Navajos for roundin' them up as he did, but he was th' only one who ever put an end to their depredations and he deserves at least some credit for putting troublemakers among them on th' path t' peace. I don't think he did it out of animosity, but he saw a need to establish peace an' went about it in such a way that it became a permanent thing. He may have been a small man in stature, but he was a giant among giants.

Mr. Bent was returning from Westport with his train when Kit died. He was a sad man when he learned his old friend was gone. That was th' winter Custer slaughtered Black Kettle and his village an' by some miracle escaped massacre himself from th' villages camped along th' Washita. He abandoned part of his command and retreated to Camp Supply.

In May, 1869, Mr. Bent took us from Santa Fe over th' old trail by way of Raton Pass with a caravan to th' States. By th' time we passed th' stage station at th' old adobe fort, he was sick and when we reached th' ranch, Mary put him to bed and called Doctor Tilton from Lyon. There was nothing he could do, Mr. Bent had pneumonia and died May 19 at the age of 60. We buried him near his old friend Kit. The train continued on to Missouri and finished up business. There would be no more Bent trains along th' trail.

★ ★ ★ ★ ★

While ramblin' around Westport, I looked in on an old junk shop one day, just killin' time. This place had everything including generous amounts o' dust. I struck up a conversation with th' proprietor, an older man whose name I have forgotten. We talked a while an' he kept sayin' my name over an' over to himself, "Zenas Leonard Meeker, Zenas Leonard, Zenas Leonard . . ." as if it reminded him of something, though I knew I had never seen him before or been in that store. Suddenly he began diggin' through piles of things on his desk. "I have something here you may be interested in if I can find it!" He dug an' dug mutterin' to himself until reachin' 'way back in a nook, he pulled out a little book. Wipin' dust off, he nodded with pleasure. "Looky here, young man," and handed me th' book.

It was old an' somewhat ragged, th' front title had faded until it couldn't be read. I opened to th' title page and read;

Narrative of the Adventures of Zenas Leonard, a native of Clearfield County, Pa. who spent five years in trapping for furs, trading with the Indians, &c.,&c., of the Rocky Mountains: written by himself.

Down below, it read;

Printed and published by D. W. Moore, Clearfield, Pa. 1839.

I couldn't believe my eyes! It was a book about Zenas Leonard an' I never knew it existed until that moment! I forgot about everything an' began reading. I don't know how long I had stood there, but I was on page fifteen when th' old man said, "What d'yuh think o' thet, young man?"

I actually jumped an' looked around, I had forgotten where I was.

"This is great!" I said. "How much do you want for it?"

"Oh, I could probably let it go for a hundred dollars."

He looked at me out of th' corner of his eye an' I knew he was teasin'. He didn't know it, but I would have considered it seriously.

He chuckled. "I suppose you could have it for a dollar four bits."

I was digging into my pocket before he had finished and handed him th' coins. Usually, a man will dicker some in a place like that, but I was too excited an' grateful to do that. He took th' book an' wrapped it carefully in brown paper an' handed it to me.

"Enjoy, young man, I hope you learn a lot about your namesake. I understand he is buried up to Sibley by old Fort Osage."

"Yes, he is," I replied. "I met him there a couple of times when my pa and I drove mules up there an' traded with him."

"When did he die?"

"In th' summer of '47," I said. "Some of his people still live around there."

"Well, enjoy the book, I'm glad you got it."

I was so excited, I almost forgot to thank him as I left th' store. As soon as I could find a quiet spot, I sat down an' read th' whole book, all eighty-seven pages! It was only th' second book I had ever owned after my Bible Grandma Ruth had given me years b'fore. Still have th' book, though it's worn an' fragile now, approachin' a hundred years old. I must have read it a dozen times or more.

CHAPTER 21
THE END OF AN ERA

Jacob decided t' visit th' folks, but I wanted to go back to New Mexico. Our work for th' Bents was over an' I would have t' find another means of makin' a living. It was then that I decided to go into th' horse and mule business on my own. I bought a bunch of Missouri mules an' joined up with a train leavin' for New Mexico. Ambrose Trimble, captain of th' train I joined, hired me and a fellow named Asa Willis to oversee spare stock and assured me that he had enough veteran drovers t' pull us through.

Those things you take with a grain of salt, for there were as many greenhorns as veterans on that trip, just as it was with every train that ever started down that trail. I had t' trust my own judgment on capabilities of men and since I was acquainted with some of them and knew they had "seen th' elephant" I decided it would be safe to go along.

It was well into a hot and dusty July when we struck out. So hot even Indians were quiet for a change. Hardly a buffalo could be seen, they having follered green grass far to th' north. There weren't many people on th' trail an' we went days without seeing a soul or a wagon. It was so quiet it was almost boring— enough to make greenhorns laugh at our caution. We just kept quiet an' went about our business assured that sooner or later on this trip they would be "eddicated" by our Indian friends.

We had crossed that cattle trail to Abilene in th' spring, but in th' time we had been gone, it had grown more than a mile

190

wider. From th' looks of that trail an' lack of grass, we guessed there must have been 50,000 cattle driven over it. Here an' there, we saw a stray steer or two, but they had gone back to bein' wild and were impossible t' catch.

When we hit th' Arkansas at Big Bend, it was barely flowing and th' higher upstream we went, th' lower it flowed. We didn't expect we could take Cimarron Cutoff, there bein' no water there. Ol' Cimmaron would surely be dry as a bone so we passed Cache Island and Cimarron Crossing.

It isn't often that summer rains get as far north as th' Arkansas, but traveling between Cache Island and Chouteau's Island, great thunderheads would build up in th' south about noon, and by midafternoon, it was raining buckets. We got in th' rhythm of things, starting out very early an' pushing through 'til it rained before stopping for rest. After th' rain passed, we would hitch up an' travel until slap-up dark.

Grass started greening and before we got to Chouteau's we figgered that cutoff just might be wet enough t' travel. A couple of days before we got there, Mr. Trimble sent me an' Asa ahead to ride down th' cutoff a ways t' see what conditions were. They were gonna wait for us at Chouteau's Island. We pushed on ahead, worried that he had put some greenhorns in charge o' my herd. Th' veterans assured us that they would keep an eye on them so we felt a little better.

At Chouteau's Island, water seemed t' be flowing more an' we were encouraged by that. If we could use th' cutoff it would take days off our trip. South of th' river, th' sand was wet, better for wagons t' pass through than heavy dry sand. Riding on, we found grass showing green an' wallows holding water. It looked like a go to us, but we rode a ways out on th' Llano t' make sure. Just as important as water was th' fact that we didn't see any sign of Indians prowling about. When we had satisfied ourselves that we could make a passage with water, we returned

191

to th' crossing amid afternoon rain.

Mr. Trimble was waiting and had about decided on his own that th' cutoff would be usable. Our report convinced him and we prepared to cross over after th' rain. Crossing any river was always a chore and this one was no different. We doubled up teams and by sundown were all across.

Asa looked back an' said, "Well, we've made a full half-mile on th' afternoon run!" We made camp and turned in early.

People always look at me like I'm crazy when I talk about th' mud we went through on that trip, but otherwise, that was th' easiest crossing of th' Staked Plains I ever made. Even that pull through sand leavin th' river was easy relative t' what it was other times. Some of th' greenhorns wondered at us even considering a longer route, but they never had seen that plain when it was dry.

As always, there was no water in North Fork of the Cimarron and believe it or not, when we hit th' main Cimarron just below Point of Rocks, it was flooding and th' trail under the bluff was underwater. We had t' stay up on top an' that wasn't easy driving. We were close enough to th' mountains that rains there sent water roaring downriver. It would rise without any warning or reason except that it had rained a hundred miles west of there. The rises didn't last long, which was good for travelers.

Stayin' up on top and camping in th' open instead of under th' bluff where we could have been better protected proved t' be our downfall, for early next morning, Satanta an' his Kiowas ran off th' cavyyard with all my mules.

We had hitched up an' just thrown th' herd onto th' trail when they hit us. I got some shots off, killed one of th' ponies. Th' rider was picked up by one of his companions an' made his escape. It was a long shot at a moving target by th' time I got my rifle out, but th' boys said I winged one of th' Indians, small compensation for losing my mules. Asa was plumb cheerful

192

about th' whole thing. "Don't worry, Zee, you can get your mules back from th' Comancheros—them that Injuns ain't et."

"Yeah," I retorted, "an' I suppose you think that Mr. Trimble's gonna pay you fer doin' nothin' the rest o' th trip!"

Truth is, I did get a couple o' those mules back down around Mora a year or so later, but I had t' whip a Comanchero for 'em. They would meet th' Comanches out on th' Llano, trade guns, lead, powder, an' trinkets for stock th' Indians had stolen down in Texas. Occasionally they would buy a slave from them in hopes of a big reward. Generally, th' Army would redeem th' price of th' slave. It was quite a business an' if every Texas outfit got their cattle back, it would affect almost every ranch in eastern New Mexico an' depopulate th' range.

Later, Jim East from Tascosa tried retrieving their cattle through th' law. It proved to be impossible, New Mexicans disliking Texians so much. Th' Texians got up a small army an' took back by force those stolen cattle they could find, but they only did it once. Guess they figured the New Mexicans'd be ready for them a second time. O'course, th' Slaughter boys got a measure of revenge when they passed through on their way to Arizona. Their herd was a lot bigger leavin' New Mexico than it was comin in!

By th' time we had to cross, Cimarron flow was down to a trickle again and we had no trouble crossing. We set our sights on Autograph Bluff twenty miles away. That night I carved a new date under th' old date by my name. Half th' train was busy carving their names for th' first time. T'other half had carved theirs on previous trips. We couldn't see mountains from where we were, but we could sure see clouds that built up over them every afternoon. Sunsets sure were pretty with th' sun below th' horizon castin' shadows of those thunderheads high across th' sky while lightning flashed on th' horizon without a sound. Those clouds would still light up even as they cooled and died. We nooned just south of old Fort Nichols next day.

I had bought into one of th' messes when our train started and so had my eats paid until th' end, but Asa was dependin' on his employment t' pay his found for th' trip an' since th' stock was gone, didn't have a job. He was in trouble with th' men he ate with and old man Trimble let it stay that way for a while. He was awful mad about losin' stock. Just after leaving Autograph Bluff, a drover got bit by a rattler an' couldn't work, so Mr. Trimble hired Asa back. Th' only cure we knew for snake bite was alcohol, so we kept th' drover drunk for about five days. It saved his life, but he walked with a limp for a long time after that.

It was fifty miles to th' second Point of Rocks from Fort Nichols with our only landmark between bein' Rabbit Ear mountain to th' south. We crossed Corrumpa Creek at McNees Crossing and spent th' night there. This was th' wet season on th' high plains an' if anything, water was too plentiful. It was hard t' find ground that wasn't rutted or cut up so much it wouldn't hold th' wagons. Our animals had to work extra hard, so when we got to Point of Rocks, Mr. Trimble decided t' rest a couple of days.

This is where Stephen Dorsey established his ranch an' built his mansion years later. I guess when we came through there, he was still a carpetbagger senator from Arkansas. There was nothing there but campsites for th' trail. Holkeo Creek was runnin' so we took that opportunity t' wash up our clothes and selves.

We climbed up on th' Point and looked th' country over. From Rabbit Ear east of us around south to th' mountains due west was nothing but open prairie as far as you could see—the perfect picture of high rolling plains in all their glory. It seemed you could see forever, Rabbit Ear looked to be a jog away, though we knew it was a good thirty—thirty-five miles away, and sixty miles west, ol' Tooth of Time bit into th' sky. North of th' Tooth was Lucien Maxwell's mill at Cimarron and a little south of th' Tooth was Rayado. Once I climbed th' mountain opposite th' Tooth an' watched a wagon train coming past Point of Rocks. Over a period of three days I watched it progress towards us looking like a string of white sails on th' prairie, disappearing in a valley, then popping up on hilltops, always getting closer, but at a great distance looking like they were standin' still. Unless you looked for a long time, you couldn't tell they were movin'.

There was a rock fort on top of Point of Rocks, probably built by some Indian group for defense, though there was no water available for them. We poked around, not minding th' sky over those mountains behind us until we heard a crackle come before it and th' boom of a huge bolt of lightning striking north of us. 'Way out on th' plain we could see antelope skitterin' here an' there lookin' for shelter. They weren't scared of rain, but they sure knew what lightning could do.

Now, a high point is not th' place t' be in a lightning storm and you can bet we set records getting down off'n that rock. By th' time we rounded th' bluff at th' bottom, it was hailing buckets so we sat under that rock and watched it storm. Hail turned t' ice water an' we near froze.

We could see our horses and mules bunched together and prayed that lightning would not find them. Rain got so heavy it seemed that cloud sat right down on us. For a while we couldn't see those wagons a quarter mile away, then it started slackin' off an' thunder seemed to move way out in the leading edge of that cloud as it moved out across th' plains. We watched it march along, dark rain slanting down an' its popcorn top climbin' an' climbin' 'til it gave out of energy and spread across a blue sky in a huge anvil, silver around th' edges, but black as sin underneath. Thunder rumbled less and less, rain drew back up an' didn't reach ground anymore.

They say that clean smell after a rain is ozone from lightning burnin' air. Whatever it is I still like t' smell it after a rain. Dust is settled an' th' air is clear as it can be.

It wouldn't have done t' wait until th' ground dried out t' move on, for another cloud would come along an' soak us before that happened, so next morning, we hitched up an' slogged on. Soon we were on rockier ground an' travel got easier. We crossed th' Canadian south of th' mouth of Little Cimarron River and Taylor Springs and camped th' next night on Rayado Creek just east of th' old stockade. From there, we turned up Moras Creek to th' divide an' down to Wagon Mound.

Two days later, Mr. Trimble delivered his freight to th' quartermaster and sutler at Fort Union. He paid off his drovers an' they headed for Loma Parda on th' run. I followed. Even if I didn't have any money, I wanted t' see that place. Well, it didn't take me long t' git my fill and Loma Parda didn't want anything t' do with a feller without jingle in his pocket, so when Mr. Trimble rode by on his way to Mora, I went with him.

For many years Mora had been th' frontier town of northeast New Mexico. East and north was Indian territory and the Utes and Apaches made it very uncomfortable for anyone passin' through. A periodic raid up Mora valley kept any thoughts of Spanish expansion out of their minds. It was a quiet little town, kinda out of th' mainstream of things with lots of farms, a couple of grist mills along th' river, a plaza with a few stores an' a couple of cantinas. Those valleys reminded me of Ozark valleys, but these mountains were taller an' it was a lot cooler.

Mr. Trimble insisted that I stay with him an' his wife did her best t' catch me up on good home cooking. I wanted t' pay my respects to Mr. St. Vrain, but he was very ill and I didn't see him before he died October 28, 1869. It seemed th' whole country turned out for his funeral and it was a great though solemn occasion. Th' Masonic Lodge conducted th' service—probably a first time experience for those Catholics—and they did a good job. All in all it was a fitting farewell to a great man.

For me, it put a final period on the end of an era. There were still plenty of pioneer Americans, but our loss of Kit Carson, William Bent, and now Ceran St. Vrain ended a personal relationship I had with those early days and I felt a little lost. A few days later, I saddled up, said my "goodbyes" to th' Trimbles, and headed back downriver to Fort Union.

CHAPTER 22
A DEAL WITH THE WASHERWOMEN

On th' road between Loma Parda an' Fort Union, I caught up
with what remained of Asa Willis. He had run out of silver and
was therefore excused from th' presence of bars, brothels, and
faro tables of that fair city and sent on his way. He was a mess
and I made sure t' stay upwind as he walked along hanging on
to my stirrup.

At th' fort, I took him around to th' laundry. We were met by
a large Irish woman who could have held her own as first
sergeant of any company in th' whole fort.

Casting a disdainful eye on my companion, she asked, "What
can we do for you *gen'lemen* t'day?"

"My friend here needs his clothes washed and mended," I
replied.

She snorted, "And wot's th' gen'leman t' wear while we try t'
rescue those rags for 'im?"

"W-e-e-ell, I was wonderin' if you might wash him along with
his clothes."

Asa backed off. "Now wait a minit . . ." but I backed my
horse against him an' pinned him to th' wall. My poor horse
trembled at th' proximity of that smelly wreck on his flank, but
held.

Hands on hips, M'Lady of Eire cocked her head an' considered th' prospect. "T'would ruin a good kettle o' water t' get th'
lot o' 'em clean, that'd be extra t' change th' pot . . ." She
began countin' on her fingers an' figuring up a cost, her eyes

198

cast to th' heavens an' her lips mouthing numbers to herself as she counted. Several other washerwomen peeked out curious at th' doin's an' gigglin' at th' prospect of a little fun. They were a rough lot, used to life in a rough man's world. and it's doubtful there was anything they hadn't seen—or done.

One of them elbowed her neighbor, "I'd wash th' waif fer free, but those clothes would cost extry!"

"Hush up!" M'Lady demanded severely, "I'm *figurin'*!"

Th' women giggled.

"I'd say that we could do th' whole job up good fer six bits."

"Mending included?"

"Mendin' included an' he can sit by th' fire while we work."

"I got four b . . ."

"It be six bits *er nothin'*, mister . . ." She cocked her head an' eyed me speculatively, ". . . up front!"

I thought a moment while Asa wriggled an' tried t' slide down under my horse. Eyeing th' dirty smudge he left on that wall, I determined six bits was a bargain an' reached for my money. "Deal, Ma'am."

Not until she had coins in her hand did she move, but when I turned th' horse she jumped like a cat on a mouse an' had poor Asa by his ear. She towered over him and I have no doubt 'til this day that she could have lifted him plumb off th' floor with that ear had it held.

Asa hollered, "Zee, you cain't *do* this!" but I ignored him.

Into that covey of washerwomen he was flung and they began work with relish. One woman tested th' water in a wash pot sitting on th' fire and added a bucket of cold water. In an instant he was naked, trying his best t' keep covered.

"Glory be, he's lousy!"

"Got crabs, too."

"Into th' pot you two legged swine!" th' sergeant ordered.

"But it's on th' *fire*!" he hollered.

The sergeant tossed a rock into th' pot. "Stand on that, now *git!*" She advanced and if it had been me an' water was *boilin'*, I would have jumped in.

Asa had th' same mind, "Yeeoowww, it's too h-h-hot!" he fairly screamed. Two more buckets of cold washed over his head an' sloshed onto th' fire, sending up a cloud of steam.

Several soldiers wandered over from th' smithy an' gathered around door and window t' see th' action.

"Don't ruin another pot o' water with them clothes, we'll bile 'em in his wash water when we're done," th' sergeant ordered.

Someone pushed Asa's head underwater an' before he could come up blubberin', his head was sudsed with a big cake of lye soap.

"It's in my eyes . . ." His holler was cut off by a hand pushing his head under again.

While a rag was applied vigorously to his face, neck, and ears, a brush was scrubbing his back and there was a scrub woman on each arm. Already he was several shades lighter.

"Stand up!"

"Not on your . . . eeyoow," and he stood straight up, trying t' cover his privates. Brushes were doing their jobs on backsides and chest.

"Grab his arms, girls, an' I'll scrub th' crabs off."

Two burly women were on each arm an' brush was applied down below with vigor amid screams of protest, which were nearly drowned out by guffaws from spectators. They must have had some experience with this sort of work, for one moment he was standing in th' tub an' next he was upended with his legs sticking up, his nose barely above water. He couldn't even yell. In a trice, his legs and feet were scrubbed and our sergeant lifted him up on his feet. There he stood in all of his pink-skinned glory, several degrees more sober than when he got in. A woman approached from behind and poured a bucket of cold water over him. He gave a great shudder and cry and would have sat down in th' hot water if th' sergeant hadn't caught him and lifted him bodily out of th' pot.

Poor Asa danced in one place, his legs to his knees scarlet, while th' rest of his body slowly turned blue from cold. A blanket was thrown to him an' he wrapped up in it. Someone set a stool by th' fire an' he was soon warming. Someone else produced a comb and scissors and he was given a much needed haircut.

"Oughta shave yer head an' git rid o' lice," th' barber muttered. When she finished, she swished comb and scissors through boiling water with her bare hand, a testimony to her immunity to heat.

That crowd was weak with mirth from th' spectacle and to a man, they tossed coins into th' washroom until I was sure that they had exceeded my price for th' job. Washerwomen and sergeant bowed to their audience as if they had just given a great performance in some play.

"Now git ye away an' let us finish our work, you scoundrels, er we jist might take it in our heads t' wash th' whole lot o' ye— fer free! Lord knows ye need it, some worse'n this poor waife."

Fresh wood was thrown on th' fire an' Asa's clothes lifted by stirring paddle and added to th' cauldron. When it came to a rolling boil, a washerwoman stirred it vigoursly. That water took on th' aspect and consistency of a mudhole. After thoroughly rinsing the clothes in fresh water, they were wrung out and hung by th'fire. It seemed our fun was over with nothing left but drying and mending. I gave th' sergeant an extra two bits (small pay for th' entertainment I enjoyed) and asked her t' keep Asa there until I returned and rode over to th' sutlery for some supplies and food. When I returned an' hour or so later, Asa was still by th' fire wrapped in that blanket. He looked much better and seemed t' have recovered from his ordeal, even joshin' with his former tormentors.

"Here's yore *patron* so you can have yer clothes back now," one of th' women said.

Asa quickly dressed under his blanket an' emerged a changed man—outside at least. He grinned sheepishly at me and we left among cheerful "g'byes" of our washerwomen.

CHAPTER 23
ASA AND THE BLUE-EYED GOOSE

It's a little out of th' order of things, but I guess this is as good a place as any t' tell you a little about Asa Willis.

He was some years younger than me, not even out of his teens when we met. He had been on his own for several years, having come west from th' Ohio region. Even when he was still a kid, he looked old and wrinkled, like those fair-skinned red-headed people are prone to bein'. I guess at his peak he would not have weighed over 120 pounds—and he wasn't at his peak when he signed on with th' Trimble train.

He may have been stunted some from hard times he had come through, but he once told me all his people were small in stature. Pound for pound, he packed more strength than any man I have known. You would tease him only once for buying his clothes in kid sizes. I've seen him take punishment from and whip men twice his size. Be around him long and you got to thinking of him as a tightly wound spring helt back by a hair trigger.

He preferred smallish horses, sat straight in th' saddle, and rode until his legs were bowed. He had bottom. I've seen him ride four days without a wink of sleep and still show "fight." His specialty was trail herdin' and he must have ridden a million miles b'side a herd. He hung on a long time an' I think he was a grandpa b'fore he quit ridin'. They talk about Texas trail herds, but we had our share o' trailin' out of New Mexico and Asa was always in high demand when a herd was gathered.

Got so he thought of himself as a vaquero specialist and he would do anything you wanted him to if it could be done from th' back of a horse. Th' minute his feet hit ground, it was work beneath him and done with much distaste. His favorite turndown was to retort, "You an' me an' a blue-eyed goose!" a term he used often.

One o' th' happiest days in his life was when he rode into th' ranch one day an' announced he had found a woman "Jist my size!" She wasn't an inch over four foot nine, as pretty a little thing as you could imagine. Her folks had settled at Eddy where her Pa had a mercantile store. Asa had wandered in there looking for a sombrero and it took him three days t' find th' right one, little Amanda Price helping. They were married a year later and raised a house full of red-headed blue-eyed kids. When long trail rides faded away and barbed wire closed up th' country, Asa lost interest in ranch work and settled down in Eddy to run th' store.

I'll tell you how we broke him from using that "You an' me an a blue-eyed goose" thing: A man named Castlebury had a little spread over here an' he had t' go back east for th' winter t' visit his wife's family so he hired me t' watch th' place for him. I needed two hands t' get things he wanted done an' I got Asa and Juan Luna t' help me. Now very little o' th' work was what could be done from th' back of a horse an' Asa got tired of it in a hurry. Hammers, axes, and posthole diggers didn't fit his hands too well an' he made it known. We got so tired of hearing that "blue-eyed" thing we made him cook while we did th' work. Problem was his cookin' left a lot to be desired.

I had just about decided I was gonna have t' fire him when Mr. Castlebury wrote to me and instructed me t' take a bunch o' steers over t' Fort Stanton an' sell them and deposit th' money in his account at th' bank. I guess he got t' spendin' too much an' run out of cash. Well, that was just th' thing for Asa an' he was in th' saddle an' roundin' up steers practically afore that letter was read. Things got better with Asa happy an' me or Juan cookin' and it wasn't long until we had a herd ready t' go.

All th' passes were snowed in an' no graze there available for the cows, so we drove them up th' basin to Carrizozo Trail an' over th' gentle pass to th' fort. It was only about sixty miles but nearabout as much work as takin' them plum t' Dodge City except for the time on th' trail. We still had t' get th' herd trail broke an' by that time, we were nearly to th' fort. We sold a hundred head to th' Mescalero agent an' thirty head to th' fort for considerably less than what spring market prices would have been, but I guess Mr. Castlebury needed cash. We found out later that local banks would not give him a loan on th' cows to be paid back after spring roundup. I had t' take th' money to th' bank at Lincoln so we all rode down there hoping t' get a couple days of relaxation before heading back.

Asa had worked up an awful thirst an' headed for th' nearest waterin' hole while Juan an' I visited th' bank an' telegraphed Castlebury. We hurried back to th' watering hole, for though he was much better after that old visit to Loma Parda, I didn't want him overdoing it an' gittin' into trouble. I needn't have worried, for we found him in a big pool game with th' Coe boys, too busy t' imbibe overmuch. (Frank and George Coe were cousins, not brothers as some may think.) We had a good time and no one got drunk. About midnight, we crawled into th' livery stable loft and slept.

After breakfast, Asa wandered over to th' pool room t' see if he could pick up another game or two and Juan and I wandered down th' street to Murphy's. It was market day and streets were full of people and things they had brought t' town to sell or trade. We got interested in th' wares for sale and Juan stepped across th' road to speak to some people he knew. In a moment I heard him call and when I looked, he was waving emphatically for me to come over. He was standing in front of a stack of crates full of barnyard birds talking to th' lady who had them.

"What's up, Juan?" I asked.

"I theenk we need some geese," he replied with a grin.

"What in the world would we need geese for? Coyotes would have them et in no time."

"I theenk we would take special carre of theese geese," his grin got bigger, "*look* at them!"

"I guess being all white is unusual for this country, but I still don't see why we need them . . ."

"Zee, *look at their eyes*!"

I took a closer look an' nearly dropped my teeth, *"They have blue eyes!"*

"Sí! Sí!" he fairly shouted, "and what does that blue-eyed Asa say?"

"You an' me an' a . . ."

". . . blue-eyed goose!"

"Better get two, Juan, he's liable t' kill th' first one."

Juan dickered with the lady an' arranged t' buy a couple o' young goslings after assuring himself they had th' required blue eyes. At Murphy's we found a small crate and hid th' geese in our wagon where Asa was sure not to see them. By late afternoon we had seen all of town we wanted and I had bought the supplies we needed, so we loaded up an' headed out of town intendin' t' camp on th' trail, but when we rode by George Coe's place, he insisted that we take th' evening with him and we did.

Juan sneaked out an' fed an' watered the geese when Asa was occupied elsewhere. We were on th' trail before sunup and by late th' second evening rode into th' ranch.

It's a peculiar thing about goslings that th' first critter they lay eyes on after they hatch becomes their "mother" an' they will latch on to them an' follow wherever they go. We hoped that these goslings would do this when they were out of th' crate, and I noticed that Juan was very careful not to be seen by them.

After breakfast next morning, he said, "Asa, wee got some-theeng in Lincoln that you need. Come out in thee yarrd an' see what it is."

Asa stood under th' ramada while Juan retrieved th' covered crate. I watched from out of sight so those geese wouldn't see me as Juan turned th' crate on its side and stood where he couldn't be seen.

"Now don't tell me you bought me one o' them sheepdog pups I was lookin at . . ." Asa stepped into th' sunlight and Juan opened th' crate. Those geese looked around blinkin at th' sudden brightness.

"What th' . . ." Asa froze in mid-stride. "Them's geese, Juan, what am I gonna do with them . . ."

The goslings had caught his movement and with chirps and squawks, wings flapping, they descended on Asa. Bonding had occurred. I almost burst trying t' keep from laughing out loud an' Juan had th' biggest grin you have ever seen.

"Git away from me, geese." Asa backed up as two goslings gathered around his feet chirping contentedly.

"They like you, Asa," Juan chortled.

I had regained my composure enough that I could step out and speak with a straight face, "Asa, you and Juan get ready and we'll start on that corral this morning. Dig postholes every ten feet an' when I get through with th' books I'll come down and help."

Asa stared at me a moment and I could see it coming, "Sure, Zee, me an' Juan an' a blue-eyed goose!"

Juan had picked up one of the chicks and was stroking it affectionately. "Ahh, Asa, I weel load thee tools while you hitch up thee wagon. Do we put a gate on thee east side, Zee?"

"Yeah, in th' middle o' that side. Be sure you dig holes extra deep for gateposts." I turned as if to go back into th' bunkhouse.

"Wait a minute, here," Asa called, "you didn't hear me, I said 'me an' Juan an' a . . .' "

". . .*blue-eyed goose!*" Juan and I said in unison.

I said, "Well, Asa, what more do you want?"

He looked puzzled, "I ain't gonna . . ."

"Ain't gonna what?" I asked and tried to look puzzled.

Juan moved closer to Asa, still stroking that goose. "I ain't gonna dig no postholes. It ain't my job!"

"But you said, 'You an' Juan an' a blue-eyed goose.' "

"That's right!"

"But Asa, wee are all here," said Juan.

Asa stepped back a little. "What in th' world air ye talking about, Juan?"

"You and me *an' a blue-eyed goose!*" and he held th' gosling up in Asa's face. That little goose cocked his head and eyed his "mother" with one brilliant *blue* eye.

Asa stared for a long moment as th' fact sank into his brain and I swear he blanched out two or three shades. "Well I'll be . . . well I'll be . . ." he stammered, not being able to complete a thought.

I looked at him an' tried my best t' look severe, though I was bustin' inside. "You got Juan an' a blue-eyed goose, Asa, are you gonna keep your word an' do that job or not?"

"I–I guess . . ."

"*I* guess you had better get busy instead of standin' there stammerin' all morning. You got a blue-eyed goose now and I expect you t' do chores same as me an' Juan or you can take those blue-eyed geese an' skedaddle!"

I turned and went into th' house where I could grin in private. It was deathly quiet except for chirpin' of geese and Juan rattling around th' tool shed.

"Well I'll be d-d," Asa muttered, an' I heard him shuffle off to th' corral, those geese fussin' after him.

To this day I don't know how Juan stood working around him with a straight face. Probably he didn't think it was as funny as I did. I watched them drive out of th' yard, Asa with his head down an' shakin' it ever' once in a while, and goslings trying to roost on a shovel handle. As soon as they were out of range, I laughed long and hard.

After a reasonable time had elapsed, I saddled up and rode down to th' corral. Asa was digging one hole for the gatepost and Juan th' other. It looked like there was an unspoken contest t' see who finished first. I didn't say anything, but dragged up big gateposts an' laid them out. Then I stepped off ten foot spacings an' laid out fenceposts around th' corral. We set corner posts and string-lined posts in between, taking turns with th' two diggers, and I will have t' say that Asa worked as hard as we did . . . well as hard as he could with two geese flapping around under his feet. If they got distracted or he moved away without them noticing, they would panic and squawk until they found him and came running to him.

We drove back to th' house for lunch and Juan penned up th' geese. He took special care of them th' whole time we worked there and when we left, he took them with him back to his brothers and sisters at Luna's Well.

We never had to use them again with Asa Willis and I only heard him start t' use that phrase once on a foreman and he caught himself and looked at me sheepish-like. He developed into a good all-round hand, but he always preferred t' do his work from a horse's back if he could arrange it.

That was just one o' th' adventures me an' Asa Willis got into. Mostly, it was fun, harmless things, but there was a time or two we done some serious scrappin', a couple I'll never tell about! Back to my tale at Fort Union . . .

CHAPTER 24
LAS VEGAS

1869

We decided after a good meal an' night's rest, t' have a look at Las Vegas, about thirty miles south of Fort Union. Asa was flat broke and we needed work of some kind before my money ran out. I dickered with a horse trader an' got Asa a pony that wasn't fit for pulling wagons. He had t' ride bareback as he had hocked his saddle at Loma Parda.

Las Vegas wasn't much more than a sleepy little Mexican placita, home to sheep ranchers and families o' their herders. Plains surrounding town were dotted with sheep by th' thousands. We hung around cantinas on th' plaza a couple o' days an' had about d'cided t' leave when I wandered into Letcher's Merchantile and struck up a conversation with Charlie Ilfeld. He was tellin' me about a wool train that left Las Vegas in May of '68 with 200 wool-packed carts and 3200 oxen, headed for th' States. They had made a successful trip and returned to Las Vegas in October.

"What did they bring back with them, Charlie?" I asked.

He shook his head. "Not a bloomin' thing, Zee, th' wagons were empty."

"Surely those Comancheros saw things they could profit by bringing back t' sell!"

"They brought back trinkets and things for their families, but not a single thing for trade. If we had known that, we would have sent them a list of things t' bring back for us, but we never guessed they would come back *empty*!"

I shook my head. Some few traders headed *east* with empty wagons except for silver stuffed in their belts, but I never had heard of empty wagons goin' *west* before.

"That shore was a waste."

"You bet it was."

"Are they gonna send out another train this season?"

"Haven't heard. Rumaldo Baca sent the most wagons and if anyone sends wagons next spring it would be him."

This was interesting to me, for I could see an opportunity for gainful employment, especially if I could fill those empty wagons with goods on th' return trip from Freeport. Wheels were turnin' in my head an' I wandered across th' plaza in a fog. I couldn't get over them returnin' empty wagons. What a waste!

Asa was squatted agin a wall soakin' up sunshine an' I joined him. "Asa, I just heard th' derndest thing, these sheepmen sent two hundred wagons o' wool up th' trail an' came back with *empty* wagons!"

Asa looked up sleepily an' said, "Aww, Zee you'd believe anythin'. Ain't no one that dumb, not even a Mex." He pulled his sombrero lower over his face, resuming his nap.

"Charlie Ilfeld just told me."

"That Charlie's full o' tales," th' sombrero muttered.

After a minute or two without any more response from Asa, I got up and wandered into th' cantina. It was run by a man named Visciano whose only talent was being married to th' best cook on th' plaza. I never saw him do any more than scratch an' serve up a beer to a customer from time to time. His wife on the other hand kept th' place clean and dished up th' best platter o' tamales and beans you have ever tasted. Her green chili was th' envy o' town and she made sopapillas as big as a plate, served hot with honey. I could hear dishes clatterin' in th' kitchen where she was cooking for th' noon crowd. Visciano was tending bar, which had no customers, much to his satisfaction.

"Picho, did you go with that wool to th' States last year?" I asked by way o' openin' conversation.

He eyed me with a "you know th' answer to that" look and grinned, "Sí, Señor Zee, I was thee Cap-i-tan."

"Must have been a long hard trip."

"Not for mee, it was just like a leettle ride in thee contry."

"Did Injuns bother ya?"

"Na-a-w, Señor, I seend word to theem that Picho Visciano was Cap-i-tan an' they stayed away."

"Bet th' trail was wet an' muddy."

"Eet was justa right, no mud, but plenty water for thee stock, jist lak I order eet! Wee take th' Cutoff an' eat fresh buffalo ever-ry night."

"How did you like th' States?"

He made a face. "Eet was too crowded, Señor, too many Gr-r-ringros!" He glanced sidewise at me an' chuckled, his belly shaking.

"Did th' wool sell good?"

Visciano threw up his hands in mock surprise at my ignorance, "Deed eet sell good? I savy so! *Ever-ry* onc come home reech, speend much peso in Visciano's cantina!"

"What goods did you return with?"

"Ahhh, Señor," he sighed, "wee geet so much seelver, thee ox not able to haul any more goods an' wee come home eemty save for that seelver." He shook his head in mock regret.

"Such a shame," I said. "I suppose Don Baca and Don Romero plan another trip this year?"

He shrugged, "I not theenk so. Thees year I am too beesy to bee Cap-i-tan an' theese Dons, they no go eef I not go."

His belly shook in mirth and I grinned at him. "May be that I will tell th' Dons *I* will lead them!"

"I don' know eef they take second best or not, but I weel put in thee good word for you, Señor Zee."

· We laughed and I ordered two plates o' huevos ranchos when Asa appeared in the door. A young girl brought out two steaming plates and a platter of tortillas. Asa patted her fanny when Picho wasn't looking an' she gave him a smile and sloshed scalding coffee on his lap. He hollered an' jumped back and Visciano laconically scolded her. She smiled sweetly at Asa and returned to th' kitchen. In a moment we heard cooks laughing and Asa blushed and concentrated on his meal.

"Asa, Picho says they *did* come back with empty wagons. We may have an opportunity to make something here," I said as we left. Asa seemed intent on continuing his siesta. "May be so," he said lazily, "I'll talk t' yuh 'bout it after my nap."

Th' plaza gradually grew quiet as people disappeared for their midday siesta, and though I enjoyed rest myself new prospects and too much leisure time made me restless and I wandered down to th' little Rio Gallinas. We would call it a creek in Arkansas, but it was th' lifeblood of th' town. I didn't have th' money t' buy wagons and stock, much less wool t' put in them, but I sure knew th' trail and something of th' trade. If I could find someone t' finance things, I could make good in th' wool trade and even better by not coming back with empty wagons.

By th' time people began stirring again, I had come upon a plan and hurried off to see Adolph Letcher. He generally left th' store to Charlie's care mornings, but spent his evenings there when trade got brisk. At my first opportunity, I approached Mr. Letcher with a proposition.

"Mr. Letcher, I heard about th' wool train that went in last year and wondered why it wouldn't be successful t' take another train to Missouri an' then bring it back loaded with goods."

"It would sure make sense for anyone to carry a load back

instead of being empty," he replied. "What's on your mind, Ze-nas?"

"I was thinkin' that if I could get up a train of wool, I could take it up th' trail an' haul your goods back and we both could come out good in th' matter."

He looked at me and I knew he was sizing me up, not knowin' who I was or where I came from. "I've been up th' trail for Mr. William Bent several times an' I know how a train operates, but I never have captained one b'fore."

"Takes a lot of money to get up a whole train, Zenas, do you have wagons and stock?"

"No, sir . . ."

"Do you know where you're gonna get the wool?"

"I thought we would buy it or take it on consignment . . ."

"Some of the big growers already have committed their crop to other buyers—but none to go up the trail that I know of. How much are you investing in this enterprise?"

"Well . . ." I didn't want t' tell him I was near broke an' didn't have near enough t' finance th' trip.

"Not much, I warrant."

"No, sir," I replied.

It was awful quiet for a moment an' I b'gan t' think it was a harebrained idea after all. "It was just an idea, Mr. Letcher . . ."

"Well, hold on there a minute and let's think this over a little."

Charlie had been listening and he peeked over Mr. Letcher's shoulder an' nodded and winked. "Sure would be nice to have our own wagons trailing our goods down, it would save on freight and be more reliable too."

"Not interested in ownin' any wagons and stock, but I sure am interested in a reliable freighter instead of depending on any one who came along," Mr. Letcher mused. "Tell you what, Ze-nas, let's think on this a little and maybe by tomorrow night we can come up with a plan. I won't finance th' whole thing, you have t' have some investment in this also, so come back with that in mind."

"Yes, sir."

I could have kicked myself for not thinkin' things through afore I opened my mouth. No one is fool enough t' trust his money to a stranger and I was certainly a stranger to Adolph Letcher as far as business was concerned. Sure, I had t' have something invested in this thing, or there would be no deal. Charlie was sweeping off th' porch when I walked out, deep in thought. I didn't even notice him until he broadsided me in the rear with th' broom.

"Good idea, Zee, but you need t' think th' whole thing out afore you come back. Meet me at Picho's after we close and we'll talk it over."

I nodded. I sure did need some advice on this one, though it might cost my slim purse a meal or two. Asa had shifted around to another wall t' catch th' afternoon sun. He had his knees pulled up an' laid his head on his arms with his sombrero coverin' him, just like I've seen a thousand Mexicans do. I sat down b'side him an' he stirred a little, one eye peekin' out from under th' hat. "Be still, I'm restin'."

Asa was one o' those who thought you could store up sleep an' he spent a good deal of his time storing it. I calculated he had about six months' worth stored at all times. Considerin' I have seen him go four or five days without sleep, there must be some truth in his theory. Just th' same, he always slept enough after one of those sleepless bouts t' make up for what he had lost.

I sat an' thought about what Mr. Letcher had said. I sure wouldn't trust my money and resources t' someone who didn't have anything invested in th' enterprise. I should have thought of that afore talking, but what could I contribute more than just my experience? I went over a list of things we would have t' have an' it came to quite a bit. Camping gear was no problem, but grub was if we ate more than meat we caught along th' way. Mr. Letcher had said he didn't want t' own any wagons or stock, so that side would have t' come from me somehow, but how? It looked hopeless and I practically gave th' whole idea up.

It sure was an opportunity for someone with a little capital t' invest, but not for me. Yet, th' idea stuck in my head an' I couldn't get away from it. I got up and started walking and soon found myself down by th' little river. Out across th' plains I could see sheep and cattle grazing. Maybe a little ride would help clear my head and I could think things through, so I went back and saddled up. My horse was glad t' be out o' th' feed lot an' I gave him his head. He loped off with me payin' little attention where we were goin' until he slowed to a walk an' I looked up t' see that he was heading north on th' Fort Union road.

There seemed t' be a herd o' sheep on every hill. Over there a herd of cattle grazed, watched over by a boy or two. These were milk cows from town that were sent out every day to graze until night and time for milking. It was fun t' watch them return to town. Every cow knew her shed, especially if she had a calf there. All the boys had t' do was trail b'hind them as they made their way down th' street and make sure they had a gate open if no one was there t' greet them, those cows did th' rest.

After a couple of hours, I turned back toward town. I say "turned back" but that isn't exactly what I did, for I had learned never to return th' same way I left—for several reasons—one bein' I had already seen that country and didn't need t' see th' back side of it agin, other times it avoided a possibility that someone who saw me ride out might lay in wait for me t' return th' same way.

("No, sir, don't never come back th' way you went!" Zenas chuckled.)

My turning back took us up a little draw that got narrower and steeper-sided as we went along, so that b'fore I took note, we were where we couldn't climb out.

My philosophy o' not turning back left me with th' only option o' goin' on to th' top o' th' draw. By and by it ended, but it was still so steep I had t' lead my horse up th' side. When I mounted up on top, I saw a herd o' steers scattered over th' plain an' there was something strange about them, so that I rode nearer t' look 'em over. They seemed tame, didn't scatter or run like range cattle, but eyed me an' then continued their grazing. Some were branded, some were not, an' I didn't see a common brand among th' bunch. These were not yearlin's or even three year olds, but somewhat older, some were even shod. It dawned on me that these were not plain steers, but they were oxen. Even stranger still was th' fact that they were a long ways from any ranch and no one was keepin' herd over 'em.

Some of them were lame and I suddenly realized that these were animals turned out and left to their own devices b'cause they had played out or gone lame and were no good to anyone anymore. This renewed my interest and I began looking them over closer. Mostly, they were fat an' sleek an' didn't look played out at all except for ones that were permanently lamed. Not much use for them except for maybe beef an' there was a lot better meat t' be had than an' old tough ox.

Turned out t' fend for themselves, not wanted an' not claimed, most likely left by some pilgrim or trader long gone from these plains, and they herded up with all th' rest that was turned loose. There must have been upwards of two hundred head scattered over several acres of prairie and it seemed t' me that full three quarters of them were fit enough t' pull a wagon again. *There for th' takin', but what good were they without wagons t' pull?* I thought as I rode slowly back to town. Who would take a chance on buyin' an animal that might be claimed by its old owner th' first time he saw he was fit agin? Still, there was a resource there for us t' think about.

It was just getting good an' dark when I rode into town and I headed for th' stable. By th' time I had put my horse up, stores were closing and there was a crowd headin' across th' plaza to Picho's. Asa was lounging around th' door wonderin' when I would come an' buy him supper. That boy sure ate good off my purse an' I would sure be glad when his purse jingled agin. Charlie waved us over to his table and we sat down.

"I already ordered us some grub and you're just in time," he said as that same little waitress approached with an armload of plates. She glared at Asa an' passed his plate from across th' table. He grinned but didn't say anything. We ate in silence, then ordered sopapillas and honey.

"Thought any more about your wool train?" Charlie asked as he poured honey into his sopapilla.

"Sure," I said as if I could think of anything else. "I got an idea where I can get a herd of oxen, but I don't know where wagons'll come from."

Asa was eyein' th' waitress an' not payin' a bit of attention to our conversation. I acted like I was shiftin' my position an' kicked his shin under th' table. He jumped an' glared at me.

Charlie grinned. "How many wagons do you plan on?" he asked.

"Don't know, probably depends on how much wool we can gather and how many drivers we can git."

Asa's eyes wandered back to th' waitress an' I shifted my feet agin. He caught th' movement an' turned sideways in his chair.

"I know a lot of little sheepmen around and it's possible we might get them to give us wool on consignment and even drive a wagon." Charlie joined our enterprise just as easy as that and

219

I was glad he did. "Mr. Letcher might be interested in investing in the train if we can convince him that you can do the job," he continued. "I don't think any big ranchers would be interested. Most of them have already committed their crop to others."

"How much wool will th' little people have?" I asked.

"A few of them may have as much as a wagon load, but most of them will have less. I know one who has black sheep and his wool will bring premium prices here. I assume it would be th' same in Missouri."

"I should think so," I said, though I didn't know a thing about th' wool market.

Charlie nodded. He understood how new I was t' wool tradin'. "I'll write to some merchants at Freeport and see if they can give us an idea about prices."

"We still have t' git wagons from somewheres . . ." I started to say.

"I kin git yuh all th' wagons ya want an' mostly fer free," Asa interrupted.

I kicked his chair. "Turn around here an' pay attention, I'm not useter talking t' th' back o' someone's head!"

He turned back to th' table grinning. "Don't think it'll cost one dime, either, but they'll be a lot o' work to it."

"What are you talking about us doin', stealin' wagons?" He could be so frustratin' at times.

"Nope, not talking 'bout stealin'. Didjuh ever look at all that junk piled up b'hind th' smithy at Union? They's enough junk t' make a dozen wagons with a little work. I heard some captain fussin' 'at th' mess had t' be cleaned up but th' men are too busy fixin' other things t' git it done. Might be they would even pay a couple o' men t' clean it up."

I looked at Charlie an' he was grinnin'. "Good idea, Asa!"

"Pieced-together wagons'd never make a trip t' Missouri an' back," I said.

"They only have t' make it *there,* Zee, then we could buy us decent wagons fer th' trip back."

"I'll have t' think this one out," I said.

"Well, while you're a-thinkin' I'm gonna go up t' Union first thing in th' mornin' an' see if we can git a job cleanin' up that junkyard." Asa slapped th' table top.

"An' I guess yuh expect me t' help you whether your idea works out or not?" I asked.

"Shore, we're partners ain't we?"

Charlie laughed. "He has a point, Zee, if you could go back up the trail a ways, there are a lot of abandoned wagons along the way. You could probably piece together several out of them and the junk pile."

Mostly, Asa's ideas were pretty far-fetched, but ever' once in a while he came up with a good one. This just might be one of them, I thought.

"I've gotta get up early tomorrow to open the store on time, so I'll leave you two to work out the details. Let me know what you come up with," Charlie said and with that he left us.

All tables were full an' there were people waitin' t' be seated so we headed toward th' door. Asa led out an' I followed until I noticed he was detourin' considerable and when I saw th' little waitress in his path, I cut straight to th' door. Just as I got there, I heard a scream an' th' clatter o' plates fallin'. I didn't look back.

I was already bedded down when Asa finally showed up. "Been sweepin' up glass?" I asked, to which I only got a grunt.

We talked a long time about our possibilities and finally decided that I would see if I could get those oxen moved to a good shelter for th' winter while Asa looked to things at Fort Union. Early next morning he was on his way as I was ridin' out to where I last saw th' cattle. They were mostly bedded down when I came up on them and I left them alone for th' time bein' while I searched out a good place t' keep them. A few miles east, I came up on top of a bluff. There looked like a small creek runnin' along th' foot of it an' I rode along th' top until I found a place to get down to the creek. There was only a trickle o' water. I rode back down under th' bluff an' looked things over. The bluff was on the northwest side of th' creek runnin' mostly northeast. It would give good shelter from storms.

A shelf of rock ran along th' bottom of th' bluff about ten to twelve feet above th' creek. There was a nice pool there an' from th' amount of water flowin' out of it, I deduced that there were springs comin' out from under th' rock. This shelf had a flat ten to fifteen feet wide, then th' bluff ran steeply to th' top. The north end tapered off to nothing, leaving the south end the only way accessible to th' shelf. It would be easy to fence off and provide a good pen for horses an' a sheltered place t' work on wagons. We could dig a dugout into th' bank for our shelter. I liked th' layout and it was remote to th' trail, so no one would be interferin' with us unless Injuns found us, which was unlikely in winter. It looked ideal for our purposes. There was plenty of grass around.

We could cut out any cattle we wanted an' they would come through th' winter fine in that little valley. I rode a little north of west from there, reckonin' th' fort t' be in that direction. It was, but it was farther than I expected, near twenty miles from th' bluff. I struck th' road from Las Vegas an' headed for th' fort. A rider was comin' that looked an awful lot like Asa, so I pulled up an' waited on him. We rode off th' road an' set our horses t' grazin' while we talked.

"You'll never believe it, but that captain is gonna *pay* us *cash* not scrip' t' move that junk!" Asa grinned. "Th' stuff was pretty picked over in places, but we can still git several wagons out'n it. Smithy said there were several abandoned wagons along th' trail from there t' Rayado Mesa. Th' hardest part will be findin' enough wheels t' go around."

I told him about th' bluff I found and how it would make a good winterin' spot. Only thing I didn't mention was how far away it was. We talked it over an' decided that we would have to hire someone t' help us an' we would have t' have a working wagon t' haul junk away. We would sort out things we wanted and dump th' rest in some ravine out of sight. Asa agreed we should keep what we were up to a secret.

That summer there had been an orphaned kid come down th' trail with some train an' they left him at th' fort. He hung around there until they run him off. Asa had seen him at Loma Parda where he picked up an odd chore here and there. He had pointed him out to me at Las Vegas and I hadn't thought anything of it, but now it occurred t' both of us that he might work out as a hand and be affordable for us t' hire. As luck would have it, there he was at th' livery cleanin' out stalls when we rode up.

"Hi there, Hard, watcha up to?" Asa called. Th' boy stopped cleanin' and grinned at Asa. "Jist aworkin fer my dinner, Asa, how er you?"

Hardy McEwel was thirteen or fourteen when I met him. He was small an' thin as a rail with black hair. Th' size of his hands and feet showed that if he growed into them he would become a big man—if he didn't starve before then. He wore someone's cast-off linsey-woolsey shirt with pegs for buttons and his ragged pants showed hide in places. He held them up by a cord tied around two front belt loops and he was barefooted. By contrast, he was surprisingly clean, a habit he kept all th' time I knew him.

"How would yuh like t' have reg'lar food an' a place t' sleep?" Asa asked.

"Sounds good t' me," he replied, "I ain't et reg'lar in a long time."

He grinned and I noted his teeth were even and white. It reminded me of that Biblical curse God made, "I will give you cleanness of teeth," meanin' they would have no food. Here stood a prime example of that.

"This here's my pardner Zenas Meeker an' we just might have a job for you. Hang around after you finish cleanin'. We'll be back t' talk."

Letcher's emporium was closed when we passed by an' we hurried over to Picho's. We almost ran into Charlie as he was leavin'. Th' place was almost empty so he returned with us an' we talked while our order was filled. I told him what I had found and Asa talked about what he had done at th' fort.

"It all sounds good if you can make it work. We won't tell Mr. Letcher about our plans until we see how it works out. Come by the store in the morning and I will give you some tools t' work with."

He hurried off on some errand an' we ordered supper. When it came, I ordered another meal t' take to Hardy an' we found him propped agin th' barn wall watchin' th' world go by.

"How 'bout some supper, Hardy?" Asa asked as I handed him th' plate.

His face lit up. "Shore would be nice."

He took a napkin off th' top an' tucked it into his collar. For a moment he just looked things over. I had ordered a double serving of lamb chops; there was a heap of still steamin' rice, Indian beans, and green chili with tortilla bread. Th' livery man—I think it was ol' Luke Evans—grunted an' disappeared inside. He returned with a steaming cup o' coffee. "Here, boy, you'll need somethin t' wash all thet down with." He winked at me.

Worst place in th' world t' talk private business is in front of a livery man. They love news and th' spreadin' of it an' they have a large audience day to day, so we sat an' visited while Hardy ate in silence except for an occasional grunt of contentment. When he finished, th' plate was as clean as if it had been washed an' lamb bones looked like they had been polished. He spread his napkin over th' plate an' said, "I shore thank you for that meal, it jist mought serve me two–three days worth!"

He gave a sideways glance at Luke who had resumed his whittling. Asa grabbed th' plate. "I'll take this back t' Ma Picho," he grinned, an' I knowed we wouldn't see him agin that night.

I stood up and stretched, "Hardy, I gotta go rub down my horse an' it looks like we lost Asa for th' night, give you a nickel t' rub his horse down."

"Why shore, Mr. Zee, I'll do that fer nothin', considerin' that feed yuh jest gave me."

We gathered up a couple of curry combs an' wandered out in th' lot where our horses were. In low tones I told th' boy what we needed an' what we could pay him for a winter's work.

"So long's its honest work, I'm yore man. I'll do anythin' that don't git me in jail er strung up!" He laughed. We shook on it an' our deal was done.

"We want t' keep quiet so's no one will horn in on our doin's," I said, "so keep this to yourself, meet us back here at sunrise, an' we'll be on our way."

With that, I turned in an' Hardy ambled back to th' front an' sat with Evans. I could still hear th' mutter o' their voices as I drifted off. Asa showed up sometime in th' night an I had t' roust him out in th' morning in spite o' th' fact we had a busy day ahead of us.

Sunrise found us headin' northeast, loaded down with provisions from Letcher's. Charlie had me sign for them. Here we were startin' out on an enterprise some would call harebrained— an' we were already in debt! Only a couple o' young fools woulda done it, and I guess we fit th' bill! Our horses was so loaded that we had t' walk an' we could see there was no way t' gather cattle, so we made tracks for th' bluff. It was near thirty miles from Las Vegas an' we didn't git there until after sunset.

I dumped chips we had gathered while th' boys unloaded horses an' Hardy led 'em to water. When he brought them back, he busied himself makin' a rope fence across th' mouth o' th' bench. It wasn't long 'til we had water boilin'. Coffee an' cans o' t'maters made supper. We talked a long time about what needed t' be done as light faded. By th' time it was pure dark, we had planned out th' next few days. It was frustratin' t' me that none o' those chores included herdin' cattle. It bothered me a lot so next morning, I said, "Boys if we git all these other things done an' don't have th' oxen safe, we're gonna be doin' it fer nothin'. I say let's git them safe an' in our control an' *then* we can settle on those other things."

They agreed, so soon's breakfast was over, we headed fer th' herd, Hardy ridin' double with Asa. He had come up with a pair of moccasins from somewheres an' tied them on when we mounted. We didn't take time t' sort th' oxen, just gathered them all an' headed them for th' little valley. Bein' half tame, they were surprisingly easy t' herd. Asa an' I kept them bunched while Hardy trotted along b'hind. Soon th' lame an' broke-down began t' drag. When it seemed they were all separated from sounder animals, we hazed them back th' way they had come an' they were glad t' go. It made th' sound oxen want t' follow an' we had a time keeping them headed right for a while.

When an ox pulled up lame an' dropped back, we would haze him back th' way we had come an' he seemed content to stay. We hadn't counted on sortin' them this way, but it worked out good for us. By th' end of th' drive we had forty-seven head that seemed sound even if not all of them were fit yet. A twenty mile dry haul made them glad t' see water an' by sundown they were bedded down seemin' content t' stay.

"I guess it's so much like drivin' th' trail that they're satisfied with it all," Asa said as he sat his tired horse an' looked over th' herd.

"Just th' same, I think we better keep a watch over them through th' night," I said.

He gave a groan, but agreed. "Let Hard have first watch an' we'll draw straws t' see who gits last watch."

"That's all right," I replied. "I'll take last watch if you don't want it."

"Good," he grinned, not realizin' that I would have uninterrupted sleep while he had t' get up in th' middle of his. I was surprised he hadn't thought o' that with all th' trail experience he had. Musta been pretty tired, but by bedtime he had rested enough t' figger it out.

"Doggonit, Zee, you flimflammed me out of a good night's sleep."

"Didn't either, you made th' choice."

Hardy ducked his head t' hide his grin.

"Just th' same, next time *I* git last watch!"

"We could draw stra . . ."

"No way!" he interrupted.

I just grinned an' headed for my bedroll, "Better git t' bed, Asa, yuh only got four hours til yore watch." I heard a gravel bounce b'hind me. "Missed me."

"Ef I'da *tried*, I wouldn't of!"

Even getting uninterrupted sleep, I wasn't ready when Asa called me. It was gonna take time t' get hardened up to this work, and I suspected he had cut his watch short just to spite me. A look at the big dipper and a long time to sunrise confirmed my suspicion.

CHAPTER 25
THE BLUE OX

Oxen b'gan t' stir with th' coming light an' I hurried up and counted them when I could see well enough. Then I counted them agin.

Hardy was watchin' from th' bench an' he called, "I counted forty-eight too, Mr. Zee." I could tell I was gonna like this boy, he was savvy.

Asa stood up from th' fire. "That blue ox that fell out last has come in with th' herd," he called pointing.

Sure enough, there he stood, fat an' sleek. We had been sorry t' see him limping along, but he would not be any good to us lame. I rode over an' looked him over. Oxen are different from range cattle in that they are used to a man bein' on foot, so he only shied a little when I got down and approached him.

"Seemed like it was his fore gee hoof," Asa called, and I had t' walk around t' th' other side to look. He didn't resist when I lifted his foot. All I could see was a little seep o' blood in th' middle of his hoof. He flinched when I touched it and I felt something hard under th' surface.

"Got a stob or somethin' in there," I called. "We'll probably have t' rope him down t' get it out."

"Breakfast's ready," Asa called.

After we ate, Asa pulled a pair of tongs out of our plunder an' I saddled his horse while mine rested. We caught Blue an' led him out of th' herd. He was some rested an' didn't limp much, but if he had t' go far, we could tell he wouldn't do so good.

"Want me t' bust him?" I asked.

"May not have to," Asa said, "let's try it with him standin'."

I got down an' we necked Asa's pony to th' ox. That horse didn't like it much but after a while he got still an' we went to work. Hardy held their heads and I lifted th' hoof off th' ground.

"Whatever that is, it's in there good," Asa said.

"Use your knife; if it's wood you can pry it out some where you can get the tongs on it," I suggested.

Asa got out his pointed blade and poked around in th' wound. Blue flinched and I braced myself for a struggle.

"Scratch b'tween his ears, Hardy,"

He started talking soft t' th' cow an' Asa worked a little more. "Hope that's th' stob an' not some bone," he muttered. He pried and pulled up an' the knife slipped out. "Didn't hold."

"Try again."

I could feel th' leg tremble when he poked with th' knife. After a moment, he said, "I think I got it," and pulled the knife up. This time something moved and he pulled it almost to the surface before losing hold.

I could see a lump in th' skin. "See if you can push it to th' hole," I suggested.

Asa pushed and the skin moved so that the end of the object poked out. "Now!"

Asa dropped his knife and reached for the tongs. Clampin' on, he pulled and a thorn came and came until he had it out. It was almost three inches long!

"Good golly, would you look at that!" Asa exclaimed as he held it up. "Looky what was in yer foot, Blue!" He waved it in front of th' ox and he showed white in his eyes.

"Think he understands you," Hardy grunted trying to hold on.

I pressed on the hoof and pus ran out until it bled. "Maybe it's cleaned out," I said and let th' hoof down.

Blue calmed enough so that we could release him from th' pony. He just stood there shakin' his head while th' horse was glad t' put distance b'tween them.

Hardy scratched his ears and nose. "Wonder how many of those other lames have th' same problem."

"We may have to find out," I said, not relishin' *that* idea.

"What now?" Asa asked, rubbin' his hands on his pants.

"First on our list was to see about th' junk at th' fort, we better get started afore that captain hires someone else," I said.

We left Hardy to tend to camp and cattle and rode for th' fort. It came in sight late in the afternoon an' we looked up th' captain t' let him know we were on th' job. "Good!" He nodded. "The sooner that mess is gone the better!"

"We'll not stop afore it's gone," Asa assured, "but we *will* have to be gone a day or two from time to time t' dispose o' th' stuff."

"I understand that," the captain said impatiently, "just keep at it. I expect it to be all gone by spring."

We asked to be paid a dollar a wagon every tenth load, which was agreeable with the captain.

"Now to find that wagon," Asa whispered as we walked away.

It sure was discouraging t' see that mess. There was maybe five acres of it all piled just where it had been thrown. Some of it had been picked over and there weren't many good wheels in th' lot, which made sense since they would get th' bulk of wear and tear and be more in demand.

"Gonna have t' build a lot of wheels," I muttered.

"Yeah, I figger that'll be our biggest worry," Asa replied.

We found a wagon bed t' serve as a wind break and laid out our bedroll, hobbled th' horses an' let 'em graze on what little grass as was left, and headed for th' sutler's. When Asa saw a crowd of soldiers in th' store, he suddenly decided t' check on th' horses an' left. Th' memory of his bath was still fresh an' he didn't want no reminders of it from them. I only stayed a minute or two; th' crowd was jolly in their cups but I knew there would be a brouhaha b'fore night was over.

Asa had a little fire goin' when I got to camp. "No lack o' firewood in this boneyard," he said as I walked up. We had a cup of coffee an' turned in early. Coffee an' canned peaches served for breakfast an' we were soon pickin' through junk. There were all brands of wagon in that pile, Studebakers, Mitchels, Conestogas, an' a hundred nondescripts made by some smithy 'way back east. I carried a spoke with me an' it was cause for more than one rattlesnake death that day.

As it turned out, th' best bed in th' yard was th' one we had slept under. We pulled out a rear axle, a front axle, an' dragged up a tongue from somewhere. There were several ox yokes an' we gathered several decent bows out of th' pile. Soon we had th' makin's o' a whole wagon but for th' wheels. Ever' one we found was busted in some way or another. Asa kept diggin' deeper an' deeper in th' piles. 'Way out in th' middle, he looked under an overturned bed an' gave a yelp.

"Kill 'im," I called thinking he had found another rattler, but he paid no mind, instead gruntin' an tiltin' th' old bed over.

"Wheels!" he called an' I scrambled over to see. Someone had piled up maybe fifteen or twenty wheels an' covered them with that old bed. O'course, none were whole, but with a little work, they could be repaired.

"Looks like we're in business, Zee!"

"Shore 'nough!" I replied. We cleared off a spot right there by th' pile an' began sortin' through finding th' best wheels. By pickin' and piecin' we had four decent wheels that fit our axles by midafternoon, only they were so dry they were loose. A good night's soakin' in th' river tightened them up an' by noon th' next day we had a wagon on its wheels.

We got a good tar bucket by stackin' two together, one coverin' holes in t'other. With a lot of scrapin' an' cussin', we rounded up maybe a half bucket full of tar, enough t' grease wheels for a while.

"Why didn't we think enough t' bring a yoke o' oxen with us?" I asked.

"Don' know, but we sure could use 'em now," Asa grunted.

We picked through th' yard for a couple of days until we had a couple of loads of gear sorted out and ready t' haul, but we still hadn't solved th' oxen problem. I kept tryin' t' solve it without makin a sixty-mile round trip to camp and back.

"May as well give in, Zee an' light out fer camp," Asa kept sayin', but I guess I had a stubborn streak about it. Still, no other solution showed up an' on the fourth day I set out for camp while Asa stayed and sorted junk. He was sure enjoyin' th' work an' I was glad he had found something he would do without coaxin'.

Hardy had been busy in our absence. He had half a dugout cut down to bedrock and a pretty neat camp set up on th' bench. It was a wonder he had time t' do all that an' still herd cattle to grass every day, but there it was. Two oxen would have done, but Hardy convinced me t' take four. "You can see what kind of workers they are; it'd be good t' have a spare yoke if you need 'em."

It made sense, so bright an' early next morning he picked out four he liked an' sent me on my way. Two had th' same brand and must have been paired together at one time. Th' other two were ones he had noticed as likely to be good pullers. Off we went northwest to Rio Mora where there was a trail of sorts along th' south bank. We were always careful t' hide our trail to camp so no one would suspect that there was anything there.

Drivin' four cattle made th' trip a lot slower an' I was obliged t' spend th' night at th' mouth of Wolf Creek where Valmora is today. We ambled into th' fort midmorning and I was really surprised t' find *two* wagons loaded and ready to go!

Asa was proud as a peacock. He had gone in to th' blacksmith t' borrow some tools an' found him ready t' junk out and discard an old trail-worn wagon. Asa had talked him into leaving wheels on it an' had pulled it out to th' yard with a "borrowed" army mule. By th' time I got there, he had loaded both wagons an' was sorting through th' yard pickin' out a third load while waitin' on me.

I sure was glad I had brought two yoke of oxen. Those two wagons had enough hardware and lumber to make two more wagons. He even had enough material to make up wheels and had wrecked out enough beds, sideboards, and overjets to make beds. There were even a couple of tar buckets filled with nails and bolts.

"They's two overjets fer ever' wagon carcass out here," he said.

"We ought to keep some o' th' best ones for our use," I surmised.

"Not a bad idea." Asa was eyeing th' oxen speculatively an' pickin through yokes. "Let's git hitched up an' go."

It took a couple of trials t' get right-sized yokes. We tried to hook up th' paired oxen backwards to what they were accustomed but they soon had us straightened out. We pulled out within an hour, takin' th' trail to Las Vegas. Asa an' I walked b'side our teams, my horse tied to th' tailgate of my lead wagon. At a likely spot past Mora crossing we turned off and headed over th' hills to camp. Night caught us on th' divide an' we made a dry camp. Th' oxen seemed to make it well but they would be sore in th' morning so we gave them a little extra time before moving out. They would be thirsty before we got to camp, but so would we, having run out of chuck and water.

That first trip to Fort Union set a pattern for our days and we spent the next four months hauling parts and building wagons. We averaged about two wagons a week, sometimes having t' wait a while until wheels could be repaired and assembled. Asa and Hardy proved to be good mechanics and I kept busy with th' herd and camp.

Charlie rode out about once a month an' brought us grub an' other supplies. On his first trip he brought us a couple of branding irons he had registered for us. It was th' Rafter CHAZ an' we set to brandin' our cattle. Hardy was proud he was included an' we made him a full partner in th' deal. We managed t' pair up an' use every ox on our trips to an' from th' fort and with one or two exceptions they all worked out well. With our first pay we bought two loads of hay and paid off some of our tab at Letcher's.

Winters can be hard on th' high plains, as you know, an' that year was no exception. We were able to work most days, either out in th' open or on th' shelf by our make-do smithy fire. Our original herd of forty-eight head gradually grew in number through th' winter as we worked th' "lame" herd for more that had healed enough t' be some good, an' by th' first of March we had fifty-two or fifty-four head, sleek and fit. By April of '69 we had twenty-five wagons ready. Camp looked like a wagon yard on th' Fourth of July.

Blacksmiths at th' fort had been watchin' our progress on th' junkyard with growin' concern an' one day th' captain came out to see us. "The Smithys are complaining that we are eliminating their spare parts pile, so I guess we had better quit the clean-up," he said, looking over the yard. We had sorted an' piled iron up in one place an' piled useless wood for burnin'.

"You men have done a good job here. Come by the office this afternoon and I will pay you off."

That was good enough for us, savin' us th' trouble of haulin' all that iron off somewheres an' savin' us three or four days' work to boot. After we ate lunch, Asa disappeared for a few minutes an' when he returned he had a big grin on his face. "I struck a deal t' sell firewood!"

"Firewood, what fire . . ."

"That pile we got there," he interrupted

"Should have thought o' that myself," I said.

"Th'washerwomen hev bought it at two dollars a cord, delivered."

I groaned at the word *delivered* but he had struck a good deal. We hauled two loads to the washroom an' stacked it by th' door. Our Irish sergeant was glad to see it, though they would still have t' cut most of it into workable lengths. We haggled a while an' finally settled on two an' a half cords an' five dollars, silver. Asa had become friendly with the women and visited them often.

("I allus suspicioned one of them was still giving him a bath on a fairly regular basis." Zenas was grinning when I looked up from my notes.)

Th' captain wasn't in his office when we got there an' we had t' wait a few minutes on him. He sat down at his desk an' pulled out an account book. "I counted eight loads that you haven't been paid for, is that what you count?" He didn't wait for an answer, just began writing as if we had agreed.

"Hold on there, Captain," Asa said, "that ain't all we done!"

Th' captain looked up with raised eyebrows. You could tell he wasn't used t' bein' corrected by a common workman.

"Oh?"

"We hauled off two loads of scrap wood this afternoon . . ."

". . . And that iron we sorted an' had t' leave would have

235

made two more loads we was shorted," I put in.

"I can't pay you for the loads you *didn't* haul."

"It ought t' be worth something bein' we gathered an' sorted it so's th' smithys don't have t' dig around for parts they're looking for," I replied.

He stared at us a minute, tapping his finger on th' desk. "How many loads of iron did you leave out there? Two loads of wood, you say, where did you haul them?"

"We sold them for firewood," Asa said without mentioning where they went, "an' they's at least three loads o' iron left b'hind."

"More like two—two and a half loads an' the wood went to the wash house, I'll bet," th' captain grinned in self satisfaction. "I'll pay you fifty cents a load for that since you didn't haul it far and got paid for it to boot."

"Most o' th' work is in th' gatherin' an' unloadin'," Asa argued.

"True, but our agreement doesn't include the unloading, the women paid you for that!"

"If you pay us half for those loads, how 'bout payin' us half for th' gathered, sorted, an' stacked iron?" I asked.

I could see patience wearin' pretty thin on th' captain's face. He stared at me for a minute an' I held his gaze without blinkin'. "What's fair is fair."

"All right, I'll do that, eight loads at a dollar each, two at fifty cents, and two and a half loads of iron at fifty cents."

"Three . . ." Asa never finished 'cause my elbow caught him in th' ribs.

"Good enough, sir," I said.

"Ten dollars, two bits." The captain nodded, writing in his ledger. He unlocked a drawer an' counted out coins. "There you are, men, you did a good job on time, and drove a hard bargain to boot."

He grinned an' I knew he thought *he* had drawn th' bargain. Asa pocketed money while I thanked th' captain and we left.

"Well, what now, Zee?" he asked as we headed for th' wagons.

"We have a couple o' days t' play with, why don't we get down to Vegas an' see how Charlie is doin' with wool buyin'?"

"Good 'nough fer me, I been hankerin' fer a good Visciano dinner!"

"Does that include a dinner *server*?" I asked. He just grunted and headed for th' lead wagon.

CHAPTER 26
A CHANGE OF PLANS

We bought two loads of hay on the way to town an' pulled into the lot after dark. I piled into the hay an' fell asleep listening to the oxen munching their supper.

There was just a little streak of light on th' horizon when I heard Asa stirrin' around an' talking to th' oxen. We shook off straw, washed our faces in th' water trough, and combed our hair. A fresh shirt from our possibles bags made us presentable an' we headed for Visciano's. The place was already filling up, mostly with Anglos, it bein' too early for the Mexican Americans. Picho was behind th' bar lookin' ruffled an' sleepy. Asa's serving girl was nowhere to be seen and we were almost seated when Visciano called out, "Seeñor Zee, we are serving huevos ranchos an' steak for breakfast, no?"

"Sí, Picho, make that three plates, all over easy," I called.

It was only a moment before three plates appeared through th' kitchen window an' Visciano called, "Heere is your plates, Señors."

Asa grunted, "Must be breakfast *without* service. What's thet third plate for, you expectin' company?"

"Nope, I'm too hungry for one plate so I thought we could split one an' it would be 'bout enough, especially since you're payin'."

He started to protest then remembered the money an' grinned. We lingered over hot coffee an' watched th' crowd comin' an' goin'. Asa took our mugs to th' bar for refills from th' "server," whose only apparent job that morning was to hold down th' bar and pass plates.

"Gets any worse an' we'll have t' cook our own breakfast," he complained.

"No, Señor, thee cook, she no let strangers een her keechin," Picho called. His serious expression made us smile.

"Charlie must take his breakfast at his boarding house. I guess he'll be opening up soon," I said. Asa wasn't listenin' too close, he kept looking around an' only grunted in reply.

"That girl ain't here, Asa, maybe she's married an' got a baby by now." That drew a dirty look, but he didn't say anything, only turned to his coffee.

We waited 'til after th' morning rush was over, then ambled over to Letcher's store. Charlie was clearing th' counter an' straightening up when we walked in. He looked up and I could see his features sag when he recognized us, "Hello, boys," he called but it wasn't a cheerful call.

I knew there must not be good news. "What's up, Charlie?"

"I haven't got any wool, and I won't get any!"

His face seemed t' get longer an' longer. I had t'stand there a moment t' let it soak in what he had just said. We had figured he would have it all bought up or committed by now.

Asa blew like he had been hit in th' gut an' his face turned pale, then got red, "Whut happent, Charlie?"

"Some Frenchman from Mexico came in here and bought all the wool on the hoof and at premium prices. I don't know how he's gonna make anything out of it. Mr. Letcher figures he's working for the French government or something like that. Anyway, he's just finishing up shearing. He's been hiring transportation now and I told him about our wagons—how they would carry more and were faster than those two-wheel Mex carts. He seemed interested, only thing is we don't have near enough wagons to carry a whole crop."

"Not much chance we can get more, either," I said. My head was kind of swimmy from takin' in all he had said.

"Mr. Letcher thinks we could contract with him—the Frenchman I mean—to fill what wagons we got."

"Ef he ain't got all he needs by now!" Asa put in. "Boy, what a mess!"

"All's not lost, Asa," Charlie said, "we still have wagons and oxen and they have value, either hauling wool or selling to pilgrims on the trail."

It was real quiet for a few minutes, each of us in our own thoughts, Charlie resumed his work an' Asa walked around th' big room kickin' an' mumblin'. I sat on a crate by th' big stove an' just thought.

"Air we gonna sit 'ound here all day mopin' or air we gonna *do* something?" Asa was always a little impatient.

"I suppose it wouldn't hurt t' go talk to the Frenchman," I answered.

"Well come on, don't jist set there." He headed for th' door.

"An' just where are you gonna find him?" I called, but th' galoot was already halfway across th' street heading for the wagon lot.

"Looks like you're on your way." Charlie smiled. "They are shearing at Romero's and Baca's. You'll find the Frenchman at one of those places, most likely. His name is Muer."

There wasn't any hurry, Asa would have to rent a horse and I would be saddled and ready before he got done at th' livery. Sure 'nough as I rounded th' corner he was mountin' up.

"Where're you goin', Asa?"

"He's at Baca's."

"Or Romero's."

"Nope, fellow jist told me he was at Baca's."

The livery man Evans stood in the doorway, perpetual pipe in mouth, hands in pockets.

"Let's go!" Asa pulled around and headed up th' street.

After our horses had loped a ways to warm up, we slowed to a walk and I asked, "What are we gonna say to th' man?"

Asa frowned at my question. "I guess we can ask him if th' moon is made of cheese, or we *might* ask him if he needs any wagons t' haul his wool."

"We *might* ask him what his rate is, or where he's goin', or how long he expects it t' take. Maybe we should ask him how we're gonna eat on th' road an' what about feed an' water for th' animals. It *might* be good t' know who gits th' wool, when we get paid, an' who pays. It *might* be good t' know where th' war is, 'cause there's *always* a war in Mexico an' I don't want near it, that's what we *might* ask!"

Talk about half cocked and Asa would fit the description to a *T*! "All them things, Zee?"

"And more! I want t' know all about this enterprise afore risking our wagons and animals when there's little risk in sellin' them to pilgrims."

"I guess yore right."

"I *know* I'm right. I won't commit to this until I know *all* there is to know about it."

"You think it might be shady?"

"Who knows? It's up to us t' find that out an' d'cide if we want in or not."

Asa was quiet and "hurry" left him. We rode a long while afore he spoke again. "I didn't think about all them things, Zee, but I'm shore glad you did. I never was long on thinkin' or slow 'bout decidin' somethin'—I'm a doer, not a thinker, I guess."

"You can always change, may be that comes with experience. I spent a lot of time watchin' Bents an' St. Vrains working th' trade business. They was always cautious an' you never knew what cards they held 'til th' deal was done—they hardly ever lost."

"What we gonna do, then?"

"Let's don't let on we have anything to offer an' just nose around a little, see what th' operation is an' if we like it. We can afford t' wait a day or two afore we commit ourselves."

"I guess we could just be two fellers that happened along an' stopped t'visit."

"Yeah, we could do that."

He spent the rest of our ride plottin' how he was gonna nose out all there was to know about the business. As we neared Romero's, I said, "Let's split up after we get there and try t' find out all we can. We can leave after a couple of hours an' mosey over to Baca's."

Asa nodded as we rode into Romero's placita. Don Casimero Romero was sitting under th' ramada watchin' th' goin's-on an' we rode up to give our respects and introduce ourselves. He rose and invited us to step down in th' gracious way of their custom, offering us water from the olla hanging on a rafter cooling. At the wave of his hand, two boys came and led our horses away. Asa excused himself an' wandered down to the shed to watch th' shearing. I sipped a dipper of cold water and the Don motioned me to a chair. We sat and visited a while. That water was good and it was cold and I commented on it.

"Yes, we have a very good spring. Some say it is the sweetest water around."

He was pleased at my compliment. His speech was perfect, not like the common Mex-English mixture an' I didn't speak *any* Spanish for fear of showing my poor grasp of th' language. A low murmur came from the shearing shed an' I said, "Looks like you will have a good crop this year, Don Romero."

"Yes, much grass in the summer and the cold winter has been generous to us."

"Are you going to take the wool to the States this year?"

"No, I have sold my crop to Señor Muer, a man from Mexico.

He has bought nearly all the wool in the country at a very good price."

"It is good that you have all done well."

"Yes, it will help the poor herders much and to sell this way is no risk for us. Are you going to offer your wagons for hire?" He glanced at me from the corner of his eye and smiled.

"I thought we had kept the wagons a good secret."

"There are few secrets in this land of few people and the herders love to talk of what they have seen on the plains."

I hadn't seen any herders around our camp and it's still a mystery to me how they knew. I have learned that what the Don said about secrets is true and the Mexican is expert at rooting them out.

"We are thinking about it," I said, "it might be a way to regain our investment," which wasn't much more than our labors, though I didn't say so.

"I think the greatest risk will be in the shipping, though the price offered is good and my people are anxious to go."

His tone said much more than his words and I took note.

"Where is the wool going?"

"He talks of Indianola or Brownsville or Vera Cruz. I think it will be Vera Cruz." He said the name as if it were two words.

"Overseas."

"Yes, maybe to Haiti, but I think more likely Europe."

"It's a long dry haul to Veracruz."

"And especially in the summer months."

"You have been there, Don Romero?"

"Once when I was young we went to the City of Mexico. It is a dry and weary trip."

"As dry as the Cimarron Cutoff, I suppose."

"Oh it is much drier and the few waterings are poor, much dust and little grass."

I wondered if the Don might be discouraging me so his

people could carry the cargo in their squealing carts instead of my wagons, but he was an honorable man and I valued his advice, though it wasn't given as such. We talked of other things and when the conversation lagged, I thanked him for his hospitality and excused myself. He nodded, and I wandered down to the shed. The work was interesting and I stood around and watched for quite a while.

Asa was nowhere in sight. Presently he appeared from behind the shed, talking and laughing with a young man who was obviously a herder. He gave me a casual wave, but continued talking with the herder. It must have been his sheep getting sheared, for periodically the two of them would herd the sheared sheep around the shed to a holding pen.

As the shearers finished with the sheep in the herd, another herd was led into the pen and after a long drink, the shearers began on the next bunch. I followed Asa and the herder around to his pen and it was amusing to see the sheared sheep turned out. They ran and jumped like lambs, glad to be free of the weight of the wool.

Asa looked at me and grinned. "You seen enough, Zee?"

"About time we moseyed on, I guess," and we headed for th' horses tied in the shade of a small elm. Giving Don Romero a tip of the sombrero, we rode out.

"Almost ever' cart in th' country has been hired an' even th' herders are rarin' t' go too. Th' Dons may have trouble keepin' them." Asa was bubbling with information. "The price is very good and they will only go to Chihuahua. We could make th' trip in half th' time of the carts an' meet them on th' way back! How was your visit with Don Romero?"

"Very good," I said, not wanting to expand on that and spoil his enthusiasm.

★ ★ ★ ★ ★

The trail from Romero's to Baca's was well worn, the two families being close and tied by intermarriages. They both go back a long ways, their families being among th' first to inhabit the new frontier of this Mora–Las Vegas district. They had ranged over much of the region, Casimero Romero later built a plaza an' ran sheep on th' Canadian where Tascosa, Texas, is now. He and Agapito Sandoval moved out there after th' Indian question was settled. In 1875, Charlie Goodnight headed east for Palo Duro Canyon grasses from his Colorado ranch with 1600 head of cattle. When he heard 'bout th' 'Dobe Walls battle, he d'cided it was best for him to stay in Colorado for th' time bein' an' wintered his herd near Twin Buttes. Th' Red River War settled th' Indian question. As he passed down th' Canadian in '76, Mr. Goodnight spent some time visitin' with Casimero at his plaza. They agreed t' split th' grazing lands up peacefully, sheep staying in the Canadian valley and west and Charlie headquartering in the Palo Duro Canyon an' ranging eastward. They kept their agreement, but new ranchers bringin' their cattle hadn't made any agreement an' Casimero was eventually forced t' convert his sheep to cattle.

CHAPTER 27
JACQUES MUER

It was a pleasant day, warm in th' sun, cool in th' shade. Typical winds for that time of year had died away to a soft breeze out of th' south and we rode along at a leisurely pace enjoyin' our ride. I was thinking about things and how we needed t' get back to camp an' spell Hardy from his chores—if we could settle on what we were goin' t' do. Topping a rise, Asa made some exclamation and I looked up to see dust rising behind a buggy fairly flying toward us.

Asa looked behind us. "Ain't no Injuns ahind him an' I don't see no smoke ahead of 'im, wonder what his hurry is."

"Could be a bank robber, runnin' ahead of th' news, or a lover outrunning weddin' bells, maybe it's Doc hurryin' to another birthin'," I surmised.

"Robbers an' lovers don't usual run away in buggies."

"Let's get out of Doc's way, it may be twins."

"Zee, you know darn good an' well that ain't Doc's rig an' he never moved that fast in his life."

I chuckled and Asa grinned. Th' rig was nearing so we split t' allow it to pass. The driver was a smallish man in strange dress for our country. He passed without a glance or nod, applying his whip to th' rump of his lathered an' winded horse.

"Well how a-bout that," Asa exclaimed at the rudeness, almost disappearin' in a dust cloud. People just didn't pass on the prairie without stoppin' to speak or give a "howdy" or wave or something. "Think there's some kind of trouble, Zee?"

246

"Don't know, let's ask these fellers followin' up."

A group of men trailing th' buggy was about a mile behind and not in near th' hurry. They were travelin' far enough behind that th' dust was settled and we squatted in th' shade of our horses an' waited for them. There were eight or nine of them, on an assortment of transportation, horses, mules, donkeys, and sandals.

As they neared we could hear their animated talk. They pulled up, dismounted, and we greeted one another. Squatting in grass and dust they began rolling their corn-husk cigarettes. One of them pulled out a sulfur match and lit up. Th' rest drew fire from the match or lighted cigarette. In time all were contentedly smoking. I recognized one or two as vaqueros and several were local sheepherders by th' looks of them, th' rest were itinerate shearers, mostly from Mexico. They would begin shearing early in the year in Mexico and "follow the harvest," so to speak, until they finished up here in th' north reaches of sheep country.

"Where was that feller goin' in such a hurry?" Asa asked through clouds of smoke.

"Ahhh, Señor, that was thee Señor Muer on his way to Romero's."

"Whut was th' hurry?"

"No hurry, Señor Muer go that way all thee time."

"Must not be his horse," I said.

"Sí, Señor, hee no have horse of hees own, must rent one."

"No one here lets heem use theirs so he have to rent one from town," th' vaquero I knew as Pepe said. His face showed the contempt for such mistreatment of horses.

We talked and smoked a while, "We were going to Don Baca's to see Señor Muer, so I guess we will just return to Romero's," I said.

"That is where we go too, Señor Muer has finished sheering at Don Baca's. He wants us to help feenish up at Don Romero's," one of the men said, "let us ride together."

They all rose almost as one and disposing of the last of their smokes prepared to continue their journey. It was pleasant riding and talking to the men and listening to their lively conversation.

We hadn't gone a mile until topping a rise, we saw ahead of us the buggy with its driver. The horse was flat on the ground. All conversation ceased.

"Looks like Muer lost his horse," Asa said, his voice flat, eyes flashing.

"Sí, Asa, now we weel have some trouble, I theenk," Pepe said.

"No, amigo, I think Señor Muer has some trouble," I said. My anger was mounting.

As we neared, the little man began yelling and gesturing for us to hurry. At my word, we continued at our own pace, Asa, me, and the vaqueros leading the party.

The little man finally gave up yelling and stood in th' middle of the road, hands on hips, the stub of his broken whip in one hand.

"In no hurry, are you?" he said without ceremony of greeting. Pointing th' stub of his whip at me, he said, "I will need your horse to continue my journey."

I gritted my teeth and tried to smile, but Asa said it just looked like a goat eatin' cactus. "You won't be ridin' any horse of mine, nor one in this crowd, Mister."

He raised th' whip, then realizing it wasn't whole stepped closer to reach me. I suddenly spurred my horse on the opposite side, a little too hard in my anger, I suppose, and he jumped and whirled, knocking the little man into the dust. Before he could rise, Asa had put his heel on his weapon hand and I had my knee on th' other arm, my face in his.

"Any man who treats an animal this way doesn't deserve to

ride!" I was fairly spittin' with anger. "You are afoot, Mister and if I *ever* see you mistreating animal or man again, I will hitch you to a wagon and beat you until you run!"

I didn't move, just stared into his eyes. He stopped struggling and his face turned from several shades of red to pale. When he closed his eyes, I stood up and Asa pulled the whip stub out of his hand and backed off, weighing it in his hand and looking at the man menacingly.

"Get up!" I said.

"I must . . ."

"You must begin walking to wherever you were going, for there will be no more riding for you today," I said.

"You don't know who you are talking . . ."

"I know I am talking to a man who mistreats animals. *And* I know that you don't do that in this country, especially if the animal isn't yours, now get going before I change my mind and start lookin' for a strong tree limb—up high!"

He stared at me a moment and turning, ordered, "One of you men . . ."

"These men will do nothing for you, on my orders! I am in charge here!" I said.

I stepped toward him and he involuntarily backed up a step or two.

"You were going that direction when you passed us, but you are free to go any direction you want," I said.

"You can go any direction you want, but yuh better git goin', you're late a'ready," Asa said. "Heer's yer stick, yuh may need it t' beat off rattlers." He tossed the whip stub to him. "On second thought, I don't think rattlers'd hev anything tuh do with a skunk like you, you'd prob'ly pizen *them*!"

The two vaqueros were working with the horse and had gotten him unhitched and on his feet. Two of the herders had hands full of grass and were rubbing him down. The horse flinched when they went across one of the many welts on his back and sides. His face and muzzle were bloody and one eye was swollen shut. My anger had begun t' go down but I started getting mad again. Muer just stood there staring at us until he saw me go to my horse and take down my rope. It was then he decided it was time to go. Turning toward Romero's, he took a few steps then turned, hesitated a moment, and started back toward Baca's. He took a wide detour around us.

"Señor Zee, eet is longer back to Baca's!" one of the men whispered, grinning.

After working with the horse some time, he seemed to rally and we led him slowly toward Romero's. The rest of the men contrived to hook up one of the mules to the buggy and the ones afoot all piled in.

When we came in sight of Romero's plaza, I stopped the procession and said to the men, "When you tell this story to Don Romero, be sure to say that I forced you to comply to my wishes. That way, no harm will come to you."

There was a chorus of *Si's* but Pepe's vaquero companion said, eyes flashing, "*I* weel not say so, Señor Zee, I weel stand *beside* you in this!"

Pepe nodded. "I too, Mr. Zee!"

"Thank you," I said, "but be wary of that man, he won't take this quietly, I imagine."

With that, we said our goodbyes and headed cross-country toward camp.

"Well, I guess we won't be goin' t' Mexico," Asa said.

"Probably not!" and we both began laughing.

It was a quiet ride to camp, each of us in our own thoughts. The only option left to us was to try to sell out, either in one lot or piecemeal. I sure didn't look forward to selling on th' road like that, but we might not have any choice about it. Maybe there could be someone who would buy th' whole lot an' we could be shuck of it all at once. That would be a lucky thing and our luck seemed to be in short supply right then. We had put in an awful lot of work without any return an' now was time t' reap some good from our labors.

Spring was Ute and 'Pache war party time and we kept a sharp eye out as we rode. It was just a natural thing for people interested in a long life back then and it's a habit old-timers still have. These youngsters today that didn't grow up with dan-ger—or curiosity—don't see half o' th' world they're passin' through.

Zenas rocked a moment gathering his thoughts, then continued:

I've thought a lot about what happened that day and what part I had in it. Now I'm not agin working an animal hard an' I'm not agin applyin' a whip *when necessary* but it should be ap-plied reasonably and with a purpose, not out of anger or mean-ness. Some would say it was none of my business what another man does to his animals, but I don't feel thataway. No creature ('cept maybe some men) deserves to be mistreated, whether he's mine or someone else's. An old philosopher once said, "The greatest remedy for anger is delay," and he was right. Th' problem then was that I saw what happened an' there was no delay afore I took action. If I had heard about what he did to that horse later, I would have been angry, but I probably would not have taken th' same action.

They's about four things that set me off that day, maybe five. Foremost was th' mistreatment I saw that horse getting, second was Muer's rude attitude. It was plain that he considered all of us bein' beneath him. Third, he was abusing someone else's property. Th' other two were things I knew by instinct, not havin' t' give active thought to them: A man that cruel to animals will be th' same to men. In other words, you can tell a man's nature by how he treats animals. And last, I knew that we would never do profitable business with this man and probably part of my anger was because our chances were all gone. The last was borne out by th' experiences of the poor folks who went with him to Veracruz, but that's another story.

We saw our herd grazing quite a ways from camp an' Hardy was watchin' them from th' shade of a cedar tree.

"Let's go tell Hardy our good news," Asa said.

"They's so much of it, I hardly know where t' start," I replied.

"Just leave that t' me." Asa b'gan laughing again and I couldn't help laughin' with him. Hardy stood up as we approached and with a little bow said, "Lite down an' come on in, gentlemen, coffee's almost ready."

Sure enough, he had a little fire goin' an' a coffee pot settin' by it. We fished our cups out an' sat down. Those oxen sure looked good for spring. They had come through winter on hay and what graze they could find and we had been able t' keep them sheltered in our little valley. It wasn't much more than a wide gulch, but it gave good shelter from winter's north winds.

"Th' way you two were laughin', you must have good news," Hardy said by way of question.

"Yup," Asa said, "but first let me tell you 'bout somethin' happened yesterday."

"I'm all ears."

"We met a stranger on th' trail with his horse down an' he was beatin' him something awful. I never seen Zee so mad. He run over that man an' afore I could git down, he was off his horse an' had that big feller pinned down, whuppin' th' daylights out'n 'im. I had t' pull him off 'fore he killed him. When that feller got up he musta been 6 foot 13 or 14 an' big as that ol' blue ox. He started for Zee with th' stub of his whip an' I had t' step atween 'em t' keep him from hittin' Zee when he wasn't looking. Well, he lit into me an' we had *some* fight. I bit off a piece of his ear an' he tried t' thumb out my eyeball, but I broke his pinky finger backwards an' he cried like a baby. Boy was he mad! He almost whipped me with only one hand, but I finally got th' best of 'im an' laid him out.

"Seein' that I had th' upper hand an' th' outcome was sure, Zee had been workin' with th' poor horse all th' time we had been fightin'. He got him on his feet, unhitched him, but th' pore thing couldn't walk . . ."

"Did he really bite th' man's ear off, Zee?" Hardy asked.

"I didn't see him do it—"

"Ha—I knowed it, yore lyin' shore, Asa Willis . . ."

"—but I seen him spit it out," I finished.

Hardy gave me an unbelievin' glare.

"Now we had two critters laid out an' after considerin' it a while, we come up with an answer. We tore th' seat out an' lined th' buggy bed with hay we pulled. Then we coaxed that horse up into th' buggy an' got him t' lay down. Zee slapped that giant awake an' got him up. We harnessed 'im to th' buggy an' made him pull that horse five mile t' town.

"You should have seen th' crowd that gathered for th' parade. Apparently, that ol' boy was quite a bully an' had whupped ever' fighter in town ('cept me o' course). They was a hundred people follerin' us whin we pulled up at th' livery stable. 'Here's yore horse an' buggy back, Evans, they's some damage t' both, but this here little feller's agreed t' foot th' expenses!' Zee told th' livery man.

"You coulda heard that crowd cheer ef ya hed been listenin' whin that big feller forked over damages money. That crowd was so happy they escorted him to th' city limits an' cheered him on his way. Last we saw o' him, he was shufflin' on down th' trail!"

Hardy laughed. "You shore can tell 'em, Asa!"

"Th' truth ef I ever told it!" Asa swore with a straight face,

"Now Zee kin tell ye th' news."

"He's th' only one o' you two who'd tell th' truth, I reckon!"

CHAPTER 28
A NEW ENTERPRISE

"Here's th' truth, Hardy," I said, "someone has come in from Mexico an' bought up all th' wool!"

"You mean . . ."

"That's right, we don't have a pound t' haul," I said.

Hardy looked from one to th' other, letting what I had said soak in.

"It's true, Hardy," I said.

"What we gonna do with all these oxen—an' those wagons?" he asked.

"Th' wool buyer is hirin' wagons an' carts t' haul th' wool t' Mexico," Asa put in.

"Good, are we gonna haul?" Hardy said hopefully, "I never been t' Mexico, can't hardly speak their language."

"Don't think we'll git t' go, that man we whupped was th' one buyin wool," Asa said from behind his cup. He took a long sip just t' make Hardy wait.

"You mean you done busted up our only chance t' make good on all this work?" We could tell Hardy was beginning t' doubt every word we said.

"It's true, Hardy, we had a run-in with th' man and we won't be going to Mexico with him." I said it very seriously and sincerely so he would believe me.

He poked at th' fire some an' asked, as much to himself as to us, "What we gonna do now?"

"Looks like our only hope is to sell out," I said. "We might be lucky enough t' git rid of it all at once, or we'll have t' spend th' summer sellin' to pilgrims as they come through."

"An' they don't have any money, only trade," he replied, "we'll be tied up from here on with used up animals an' broke down wagons."

"Might be used-up wagons an' broke-down animals," Asa muttered.

"Well, darn nation, couldn't Charlie have bought up some of that wool?"

"He didn't have any cash, we was gonna take it on something called 'consignment,' means on th' cuff t' us," Asa said.

"When this man showed up with hard money offering premium prices, we were washed up," I said.

"Man oh man, what a mess. Asa, you really messed this up shore. How come you two t' do that?"

"I won't do business with a man who treats animals like that, Hardy. He's just as likely to treat men th' same way," I said.

"I guess you're right, Zee, but it shore is a mess, What did Charlie say?"

"He's looking around for a buyer, but we don't hold out much hope."

"We could shore plow up a lot o' ground with them oxen," Asa said.

"What good would that do, you cain't grow nothin' 'ithout'n water," Hardy replied.

"Those Pueblos do all th' time."

"But they got water, dug ditches an' such."

Th' sun was just sinkin'. It was time t' go back to camp and I interrupted their conversation t' say so. We rounded up cattle an' they headed for th' valley on their own. After a long drink, they would bed down an' chew cuds for a while. They sure enjoyed their routine. It would be hard t' convince them t' move on. It was early to bed for us an' I lay thinkin' for a long time, 'til I just drifted off. I've learned since then not t' worry so much, things generally work out in th' end—an' if they don't, there's not much I could do about it.

After breakfast, I said, "Why don't you two go into town and pick up our two wagons? Asa has t' return his mount and you could talk t' Charlie an' see if he has any news for us."

"Suits me just fine!" Asa was always ready t' move. Not that a certain little girl was any motivation for him, no sirree.

Except for a few trips to the fort, Hardy hadn't been t' town once all winter. His clothes were wearin' mighty thin an' raggedy so I told Asa on th' sly t' get him a new outfit. It was little pay for what he had done, but all we could afford. Not that any of us had any more. They hustled around an' by th' time th' herd was ready t' move they were ready. They helped me move them t' new grazing ground and went on their way, leading Asa's horse for a spare

Th' next three days were quiet and I enjoyed th' routine of camp life. It made me realize how much I had missed it with all th' bustle of diggin' out parts an' buildin' wagons, dealing with people at th' fort and all. I thought a lot about our set-to with Muer an' almost regretted what I had done, but I knew I would do th' same if it happened again. Th' sad part is that I doubt it changed th' man one bit. He prob'bly spent th' rest of his life just like he was, abusing animal an' man t' meet his ends. Th' story told by th' survivors with him bore out th' truth of my notions. With men like that it's best t' leave any retributions to th' Lord. He can deal out justice better than any man or court. I've seen it happen.

By noon of th' third day I had decided that I was gonna shed this project as soon as possible even if it cost me and get back to some sort of ranchin' where I would be much happier. Even a trip or two up th' Santa Fe looked inviting.

It was long after dark when I heard wagons rattling down th'

257

valley an' I lit a lamp an' went out t' meet them. Hardy an' Asa were riding their horses and drivin' one wagon b'tween them.

"Where's th' other wagon?" I asked.

"Sold it," Asa said, "Charlie had a man in need of a wagon an' we convinced him that oxen pullin' it was th' way t' go an' he took th' whole outfit."

I held th' lantern while they unhitched and Asa whispered when he got a chance, "Look at Hardy."

He was working outside th' circle of light an' I moved over as if t' give him some light. He had on a new gray flannel shirt, a pair of cotton overalls, an' a new pair of boots peeked out from under his pants cuffs.

"Where'd you git that outfit, Hardy, rollin' some drunk in an alley?"

"No, sir, Asa bought'n it for me." He said it apologetically like I might not approve.

"We thought you deserved a little pay for your work, even though it ain't much. B'sides we was tired o' seein' all that skin peekin' through your old clothes." I laughed.

"Well I thank you," he said, a little embarrassed.

It didn't take us long t' get to bedrolls after they had a bite t' eat. Hardy pulled off his new clothes an' carefully folded them. He tucked them under his blanket and I noticed that he had on a new pair of longhandles.

"New underwear too? Man you really made out, Hardy!"

"Asa made me get them, Zee, I didn't have t' have them."

"Do they itch?"

"A little." I could see his teeth shining as he grinned.

"You deserve it all and more," I said, "But I don't know if th' 'more' will come."

"Will you two ladies hush up, there's people tryin' t' sleep here!" Asa growled.

I threw a rock at him. It hit with a satisfyin' thump.

"Bunch of kids," he muttered.

Morning broke bright and clear an' we lingered around camp later than usual. They had gotten a reasonable price for th' wagon outfit an' were fortunate enough to make a deal in cash. Asa had put it all in on our bill at Letcher's, after takin' out for Hardy's outfit. Charlie told them about some fellers planning to set up a road ranch at Taylor Springs for th' summer. He said they were good men and it would be a good place for us to sell our wagons an' oxen. Asa knew a couple of the men and he had a good opinion of them too, so we talked it over an' decided it might be a good place for us. Asa had told them we would meet them somewhere along th' trail north of Fort Union if we decided to join them. I agreed with th' plan and we set about making ready.

With twenty-four wagons and over fifty head of cattle, we were gonna need help moving, so we sat down an' discussed our plans. We decided we could hitch three empty wagons together and pull them easy enough and we would have around twenty head to drive.

"Don't see how we can make it in one trip without six or eight extra hands," Asa said.

"What can we pay them?" I wondered.

"That's just it, we don't have money."

"Could be we could work out something with them on shares," Hardy suggested.

"No-o-o, I don't think that's gonna work, our business is too risky fer anyone t' trust like that," Asa said.

"I would guess it's fifty–sixty miles to Taylor Springs from here," I said, "A three or four day trip with th' wagons dependin' on travel conditions. If we made two trips out of it, how many men would we need?"

"Four drivers an' maybe half th' spares . . . one man could handle th' spares, that's five, less us three an' we would need someone here t' watch things an' keep th' animals t'gether . . ."

"Someone would have t' stay at th' Springs t' watch our outfit an' hopefully do business," Hardy said.

"So only four would come back for th' second trip, but th' one left here would be available for th' last trip." Asa rubbed his chin.

"You think we could do it with just five?" I asked.

"Maybe . . ."

"We don't have enough yokes to make two trips without bringing some back," Hardy put in.

"Danged if you ain't right," Asa groaned.

It was quiet a minute while we all thought out this new problem.

"So-o-o it means that we have t' haul one wagon back full of yokes after our first trip and on one trip or the other we will need t' take thirteen wagons," I said.

"Think we could hire someone on one of th' trains t' haul them back?" Asa asked.

"Not likely, they'll all be loaded to th' gills, then they'll probably double up t' avoid a lot of taxes."

"Too bad we don't need something shipped out, those wagons goin' east won't have much of a load," Hardy said.

"Won't help at all, will it?"

"Now, *they'll* have a bunch of extra yokes t' carry back, 'cause they won't drive as many oxen east as they came out with," Asa exclaimed.

"I guess they would have, but would they be willin' t'loan them to us to Rayado?" I asked.

"I wouldn't count on that. It's not likely they would be available when we needed them." Hardy was a good thinker.

"Surest thing is for us t' rely on ourselves," Asa said, and he was right.

"All right then, we need three or four helpers and we will need to take thirteen wagons on one of the trips. I think we should do that on the first trip out, then that second trip would be easier," I said. "I think I should go looking for help, maybe there would be some at Baca's and if not, Romero's is on th' way to Las Vegas. Surely one of those places will have some men wanting work."

"While you're doin' that, Hardy an' me will round things up here. We need t' be movin' in four days t' meet those boys on th' trail."

"What are we gonna pay them with, Zee?"

"I don't know, Hardy, but it ain't likely t' be hard cash, seein's we don't have any!"

I left camp just before noon and th' sun was getting low when I rode into Baca's plaza. Señor Baca emerged from th' sheds and greeted me, "Step down, Señor Zenas, I was just going for a drink of water."

He called the ever-present boy to take my horse and we walked to the house. Water from the olla hanging on the ramada was cold and sweet. We lingered there and my host motioned to chairs.

"Señor Muer has told me how you mistreated him the other day," he said rather seriously.

"I did treat him, but it wasn't abuse he didn't deserve," I said.

The Don chuckled, then laughed out loud. "You should have seen him when he came dragging in here, it would have done your heart good! His clothes were ragged from his knees down where he had wandered through cactus trying to take a shortcut and his fancy boots were ruined. He was skinned and covered with dust and dirt from falling down a bank, and his tongue was beginning to swell for lack of water. He almost drank the olla dry before I could stop him, then he threw it all back up.

"I was alarmed when I heard his story how crazy Americans attacked him without provocation and thought it was some of the road agents roaming about, but when he said the attackers didn't want money, only his horse and buggy, it puzzled me. It took him some time to recover and the next day he asked me for a horse to ride to Romero's. I had seen him drive and offered him a buggy and driver, saying I needed the buggy back right away. My driver had strict instructions not to abuse the horse and to pay no attention to Señor Muer's demands. He is a smart man and pretended not to understand anything Mr. Muer said. It seemed like the man would have a stroke yelling at my driver, but he got to Romero's in due time.

"The sheepmen who were with you told Don Romero what had happened and he got a good laugh out of it. He was prepared for Muer when he arrived. You must get him to tell you about it." He laughed.

I told him how he had passed us on th' road and then how we had found him beating the horse with his whip until he had broken it.

He nodded. "I have seen some of that myself, even warning him a time or two about it, but Señor Muer is not one to listen."

Then I told him Asa's tale, as much as I could remember, and he got a good laugh out of it. "This Señor Willis has a good imagination, no?"

"He can sure tell a tall tale or two," I replied. "Don Baca, we had planned to propose taking another train of wool to Missouri until Muer bought it all up. Then when I accosted him about his abuse, we lost all chances of hiring our wagons out to him, so now we are planning to go to Taylor Springs and trade with th' trains coming through. To do that, we need at least three more men to help us move."

"I have heard that some are planning to go there, it is risky business with the Comanche, Kiowa, and Cheyenne roaming about. Do you have any other recourse?"

I shook my head. "Not that we see unless someone wants to buy us outright."

"That would be fortunate, but not likely."

"We have very little cash and I am not sure how to arrange to pay the extra help."

He thought for a moment, then said, "It seems to me that you are risking everything taking your whole business to Rayado. Why don't you take a few wagons and see how business goes, then you can come back for more if you need them? Otherwise, if you move everything up there and don't have any business, you will be stuck with all you have accomplished in a place where you can't profitably dispose of it."

I felt like hitting myself between the eyes, why hadn't we thought of that? Even knowing how th' Bent–St. Vrain Company did it, I had overlooked one of their basic rules of not putting everything into one pot. Of course, we three could do that without hiring other hands with money we didn't have!

"I should have known that, Señor Baca, I just wasn't thinking."

"I find it helps to seek other opinions in my endeavors. It is wise."

"The only thing I have to solve now is how to keep our property we leave behind safe while we're gone."

"It may be that I can help you there," he said. "Don Romero and I have been looking for a good place to pasture our sheep for the summer and your area looked very good. You have good water and a very good camp. Your dugout would provide shelter for our herders," (he could have added safety from raiders as well), "and with some small fencing, the sheep would be safe in your little valley. We could keep several flocks there and the men could watch over your wagons and pasture your stock as rent payment for using the camp."

I could have jumped for joy, there it was! The solution to our puzzle. "I am sure we can make those arrangements, Don Baca, if you decide that is what you want to do."

"It is settled, then, I will have two flocks ready to move in tomorrow. There will be four men with them at first, then two more flocks will be out in a few days. Don Romero will have his flocks ready quickly also. There will be six to ten flocks in the area and one or two men to tend to the camp, so someone will be there all the time."

I realized then that those two had this all planned out ahead of us. They anticipated our moves before we did and set their plans accordingly. If we had moved off entirely, they would have just moved in. Watching over our stock wasn't anticipated, but it was small trouble for the good it would do them. It was another lesson in how to be a good businessman. We were just fortunate that it went to our good rather than against us.

He rose, "I must not be rude, Señor Zenas, but if you agree with my proposition, we both have much to do before tomorrow."

"Yes," I said, "I must get back to camp and get things done."

He clapped his hands an' that boy appeared as if by magic. "Go to Maria and have her fix some tamales for Señor Zenas to eat as he goes."

The boy was scurrying before he had finished talking, "Now, hurry!" Turning to me he said, "I need to get to my flocks and send word to Don Romero of our agreement, if you will excuse me, the boy should be back soon."

"Thank you very much, Don Baca, I will be leaving as soon as I can." He turned and strode toward the sheds, calling to someone inside.

The Mexican Americans are slow moving and relaxed in their actions, this makes some think they are lazy, which is not true. By contrast, Castilians such as the two Dons were not many generations from Spain and their blood was not mixed with the natives of Mexico. They were active and energetic compared to the natives.

The same boy came around the house leading my horse. He had a package in his hand and when he handed it to me, it was very warm.

"Don Baca has promised me that I can go to your camp this summer, I weell take good care of your oxen, Señor Zee!" His dusty bare feet danced with joy.

"I'm sure you will, what is your name?"

"Tomaz." He said it with a *z*.

"Well, Tomaz, I have a special ox I want you to watch after. He's a big blue ox and seeing that you will be there I will leave him in camp."

"I weel take good care of heem." His eyes were big and bright.

"I know you will. Be sure to tell the others about him if you have to leave before I get back."

"Si, Señor Zee."

I mounted and the boy trotted along with me to the edge of the plaza.

"Goodbye, Señor Zee!" He waved until I was out of sight.

CHAPTER 29
POKE DRANNAN

There were six tamales and I ate every one of them—well, except for the last one I gave my horse. He sniffed the air while I ate an' I couldn't ignore him completely. If I had given him one earlier, I would have had to give him more, so long as he smelled them. With the scent gone, he bent himself to his chore and we rode into camp late in the evening.

"Rouse up, you lazy slugs an' get busy, we're in business!" I called, but the only answer I got was a boom and the spang of a bullet crashing into the bluff behind my head.

Fortunately my horse was quick to move and fortunately for me, I had my hand on the horn in the act of stepping down or he would have left me in the dust. I rode fifty yards with one foot in the stirrup and hanging on to the horn before I could get him under control. Another boom and th' whiz of lead sent him on another run, and this time I was in agreement with him. In an instant we were around the corner of th' bank and out of sight. Without hesitating I spurred up the steep side and scrambled up th' steepest on hands and knees, my rifle slung on my back. I lay there catching my breath for a moment, then keeping below the crest, crept to a spot over the dugout. Th' chimney was cold as it should have been, so I stuck my face into it and called softly down, "Is anyone in there?"

There was a soft shuffle and Hardy called back, "We're both here, Zenas."

"What's goin' on?"

"Some feller with a Buffalo gun comes walkin' in an' said t' vamoose, he was takin' over camp. Of course we resisted and he's been takin' potshots at us from th' other side. We're nearly out o' bullets so we haven't been answerin' his callin' cards."

"Where is he?"

"He's forted up b'hind some rocks just to the right of that twin cedar on th' ridge. Since he's above us, we can't get a good shot, but you should be above him up there."

"Hold on. I'll look."

I could barely see that rock fort he had built up. It wasn't high, just enough so he had shelter from th' cave below. He must have been well hidden, for I couldn't see anything of him, though I knew he would be visible in enough light. I crept back to the chimney.

"Give me a moment t' get in position, then try t' draw his fire so I can locate him," I whispered.

"Ok," came a muffled reply.

Even in that short time, it seemed it was darker. If I was t' have a shot, it would be a blind one and I would have t' depend on th' flash of his gun and luck if I hit him. I propped my rifle on a rock and waited. It was just a moment before a shot rang out from below. Even expectin' it, I flinched a little. Nothing. Another shot from th' cave an' I heard it hit rock. Almost instantly there was the flash and boom of the buffalo gun, almost directly in line with me. I sighted on the flash, then raised it a little to where I guessed th' stock was. He would be reloading and I heard th' bolt click home. One more moment and he would be back in position, th' same position, I hoped. I could see a faint gleam from my bead sight and I kept it steady on my invisible target. A trickle of sweat rolled down th' hollow of my spine. Three deep breaths and exhale, squeeze slowly. Th' bang of my gun startled me.

Not expectin' it, he might not have caught th' exact location

267

of my flash, but I ducked anyway and moved down-ridge a couple of yards. Silence. Not a sound. Now I really began t' sweat! After a long wait, I moved back to th' chimney and called, "Anything?"

"We heard a clink an' something slid down th' hill, but not a sound since then. He could have pushed a rock over t' fool us an' be waitin' for us to make a move."

"We'll just have t' outwait him, keep out of sight, and don't give him a target."

"You don't have t' tell me! Asa took some rock splinters with that last shot. We're gonna go around th' angle an' light a candle so's we can stop him from bleedin'."

"Ok, but be careful an' get back t' guardin' that door, you don't want him t' sneak in on you."

"Ok, Zee, what are you gonna do?"

"Wait."

And wait we did, from about an hour after sundown til sunrise, we waited. I forted some rocks up and made myself comfortable, as comfortable as I could be in one place. I felt as trapped as those boys in th' dugout, not moving around, but in that dark it was th' only thing t' do. As it got light, I peeked through a crack at th' rocks across th' way. There was no movement. By th' time it was light enough, my eyes were burning from staring at that rock pile, still nothing moved. From my position, I could tell if there was anyone behind that low wall of rock and there was nothing. He wasn't there. Where was he? I rolled over an' searched th' slope behind me. It would be to my eternal shame if that bully had sneaked up an' back-shot me while I was layin' there.

Hardy said something slid down th' bank, what was it? Carefully, I scanned th' hillside. Grass was tall, but I could see even from here that something had bent grass below th' fort. A breeze stirred th' grass an' I glimpsed something out of place beneath them, but it was gone in a second. I watched that spot, but th' wind didn't cooperate for a long time. When it did, I saw a rifle barrel laying there.

Still, I was cautious, that owlhoot could still be around and th' gun could be a blind t' make us think we were safe. For a long time I lay there looking things over. When I was satisfied he wasn't in my range of view, I scooted up an' stuck my head over th' rim further.

My new position brought me a view of th' whole bench right up to th' dugout mouth. Again, I examined every inch of it, but found nothing. If he was still there, he would be under th' bank standin' in water. He couldn't stand perfectly still there and when he moved, he would make waves. I watched a long time, but nothing moved but cattle who were getting restless and had started out of th' valley, grazing as they went.

Asa was calling up th' chimney when I got there, "Where you been, we been callin' fer two hours! We're getting cabin fever cooped up in this hole!"

"Have you seen hide or hair of that feller?" I asked.

"No, have you? I think he may have left."

"Only place he might be is in water under th' bank."

"That's mighty cold water, Zee."

"What'd he look like?"

"A dirty buffalo hunter, 'bout my height, a little heavier. Wore buckskin and carried his canon in a sheath decorated with beads an' such. Probably an ol' mountain man tricked out t' hunt 'bufferler'."

"That bein' so, he don't have any feelin' b'low his knees an' could stand in that water all day without discomfort."

"Yore right there, I seen 'em do it."

"It's clear right up to th' doorway, think you could crawl up there an' look around?"

"I'll send Hardy, don't want my hair parted by no Sharps."

"Don't you dare send that boy, this is a man's job. If you're too . . . cautious t' do it, just let it go!"

"Just joshin', Zee, I'll go look an' whistle if it's clear."

I resumed my vigil an' it was a long time before I heard Asa give a whistle. I couldn't satisfy myself that an old mountain man would give something up that easy, but maybe I got a lucky hit an' he had t' leave. Finally, I stood up in plain sight. If he was there, I would be too good a target t' resist. I kept movin' but even then my hair stood on end—back o' my neck—and sweat rolled. Nothing. I found my horse grazing where I had left him. We made a big circle, comin' up b'hind th' bushwhacker's fort. It was empty an' peekin' over th' ridge I could see no one was standin' b'low th' bank. Stayin' where I was below th' ridge and out of sight, I called out, "It's ok, Asa, all's clear."

After a few seconds he called back, "Show yourself, Zee."

Cautiously, I walked up to th' ridge holdin' my rifle over my head with both hands. It would be something t' be shot by my own partners after all this. "He's gone, saddle up an' come on around here."

I had looked over things good by th' time they got to me. There was blood in th' fort, goodly amount, but not enough t' be fatal. I could see where he had crawled and walked to his horse. Th' ground was trampled good there, and I could tell he had spent time to bandage up some before he mounted. There was a plain trail toward the river.

"Looks like yuh winged him, Zee," Asa said, rubbing his hands on his pant legs. Hardy scrambled down th' hill an' picked up a Sharps fifty caliber rifle, "We got his gun!" He waved it over his head, heavy as it was.

"Got skinned a little bit," Asa said, examining th' gun an' wiping it clean. He ejected a bullet and left th' bolt open.

"Now what?" Hardy asked.

"We got t' follow him an' see what he's up to an' at th' same

270

time we got t' guard this place," Asa said.

"I guess he got a good look at you two," I said.

"Yup, nose t' nose almost."

"Have we seen him b'fore?"

"Not that I recollect," Asa said, "an' I think I would remember that character."

"I didn't see him in town," Hardy said, "I'm sure I would remember if I had."

"There's a good chance that I don't know him either, then," I said. "If I do know him, he isn't likely t' associate me with this place. I'll follow him up an' see what he's up to—"

"—or bury him," Asa put in.

"You two stay around here and be on guard. I may be gone a couple of days, so don't look for me soon."

Hardy traded me a full canteen for mine an' Asa traded horses with me. I took off from right there. Those tamales would have t' do for a while.

His trail led northeast down th' creek a ways an' after a while turned left up over th' divide down to the Rio Mora. My man stopped and washed in th' river. He must have worked more on his bandages. I found where he had led his horse to a boulder he stood on t' mount. From blood drops I deduced he must have been hit on th' left side. It was easy following him from there and it soon became plain that he was headed for th' fort. I rode fast, checkin' for signs only once in a while to be sure.

It was midafternoon when I rode into Fort Union and tied up in front of th' sutler's. The place was busy and I just stood around listening to gossip. A tall soldier in a white smock smeared with blood was saying, ". . . first time I seen a man riding standin' up since Sergeant O'Reily got hit when Injuns attacked that immigrant train. He come ridin' in here with th' arrer still in his be-hind an' he looked like a rooster with tail feathers. Doc pulled th' thing out'n him an' he never sat down for near a month."

"How'd this feller git shot?" the clerk asked.

"Said he was bushwhacked in his bedroll. Killt th' varmint an' rode all night t' git here."

"Hit him in th' rear, did he?"

"Yup, bullet went plumb through his ham, skipped his thigh an' hit th' fat o' his calf. Doc cut it out from th' front where it come t' rest agin his shin bone. Made a blue lump in his skin, it did."

"Bet that hurt," another soldier said.

"You bet, an' it hurt agin when we run a rag through th' hole in his rear. Near bit that stick in two, he did."

"Where's he now, in th' hospital?"

"A-layin on his side!" the doctor's aide grinned, "gonna be there some time, I imagine."

"Who is he?" a grizzled sergeant asked b'tween puffs on his pipe.

"Some old mountain man, said he was tiret o' shootin' buffalo an' was headed for Taos when he got it, name's Poke, Poke Drannin, er somethin like that."

Poke Drannan! I knew him when he used to hunt meat for Bent's Fort. He was a dirty old rascal then, but a good hunter. He kept th' fort in meat almost as well as Kit Carson could. He had a Nez Perce wife an' 'bout a dozen kids. Wouldn't sleep in th' fort, they had a tepee by th' river. I heard him brag once that he took a bath once a year on th' Fourth of July whether he needed it or not.

I walked out on th' porch an' looked across th' parade ground. All was quiet except for some soldiers policing grounds an' th' clank of hammer on iron from the blacksmith's shop. I left my horse at th' rail an' walked over to th' hospital. There was a corporal sitting at a desk. He looked up at my footsteps an' asked, "May I help you, sir?"

"You have a man here that has been shot?"

"Got two, actually, one of those raw recruits who shot himself and a civilian who came in just this morning."

"That's the one, Drannan, I think his name is?"

"Yes, he's in the ward, third bed on th' right."

I walked back to the ward. He was there, all right, layin' on his right side, sleeping restlessly. I didn't bother him, knowing he had had a hard time of it. I would check back later when he was more rested.

I spent th' rest of th' day visiting around, sayin' hello to people I knew. There had already been a train or two come through and th' smithy was busy repairing wagon iron. Th' junkyard showed signs of reviving.

Th' harness shop had a pile of harnesses t' repair, bearing witness that the trains had been pulled by mules. It made sense, an ox train would be slower and not likely to be in this early in th' season.

The washerwomen remembered me, calling out, "Do ye need that boy washed agin?"

"Next time we're in!" I called. I left them chattering and gigglin'.

Late in th' evening, I checked back at th' hospital an' found Poke awake. Even through th' dirt, he was pale an' I could tell he was in quite a bit of pain.

"Poke, it's me, Zenas Meeker, remember?"

He looked up and after a moment said, "Yeah, I 'member you, Bent's Fort, wasn't it?"

"I was mostly at Purgatory Ranch, but at th' fort some."

He nodded his head and winced. "I 'member."

"How are you feelin'?"

"Oh, I'm all right, been through worse, I guess."

"What happened?"

"I *told* them I got bushwhacked in my bed," he whispered,

looking to see if anyone was near, "but that ain't so. I went to a place I knowed down th' river, a good place t' stay, but some fellers run me off."

"Run you off?"

"Shot me an' run me off."

I squatted on th' floor so's we could talk eye-to-eye and I pretended t' get angry. "Why'd they do that?"

"Wanted th' place fer theirselves, I reckon." He stirred some and winced.

"How bad are you hit?"

"Took one in th' ham an' one in my laig b'low th' knee."

"Think you'll be here long?"

"Nah, this nigger'll be up soon, I reckon, *wagh!*" He reverted to the old mountain vernacular, something that's died out 'most completely now.

"When yore up, may be we'll hafta visit them outlaws an' teach 'em a lesson er two. Must hev been a dozen o' them t' git th' best of you this a-way."

"Fourteen, I reckon. They near surrounded me, but I got t' ol' Silverback an' we hied ourselves out'n there. I wouldn't hev left, but they shot Coliga out o' my hands an' he rolled down th' bluff outta reach."

"Yuh had t' leave him there?" I was incredulous and saddened.

"Hardest thing I ever had t' do—'cept maybe whin I had t' carve up my 'paloose an' eat her out on th' Mojave—that was a time, *wagh.*"

"I 'member th' story," I said. "Think I'll back track yuh an' get ol 'Liga back fer yuh, where'd yuh come frum?"

"Down th' Mora a few mile, yuh know where that little lake is south o' th' river? Well southeast o' th' lake over th' divide is a wash with a spring-fed pool in it under a bluff. Me an' my Cheyenne wife wintered there several years, dug a dugout in th' hillside on a bench an' we was snug as bugs. These scoundrels musta found it an' claimed it fer theirselves. Had a herd o' steers, bet ever' one o' 'em was stole."

"I'm goin' atter 'em!" I cried, slapping my thigh, "an I'll die afore I come back without yore Coliga!"

"Don't do it, Zee, less'n yuh can take ten men er one er two old mountain men with you, they's *some* mean fellers!"

"Right now, I'm mad enough t' take 'em on myself, but reckon I'll take yore advice an' nose out a mountain man er two. They's better'n ten o' these girls livin' 'round here!"

"Give me a coupla days an' I'll ride with yuh, ef I hafter stand up all th' way!"

"Nah, ol' hoss, we'll do this fer yuh while you heals up!" I rose like th' matter was settled, slapped th' old man on th' shoulder, an' said my "goodbyes."

"Take lotsa lead, ol' hoss," he called as I walked through th' door.

Now, you're thinking I was deceiving goin' along with his tall tale but in those days yuh didn't challenge a man on his stories unless you wanted a mortal enemy. At that, we were both enjoyin' our conversation even if I knew he was lying. The spinning of tall tales was a special talent of men of th' mountains— an' plains too for that matter. In this way, Poke got t' save face. He knew I would keep my word or at least try, and he also knew what I would find. Aside from some mischief afoot, it would not come to much. There was even a slim chance I might come back with his beloved rifle.

While we're talking, let me tell you how it was shooting people back then. When lead started flying an' it was headed your direction, you didn't ask any questions, you just shot back an' hoped to live through it. If you had to kill a man, you did what you had to do and went on. Would I have shot if I had known it was Poke Drannan at the time? You bet! Would I have shot to kill? You can bet on that too. When it's my life or his, I'm gonna do my best to preserve mine. Am I glad I didn't kill him? Yes. But I'm not sorry I shot him and I'm not going to feel bad about it. The aide at th' desk was rather wide eyed when I passed through. I'm sure he heard (and believed) every word Poke had said, if he could have deciphered th' language. "Goodnight, Mr. Meeker," he said quietly.

Me an' horse rode out on th' prairie a ways where it was quieter an' I rolled up in his blanket while he grazed on a picket line all night. Next morning I went to the sutler's and bought a pad of paper and pencil to write a note to Poke. This is what I wrote:

Friend Poke:

I take pen in hand to tell you of the events of the last days. Taking your advice, I was lucky enough to find a mountain man at Loma Parda and when he was sober enough we lit out down the Mora. We found that camp just as you said. There were only five or six men there and the herd was gone. After some persuading they gave Coliga to us and we invited them to return to the safety of their dugout, after which we blasted the bluff down on the mouth of the cave with a half-keg of powder. It will be some time afore they dig out of there. The good doctor has agreed to hold Coliga for you until you can get up and around. It goes without saying that my friend and I have *urgent business elsewhere* or we would spend some time with you. I hope this finds you healing and will see you on down the trail.

Your friend,
ZLM.

(Doc agreed to wait a week before reading th' note t' Poke, but five or six days later, Poke was up and about t' leave and the doctor gave him Coliga an' read him th' note. Poke got plumb choked up about it an' took th' note with him when he left for Taos. Doc said he was ridin' awful high in th' saddle. I never saw him again. I heard a rumor that he died of lead poisonin'—th' .45 caliber kind, ya understand—up Elizabeth Town way.)

CHAPTER 30
TAYLOR SPRINGS

Word around th' fort was that th' bunch settin' up a road ranch at Taylor Springs would be in any day and th' Army was sending a squad of troops t' guard an' patrol th' trail all summer. That put a burr under my saddle an' I made ready to make tracks back to camp. Before I left, I wrote a note to Charlie Ilfeld.

Dear Charlie:
We are leaving for Taylor Springs with six wagons and some oxen and will try to trade with the pilgrims coming through. Dons Romero and Baca will be using our camp for their sheep camp in exchange for watching our property left behind. If you get a chance to sell anything we have left at camp, take this letter to either man so they will know you have our permission and will allow you to take what you need.

Your Friend,
Zenas Meeker

I posted it as I left. We made a hard day's ride and rode into camp late afternoon. I saw a flock of sheep grazing on th' hills past the valley and knew some herders were already there. That was good news. Now all we had t' do was pack up and leave. I was greeted by th' fragrance of fresh meat cookin' an' when I came up from th' creek an old man was cookin' over th' fire.

He had a quarter of meat turning on a spit. It looked like antelope, but most likely it was goat. Asa an' Hardy were not in sight, so I made myself at home an' visited with th' cook for a time. Soon oxen came trailin' over th' bank, glad t' be home. Asa an' Hardy were bringing up th' drag.

"Hi, there Zee!" Hardy hollered. They hurriedly unsaddled an' came up, anxious t' hear what I had found.

"Yuh bury him on th' prairie?" Asa asked, squatting by th' fire.

"Nope, he made it to th' fort," I said.

"Not a clean shot, huh?" he grunted.

"Hell's bells, Asa, it was a shot in pure dark. I was lucky it hit anything!"

He chuckled.

"What happened to him?" Hardy asked. He was all ears an' eager t' know.

"Th' doctor fixed him up an' he was in th' hospital when I left. Turns out, I knowed him, it was Poke Drannan, Asa."

"Drannan? Poke Drannan? Was he th' Poke that hunted meat for Bents?"

"That's him."

"I heard talk of him, but I never seen him. Said he was a good hunter, but they suspected some 'elk' he brought in had been shod at one time."

"Was he hurt bad, Zee?" Hardy asked.

"Not too bad, th' bullet went through th' fat of his left hip and lodged in his calf by th' shin bone. He left a lot of blood laying around, an' hopefully it hurt a lot. I don't think he'll be visitin' us any time soon." I told them how I had visited him and about th' letter I had left with his rifle.

"That should keep him off our trail for a while," I concluded.

"Claimed he dug th' cave, did he?" Hardy was indignant. "Let him come on back, *I'll* show him who dug it!"

279

I laughed. "It don't matter *what* he *claims*, we know th' truth an' you get credit for doin' th' bulk o' that work!"

"Yuh could tell he was new at it, he left a lot o' lumps on th' bed ground," Asa said.

"That was just on yore bed, Asa, our others were just fine." Hardy threw a chip at him.

"What's been goin' on around here?" I asked.

"We're packed an' ready t' go, pullin' out early in th' morning—with or without you!" Asa grinned.

"Your roll is in that front wagon." Hardy pointed to wagons lined up on th' valley floor. There were six of them, hitched three and three, an overjet on each one and several spare yokes and bows in one of them.

"Who'd ya think was gonna drive th' cattle?"

"We was thinkin' t' hire one o' th' extra boys around here, but didn't know what t' pay him with." Asa stretched, "Shore am gittin' hungry smellin' that meat."

"If *you* was a decent shot, we could have had that all along." I was still piqued at his little comment about my shootin' skill.

"I was just funnin' ya, Zee."

Th' sun was below th' horizon when we heard bell goats bringing in th' flocks. There were three of them, two Baca's and one Romero's. Herders are quiet people by nature an' they didn't talk much around th' fire. You could tell they were uncomfortable with us bein' there. We ate in th' dark, th' only light a dying fire. A few words about tomorrow's work an' herders were off t' sleep. We turned in too.

There wasn't a crack of light when Cookie stoked up th' fire, but already camp was stirrin'. We dressed, an' rolled up our beds knowin' we most likely would not see this home of ours for a while and probably never live here again. It had been a good place an' a good time and we left reluctantly.

"Who's drivin' wagons an' who's drivin herd?" Asa called as

we descended th' bench.

"If we're gonna split this herd, we better all drive 'em 'til we get them separated an' settled down," I answered, "*then* we can decide who drives what. First of all, we'll yoke up th' ones pullin', then we'll git th' herder boy t' help us split up th' herd. Two of us can go with each bunch until they are out of sight of one another an' not inclined t' get back together."

"Sounds easy enough," Hardy said, but he soon learned it wasn't as easy as it sounded.

Th' sun was well up before we got two bunches divided up and settled down. We expected th' yoked oxen t' wait until driven, but to our surprise, they followed our herd, being they were pointed our way. We drove the herd a couple of miles before they settled down. When they were quietly grazing, we started t' return for the wagons only t' find they were only a half-mile behind.

"Well I'll be switchered, would ya look at that!" Asa called. "Maybe we don't need any wagon drivers!"

It was obvious we had th' order of our train set, but we would still need a driver with each set of wagons, if nothing else but to assure someone didn't drive them off. I don't remember ever seein' an ox train with a herd leading, but it worked well for us all th' way to Taylor Springs—and th' rest of th' summer for that matter. We kept bunched up a lot closer, which meant th' herd had t' go slower than their usual pace in order for th' wagons t' keep up, but that was good in that none of them got sore and they arrived sleek and fit.

It was high noon when our wagons caught up so we unhitched an' let them graze a while, then hooked up fresh teams and were on our way. Noonings didn't take as long as on th' trail because we could change teams and th' herd had time t' graze as they went. It was almost like drivin' a herd of steers t' market. We decided to rotate through, drivin' wagons two days an' th' herd one. By driving wagons side by side, we were able t' teach Hardy th' fine art of drivin' oxen. Bein' they were more docile than mules, he didn't learn mule skinner language, and that was good too.

We didn't catch up with our train until th' third day out of Fort Union and by that time we were only a half-day from Taylor Springs. It was an anxious time because of th' Indian threat, but I guess they didn't see much profit in a bunch of oxen and empty wagons. We were not foolish enough t' think we were not observed. Maybe th' nearness of th' cavalry was a determent, but I doubt that. Indians didn't have any more respect for th' Army than for a train on th' trail. In fact, more likely than not, th' train would have better weapons than th' Army and could do more damage. It wasn't unusual for th' Army to be up against Indians with old single shot Springfields while th' Indian had Winchester repeaters. Says a lot about our government, don't it?

I was pleased t' see Mr. Ambrose Trimble was one of th' bosses with th' ranch. T'other boss was a feller named Gordon McNeely, as fine a man as Mr. Trimble, but a little more th' nervous type. Their crew was mostly Anglo and new to th' country, Mexican Americans bein' too wise t' expose themselves to Indians. We was exposed to Apache, Comanche, Kiowa, Cheyenne, Arapaho, Ute, and most any other tribe in two hundred miles that took a mind t' "visit." Even Navajos gave a visit occasionally on their way to an' from buffalo grounds. That was th' reason Kit and Lucien Maxwell had t' abandon Rayado th' first time they tried t' settle there. I don't think anyone was there permanently until those Indians were subdued an' then they were mostly at Cimarron.

Our first order of business was t'put up a corral for our animals. With all of us working together, it was done in no time.

We would keep all cattle there at night. It sometimes got crowded for them, but it was a lot safer than out in th' fields. We spent some time repairin' an old shelter and makin' it fit for our quarters. Th' whole bunch of us slept there. An arbor served as th' smithy an' it was soon in shape for business. Mr. Trimble had even thought enough t' bring along a stock of coal for th' forge.

Mr. Trimble and Mr. McNeely set up a schedule where two of us were on night guard all th' time. It wasn't too bad with as many of us as there were. Even with guards out, Mr. Trimble made rounds a couple of times a night an' Mr. McNeely was always up before dawn making rounds. He believed that was th' most dangerous time for an attack and that was generally true. We all went armed at all times. It was our primary nature.

Ever' one was anxious t' see trains coming in an' on th' fourth day there, a train rolled in from th' north. They had come over some pass east of Raton because of high water at th' Cimarron Cutoff an' we had little warning they were near. It was a mule train so we didn't have any business from them. Trimble, McNeely and company did a brisk business, even selling a couple of mules t' replace ones that had died on th' trail.

In an effort t' save grass around th' fort, we had fenced off a draw about a half-mile south of camp for th' trains. They were glad to use it since it gave more security for their herds than open prairie. We even made an arbor for sleeping quarters there, but I think most slept under their wagons like they were accustomed to. Th' arbor provided good shade if they stayed over a day or two. Taylor Springs was sort of a dividing place for th' Santa Fe Trail. From there, trains could go on west to Cimarron, or angle for old Rayado an' th' pass west of Rayado Mesa, or if water was plentiful, they could aim for a point south of th' mesa. It depended a lot on th' availability of water. Cimarron bein th' distribution point for th' Mescalero Apaches, a lot of trains were destined for there.

We were all nervous about our business, but it was still too early for ox trains. All we could do was wait an' none of us was used t' that. Finally, on May 10th we saw an ox train coming from Point of Rocks. Asa an' a couple of others rode out t' meet them an' let them know we were at th' Springs. Asa rode back alone, th' T&M men staying with th' train. I chastised him severely for takin' a risk like that, but he was too excited t' sit still.

"They're needin' a hind wheel bad an' I want t' take one to 'em. They're also needin' oxen an' I wanted t' let you know so they would be in when they git here," he explained.

He and Hardy loaded up one of our wheels in a wagon and drove out t' meet th' train. They got a good price for it and th' old wheel thrown in for good measure.

"A couple o' new spokes an' some forge work an' she'll be good again," Hardy said. He was enthusiastic about prospects of more business.

That train pulled into th' south yard just afore sunset an' some of th' drivers walked over t' see what we had for sale. Mostly, they were looking for drink, but T&M did not bring any. It would have been a disaster if they had and those drivers got ahold of it. When future trains got word we were selling alcohol, they would avoid us, not wanting their men t' start their carouse while on th' trail.

We talked about driving our oxen over to camp, but d'cided not to appear too anxious t' trade and early on th 11th two men came over t' look at our stock. They picked out a team an' we dickered a while. I rode back with them t' look at th' stock they wanted t' trade. One of them was skin and bones an' looked like he was on his last legs. The rest of th' herd looked in good shape so I knew he wasn't skinny for lack of forage, but something else was wrong with him. He was probably too old t' even start th' trip an' I decided I didn't want him for trade. Th' other ox was in better shape, just had thrown a shoe an' gotten sore-footed.

We settled on a price and they paid th' difference in cash. That was a good thing about traders on th' trail, they always carried some cash and it was easy t' do business with them. Not so with immigrants comin' in, most o' them were short on gold an' long on tradin'. They would trade anything they had and we had to be careful about that. We would take anything of value, but we would not take a man's weapons in because we knew they had need of them down th' road—not only for provender, but for sure for defense. We were satisfied with our first trading experience.

Next day when that train pulled out, th' old ox was left in th' pen. Hardy took pity on him an' brought him up to our herd.

"Bet you ten t' one that there boy is wormy," Asa said, "an' I know just what'll fix him up!" He took about a pint of our precious kerosene an' poured it down his throat. "Now we don't want him near our boys 'til th' medicine works, else they git worms too."

So Hardy spent th' afternoon under th' south camp arbor carving out wagon spokes and watching Ol' Methuselah, as he called him. It wasn't long until medicine b'gan t' work an' Old Methuselah b'gan t' scour. Late that afternoon, Doctor Willis went over with another dose and when they rode in, Hardy was all enthused.

"I never saw so many worms in my life!"

Asa was smug about th' deal, "Told yuh so! You be sure an' pick up all those piles an' haul 'em 'way off. We don't want t' spread those worms all over creation."

"Yes, doctor," Hardy said, ducking an expected swing.

Worming did th' trick and from then on, Old Methuselah

gained weight and strength. By July, he was as good-looking as th' rest.

After that first train came through, trade really picked up. Sometimes there would be three trains in at once an' more in sight. We took trade-ins on oxen, usually two used-ups for one good one, or one and cash boot, which we really preferred. Our wagons went fast an' before we were quite ready for it, we had t' go back for more of both. I hired a couple of men who were wanting t' get back south an' we drove th' worst of those used-up oxen back to camp.

It was a frustration hiring some men t' drive back to Taylor Springs with me, but I finally convinced three Mexican Americans t' go with th' promise of a quick turnaround and maybe another trip out. I paid them white man's wages and that was an incentive. It is something I have always done, and I have always gotten good return for my investment. These people who pay less get what they pay for an' maybe a little bit less, considering th' resentment of their employees at being discriminated against.

It seemed I was on th' trail all summer, hauling wagons an' drivin' cattle back and forth and th' men I hired stayed with me all summer. We made a good trail crew and by early fall they had earned what would normally have been six months' to a year's wages for them. We even made a couple of trips for Mr. Trimble driving his excess mules back to Fort Union, where one of his crews picked them up and drove them on to his Mora ranch.

For some strange reason, Indians didn't bother us much. We heard there was much trouble along th' trail, especially around th' Arkansas River. I guess they were too busy up there t' bother with us. Some young Apache bucks ran off with th' mules an' oxen, but they bit off more than they could handle an' we got all th' oxen back because they couldn't keep up with mules. It seemed th' mules were lost, but a few days later, here they came back, driven by men from one of th' trains that had passed through earlier. They had seen th' herd out on th' plain an' surmised what had happened. That night, they sneaked up on th' Indians while they were sleeping off their mule meat feast and retrieved th' herd, driving them right through th' Indian's camp. For good measure, Indians' ponies went with mules and we all wondered what they told when they walked into th' reservation without them.

Asa and Hardy stayed busy trading an' fixin' up trade-in wagons. Under Asa's guidance Hardy became a good trader an' by midsummer he was handling most of th' trade while Asa concentrated on repairing wagons and watching cattle. Hardy even acquired a few mules in his dealings, though by fall they were gone, traded back to other trains coming through.

We could have used a blacksmith but we didn't have access to one. Th' smithy T&M brought out stayed busy from before sunup 'til after sundown on things of their business an' by th' time traffic tailed off was worn to a frazzle. Th' rest of us were not too far behind him an' when that last train came through we were all ready for a rest. On our last trip from th' fort, I brought back a keg of beer an' th' night before we abandoned camp, we had a big bar-b-que an' I brought out th' keg. There was enough for a cup or two for all, but not enough for anyone t' get drunk.

I remember th' fall colors of those hills as we rode home. Shinnery Oak was turning red and brown and higher up, aspen were so bright it almost hurt your eyes. When I looked back from up on Rayado Mesa pass, I could just make out fresh snow on Mount Baldy. Th' air was crisp an' nights chilly. Cooler weather made man and beast more active and we made good time getting back to Fort Union where we broke up, each going his own way. We had a good summer, trading off all our wagons except four fix-ups loaded with spare parts and with more oxen than we had started out with. By spring, with good care they would be ready for more trade. In addition, we had over five hundred dollars in cash after paying off all our debts.

Asa and Hardy were enthusiastic about another year of trading, but I was restless for something different. I was twenty-six years old an' still knockin' around without a plan or idea of what I wanted t' do. I had a need to settle some an' quit bein' a nomad. I also needed a trade and I knew it could not be in any business with th' trail. Things were too unsettled and depended too much on th' whims of weather, Indians, and other men. I had really enjoyed working with cattle an' maybe, I thought, that would be where I could find an occupation to my liking.

CHAPTER 31
A NEW RANGE

1870

After a few days at th' dugout we all rode in to Las Vegas to settle up with Charlie Ilfeld and relax a little. We spent a few days there, visiting and enjoying ourselves. Asa and Hardy stayed in th' hotel, but I wasn't comfortable there and preferred th' relatively quiet comforts of th' livery loft.

Asa wasted no time in visiting Visciano's and th' waitress he was sweet on. He found her married and large with child. He moped around for a couple of days, but soon fell in love with another waitress and was happy again. The girl turned out to be the younger sister of waitress Number 1 and was prettier. He pursued her with just as much ardor as before and she managed to keep out of reach just enough to keep him "on the hook,"

This would be a good place t' tell you a little about Charlie Ilfeld. He emigrated from Germany in 1865 and soon was hooked up with Adolph Letcher in a store in Taos. They became partners and in 1867 moved to Las Vegas, their goods on th' backs of 75 donkeys. Their store was on th' plaza in Old Town and right off they did good. Charlie slept many a night under th' counter to protect th' store from thieves. He was still sleeping there occasionally when I first met him.

To say he embraced his new surroundings would be an understatement. Unlike most Anglos, he became involved in th' Spanish American community, learning Spanish along with th' American brand of English. He always had a German accent, and in those first years, it was heavy. Have you ever talked Spanish with a man with a German accent? I haven't, either, but I could understand *English* with a German accent and we got along very well there. The Mexican Americans loved him and called him Tio Carlos or Tio Charlie in his later years.

A few years after our wool adventure, Charlie bought out Letcher and established the Charles Ilfeld Company. It seemed he was always importing family from the old country, even bringing his wife, Miz. Adele from there. He had a long and successful career, active in community and state affairs. His brothers established another trading company and operated out of Farmington. All the Ilfelds were hard-working industrious people and their descendants are still prominent in their communities. I enjoyed a long association with Charlie up to th' time of his death in 1929 and I still have ties of friendship with his family.

I tired quickly of life in th' city but Asa and Hardy were both happy there, so we divvied up our profits with me taking my portion in silver and good horseflesh and th' boys keeping all of th' hardware. They were set on returning to Taylor Springs and tradin' and continued t' do that for several years until th' railroad put them out of business. I think they did pretty good for themselves. Asa went back t' cowboyin', but he had a good stash of silver tucked away somewhere for his old age. Hardy had tradin' in his blood an' was successful in a trading post he set up on th' Navajo Reservation. I ran across him several years ago. He had a passel of kids an' was expectin' a bumper crop o' grandkids t' spoil.

So it was that I found myself "footloose an' fancy free" with three good horses and jingle in my pockets—and not an idea in th' world what I was gonna do! After a day of payin' my respects and saying my goodbyes to friends, I took up my bed and rode out early one mornin' without any destination in mind . . . well I did have some idea about where I was goin'. If my luck was good I would meet up with a gang of cowboys, just returning from driving a herd to Fort Union. I had met these fellows a time or two before when they drove cattle to th' fort and they were a likeable bunch. We got along well.

They were from th' Rafter JD ranch in th' Sacramento Mountains somewhere south of Tularosa. Several times they had invited me t' ride with them and I had made up my mind to do that if I could. The foreman was a man by th' name of Bob Green, his wranglers at that time were Lon Sims, John Jones, Tom Washington, and Van Hunsucker. Manuel Lutz cooked an' drove th' chuck wagon. Others came and went, but these were the ones I remember as bein' in th' bunch when we first met.

About midmornin' I cut th' trail of an outfit headin' south an' by th' number of ridden horses and th' wagon, I was pretty sure that it was my friends headin' home. They always visited Loma Parda after deliverin' th' herd and by their leisurely pace, I surmised that is what they had done. There would be quite a few headaches in th' bunch and maybe a battered face and body or two. Like any outfit at th' end of a drive, they had a good time.

They couldn't have been far ahead and I was sure I could catch them before dark, so I matched their pace, enjoyin' scenery and good weather. It was about as pleasant a ride as I can remember, and sure enough, I found them noonin' on th' Rio Gallinas.

It was late for just a noon rest and all were sacked out except Bob and Manuel, who were takin' it easy under th' shade of a nearly leafless cottonwood, watchin' their horses as they grazed along th' bank.

"Hello, there, Zenas, come on in an' have a rest," Bob called.

291

"You'll have t' excuse th' sorry state o' th' rest o' this outfit, they're mostly out and *not* fit!"

There was a groan or two and Lon Sims lifted his sombrero from his face and gave me a cockeyed grin. One eye was swollen shut an' there was a gap in his front teeth. "Howdy, Zee, pull up a chair." The sombrero lowered gently and he resumed his rest.

"Don't know if I'll git all of them home afore one or two o' them expire," Bob said, "May have t' bury 'em on th' prairie."

"You just be shhure I ain't breaphin' afore you bury *me!*" Lon's sombrero said.

"Where yuh been an' where yuh headed?" Bob asked.

"Shhhh!" a lump said. "Do yuh *have* t' yell?"

"I think this is as far as we're gonna get today," Bob whispered, grinning, "let's go down by th' river and see if fish are bitin'." He fished a line out of his saddlebag and we walked to th' river, catchin' a couple of grasshoppers along th' way. Bob cut a long willow switch and tied his line to it. He swung his line out over th' water, hopper on hook, an' let it settle. A bite or two and bait was gone.

"Must be a little one."

"Or maybe a mud turtle," I said.

We sat an' watched th' line for a while, not talking, just enjoying warm sun and clear air. 'Way off came th' call of a goose an' looking up, we saw a large south trending vee flyin' over, very high above us.

"Must be a hundred of 'em," I said.

"Yup."

We listened until their calls faded into silence. Ripples in th' stream lapped against rocks, making me sleepy, and I must have dozed when Bob gave a start an' jerked th' pole.

"Got one!" He pulled th' line up and hooked on th' end was a nice pan-sized trout. "Half-dozen more o' these an' we'll have supper." He re-baited and resumed fishing.

I lay back, pulled my hat over my eyes, and napped while he caught several more fish. Manuel came down and gathered them up. He gutted them and packed each in a clay wrapper, placing them in th' fire coals. Soon th' aroma of supper was wafting over prone bodies and they began t' stir, some wandering down th' river t' relieve alcohol-sotted stomachs and wash, some just t' sit and stare. They sure were a sorry lookin' bunch, but I didn't waste a bit of pity on them. They didn't deserve it.

"Come an' geet eet," Manuel called.

There was a baked fish for each of us along with biscuits and ever-present beans and black coffee.

Tom stared at that lump of clay on his plate and asked, "We eatin' dirt for supper, Man'l?"

"Eef you want too, Señor." He rapped th' clay on th' edge of his plate and peeled off th' top side, scales and all, and with his fingers began to gingerly eat steaming meat. After a bite or two, he said to Tom, "Geeve me thee clay an' I weell take care of it for you."

"No way," came th' prompt reply.

"Did yuh *hafta* leave th' head on? He's starin' at me," Van asked. He looked pale around th' gills.

"Tis best that way," Manuel purred.

"I don't care what's *best*, I just don't like my supper watchin' me eat him!" He covered th' head with a biscuit. "Ain't eatin that biscuit, neither!"

"I ain't eatin *nothin'!*" Lon said. "Ennythin' goes down this gullet'll come right back up. Here, Zee, You can have my fish."

"Bob did all th' fishin, give it to him," I said, "This is th' gloomiest camp I ever been in. You girls sure cain't hold your whiskey 'thout whinin'!"

There was a chorus of groans at that. "You don't hold *yourn* any better," Jones said.

"I don't hold *any* an' I have as much fun if not more than you do—and I don't suffer for it next day, either!"

"Just what kind o' fun can there be sober?" Tom asked.

I told them about th' washerwomen cleaning up Asa, embellishing it a little. By th' time I finished, they were in a better mood.

So you're th' one that done that!" Bob said, wiping his eyes, "I heard about it at th' fort."

"We heard you was up on th' trail runnin' a road ranch," Lon said.

"How'd that go, Zee, d'yuh hafta fight off Injuns all summer?"

"No, Jones, they was purty quiet this year. We only went to Taylor Springs and they were a lot further east. Caused a lot of trouble from Big Bend to Bent's. I heard young Charlie Bent was a ring leader in th' Cheyennes."

"We heard he was purty wild an' hated all whites," Bob said.

"He musta got all th' red blood in th' family."

"No, not all," I said, "George and Mary show their Indian traits too."

"Is it true that Charlie tried t' kill his father?" Tom asked.

"More than once. He hated him for some reason. Mary used t' put a light in th' window when Mr. Bent was away an' Charlie would come in and visit. He never stayed long. I don't think he ever stayed overnight. There sure was enmity a'tween 'em."

"Eet ees not good to have bad blood in thee fam-i-ly." Manuel shook his head sadly.

"That's fer shore, Manuel. Seen it in my own family, some's on th' North an' some's on th' South," Lon said.

"War's over, Lon," Bob said.

"Yuh jist don't want t' go sayin that in Louisiana or Atlanta!" he replied.

"Er Texas fer that matter," Jones said from beneath his sombrero.

They all seemed t' be sinkin' fast and we watched shadows creeping across th' plains. By sunset they were all rolled up in their beds asleep. I watched night come rolling in from th' east, lighting stars as it came. They are like a pan of popcorn, first there's one or two, then a dozen, then a whole avalanche o' stars pop out 'til they are out in all their glory. Many's th' night I've watched it happen an' I've never tired of it.

Up here in this high atmosphere, they shine their brightest. If you aren't in a hurry, they shed enough light t' travel by, see your shadow, or watch some critter out prowlin' 'round. Nights when th' wind has been still or after a rain, they give a steady light. When winds blow, they will twinkle like a candle. I know it's not wind makin' 'em do that, they say it's dust in th' air, but some think th' wind makes them flicker. I ask 'em, "D' yuh ever see it blow one out complete?" but few will say they have.

Th' last thing I did was saddle one of my horses an' picket him near my bed. It was a habit I got into on th' trail and many's th' time it has paid off.

At first I thought it was grasshoppers or some other bug hitting my cover, but when they persisted, I realized it was pebbles and sat up. By th' dipper it was after midnight, probably goin' on two or two-thirty.

"Señor Zee, listen!" Manuel sat in his bedroll nearby.

There wasn't a sound, then I started, "Th' horses are gone!"

"Sí!"

I pulled on my tether and my horse was standing there, staring down th' valley, ears cocked forward.

"You theenk they have run off, maybe?"

"My horse don't think so!"

"May be thee In-juns?"

"Not likely, they would have tried t' git my horse too." I found a rock an' tossed at th' nearest form. It landed with a thunk and Jones grunted. After a moment he slowly sat up an' looked around. "Horses er gone!" he hissed.

"My horse tells me they didn't jist stray off," I answered.

"Better git atter 'em."

"I'll start out down th' river, but they's really no telling where they went."

"I'll go with yuh," he said pullin' on his pants.

"I can go a lot faster and longer if we don't ride double," I said.

"Don't aim t' ride double, Zee." He was rummaging through his roll and I heard him slip on moccasins.

"Manuel, wake up Bob an' tell him what we're gonna do," I said, "he may want t' send someone upriver."

I tightened girts an' mounted. Jones hung his gunbelt over th' horn and handed me his rifle, "Let's git!" He turned an' headed downriver at a good trot.

My horse seemed eager t' go an' I gave him his head. A horse can scent a trail 'most as good as a dog an' I was bankin' on this one t' do his job. It seemed he was, for after a couple o' miles, he suddenly turned up a draw. Jones turned and followed. I stopped at th' top t' let Jones get a breather. He was hardly out of breath.

He dropped to his knees and on all fours scoured th' ground. Feeling with his fingers, he found a track. "Dirt's still crumblin', they ain't too far ahead."

We scanned th' country. "There!" he said pointing eastward.

I could just make out a darker blob moving across th' ground. It had t' be our horses.

"Where are they headed?"

"T' market, t'market," he chanted, "Prob'ly Las Vegas."

"They'll turn them faster at th' fort or maybe even along th' trail," I said.

"Not many customers on th' trail."

"I guess you're right, but I don't see 'em takin' them to Las Vegas."

"Well one thing's fer shore, they ain't gonna get anythin' by goin' east, 'cept maybe a scalpin'."

Even while we watched, it seemed they turned northward in a great arc before they disappeared entirely.

"Let's head north toward Las Vegas an' I bet we cut their trail about daylight," Jones said.

"You want t' ride a while and let me run?"

"Nah, you'd slow us down, prob'ly break a leg an' I'd hafta shoot ya. I can run like this all day long." He turned north and trotted off. My horse wanted t' follow th' scent an' I had t' reassure him that we were gonna get them by following Jones, so reluctantly he followed.

By then we must have been twenty miles southeast of Las Vegas. We could see Mesa Lauriano a little north of east and it looked as if th' herd was headed for th' east side. If that was so, then th' only choices they had were to almost circle th' mesa or climb th' gap in th' bluffs to th' flats northeast of Lauriano. Neither route made much sense if they were taking horses to sell.

Maybe they were hopin' t' throw us off or maybe they felt we were afoot an' wouldn't follow. We were taking a gamble by not following along their trail, but that would also mean that we would always be behind them and they could have th' bunch sold before we caught up. And th' only way we could retrieve those horses after they were sold was with silver or lead. More times than not lead was th' "medium of exchange."

Our route to th' top had t' be Canyon del Agua and it was a treacherous route. Jones must have run fifteen miles by th' time we rounded th' bluff at sunrise. I marveled at his endurance.

"Raised by 'Paches, had t' run or die," he said.

Northeast were wetlands and ponds around Laguna la Monia. There was water in th' sinks, but th' wetlands were mostly dry.

"Let's go a little west of due north and see if they went in to Vegas," Jones said, and off he went.

After a couple of miles, I spotted th' herd far to the east of us crossing th' wetlands. "Looks like they are headed north," I called.

"Think you're right. They may go to Fort Union, Loma Parda's more likely, folks won't ask many questions there an' they would know th' horses from th' time we spent there."

"They aren't likely t' see us small as we are, so let's just parallel their path an see what they do. Sooner or later we'll meet up with them."

Our good luck held a little later on when we came upon a man with a few head of horses. I paid more than he was worth, but Jones now had a mount an' we might even make more time, though he had done almost as good afoot as he would have riding. We rode on chewing on some jerky from my saddlebag, Jones bareback with only a hackamore for reins.

"Herd's getting closer," he said.

"It almost has to," I said, "think we can head them now?"

"Yeah, we better make a try for it afore they get into a crowd where we might be cramped for action. Hand me my guns."

We broke into a lope, Jones buckling on his belt an' checkin' th' load in his rifle as he rode. Our paths converged quickly and we rode hard t' get ahead of the herd. By now they had seen us an' pushed hard, but they were as tired as we were. Jones with th' only fresh horse soon outdistanced me and when he got ahead of the herd turned and rode full speed at them. This forced them t' turn sharply west and much closer to me so that when we came together, Jones was on th' north side of them and I was on th' south side.

There were four men, two were unarmed Mexican Americans an' they broke and headed east at a high lope. Th' one closest t'me showed fight an' when he raised his gun I shot him out of th' saddle. Th' fourth man broke an' ran and we had our hands full getting th' herd rounded and stopped. They were winded and going nowhere so we rode over to th' man sitting on th' ground tying up his wounded arm.

He was dirty and disheveled an' when he looked up he grinned and said, "Nice shootin'; yuh just knicked th' bone I think, but my back hurts something awful."

We got down and I saw where th' bullet went through his left sleeve and entered his coat. When we took off his shirt, there was a long ugly welt where th' bullet had made a furrow across his back and left a hole where it exited his clothes. Blood seeped from a couple of places, but it wasn't a serious wound, just awful painful.

"Not much damage back here, just a furrow or two," Jones said.

I finished wrapping his arm and th' bleeding stopped. "Think you can stand up?" I asked. He picked up his sombrero an' nodded.

We helped him up an' he turned paler, so we held him a moment.

"Whoowee, don't git downwind o' this critter!" Jones said.

"Ain't any better upwind," I said. "How'd you git this way, cowboy?"

His knees buckled and he sat back down. "Celebrated too much in 'Parda, got rolled by a coupla tinhorns, an' turned out t' pasture. They outnumbered me an' I was tryin' for a stake t' go back with an' clean house."

Jones squinted at him and said, "I seen you there. Was it those two hombres with you done it, th' tall skinny one with th' silver buttons an that fat-assed gopher?"

"Very ones, took ever'thin' but my clothes on my back an' one o' my guns." He held up a fine engraved Remington revolver with black ebony handles. "Her twin is still in 'Parda, I 'magine."

Now I admit it ain't often a feller would sympathize with a horse thief, but here was a cowboy in a heap of trouble not his makin'. He showed poor judgment by followin' th' boys an' stealin' their horses, but sometimes you don't think too well with a fogged mind an' in th' straights he was in. Not much harm was done except for runnin' him down an' getting th' horses back. Jones sat back on his heels an' frowned.

"Don't seem right a feller should be treated thataway. If it weren't that there was a bunch o' us, we would have gotten th' same welcome. *Throwin'* yore money away is one thing, but someone *takin'* it is another."

"I'd already spent a lot on them two s.o.b.'s enyway." His head sank to his chest an' his eyes were closed. I imagine if anything had been in his stomach it would have come up by now. He looked awful.

"Think we better bed him down here, Zee, he ain't in no shape t' go far."

There was a pond nearby and we led him to a spot under th' willows an' made a bed for him. I lit a fire, an' made coffee in my cup. It was strong, but he drank it all and I put on another "pot."

All the while, Jones and I were discussing our situation an' wonderin' what t' do about it.

"I'm all fer goin' in an' wiping out that whole nest o'vipers," he said.

"Th' three o' us could do it, but our partner ain't up to th' job jist now."

"Don't go without me," The Rustler said.

"We clean out th' town an' th' whole army'd be on our tails fer ruinin' their recreation," I said. "And they would be very intent on catchin' us, 'specially th' non-coms."

"Yer right, but I bet th' gen'ral 'ould like it."

"What say we concentrate on those two scalawags an' try t' git The Rustler's money back?"

"Don't care 'bout th' money s' much as th' guns an' rig."

We were quiet for a while and I mulled over an idea in my mind. "Jones, why don't we sell that herd?"

Now, he didn't know me well enough t' know I wasn't th' stealin' kind an' th' question caught him flat. He set his cup down out of his gun hand and backed up a step or two. He less than casually let his hand drop to his side. "What you got in mind, Zenas?"

I could tell he was a straight-up sort an' my admiration for him grew a little more. I grinned.

"If we could convince Silver Buttons we had a good herd of questionable ownership that we would sell at a bargain, maybe he would want t' come out an' see them, maybe buy th' bunch. Atter he bought them, we could set him free on th' prairie, take th' horses back."

The Rustler chuckled, then grimaced at th' pain it caused.

Jones rubbed his chin—with his left hand—and thought a moment. "That idée has some merit, but it may need some refining."

"Maybe we could git into a game with him, we're shore t' lose . . ."

"Speak fer y'self, cowboy." Jones must be proud of his card playin' abilities.

". . . Then tell him about th' herd out here an' offer him a good deal."

"Better yet, let's drive 'em into town, let him see 'em there. He'd remember *them* an know they was stolen, prob'ly remember me an' know we was outside th' law an' in a hurry t' turn 'em at a bargain rate."

"Then we could drive 'em out here t' finish th' deal?"

"Yeah, Zee, an' relieve him o' his earnin's. Somethin' like that could work . . ."

"I have a couple of friends nearby that could help us."

"Who be they?" Jones' suspicions were rising again.

"Two vaqueros who work around here. They're good men."

I met his eyes and held them, "I'm not a crook, Jones."

After a moment, he nodded. "Can't be too careful with another man's property. Zenas, if this is straight up, I'm fer it, but let's be careful."

CHAPTER 32
SILVER BUTTONS

For sure *I* was gonna be careful! Jones showed potential of bein'
a powerful enemy an' I didn't want t' be on th' receiving end o'
his anger. After cussin' an' discussin' th' deal a while, I headed
for Baca's. If Pepe and Ignatio weren't there, they would know
where t' find them. I found Pepe lounging around th' corrals
looking bored an' told him what I needed. He was interested
an' said he would find Ignatio and come to th' flats. By th' time
I got nearly to th' herd, I could see them a couple of miles
b'hind. Not long after I got t' camp, they rode in. Ignatio had a
goat carcass slung b'hind his saddle. It was a welcome sight, th'
only thing we three had eaten in a couple o' days was jerky—an'
I'm not sure how much longer The Rustler had done without.

We soon had meat roasting and I told the two vaqueros our
plans. When I finished, Pepe grinned and nodded. "Eet sound
like a gr-r-r-eat venture, Señor Zee, wee eenjoy such fun weeth
thee Loma Parda gr-r-r-eengros!"

Ignatio nodded. "Suure we have thee fun too!"

The Rustler was all up t' go with us, but he just wasn't in
shape t' do it. His fever was up even though we had washed his
wounds an' wrapped them carefully—at th' expense of my only
white shirt—it looked like he was getting some infection.

"I know a woman who is good at healing such," Ignatio said.
"I weel take Señor Rustler to her, then return to where you
are."

"Most likely that will be Loma Parda. If so, stay back and

just watch us. You may have t' step in an' help if things git touchy."

"Si, Señor, I weel be thee ace in thee hole."

With that, we got The Rustler up on his horse an' they rode off toward th' plazas. We rounded up "our" horses an' corralled them at Loma Parda just after dark. Our arrival was noted, we even saw Gopher standin' on th' porch of La Cantina.

"Least we know where Silver Buttons is operatin' tonight," Jones said.

We left Pepe t' watch th' horses and ambled into town. After a couple of hours, we wandered into La Cantina and ordered a couple of drinks at th' bar. I pretended t' drink mine and Jones took a big sip of his and washed it around in his mouth b'fore swallowing. Th' rest he spilled down th' front of his shirt.

Silver Buttons an' Gopher were slowly strippin' a couple of soldiers of their silver in a game of cards. Gopher was th' designated winner with a pile of chips in front of him. Silver Buttons only had a small pile an' he lost it th' same hand those two soldiers lost all of theirs.

"That does me in, fellows," he said, "is the winner buying?" He looked questioningly at Gopher.

"Belly up, boys, I'm buyin'!" Gopher said.

They all rose an' came to th' bar, soldiers rather unsteady on their feet. Silver Buttons eyed us and gave Gopher a nod.

"Set us up a round, George, an' don't leave out those two gen'lemen!"

Our glasses were refilled and we had a time emptyin' them without swallowing any—well, swallowing much would be more accurate. Th' soldiers soon left, no jingle in their pockets, and Buttons turned his attention to us. After some small talk, Jones said, "I have a yen fer a good game an' they don't seem t' be anyone else available here. Too bad yuh got cleaned out." He pushed away from th' bar as if to leave.

"Thanks for th' drink." I nodded to Gopher. "Too bad yore through, an' it's so early at that."

"Oh, I'm not cleaned out," Buttons said, "I just set aside a certain amount I'm willing to lose on any given night and when it's gone, I'm through. Don't want to risk everything just for some entertainment, though my money didn't buy much of that tonight."

"I'm good for another game if we can find a fourth," Gopher said, not hiding his eagerness very well.

Buttons feigned reluctance, then said, "Tell you what, I might risk a little bit on another game. This fellow's luck can't last all night and I would like to win back a little of what I lost."

"Hah!" Gopher scorned, "that last deck was so hot it near scorched my hand. I bet I'll clean yuh all out!"

"That does it!" Buttons exclaimed, slapping th' bar. "A fresh deck, Keep, and I'll buy the next round!"

We found another table farther back in th' room an' Buttons unwrapped a new deck. With a flourish he spread it out on th' table to see that it was whole, then began to shuffle.

"What will it be, gentlemen, a little five-card to warm us up?"

"S'good with me," I said, and we began to play.

No one gained much the first few hands and the talk was lively and friendly. I kept a keen eye out, th' fun for me when I played a tinhorn was t' figger out how he was cheatin' me. 'Course, Gopher might be as sharp with cards as Silver Buttons. He was sure good at pretendin' to be awkward.

No use goin' into details about how we lost, th' ending was sure before th' beginning, an' before sunrise me an' Jones was drained. Th' piles in front of th' two others were about even an' Gopher kept gloatin' about his good luck.

"We better go, Jones, an' see if we can sell some horseflesh er we ain't gonna eat well for th' next day or so," I said.

Jones just grunted.

"Got some for sale?" Buttons asked. "I might be in the market for a good horse if you know of one."

Jones glared at me an' shook his head slightly. "Just a herd we got t' push on up t' Mora, an' we need t' be goin'."

"Nothin special," I said hastily, "we better git."

"Not even one good one in the whole bunch?" Buttons persisted.

"Just old rannies an' cow horses." Jones muttered, "Let's go," looking at me.

"Well, so long, come back when you hanker for another game," th' tinhorn said.

We made a hasty exit and as we crossed th' plaza a shadow moved from under one of the ramadas. Ignatio was back. We hazed th' horses out an' headed northwest *away* from th' Mora Road. About midmorning we stopped to let th' herd graze down in a draw. We took a long break hopin' th' bait would be taken and sure enough, it was. I watched from th' top of th' ridge as a rider came following our trail. When he saw it turn for th' draw, he came on th' run. It was Gopher. I put a warning shot in front of him, he skidded to a stop and I stood up, rifle in hand.

"Don't shoot, it's me," he called, removing his hat.

I pretended to just then recognize him and waved him on in. "I didn't recognize ya," I said by way of apology.

Without ceremony, he blurted out, "There's a deputy in town askin' about a herd o' horses he said was stolen. He's on your trail not three miles back an' ridin hard. You better git goin'!"

I pretended confusion, "Where can we go? How many with him?"

"They's eight or ten an' some o' them's th' owners of th' horses. I saw lots of hemp hangin' on their saddles!"

I began t' run down to where th' boys was settin' an' Gopher rode beside. "Sheriff's comin', git goin'!" I yelled.

All was confusion for a minute. "I ain't leavin' th' horses,"

Jones yelled. That was funny considerin' where they came from.

"We got to," I yelled

Jones faced me, his rifle in his hand, *"I ain't leavin th' herd, Zee!"* It wasn't an act.

"What are we gonna do?"

"Head em fer th' river, I know a place," Gopher called.

We pushed them to th' river an' instead of wading up or down, Gopher yelled t' push them straight across and on to Mora Road. Up th' road at a run we went, stirring up dust you could see five miles away. Suddenly, Gopher turned th' herd back into th' river and up Coyote Creek. We splashed for a mile or more, then out of th' creek onto a trail heading northwest. After a mile or so, he turned them into a pretty valley surrounded by five hills and there we stopped.

"You'll be safe here," Gopher called. "I'll go lead th' posse astray." Which was easy t' do considerin' they didn't exist. It was a big joke to us, with a trail a blind man could foller, no posse bent on catchin' us would be deterred. He rushed off back down th' trail. We gathered t'gether an' had a good laugh.

"Does he expect us t' b'lieve him?" Jones asked. "What now?"

I had been thinking hard on th' subject an' a plan I came up with was simple but it would work—I hoped. "Pepe, you an' Ignatio go hide out . . ." I looked around, ". . . behind those rocks up on that bluff. When th' deal's done, I will remove my hat an' you commence shootin' at us, but don't hit us. We'll panic an' run our horses out th' upper end of th' valley there. We'll be sure t' leave Gopher an' Silver Buttons here afoot. You can catch up with us on th' way back downriver."

They nodded and after changing to fresh horses moved off.

"This may take some doin', Zee, but I think it's possible," Jones said.

"I shore hope so," I replied, but my stomach was churnin' as much as my brain was working.

Jones guarded our back trail and I rode up to th' west end o' th' valley to "watch" but mostly to scout out th' land. There were two passes between those hills, one to the northwest an' one to th' southwest. Taking either would do, but southwest was our most direct route to where we were headed.

It wasn't long until Jones saw two riders approaching. It was Silver Buttons an' another feller that looked far worse for th' wear. We surmised later that he was a town drunk hired by Buttons. As they rode up, he called to Jones, "No warning shot to keep us away?"

"Naw, I seen those silver buttons flashin' an' knowed it was you. They'd sure make a good target if someone wanted t' shoot you!" Jones said.

Buttons looked startled, then laughed. "You're surely right there."

"It'd be smart ef yuh took that fancy vest off if yer gonna associate with hoss thieves," Jones said pointedly. "It says who you are an' attracts too much attention. We don't like attention."

He shrugged and got down, an' removed th' vest, revealing a fancy black-handled revolver in a shoulder holster. Tying th' vest b'hind his saddle, he let th' horse graze off a little ways. Jones noted th' brand was a Texas brand well known to him.

"Nice horse."

"Yes it is," Silver Buttons replied. "I won him and that fancy Texas rig from a cowboy passing through a couple of weeks ago."

I'll bet you did! Jones said to himself.

"Our card-playing partner" (*meaning th' Gopher*) "convinced the deputy that he knew where you were going and that he knew a shortcut to get ahead of you and set up an' ambush. They're out of the way for now, so you have some time. Sw . . . John and I were in the posse and we volunteered to follow your trail to make sure you didn't take off some other direction." *Yuh could jest as well hev said Swamper,* Jones thought. Swamper John slumped in th' saddle, chin on chest, dozing.

"Not a bad-looking herd," Silver Buttons commented.

"Just cow ponies an' right now I'm wishin' they were somewhere else."

"Have you got them sold?"

"Naw, just prospects."

"Must be near fifty head."

"Fifty-six countin' our personal hosses." All th' while they were talking, Jones kept an' anxious eye on th' back trail.

"I may be able to help you out of this little bind," Buttons said, ". . . tell you what, I'll give you a hundred fifty dollars for the bunch."

"*A hundred fifty! Three dollars a head?* Why at that price, *I'd* hang *you* fer horse stealin'!" Jones said angrily. "Those horses are worth fifteen a head easy an' on a good day would go twenty–twenty-five a head!"

"You can't haggle price too much with a posse on your trail and no place to go. I can take them off your hands and dispose of them safely where you can't. I'll go five a head and not a penny more."

"I won't take less than ten an' you can go to . . ."

"Don't burn your bridges just yet," Buttons soothed. "I can split the difference with you at seven fifty, but that's my last offer."

Jones stomped and cussed while Mr. Silver Buttons looked on smiling. Gradually he cooled down and looked thoughtful. Taking a stick he deciphered th' amount at seven fifty. Rubbing it out with his boot, he thought some more.

"That's a mighty poor price fer th' work an' risk we been through, but I don't see a easier way out'n this. Yer robbin' us, Mr., but if you can git away with th' herd, it's prob'ly better'n we can do. It'd be your neck yer riskin' an' not ourn. I guess I'll take your deal, hard cash, no paper an' right now on th' barrel head."

"I figured as much and I have money in silver, if that is all right with you."

"Fine," said Jones, "but hurry it up!"

Now, I have t' interrupt this transaction t' let you know what I had been up to during this conversation: I saw two riders come in and start talking to Jones. A flash or two told me our friend Silver Buttons was one of them. When he dismounted, I worked myself behind brush and boulders down th' opposite side of th' valley from where Pepe and Ignatio were, makin' sure they saw me on th' way. When I was opposite Jones and company, I made myself comfortable and waited.

After a while, Buttons went to his horse an' brought back a heavy saddlebag and a blanket. He spread th' blanket an' was just unbuckling th' flap on th' bag when I let them have a couple of shots with my pistol. Hearing that, our two vaqueros let loose too. Th' effect was instant. Later Jones told me what happened.

"I near jumped out'n my skin when I heard that shot comin' from opposite side o' th' canyon, then I realized it must hev been you and I hit th' ground, pushing Buttons down as I went. Swamper John revived miraculously an' departed th' scene.

" 'You dirty dog,' I yelled, 'you set us up fer a trap!'

"Mr. Silver Buttons was pale as a ghost. 'No, I didn't . . .' But that's all he got out b'fore I buffaloed him b'hind th' ear an' he fell asleep."

We stopped shooting when Jones stood up. Grabbing th' blanket, he rolled Buttons up like a cocoon an' tied him tight, blindfolding him. With th' saddlebag, he sprang into th' saddle and we all scrambled down to start our horses homeward bound. I would have loved to have seen their faces when Gopher an' his hired hands rode in t' move th' herd—at a leisurely pace—out of th' valley, if they even planned t' move them at all. We had a long ways t' go an' not much time t' do it in. There was still a danger that we might be caught with th' herd, an' no papers or authority t' have it would probably get us a rope stretching job. We took a straight line for camp on th' Gallinas, hopin' someone was still there. It was past sunset when we passed east of Las Vegas and we were glad of that. After dark we felt safer and slowed down considerable.

Camp was dark except for a spark or two from th' fire. Th' chuck wagon was still there, as was Manuel, but everyone else was gone.

"Who goes there?" Manuel called from somewhere near th' wagon.

"It's me, Jones, and th' herd."

Still no movement. "Who is that with you?"

"That feller Zenas an' a couple o' vaqueros."

Pepe spoke in Spanish, "We are hungry friends, amigo."

"I'm gonna stoke up th' fire so's you can see us, Manuel," Jones said.

When th' fire was bright enough, we were all sitting in plain view of th' wagon. Slowly, he moved out of th' shadows. His double-barreled shotgun ready. When he had satisfied himself that we were who we said we were, he relaxed.

"Good work, Manuel, yuh cain't be too careful out on th' prairie like this. Whur's ever'body?"

"Looking for thee horses—and you!"

"Well here we are an' there's our horses an' we're hungrier than a old mama wolf. How's about breakfast? Them boys *walkin'* atter th' horses?"

"No, Señor Jones, they borrowed horses."

"Th' whole bunch of 'em?"

"Sí, they not too good horses, I theenk." Manuel began cooking while he talked.

"Well, if they trail us all over th' country, it'll be a *while* afore they git in, I reckon. How long we been gone, Zee, two er three days?"

"We left in th' night, caught th' herd an' pulled into Parda next night, left an' ran all th' next day, was that yesterday? Then drove all night t' git here. I guess only two days an' three nights."

"Sí, that ees r-r-right, Señor."

That's th' last thing I remember anyone saying and I didn't know anything else until Jones shook me an' said, "Chow's on!"

All I remember o' that meal was black coffee an' hot biscuits. Manuel said I fell asleep with my plate in my hands an' my knee was wet where I had spilled my coffee. I slept there all day an' didn't wake up until th' sun was settin'. I sure was confused for a while until I got reoriented. Jones still slept and three Mexicans were playin' cards on a blanket in th' shade o' th' wagon. When I stood up, I think I creaked like an old rusty gate. Boy, was I stiff and sore!

"Is that herd safe?"

"Sí, they are a little tired but fine," Pepe said.

"We better pull them close for th' night while Manuel cooks supper."

"Supper weell be ready when you geet back." Manuel was touchy about common cowboys givin' orders.

There were four fresh horses saddled and I took th' one with my saddle on it while Pepe and Ignatio mounted.

We rode out. "I noticed th' saddlebag wasn't in sight."

"Señor Jones say he need a pillow."

"Good."

I was relieved. Now that we had it, our problem was what t' do with it. I thought about it as we rounded up th' horses. Jones was up and around when we got back. "Smelled chow, did you?"

"*Earned* chow while you slept," I retorted.

After supper, Jones and I rode out to check th' herd once

more. He had th' silver with him.

"Zee, we cain't tell that we risked th' herd t' save a rustler's neck er we'll be in a peck o' trouble ourselves. We gotta make up some tale t' cover ourselves."

"I been thinking along th' same lines," I said. "Maybe we should dispose o' that money quiet-like afore th' others get back."

"Wonder how much there is?" We spread out a blanket and dumped th' silver out. When it was counted, there were five hundred dollars.

"Whooee!" Jones exclaimed, shaking his head. "What we gonna do with all that?"

It's funny now that neither of us had any desire for th' money, but our main problem was to *get rid* of it! I kicked back on my heels and thought.

"Ignatio an' Pepe deserve pay for their work, let's us pay them each fifty dollars and us fifty each. We'll give The Rustler th' rest t' dispose of as he pleases."

"I don't hanker t' keep any of it myself," Jones said.

"Me, neither, but it don't b'long t' that theivin' Silver Buttons either."

"Yore right, but just th' same . . ."

"Say, how much did ya lose in that card game?" I asked.

"Thirty two dollars an' fifteen cents," he said immediately.

"Well, I lost 'bout th' same, more er less, so we aught t' get that back, an' we was out some trouble doin' it all, so we deserve a little pay for that."

After a minute mullin' it over, he said, "All right, Zee, yore right, we'll take our losses plus fifty each and leave th' rest to The Rustler. He can worry 'bout what t' do with it."

"I'll stay out here with th' horses an' you git Pepe an' Ignatio t' say they needed t' git back home an' send them out here t' me. I'll pay them, go with them to wherever The Rustler is, an' give him th' whole outfit. I can catch up with you later."

We plotted out what we was gonna say happened on th' trail with those horses, leavin' out anything about The Rustler an' money.

"Looks good t' me," Jones said, "Now Zee, we *gotta* stick to our story. Word gits out what I risked that herd for an' my hide'll be decoratin' th' barn wall shore. Yuh gotta stick to our story ef we meet up agin!"

"Ok, saddle up The Rustler's rig an' I'll see that he gits it."

Jones went to his possibles bag an' brought back th' second black-handled pistol. He opened it an' thumbed out shells.

"That greenhorn had six shells in here! It's a wonder he didn't shoot hisself or his horse!"

"Greenhorns'll be greenhorns."

"That's shore," he said disgustedly. He put th' gun and loose shells in th' saddlebag with th' money.

I found two cloth pouches an' stuffed money for th' vaqueros in them while Jones rode back t' camp. In a while, Pepe and Ignatio rode out and we headed up th' river trail. Now I was pretty tired of night ridin' an' my companions hated it so after an' hour or so when it was good an' dark, we cut into th' brush an' bedded down. I gave th' boys their money and they were shore taken aback, but grateful. In my estimation they had earned it, though I'm sure neither had ever had that much silver in their hands at one time—and maybe not again for a long time after.

We talked about what we had done and how we would have t' keep quiet about it, especially them since they were around Loma Parda country an' Silver Buttons was probably gonna make a lot o' noise about bein' robbed. I warned them about flashin' silver around an' t' be careful where an' how much they spent at a time. They must have heeded my warnings for I never heard of them getting in trouble over th' deal.

It seems that Silver Buttons did make a lot of noise, but no one paid much attention an' after a while he just rode off. We heard he was following railroad construction, but when Helltown got to Las Vegas he wasn't in th' crowd. Rails ended in Las Vegas for several years an' it got a reputation o' bein th' roughest town in th' west. It was a shame an' I was glad people got together an' cleaned out th' mess.

I did see Gopher several years later. He had been "promoted" t' Swamper John's position, probably when John cashed in. It was plain he had acquired th' swamper's taste for alcohol an' he didn't recognize me.

We were in th' saddle early an' by noon rode up to th' jacal where The Rustler was healing. He was sittin' under an arbor in th' yard all cleaned up an' bandaged proper. It was funny seein' him in peasant dress with white duck britches and his fancy sombrero on his head. Someone had even given him a haircut.

His eyes really lit up when he saw his horse an' rig. "How'd yuh come 'bout them?" he asked.

"Oh we found th' horse wanderin' 'round Parda an' knowed by th' fancy rig it was your'n," I said.

"I gotta hear this story!" he exclaimed.

"No you don't and I recommend you stay away from Loma Parda *for a spell!"*

"You can count on that!" he said, "I'll never enter those portals solo agin, even then I'll keep my facilities about me."

A boy appeared from the house with an olla of water and a dipper and we enjoyed a cool drink. An elderly lady stood at th' door wiping her hands. She nodded and disappeared into th' house. Soon a steaming bowl of tamales and tortillas arrived and we all ate gratefully.

"Seems you are getting good treatment," I said to The Rustler.

"Best ever," he said. "I'm feelin' so good I'm gittin' restless."

"Well, you have transportation now. Your other sidearm is in th' saddlebag along with some money t' pay for your hospital stay. I'm headin' for other ranges fer my health an' well bein', must be on my way." I said.

"Say, I never knowed yore name."

"And I never knowed yore'n. Might be best we keep it that way fer th' time bein'," I said. He just grinned. "Be careful, cowboy, "I'm much obliged."

I left right away, taking th' trail to Anton Chico thinking I could head off th' outfit or cut their trail. We (me an' my horse, that is) watered at Apache Springs and rode another mile or two before we camped for th' night. I didn't build a fire and it was sure hard gettin' going next morning without coffee. I hadn't cut any trail an' when we rode down th' creek from Spring Branch to th' crossin' of Tecolote Creek, no herd or outfit had crossed it. This was a puzzle to me until I got t' figurin' times an' such. Bein's th' outfit couldn't follow our trail at night, they would have t' delay their trailin'. It would also take some time t' find th' trail o' th' herd out of Loma Parda unless someone saw us an' told them which way we went. Not much chance o' that happenin', so they would have t' make a big circle t' cut trail. More time wasted. Manuel said it took them a whole day t' get mounts, so it would be after th' second day afore they started out. That would mean they were only twelve to eighteen hours on their way when we got back to camp. A hard day's ride would have caught up with them at Loma Parda if we had known. Another two days determining that th' herd was headed back to th' Gallinas camp and I realized they probably hadn't left there yet—either that or they changed their route. I was pretty sure of th' former so determined t' wait at th' ford a day b'fore doin' somethin' else.

Ol' hoss appreciated th' break an' spent all day grazin'. I

watched him close an' in th' afternoon wet a hook in th' stream. Two pan-sized catfish I caught made a tasty supper.

After breakfast I rode back to th' bluff above Apache Springs to look for any sign of th' boys. It seemed I could see a dust rising northeast of there, so I watched a couple of hours an' when th' dust got to Aguilar Creek just west of Cuates Mesa I was sure it was my outfit. We took a leisurely ride back to th' ford and got there th' same time they did.

"Hallo there, Zenas, where ya been?" Lon called.

"Waitin'. Where *you* been?"

"Oh, we took a little circle 'round Loma Parda looking at th' scenery up there," Van called.

"Zee, can you believe it took them *four* days t' take that ride? an' t' think we did it in two days an' three nights! *Zee!* They even *slept,* never missed a night!" Jones shook his head in misbelief an' disgust.

"You don't mean it!"

"I *do,* an' look where we are! This is th' *seventh day* after th' herd left us an' we only made it t' here."

"It's always thata way, Jones, some men do all th' work while others lay around camp an' take joy rides across th' country."

Van picked up several rocks an' I ducked behind his horse. "Don't stone th' prophet for carryin' th' gospel."

"Gospel, my foot," Tom said. "I done rode my rear raw chasin' you two only t' find you lollin' around camp. I'll bet no one stole those horses, yuh jist taken 'em fer a little run!"

"Ef yuh rode yo'self raw, sleepin' ever' night, you're too soft!" Jones called from out of throwing range.

We only paused long enough t' eat some warm beans an' cold biscuits before pushing on to th' Pecos at El Viandante Ruins where we spent th' night. Dark was coming earlier and earlier. You can imagine banter that went on all afternoon and evening, but it was all in good humor an' no one got mad, though some of th' remarks were pretty pointed.

After supper, Bob said, "Zee, we sure would like t' hear th' truth about your adventure. We've heard enough o' Jones' tales t' know it was blown up considerable, tell us th' barebones truth."

"I don't know how long th' herd had been gone, but Manuel woke me up an' I woke up Jones t' tell him I was after 'em, but he insisted on goin' too. He made me run an' he rode my horse, nearly run me t' death afore we found another hoss . . ."

"I *knowed* it, he wouldn't run fifty yards t' catch his own horse . . ." Tom began.

"You hush up, it was *me* what done th' runnin'!" Jones said fiercely.

"Anyway, I convinced Jones t' go north, thinkin' they would head for town or Fort Union. He was all for goin' east, said they would hide in th' hills there . . ."

"Zee, ef ya don't stop lyin', th' hull outfit'll hang your hide out t' dry—if there's eny left atter I git done with it . . ."

"Sure enough, those fellows had gone east of Lauriano . . ."

"Went up th' gap in th' bluffs," Tom put in.

". . . and we gained on 'em when they headed north. We paralleled their path 'til they turned west an' we headed them off. We had one heck of a battle, but bein' there was only eight or ten o' them . . ."

"I counted thirteen," Jones interrupted, "two had Sharps .50's."

"Weren't more'n four," Lon snorted.

"*You* weren't there duckin' bullits, how'd you know?" Jones challenged.

" 'Cause I can read sign, that's how!"

"My ol' half-blind granma kin read sign better'n . . ."

"Hush an' let Zee finish, he kin tell tales as good as Jones,"

Bob interrupted.

"We had a little runnin' gun battle there . . ."

"An' I winged one o' them from a hundred yards on a dead run just like I told you!"

"Jones, if you don't shut up . . ." Lon and Van both glared at him.

"*I* winged him," I said giving Jones a hard look, "but th' rest got away with th' herd. We went back to see about th' one *I* shot, knowin' where th' herd was headed an' I rode t' git him help. I picked up two tough vaqueros I knew and we followed that herd in to a corral at Loma Parda, but they kept them well guarded an' we couldn't do nothin' but wait for you to catch up. When they drove them out afore daylight an' we hadn't seen you, we just followed. By th' time they holed up in that valley, we knew we couldn't depend on you-all for help an' we ambushed them ourselves, got th' herd, an' headed south on th' run."

"We saw blood where yuh caught them on th' prairie, but they weren't none in th' hideout," Van said.

"We made it pretty hot fer them an' when they saw I had captured their boss, they cut an' run."

"*Who* caught th' boss, Zee?" Jones asked.

"Me," I said calmly.

"I b'lieve 'im!" Tom crowed.

"By th' time we got back to camp with th' horses, we had gone three nights an' two days without sleep an' little food. It hurts an' saddens me greatly t' know what a lark you fellers made of it all," I concluded.

Bob rubbed his chin. "We'll study on it tonight an' vote on who is th' biggest liar in th' morning."

"Jones got it, hands down, that long shot on th' prairie proves it," Van vowed. "I seen him shoot!"

There followed a long argument among th' four of them over

truth and merits of th' two stories. It continued even after we were all in our rolls until one by one they drifted off t' sleep.

There was no use trying t' fool them with a tale that wasn't close to th' truth because every one of 'em could read sign easy enough. We just hoped that by only eliminating the part about The Rustler an' bankin' on our tracks bein' harder t' follow after th' gunfight, they wouldn't dope out th' whole truth.

From then on, there was a man on guard duty with th' horses all night. Since I wasn't on their payroll, I didn't stand watch, though I volunteered to. This galled th' rest an' that's where I got my nickname Daylight, them sayin' I was no good on night watch. I sure put in a lot of nighttime hours in later years t' dispute that, but th' name stuck anyway.

We made a leisurely ride of two hundred miles t' Tularosa. Th' only thing we had t' worry about was water an' a couple of nights we did without. Th' Capitans were white an' we got snowed on goin' through Capitan Pass. From there we went west past Church Mountain and turned south again b'tween Diamond and Cub Mountains. By that, we avoided high mountains and more importantly th' 'Pache reservation where we would have been sure of losin' horses.

We found ample water at springs an' streams along th' foothills. I was struck by th' openness of Tularosa Basin an' near wore my eyes out looking. Th' boys kept me up on landmarks and sights. There was carvings an' pictures on th' rocks ever'where, but no one could decipher them. They tell us now they were made by prehistoric men, maybe cave men. I think Indians did it, long before white men saw these shores.

We pulled in to Tularosa midafternoon twelve days after crossing th' Pecos. Ever'one was sure dry. After horses were corralled and we cleaned up some, they scattered like quail, mostly to th' saloons, but a couple sneaked off to see sweethearts at La Luz. Bob an' I watched them go.

"You'd think those fellers would have a belly full of ridin', but off they go. They'll ride twenty miles t' see some gal who'd as soon not see them!"

I didn't mention that I would have done th' same thing if I had a girl. Come t' think of it, I saw Bob do it a time or two afore he married.

"Zee, Manuel says you had a good horse an' fancy rig when you rode in with th' herd, but it wasn't there when we got back."

"It was th' rig of th' boss rustler, we took it when we left."

"I sure wish you would have strung him up when you had him."

"We considered it, but there wasn't a convenient tree big enough t' hold him an' we wanted t' make tracks afore that gang found out there were only four of us."

Bob nodded. "What happened to th' fancy rig?"

"We had t' pay th' vaqueros something an' I went with them to sell it an' give them th' money, got a good price an' split it atween them. They were happy an' I warned them to keep their lips sealed an' not flash money around."

"What about a bill of sale?"

"Th' man that bought it didn't ask for one. I told him th' sale was safe only if he rode south or west. He understood."

Bob grinned, "You two did a good job and I'm grateful. We won't have work this winter, but if you come by th' ranch next spring, you'll have a job."

"Thanks, I will if I'm livin'."

"Come on, I'll buy you a drink," he said and we turned in to th' saloon. Jones was leanin' agin th' bar explainin' our adventure to Barkeep. He was wearin' a black leather vest with silver buttons.

This basically ends the stories of the family's adventures on the Five Trails West. Volume IV is primarily concerned with Zenas' life in and around the Tularosa Basin. The trails he follows and cuts there do not involve a migration, but an end of the western odyssey begun so many years ago by his forefathers.

ABOUT THE AUTHOR

James D. Crownover has been a student of the American westward migration for many years. Upon retirement from an engineering career, he has found time to write about the times. Inside every major event in history are hundreds of smaller events performed by men and women with little notice from the historian. The two-time Spur Award winner is convinced that these unnoticed people and the aggregate of their unnoticed labors are the essence of any great event in history.

These are the people he wants to recognize and write about.